AS LONG AS THERE IS CHOCOLATE

TANA LOVETT

To Carly.
Enjoy!
Tana Lovett

First Edition: January 2018

ISBN-10: 0999668757
ISBN-13: 978-0-9996687-5-7

For my mother, Dolores Meyers, who hoped I'd finish the book before she left this earth. I'm sorry I didn't. I miss you every day.

For my Captain Awesome Man, who read all incarnations of every scene without apparent exasperation. Thank you for talking me down from Impostor Syndrome a million times. I'm grateful for you every day of my life.

1.

Falling for Fabio

"You are not going to fall. You are not going to fall. You are not going to fall." Muttering this mantra around the pencil in my teeth almost kept me steady. Almost. Funny, my little altitude problem hadn't occurred to me before now. I was perfectly capable of adhering the vinyl artwork to the wall, and there was no way I'd be hiring it out. I clutched the ladder with my left hand, careful not to crush the paper roll under my arm. Wearing the tape bangle bracelet on the arm clutching the tools, I made it to the first step.

"Good job, Kate. Well done." Stalling, I rearranged the curls sticking to my damp forehead with an upward breath.

A noise across the street caught my attention, as if I needed an excuse to look. It was a sickness, really. An obsession. I felt like I spent half my life staring out that window. Gawking at the cute deli guy every day blew a hole in my productivity— and my dignity—yet here I was again, wanting to turn at the Pavlovian stimulus of his voice. I refused to give in to the temptation to stare at Gio DiMarco this time.

His laugh exploded.

I shook my head. "He is the loudest man."

He was probably in the middle of a swarm of girls too young to know better than to loiter outside Mangia Italian Delicatessen. I had work to do, and the last thing I needed was being distracted by *him*.

A little acrophobia was nothing compared to some of the stuff I'd conquered in the last few years, and I was proud of how far I'd come. Even if a lack of social life had me talking to myself. "I am strong. I am invincible . . . "

The total gut-job in my shop space was finally showing signs of being turned around. The early-twentieth-century crown moldings had been rescued from years of obscurity behind a hideous popcorn drop ceiling. The old brick of the exterior walls was exposed, and the interior walls were plastered just as I'd imagined they'd been back in the day. The painters finished up yesterday with a rich caramel and raspberry scheme. Tomorrow, gold embellishments would be applied here and there. The gourmet *chocolaterie* of my dreams would open soon. Watching my baby take form was my single most soul-satisfying accomplishment to date.

I took another step, pausing to check for swaying. "You're only going to be six feet off the floor. No big deal." I breathed in through the mouth, out through the nose, like in yoga. Or was it *in* through the nose?

"Even if you did fall . . . which you wouldn't . . . probably . . . it wouldn't be fatal." The pencil was making saliva pool in my mouth, causing my speech to gurgle and hiss. "Compound fractures aren't nearly as hard to fix as they used to be."

My positive affirmations really needed work.

Smacking the solid aluminum for reassurance, I soldiered on. "Just keep looking up, Kate. You've got this."

The room went to spin cycle when I turned at the sound of the front door opening. That low, booming voice called, "Special delivery for Kathleen Hannity."

The ladder danced while I struggled for balance.

It was the man-harlot from across the street, holding a parcel, shouting as usual. "Wait! Whoa!" He dropped the box and darted toward me.

I don't know why I let go, exactly. Maybe I was trying to *not* commit assault with a deadly ladder. Instead, I only sacked him like a linebacker with the full force of my body.

Beneath me, flat on the floor, nose nearly touching mine, he croaked, "Are you all right?"

I'd just become a human ton of bricks pinning him to the ground, and he asked *me* if *I* was all right.

"Yeah. I'm fine," I lied. The drumming in my head became louder as blood seeped back in, and I remembered to breathe. "I get woozy sometimes when I work up high. I'll be okay in a second."

My scalp tingled and the rest of me felt like it was being nuked in a microwave, warming with a low vibration from the core outward. *That* was something new. The scent of spearmint and soap and . . . man filled my nostrils as my vision cleared.

I drew back and saw the classic Roman lines of his face, his perfectly chiseled nose, lips that had had their share of action, I had no doubt. His muscled chest and abdomen were considerably harder than I'd imagined, having mostly only seen him wearing an apron. His eyes were dark and all but vanished behind ridiculously thick, curly lashes when he smiled. And he smiled a lot. But when he wasn't smiling, those eyes latched onto my face like a magnet, no matter how many times I tried to look away.

I could only stare back, rendered temporarily mute until I thought to ask, "How about you? Are you all right?"

"Hmm. Not sure," he rasped. "I'm having trouble breathing."

"What?" *Oh, Sweet Lord of the Dance*. My eyes flew open and my jaw dropped. "Did I break you? Your ribs? Crush your windpipe?"

"No. Here, just let me, uh . . . " He rolled to the side, depositing my weight onto the floor next to him, then got up on one elbow and looked down at me. "There. That fixed it."

"Oh." At last, the bulb of recognition lit and I saw we'd just been sandwiched together like an Irish/Italian panini. My cheeks flamed with him lying next to me now, in a way that seemed even more intimate. The absence of his warmth made me realize what—or who—had been responsible for the hum still buzzing deep in my belly. "Oh, holy . . . "

I jolted up from my prone position. "I am so sorry." I brushed back a springy red curl from my face. "How are you feeling now? Does anything hurt?"

"I'm good," he said, rubbing the back of his head. "Just conked my melon a little."

"Are you dizzy? How many fingers am I holding up? I should take you to the ER." I rose to my knees. "You could have a concussion or something. No, wait. Stay right there." I patted my pockets, thankful for the Cadillac insurance policy I'd just taken out. "I'll call an ambulance."

The cell phone nearly fell to the floor before I got a good grip and began tapping. "Where is the phone on this thing? It's a phone, for the love . . . Why do they even *call* them phones when phoning's the last thing we use them for?" *Stop blathering, Kate.*

A shriek came from the device in my palm. "Sorry," I yelled over the squall, before figuring out how to make it stop. "It's a whistle app. You know, for personal safety."

I located the keypad. "Stay put until the EMTs get here. You could have a spinal injury. Don't move."

His brows wiggled over twinkling eyes. "Are you sure I don't need CPR?"

I considered for a second, picturing my mouth on his . . . "No, you are clearly breathing. That's good. I think I'm a little rusty on CPR." *Especially the mouth-to-mouth part.*

He stood at once and extended a hand to me. "Calm down, Kate, I'm fine. My head's my toughest part."

His hand dwarfed mine when he helped me up, aiming that piercing gaze with heart-stopping accuracy.

I flushed again, hating how the red patches on my pale

cheeks flared with a hair-trigger of the slightest provocation. It was like wearing a blinking sign, advertising every private thought. "I feel like I need to compensate you or something. I could have killed you."

"Compensation. Hmm." He scratched his chin. "I'll have to think about that." He looked me over just enough to crank up the wattage on that microwave. "But that's crazy. A delicate little thing like you is not going to hurt me."

The eyes crinkled into that disappearing act again with the return of his quick grin. "Tell you what," he offered. "Why don't I stay and help you? You can give me a sample of chocolate, and we'll call it good."

He called me delicate—even if he had implied I'd squeezed the breath out of him—and he offered his help. Eddie always needled me about my weight, which was well within normal range, thank you very much. He would never have offered his help. He would have thought my project was ridiculous.

Delicate. My waist was small, but the hips and thighs more than made up for it. And breasts too, as long as we're over-sharing. I loved to cook and I made candy for a living. *Delicate.* I was no match for the deli guy, with his smiles and his flattery and—why did he always have to smell so good? There was no way I was letting him stay.

"I'd be happy to *send you away* with some chocolate, but I can handle this myself."

He was tall. Judging by the proximity of my forehead to his sternum, I'd guess about six-four, with broad shoulders and narrow hips. At five-foot-two if I stretched—if I wore heels and stretched—I wouldn't stand a chance in a struggle. And if there were a struggle, at least I knew the rape whistle on my phone worked—if I could find it on purpose next time.

He wouldn't budge. "You know what? I was just going to run a few errands. Your package was one of them, actually. Got delivered to my place. Seriously. The deli is covered for several hours. I'd be happy to stay."

"The handsome ones will break your heart every time, Kathleen," my mother's words looped in my head, "like your father." He *had* broken our hearts. Our hearts were broken by a succession of the handsome men she'd welcomed into our lives. She'd never learned.

But I did.

I climbed faster this time. "The vertigo is really getting better now, I think." I looked upward again, trying to make it so.

"Kate, you're scaring me." I jumped, and his voice quieted. "I can't leave you up there by yourself. I'd feel like a big jerk." He planted his feet. "I'll stay down here and be your spotter. How's that sound?"

I knew just what he'd be spotting, too. His fixation with my bottom had been impossible to miss over the past weeks. *Thank you, God, for not letting me choose the yoga pants today. They make my rear look enormous.*

Why did there have to be so much raw sensuality about him? He was always polite and appropriate with me at the deli. I was his best customer; he'd better be. Even so, there was this *maleness* oozing from every pore that triggered something primal in me. I didn't know what to do with a body that produced a chemical reaction without my brain's full consent. One thing I did know—I wouldn't be joining the ranks of the Barbie battalion that seemed to find him wherever he went.

Besides, I was more comfortable with the highly driven, cerebral type. At least I had been once. From what I'd seen, he wasn't in danger of growing up anytime soon. That wasn't the guy I was looking for. I needed solid, motivated, achievement-oriented.

What was I thinking? I wasn't looking. I'd failed Relationships 101 and wasn't ready for a retake. My judgment was all wrong when it came to men. I needed to be happily independent before thinking about happily ever after.

"And speaking of the fan club . . . " I muttered, glancing out the window. I swear. The man attracts women like a weepy-day carton of Ben & Jerry's.

Gio waved to three matching girls on the sidewalk, with hands shading their eyes and noses nearly pressed against the one window that wasn't protected by antique metalwork. "Haha! It's the triplets."

As usual, my most menacing glare went completely unnoticed, while the three little piglets slimed the clean window by flattening their snouts against it.

It reminded me of the morning I heard voices and scratching at that window. When I came downstairs from my apartment to investigate, I found Gio overseeing three boys—with rags, scrub brushes, and grudgingly penitent faces—as they removed what appeared to be graffiti. I was too late to see the intended message, only smeared paint, accompanied by an overwhelming solvent odor. That had been the first time I'd thanked him with chocolate. I sighed. How bad could he be, right?

Since he refused to go away, and I couldn't exactly pick him up and carry him out, I decided I might as well put him to good use. I probably was safe enough, with curious small-town eyes everywhere. He could at least call 911 if I fell, maybe mop up the blood before the floor guys came tomorrow. "I guess you could hold the ladder, if you're sure I'm not keeping you from something important."

His gaze trailed the girls until they were out of sight. "Can't think of anything more pressing."

This is why you choose your head over hormones. Keep away from the fire and no one gets burned.

It was time to ignore the testosteronic time-bomb at my feet. I used the level and pencil to align the decal sheet. Getting it positioned properly was the most crucial step.

"I'm not sure I understand what it is you're doing up there," he said. "Is that, like, wallpaper?"

"Sort of. It's kind of like individual stickers that make up the lines of a drawing, sandwiched between two sheets of slick paper. The idea is to line the sheets up just right and tape them in place. Then I start peeling off the under layer, while I smooth the sticky pieces into place with this." I held up the kitchen spatula. "When I'm all done scraping them into place, I peel the outer sheet off, and *voilà*! It looks like the picture has been drawn right on the wall."

"I probably have something that would work better than an egg turner," he said—like a man. "Want me to go get it?"

"Don't let go!" I closed my eyes and counted to five to modulate the desperate, shrill tone of my voice. "This will work just fine."

Gio shrugged. "Okay, chief. You're the expert."

In order for him to look up into my face, he had to take in the entire length of my body. My upper lip dampened with perspiration. "Would you mind handing me that bottle of water? It's getting hot up here."

As he made small talk about the weather and calendar of upcoming community events, the tone of his voice softened and crescendoed in animation. I responded with hums and monosyllables while I concentrated on what I was doing. Surprisingly, the continual chatter did seem to have a calming effect.

Leaning in closer to the wall, I bumped the level off the top step. With lightening reflexes, Gio caught the flying object in his right hand before it had a chance to cave in his skull. "Whew." He gently laid the tool down without losing sight of me, making sure I didn't follow its downward path. "Give it up, Kate," he said without missing a beat. "It'll take more than that to make me level-headed."

I should have groaned, but his deadpan delivery of the cornball joke actually made me laugh out loud. Okay, maybe I couldn't help but like the big doofus a little. I'd probably like a Great Dane puppy too, but that didn't mean I wanted its paws all over me.

When I had squeegeed everything one last time, I climbed back to the top of the ladder. "This is my favorite part. The unveiling." I removed the tape and began peeling the outermost panel downward, careful to not take any of the smaller vinyl pieces with it. As soon as the drawing was completely exposed, my foot hit the edge of a lower step just unevenly enough to make my body stiffen and sway off balance.

Gio put his hand at the small of my back to steady me. "Hey, easy," he soothed. It was a small gesture, really, but the tone of his voice made something inside of me *brighten*, for lack of a better word. The touch, the words—they seemed so familiar—yet, for the life of me, I couldn't think why.

Stop it, Kate. You don't need anyone to take care of you, and if you did, it wouldn't be Fabio, the sandwich boy.

"Would you look at that," Gio bellowed, smiling broadly. "Fantastic, Kate."

Despite his overblown enthusiasm, it was nice to have someone appreciate my idea. Now that I was safely on the ground, Gio moved the ladder away so we could get a better look at the artwork. It was an outlandish caricature of a French chef, complete with goatee, curly mustache and a ridiculously huge hat. The caption read, "Every Day Is A Good One, As Long As There Is Chocolate. – Chef Henri Leveque"

With Gio standing next to him, Henri didn't look nearly so high on the wall. "Are you the one who drew it?"

"I am. I must have made a hundred scribbles of him. Such an expressive face. Chef was my favorite instructor in culinary school. Without him," I held my arms outstretched, "I wouldn't be doing any of this."

Dumping my half of the marital assets into this place was so uncharacteristic. I was not normally driven by impulse. My mother called me "an old soul," which was code for "stick in the mud" or "party pooper." One of us needed to be sensible, since the other had been prone to flights of fancy. It was years before the root of her fanciful flights was properly diagnosed and medicated, and, by that time, there was no going back.

Becoming a chocolatier was the first major rebellion of my life, and this insurrection was against no one but myself. I was shedding the cocoon of willing codependency that had held me suspended. My newly emerged wings were stretching and strengthening, and it wouldn't be long before the new Kate would launch into the next phase.

I returned my attention to the artwork. "I wanted to put this one up there, to take advantage of that jut in the ceiling. I need to find something cool and vintage to go underneath. Something that will give a sense of weight and balance and tie in with the original architecture." I looked at the other walls. "I don't think I'll need a spotter to do the rest. Thanks so much for your help."

"Are you sure? Because I can stay if you'd like."

Watching that full mouth as he spoke made me think of things I'd like. But liking didn't make them good for me.

"No good . . ." I cleared my throat. "No, thank you. You have errands to run, and I'm sure I can handle the rest."

"Okay, but promise me you'll give me a yell before you go climbing to the top of that thing again. All right?" Those 80% pure cacao eyes fixed on mine again.

Full-body goose bumps sprang to attention. "Yeah. Sure," I breathed, knowing it was unlikely.

"See you for lunch?"

I hesitated. "I might try something else today. I mean, every day the same thing, you know?"

"All right, then." His brows knit together. This time, he was the one who looked away first, putting his hands in his pockets. "Maybe tomorrow then."

"But, hey, I could change my mind. I seem to have a Mangia Deli addiction."

Oh, Kathleen, you are in so much trouble.

2.

Mass Confusion

The bells rang from the center of town. I followed their sound past the colorful Oldtown storefronts that helped make Castle Springs, Colorado, the charming little tourist attraction it was. The crisp morning air helped chase away some of the early-hour brain fog I was experiencing more and more since I'd moved in.

Even with my hurried pace, I had to stifle a yawn. I loved my building, and restoring it made me love it more every day, but old buildings had their quirks. Combined with a million details of the remodel ping-ponging inside my head, the little creaks and groans of the old girl had kept me from sleeping well for weeks. And when I woke in the mornings, I always had a feeling I should be remembering my dreams, but I never could.

I'd intended to arrive at the church about ten minutes before the start of Mass, but that morning I seemed to have attracted every sticky substance within ten feet of my person. The fluttery layered maxi skirt—maxi for me, anyway—wasn't my first choice, but it was orange-juice-toothpaste-and-mascara-free at the moment. You'd think I'd never been the new kid on the block before. Some things didn't get easier with practice.

If I was going to have a successful business in a new

location, I had to make an effort to meet people. I couldn't think of a better place to start than church. I swallowed hard and dabbed at my chilled nose with a tissue. *They're just people, Kate. People don't usually bite. Not at Mass, anyway.*

Father Michael Castaldi, looking like he should be wearing a retainer and acne cream instead of a Roman collar, had welcomed me warmly the day before. After confession, which I had put off for too many weeks, he said he would look forward to seeing me at church and assured me I would love the people of the parish. *Me* loving *them* wasn't what I worried about.

Rounding a corner of the square, I spotted a group of twittering women, all decked out and giggling excitedly around Gio DiMarco. His big booming voice could be heard half a block away, expounding some fascinating bit of wisdom, at which the girls gasped and emitted a collective, "Ohhhh." Before I crossed the street, Gio looked at his watch and said something more quietly to his assembled audience. They formed a queue and followed him inside like a row of adoring goslings.

Not goslings. What do you call the babies of a strutting peacock?

This was the last place in town I expected to see him. If I weren't already late, I think I might have been sick right there.

Reverence was dispersed into the high-ceilinged chapel by an ancient pipe organ, played by a veiled nun, nearly as ancient. One by one Gio and his little gaggle dipped fingers into the font and made the sign of the cross before joining a group in a pew near the front.

I quietly did the same, choosing a seat as close to the exit as possible,

Gio's head sat taller than anyone else's in the congregation, and his shoulders seemed to take twice the space of one of his girls.

A harem at church. Classy.

I should have spent the last few minutes of the prelude in introspection, yet my clasped hands felt anything but prayerful. I willed my wiggly foot to stop its fidgeting.

Parishioners sitting nearby softly greeted him. After Gio motioned to a dark-haired woman, she passed her baby down the pew. He lifted the little girl over his head and dangled her there for a few seconds. She gazed adoringly down at him and drooled a smile that looked so much like his own.

None of your business, Kate.

Gio put the infant over his shoulder and patted her back as the service began. She was beautiful, dressed in pink, with eyes just like his. She had a full head of dark curls and chubby little dimpled fingers. I caught myself turning my head and drawing in breath, as if I could smell her sweet scent at my own shoulder.

I needed to focus my attention elsewhere.

The stained-glass windows were intricate, from the late 1800s or possibly the turn of the century. It was quite a grand cathedral for what must have been a very small town at the time. The windows were surrounded by the original gray stone of the building. It looked as though a later generation had covered up the remaining stones with plastered walls, probably for insulation.

One window in particular caught my eye. It depicted the Immaculate Heart, a portrait of the Virgin Mary with a large, haloed heart on her chest, but it was unlike any Catholic iconic image I'd seen before. In similar depictions, the heart was always red. This one's was of metallic gold, emitting long shimmering rays. In the foreground of the picture, eclipsing the lower part of her body, was what seemed to be some sort of foliage or petals of a flower that pointed toward her in a rough semi-circle. The mottled gray-green of the petals gave an impression of being more mineral than vegetable. I wondered if those pieces of glass had faded over time from a richer hue. I would have to ask Father Michael about it later. Once an art major, always an art major.

But this wasn't an art history lecture. I returned my attention to the service. I stood and sat and knelt and recited in all of the correct places, but practically on autopilot.

The pull of Gio snuggling the baby was stronger than the pull of the liturgy. The girls on his row fussed over the infant, but I wondered if they would have given her a second thought in the arms of her mother.

Kate, stop looking at that baby. Stop looking at him. Pay attention.

By the time lines were forming for communion, I had given up. The baby slept on Gio's shoulder with damp curls sticking to the side of her pink face. Her mouth hung open in a tiny 'o,' and her little arm dangled limply. I imagined her softness as he turned his head to kiss her cheek occasionally. I could remember *his* scent too, from our close encounter on the cold cement of my shop's floor. I didn't know which produced a pang of longing more, the man or the baby, but the combination of the two together was lethal. I was pretty sure I heard the sound of my ovaries imploding.

"Cute, aren't they?" someone whispered.

I turned to find Sylvia Giordano, the real estate broker who had sold me my building, smiling behind me. I gave her a blank stare, as if I didn't know who she was talking about, but my warming cheeks gave me away.

In the line ahead, Gio, still holding the sleeping baby, knelt to receive the altar bread.

Maybe he brought the baby to the front with him to draw more attention to himself. It wouldn't surprise me, but that's not what it looked like. He clearly was very attached to her.

When he turned to go back to his pew, his expression was frozen in solemnness until he noticed me. His smile beamed in recognition and he winked as he passed.

The base of my neck thrummed so forcefully, I was afraid my heartbeat could be heard over the music. Why was I being so stupid? He was just a man with a pretty face, and no one was more aware of it than him.

Was that a knowing look in the young priest's eye or was I imagining it? If I thought my cheeks couldn't generate any more heat, I was wrong.

At the final Amen, I jackrabbited toward the door, but Sylvia caught my arm.

"Kate. It was so good to see you today. How are you settling into our little town?"

Sylvia and I had clicked from our very first handshake. We were so dissimilar. I couldn't understand why we'd get along so well, but we just did. She wore a tailored black skirt, barely long enough to be considered tasteful, a jade green silk blouse, and mile-high green designer heels that most certainly were not bought in Castle Springs. But despite my cobbled-together ensemble and comfortable flats, as always, she put me at ease. It was a shame I had been so busy with the shop remodel, I hadn't taken her up yet on her lunch invitations.

"I haven't had much time to assimilate yet. I'll get to that after the opening."

"Promise you'll call me this week, for sure. I know you've been working hard, but everyone has to eat. I'll take you to this really nice place over on Elm Street. My cousin owns it. It would get you away from the stress for a little while. We can catch up."

I was annoyed by my first emotion, which was a moment of panic that I would miss a day of eating at the deli. Of course I could do something else. "I promise." I saw Gio returning the baby with a kiss on the mother's cheek. "Better yet, why don't we decide right now? Can you do it on Tuesday?"

Sylvia took a phone out of her expensive-looking little

bag. "Tuesday?" She scrolled down the phone's screen. "I'm expecting a big client that day, but Wednesday looks good. How about you?"

I found the calendar on mine after only three tries. "I should be able to leave the trim guys alone for a while. I don't think I'll have a delivery until after two. Yeah," I said while I tapped in the appointment. "Let's do Wednesday."

"Kate!"

I cringed at the deep-voiced outburst behind me and the attention I was sure it was attracting. Didn't he know he was supposed to use his inside voice at church?

"Oh, hello." I did a miserable job of acting surprised to see him.

"What are you ladies up to?"

Seeing familiarity between them, I said, "You must know Sylvia, then. It wouldn't be rude if I failed to introduce you."

Squinting her eyes and pursing her lips in inspection, Sylvia asked, "This guy?" She tilted her head like a curious puppy trying to get a better look. "Yes, it would be safe to say we know each other."

Great. I chalked up one more conquest in his past—or present, for all I knew.

"I'll leave you two to talk." She hugged us both, nudging us closer together in the process. "I'll come pick you up at a quarter to twelve on Wednesday."

"Sounds good. I'll see you then."

Gio held up his hand in a wave as she left, and leaned in to open the door for me. "Are you headed home? I'll walk with you."

"Yes. And all right, I guess."

"Don't sound too excited, Kate. I might think you like me or something."

"I'm sure you're used to that."

Puzzlement dimmed his eyes.

"Women getting excited if you pay attention to them? Women liking you?"

"It's a friendly town. That's all. I have guy friends too." He followed me down the cement steps. "You know, I'm pretty easy to get along with, once you get to know me."

The steel stair rail was cold against my hand. "You *are* easy. Yeah, I totally get that about you."

"I can't quite figure you out." He put his hands in his pockets and slowed his steps to the pace of my much shorter legs.

"You've been trying to figure me out?" I crossed my arms in front of me, though the day was warming up.

He laughed in his thunderous way. "You might be surprised at how much I've been trying."

"Why would you be doing that?"

"You are a pretty fascinating woman."

Oh, what a steaming pile of Crêpe. I twisted my mouth to one side.

"Besides being beautiful, you have this quick, dry humor that cracks me up every time, even though you're usually busting my chops with it. You come into town and you know exactly what you want. You handle those workmen like a general—all five feet of you—but you've got them eating out of your hand."

"I pay them very well. Biting my hand would be foolish."

"Sorry, Ms. Vanderbilt, but there's not enough money in the world to make those guys put that much love into a place. They've done some really beautiful work over there. They obviously want to please you." He tugged at my sleeve and put his hand on the other shoulder to guide me around a puddle at the crosswalk. "You try to be the tough guy with them—with me—but I've seen how you react when a kid, or an animal, or an old couple pass your door. You're a softy, Kate. You know you are."

I suppressed a smile. "I can neither confirm nor deny your statement at this time."

"HA!" He threw his head back and brayed. "You're such a hoot."

We walked in silence for a few beats.

"It is becoming beautiful, though, isn't it?" He knew I couldn't resist talking about my baby. "The building has good bones. I knew it could be great, but those guys have taken all my ideas and run with them. It's really beyond my wildest dreams now."

We passed another group of smiling women.

Gio returned their grins as they passed. "Hi. How's it going?"

I heard a snippet of their quiet conversation after we passed.

"She bought the old flower shop. She's not from around here. She's not even a third-cousin to a Square."

I sighed at the familiar sound of those words. Being "not from around here" had been the story of my life. I'd heard the term "Square" a number of times since coming to town, and not used in a familiar way. From what I could gather, it was a word to describe some sort of good ol' boy network that gauged one's acceptability into the community.

The electrician rewiring my building had wondered why it had been sold to me. He said something like, "Squares only sell to Squares. These places never even go on the market. They are always sold privately."

Gio brought my attention back to the conversation. "I've never seen the florist's building look so good; that's for sure. Of course," he leaned a little closer, "anyplace would look better with you in it."

"Smooth." I rolled my eyes. "I bet you get four-wheel traction with that pickup line."

He blinded me with his big smile. "Hey. It worked in high school."

"Yeah." I unwillingly smiled back. "Maybe you need to work on that one. It's not aging well."

We turned the corner onto 2nd Street. The morning sun cast a spectacular golden light on "The Keep" beyond. A rock formation that from a distance resembled a castle on the hill, The Keep was one of the main attractions in Castle Springs.

"Oh, now that's just plain gorgeous." I groped inside my bag again for my phone. "Darn. I wish I had my good camera with me."

"Here, let me hold that for you." Gio took the purse that had slipped down my shoulder when I lined up for a picture of the mountain.

Secure enough to hold a bright red handbag. I put a mental check mark in the plus column, then berated myself for keeping score. Holding my breath as I lined up, I took several shots of the cliffs.

"I've lived here almost my entire life, and I still get goose bumps when the light hits it just right. Sometimes you can almost see God's fingerprints on the side, like He'd sculpted it out of clay."

I closed my eyes momentarily, to get the image in my head, then looked back at the mountain.

"Not quite today," he said. "But, I'm telling you, sometimes it will really knock the breath out of you."

He was obviously expert at this—this flirty, amiable chitchat. I could come up with no response whatsoever. I nodded, retrieved my purse, and resumed my pace. He held his position by my side, waved at people as they drove by, saying hello to everyone we passed.

"You should see it from the other side. It's much more impressive."

"The Keep? I wasn't aware you could get to the other side."

"Oh, you can't, really. It's all private property back there for miles. But I could take you there. It's an amazing hike."

"What about it being private property? You just said—"

"I know the owners. They'd be happy to let me show you

around over there."

Eager to squelch that idea, I responded, "I'm just so busy right now—"

"I know, Kate. Whenever you're ready. No pressure."

Cheerful, bright awnings on the red brick buildings fluttered in the breeze like handkerchiefs waving from the railing of an ocean liner. Even the buildings in Castle Springs waved when Gio DiMarco passed. I could swear I saw the sun glinting off of his teeth, and a singing bluebird flitting around his head. Why did everyone think he was so great? Other than his winning the lotto of genetics and being heartbreakingly beautiful? And happy. And nice, really.

I was a firm disbeliever in the existence of a perfect man. My experience with "too good to be true" was that it always was. If I could just calm the quiver inside, as he said goodbye and crossed the street, I might get a grip on reality.

"See you, Kate. Thanks for letting me walk you home," he yelled from the other side.

I lamely wiggled my fingers, watching a very good side of him walk away, and whispered, "No. Thank you."

3.

Slipping Away

While I wiped down every inch of the new stainless steel counters and work tables that had just been delivered, a sedan, equally shiny and silver, pulled into the alley behind my shop. I tossed the cloth into the sink, brushed hair away from my face with my sleeve, and investigated through the screen door.

Sylvia Giordano emerged from the car, one long, tanned leg at a time, nude, spiky, peek-toe pumps extending their length by about a mile and a half. The remainder of her body followed the legs gracefully as she stood. Tall and sleek in a short taupe skirt and persimmon red jacket, a waterfall of highlighted hair streamed past her shoulders. Forget small-town Colorado. Sylvia looked ready for the Trump boardroom. Her professional polish reminded me of some of the barracuda executive clients of my former life in Manhattan. The only thing small-town about Sylvia was that, once you got past that shellacked veneer, she was genuinely, deep-down nice.

"Good gourd, Sylvia, I forgot all about lunch." I held the door as she clicked up the steps. "I got distracted by my sparkly new stuff."

"Beautiful, Kate." She slowly panned in a circle to take in every detail. "This is so nice, it almost makes me want to cook." She reached out her perfectly manicured hands to give me a quick but very real hug. There were no air-kisses from Sylvia. "Almost makes me want to cook, but I wouldn't starve myself waiting for it, if I were you."

I looked down at my jeans and work boots. "I'll run upstairs and throw on something nicer."

"Don't bother, honey. I'm not going to have much time today anyway. Why don't we have lunch at the deli? It will be like old times."

Our "old times" dated back to just a few months before when Sylvia had taken me to Mangia after a long morning of looking at properties. There had been many commercial/living spaces to choose from, but there was no contest. It was love at first sight for me and the old flower shop from the moment I'd driven by it the week earlier. That's what everyone called it, the flower shop, but a long trail of businesses had come and gone since the days any bridal bouquets had been arranged here.

"The deli will be fine." As silly as it seemed, relief that I wouldn't break my long-running daily routine spread over me. "I think I should purchase stock in that place to get a return on my investment."

"I told you I'd take you to my cousin's place, didn't I? We'll just go to a different cousin's, that's all."

It took me a while to comprehend. "You and Gio? You never told me that . . . did you?"

"I'm pretty sure I did," she smiled. "You might have had your mind on other things."

I blushed, remembering the first time I had seen Gio DiMarco—and not remembering a word of our conversation about the property tour. I deliberately misunderstood her innuendo. "My head was very full of real estate that day."

Sylvia patted me knowingly on the shoulder and all but winked. "Mm-hmm."

I skittered into the small bathroom and looked in the mirror. Not horrible. I just needed to tame the red beast a bit. I washed my hands and ran damp fingers through my hair, then took an elastic band out of the medicine chest and made a loose bun on top. I never had to try for the stylishly messy look, and no amount of product could produce anything but. I retrieved the tube of lip balm from my front pocket and applied it, rubbing my lips together and ending with a final smack. It didn't matter that I was no Sylvia. I was me, and I was good enough. There. I'd looked myself in the eye and thought it. I am good enough. I could cross that off my mental to-do list for today. I straightened to my maximum height and returned to the kitchen to find it empty.

The only thing in the alley was a green dumpster loaded with construction debris and Sylvia's car. I followed her low, throaty voice out into the shop. She was berating the finish carpenter for an imperfection in the trim.

"That is completely unacceptable. Kate hired you to do a job, and it's your responsibility to get it right. If it's not right, it just isn't. You need to replace this piece. The grain blends in like a nun at a biker bar."

The carpenter and I had already had this conversation, but with a little less aggression. We'd agreed that the piece should be changed. I looked at the man on his knees with the cat's paw crowbar in his hand. I hoped he would use it to pull the baseboard away, and not as a lethal weapon. I smiled and shrugged behind Sylvia's back.

She turned to me. "You ready?"

"Yeah. Am I all right?" I circled for her inspection.

"Gorgeous. Everyone loves a petite woman, and that red hair? Women want to have it and men want to have the women who have it. But then, Gio would think you looked great in a potato sack with a paper bag over your head."

"Who? Oh, you mean your cousin, the deli guy?"

"Mm-hmm. Kate, you and I both know that you are well aware of whom I speak."

"He makes a very good antipasto, that Geno man."

"You are so full of it." Sylvia opened the door. "Let's get out of here." To the workman, she scolded, "and I'm going to make sure this is fixed before I leave."

It was a warm September day, and all of the outdoor bistro tables were already taken. Gio was delivering three paper-lined baskets to a group of chattering women near the door. "Here you go, ladies. Enjoy."

I certainly did not have to strain to hear every word he said. The man simply had no volume control.

He saw us waiting at the crosswalk and waved violently. "Hey, Kate." he shouted, making everyone along the street turn to look. "I've got a table saved for you inside."

I smiled sheepishly at Sylvia's murmured, "Mm-hmm."

We were ceremoniously escorted to what I had come to think of as the "special" table in back. I'd never seen it without a spray of fresh flowers. Coming in to find Gio there in deep conversation with someone had piqued my curiosity on a number of occasions.

He stood now at attention with a towel folded neatly over his arm, imitating a waiter in a five-star restaurant. "Here you go, ladies. Today's specials are the smoked pulled pork sandwich. Or if you are feeling more traditional, we have the Italian sausage sandwich with a spicy marinara. There's a chopped salad with marinated cucumbers, onions and tomatoes on a bed of mixed greens with arugula. We've also made up some fresh strawberry lemonade that's been very popular today."

I looked at Sylvia. "I already know what I want. How about you?"

She turned to Gio. "You know what I like, G, and I'll take some of the lemonade too."

"And the usual for you, Kate?"

"Yes, please."

He turned to his crew behind the counter. "Two antipasti with extra artichoke hearts."

A handsome young man with black curly hair and dark eyes, struck up the crew with a "One, two, three, four."

They all began *dah-dah-dah*-ing the instrumental part of a familiar oldie, using utensils for percussion. Gio ended each of the three stanzas with a loud cheer of, "An-ti-pas-to." He bobbed his way back behind the counter to help prepare the meal.

Sylvia's eyes twinkled at me. "How did I know we'd get the same thing? Really, Kate, I think we are two peas in a pod, you and me."

I couldn't imagine a pod that would include two such dissimilar peas, but I did like spending time with her. I felt a little beige and bland next to her, but I was partial to the anonymity beige-ness afforded.

Sylvia sipped the ice water that had just been delivered by a girl of about sixteen. "Hey, Lolo, when did you get old enough for gainful employment? I remember when you had the cutest little dimples on your . . . knees."

Lolo rolled her eyes. "Aw, Syl, you say that every time. You were at my sweet sixteen party two months ago."

"That was you? I think you must have grown an inch since then." She spoke more softly to me as the girl left. "My niece. If there is one hint I can give you about Castle Springs, it is that you really have to watch what you say about everyone, because you never know who's related to whom."

"It sounds like you are related to just about everyone in town."

"We're all pretty tight that way. If you didn't know the truth, you'd think our family was so close it was kind of, well, icky— and I guarantee we're not that close. But there's something comforting in knowing who your people are, you know?"

I wished I did. My father had been almost a missing person

in my life, and my mother had alienated her family by running away when she was a teen. We'd never stayed put long enough to develop deep, lasting relationships, but she was always good at meeting new friends wherever we went. Belonging to a tight-knit community like this one? Knowing who my people are? That was a concept I definitely wanted to explore.

I surveyed the lunch crowd and rolled my eyes. "As usual, the place is hopping with women."

Sylvia tilted her head. "Well, the owner is quite a treat to look at." She laughed. "And I mean that in a from-your-point-of-view way, not an I-just-called-my-cousin-hot, icky sort of way."

Gio delivered our platters and drinks, with the addition of some gooey brownies. "I thought you both looked like you needed a little treat. You're wasting away to nothing."

I snorted in derision.

"What? You've been working hard over there. You need to keep up your strength."

"I doubt the brownies will be going to my muscles. They'll go straight to my great big, fat—"

"But . . . everyone needs a little reward once in a while." He winked before returning to the prep area.

"Talk about a load of—"

A customer ordered the macaroni salad and the crew fired up a rousing, dancing chorus of the Macarena with, of course, the ending words, "Hey, macaroni!"

"Honey, having a little extra junk in the trunk is a good thing. Just look at those poor little rich girls on reality TV. The ones with big behinds? Work what you've got, sister."

"Yeah, like you would know anything about that, Miss Zumba Magic."

She looked over at her cousin. "Not everyone is a fan of the tall skinny girls, you know. And some of us have to try really, really hard to look good. You don't."

I examined the room full of all types of women with a sardonic grimace. "It doesn't look to me like some men have much in the way of discriminating taste."

Sylvia put her hand on top of mine. "He's got his fan club, all right. Things are seldom as they seem, though, sweetie."

Gio and his staff had just finished a round of "Three little fishes in a little bitty pool" as he handed a customer a tuna on rye, when Sylvia looked at her watch and our empty plates. "Are you ready? I have a meeting up on the ski hill in about an hour and I've got to swing by the office first."

"Yes, that was wonderful. Thank you so much for making this happen. I've been working with construction crews so long, I was beginning to think I'd forgotten how to do girl talk." I dabbed at my lips with the napkin before laying it on the plate. "I've got to get back too and check on the progress over there."

Glancing back as we went through the door, I noticed Gio, stopped still amid another display of adolescent exuberance. He was watching us walk away and didn't seem to notice he'd stopped singing along.

As we entered my store, Sylvia walked around the perimeter of the open room. "This is looking much better, Mike. Much better. Good job."

Mike answered, "Thanks, Syl. Glad you approve." He looked at me and rolled his eyes.

Sylvia answered. "Smarty pants. Are you and Angie coming over for dinner and games on Friday with the rest of the family?"

"Yeah. Wouldn't miss it." He began picking up tools and wood scraps.

Sylvia answered my confusion with a smile. "My sister's husband." Inspiration lit her face. "You should come, Kate. We turn into a bunch of lunatics when we play games. You'd have fun and get to meet a few people."

I couldn't imagine feeling comfortable in a big, loud group. And besides, I'd made up my mind to avoid Gio whenever possible, except for lunch. If he was Sylvia's cousin, it was likely he'd be there. "I think I'll have to pass this time, Sylvia. I've got so much to do."

"You won't be able to use that excuse for long. The remodel is almost done. You'll have to come play sometime soon. You'll have a blast, I promise."

"Maybe after things settle down." Across the street I could see Gio serving another al fresco order with a big, cheesy grin. I wasn't sure if things were ever going to settle down, as far as some things were concerned.

4.

A Better Picture

I set the tripod down between two of Gio's bistro tables covered by brightly colored umbrellas. Mangia hadn't opened yet, so I had plenty of space to maneuver in, and I was hoping to finish and get out of there quickly. Behind the neat row of buildings, The Keep was bathed in early autumn light, making the perfect backdrop. I raised the camera about a foot, tightened the knob to hold it in place and leaned in to frame the shot.

"Hey, lady. What are you doing?" Gio poked his gorgeous head out the door and startled me.

I shot him a look that told him it was obvious what I was doing. I tried to picture his view of me just a moment before when I stood bent away from his front window. And . . . there it was, the giveaway patches of red on my face.

Since the walk home from church the week before, I'd been taking drastic measures to avoid him, other than my daily lunch habit. A girl had to eat, after all. All right, I couldn't stay completely away, but sometimes I deflected him with full-body emotional armor to the point of near nastiness. Even though—or maybe because—he seemed to be growing on me, I couldn't afford to let him find that chink of vulnerability. I didn't have time to waste on his flirtation, and I *really* didn't have time to recover again from a pummeled heart. Of course, he didn't seem to recognize the existence of any sort of personal boundaries, so I didn't know why I bothered.

Without looking up, I answered, "I'm taking a picture of my baby. Is that all right with you?"

I zoomed in on the shiny gold and black lettering, Mon Petit, my little one. Just below the sign hung a tan and black striped awning with "Chocolaterie" woven into its border. The unique metalwork over her windows was scattered with ornamental floral sprays, a beautiful piece of artwork that had survived since the flower shop days.

Except for the weird noises, I loved everything about the place. Last night I could swear I was awakened by someone whispering, only to hear wind blowing, or water in the old pipes, or . . . I could never quite figure it out. The noise was the next thing I was going to tackle, now that the shop was done.

Ignoring my attempt at rudeness, Gio persisted. "She's looking great."

I looked up from the camera then, to make sure he was looking at my shop and not referring to me. Not that his continual use of poorly disguised double entendre wasn't flattering—it actually sort of made my day—but feeling flattered only made me more annoyed with myself.

He eyed Mon Petit with obvious appreciation. "You did a first class job, Kate." His smile pushed those lashes up to veil his eyes again. "First rate, all the way."

"Thank you." I stood tall—for me—with hands on hips. "She's looking ready to open tomorrow, isn't she?"

"Oh yeah, hundred-ten percent, and the timing is perfect. It'll be ski season before you know it. You've got plenty of time to get cozy with the locals. They'll be your best advertisers."

"I've got a head start. I've delivered samples all over town. I imagine a collective weight gain in Castle Springs this week."

"Ah, but I thought your samples were just for me." Gio stuck out his lower lip and tilted his head with faux-sad eyes.

"Well, to be honest, you've gotten the most." *Without gaining an ounce. Not that I've noticed.* "I've had to do something to make up for all the extra artichoke hearts you've added to my lunches. Yum." *Seriously, Kate, did you just say 'yum'?*

"Old family recipe." He glanced at the camera. "So, what're the pictures for?"

"Gah. I've been so busy I haven't had time to get the website working. I've got to get something up tonight, if I can get it figured out." I took several more shots, making different adjustments to the camera. "Opening a business without a website is suicide. Even if I'd had time to make the Yellow Pages, people don't really use them as much, anyway."

"You've got that right. They make nice doorstops, though." Gio put out his hand to steady the tripod as I clumsily moved it forward, hanging one of its feet off the curb. "Easy there," he whispered, so close to my ear I could feel his breath.

Back off, Fabio, I thought, shooting him my best incendiary glare. Gio, as ever, seemed oblivious.

"You should let me have a look, Kate—at the website. I'm pretty good with stuff like that."

I eyed him skeptically.

"Aw, come on. You think that because I work behind a counter, I don't know anything else? You're not one of those women who judges a book by its cover, are you?"

Actually, I am. If it looks like a player, and sounds like a player, and smells—Holy cow. Heaven. "Really, I think I can figure it out. I just need to make myself sit for a couple of hours and concentrate—"

"Well, whatever, but if you get stuck," he pulled an order pad out of his white apron's pocket and scratched something down, "give me a call. I *am* right across the street, you know."

After a lengthy pause, I hesitantly reached for the paper and, turning back to the camera, shoved it in my hip pocket, subtly indicating the place he could kiss if he thought I was going to call him any time soon. "I'll be sure to do that."

I glanced back to find his gaze had followed my hand to its destination and rested there. I cleared my dry throat, and he looked back up to my face.

"All right, then." Gio put his hands in his pockets.

"All right, then." I bit my lip.

We both stared across the street for a few awkward moments.

"See you at noon?"

I bristled inwardly at his assumption, even though he had me pegged. "Yes. Noon."

"All right, then," Gio repeated as he turned to go back to the shop. His voice lilted, as though he were tempting a small child. "I've got a surprise for your antipasto today . . . "

Involuntarily, the corners of my mouth curled up, only slightly, as Gio disappeared inside.

"Ahhhhhhh!" I kicked the card table that was serving as the home office of my upstairs apartment, barely catching the laptop computer mid-flight as I screamed at it, "You're killing me!"

As if in response, that annoying tapping, scratching, whooshing noise came from the wall again. *Stupid decrepit pipes.*

I had tried for hours to make the website work, but was getting nowhere. "I can't *do* this." I whined and pouted, rubbing my temples with my knuckles.

I heard soft whistling outside and looked down to see Gio hosing the sidewalk in front of his shop. He'd changed into street clothes—a fitted t-shirt and jeans—which he had to know showed off his . . . assets.

"No," I muttered. "No." I watched him slide the metal chairs under the tables. "Not only no, but . . ." I stuck out my lip and narrowed my eyes. "I am not going to call him."

I returned my gaze to the pathetic attempt at a web page. The hosting site claimed the program was user-friendly and that anyone could do it. "Liars."

I sighed as Gio let the umbrellas down. "He'd probably screw it up worse. All he really wants is an excuse to come over."

I woefully eyed the computer again. It was hopeless. There was no use denying it. I removed the note from my back pocket. "Gio DiMarco, 555-5604. Mangiadeli.com (I did it myself)."

"No way," I mumbled as I navigated to the site listed on the note. "Get the heck out!"

On the website was a photo of Mangia Deli, taken from almost the same angle I was seeing it fr—wait. It was *exactly* the same angle.

While I was wrapping my head around someone standing right here taking the photo, it struck me just how polished and professional his website was. I'd expected to find a simple menu and contact information, but this was far more sophisticated and imaginative. He'd paid a lot for it, I was sure. I wondered which part he'd done himself if, in fact, that claim was even remotely true.

When I clicked through to the "About" page, my jaw dropped. After several minutes of reading, I picked up my cell phone, punched in the number that was on the note, and heard a musical ringtone from the sidewalk below.

He was coming at seven. He was bringing dinner. He refused to take no for an answer.

"Of course I'm bringing food. That's what I do."

"Really, you're coming over to help me. I should be feeding you."

"Maybe, but you've been busy and I have a whole shop full of food. I'm bringing dinner and that's that."

I had been working frantically all day. I smelled like a mixture of cocoa butter and freshman-year locker room. A shower and scented lotion was more a public service than an attempt to impress (wasn't it?) and shaving my legs was because, frankly,

I'd let them go well beyond the free-spirit stage.

I thought about the whiff of *eau de DiMarco* I'd gotten earlier today. He smelled of soap, fresh baked bread and what had to be pure pheromones. *Geez, Kathleen.*

I put on my favorite jeans and the new ginger-colored cotton sweater my mother had picked up. She always tried to coordinate my clothes with my red hair and green eyes, which never ceased to amuse me. I was not even remotely that particular. Personal shopping had never been high on my priority list, but had been nonexistent for me the past few months. I was thankful that, at my age, I was still the recipient of the things my mother picked up now and then. Otherwise, the only decent thing I would have had to wear this evening would be one of my new chef's coats. I actually loved their boxy, shapeless, comfortable design, even if they made my short, curvy frame look like a half-roll of Charmin.

This was not a date. This was—what—a business transaction? If you called a refusal to take payment in any form but chocolate a business transaction, I guess.

I brought my laptop and all of the related paraphernalia downstairs to the commercial kitchen. With my energies focused on the store, I hadn't had time to properly move into my apartment. Nobody, especially not Gio, was going to see the chaos I had going on up there.

I covered the kitchen's stainless steel work table with a cloth, pulled up some tall stools, set out a plate of my most decadent dipped strawberries, and suppressed an urge to find some candles.

"This isn't a date. This isn't a date. This isn't a date," I repeated.

I was pretty disgusted with myself for my abrupt change of tune where he was concerned. The biography I'd read earlier taught me as much about myself as it did about Gio. Was I really that shallow? I'd assumed all the wrong things based solely on superficialities. Or I was pretty sure I had, anyway. I hated it when people presumed I was a certain way because of the color of my hair, or my short stature, or because of how I was raised—and here I stood, guilty of the worst kind of reverse snobbery.

In my mind, as much as I hated to admit it, every great-looking man lacked intelligence. He was a lothario, not to be trusted. He took advantage of every stupid, gullible female who threw herself his way. He lacked depth. He never had to reach and grow as a human being, because everything was given to him for the price of a smile. That's exactly the person I thought lived across the street from me, the guy who sliced my salami, the man who, despite my resistance, made me feel things I didn't want to feel. Of course, I had no way of knowing if any of the bio was true, but I liked to think of myself as someone who gives people the benefit of the doubt. Even if my behavior of late indicated otherwise.

How could my image of him instantly turn into something so different, with one little click of a mouse? What changed my mind wasn't his list of impressive accomplishments, though they were many. It was because he never once—not even with all the blatant flirtation—tried to impress me with any of it. His now evident kindness and humility were the things that surprised and impressed me most.

The "About" page had read:

"Mangia Deli, family-owned and operated for over seventy years, was opened by Giovanni and Sophia DiMarco in 1940. The restaurant has employed four generations of DiMarcos."

I skimmed the history to the end.

"Gio DiMarco, great-grandson and namesake of Giovanni, took over the business with his late wife, Susan, near the end of her life, so they could spend more of her remaining time together. Gio has stepped away from day-to-day operations of GDM Enterprises, as he continues to do what he loves best—

feed hungry people."

I followed the link before realizing why the name sounded so familiar. GDM Enterprises owned real estate all over town, but particularly within several blocks of this neighborhood. Gio DiMarco was founder and President. Not surprisingly, I had purchased my building from GDM.

Another quick search revealed expressions of gratitude from various charities and nonprofit organizations for his generosity and participation in their causes. Yes, it was becoming obvious I had judged a book by its cover, and I had judged wrongly. Except for the part about the women. I was still trying to reconcile my newfound respect for him with the issue of all the women in his life. That was a barrier I was sure I couldn't get past.

A knock came from the front door. I found Gio on the other side of the glass, carrying three bags in one hand and balancing something large and awkward behind his back. The shop keys rattled as I took them from my pocket and unlocked the door. The jingling of the door's bells accompanied his teetering dance inside. I took the sacks from him as he steadied the hidden object with both hands.

"I brought you flowers," he announced, grinning ear to ear.

Whoa. I had just decided he probably wasn't all that bad as a human being. I couldn't go straight from there to romantic gestures without even shifting gears. "Gio. No. Not flowers. I couldn't—"

He produced from behind him the surprise he'd been concealing. It was a beautiful shelf with floral metalwork brackets. "It's sort of a shop-warming gift."

"Oh, wow." I gasped. "They look just like the flowers on the shop's window grate." I inspected closer. "Just exactly like . . . They aren't. . ."

"Yep." Gio carried the shelf over to the blank space on the

wall behind the cash register. It belonged there, as though it were custom fit. "These pieces I used for the brackets were removed from the window several years ago. They needed some restoration. I saved them knowing I'd find a use for them someday."

"You made this?" I laid the shelf on the counter to inspect it more closely.

"That day you were working on the ladder, you said you wanted to put something special in this spot. I just got to thinking."

He had remembered. I smiled at his thoughtful gesture.

"My grandparents used to own this place, you know," Gio said.

"Giovanni and Sophia?"

I felt my face inflame at his surprise. "I've, uh, done a little cyber-stalking today," I confessed lamely.

"No." His grin lit up. "My Castaldi grandparents lived and worked in this building their entire married lives." He took a look around the shop with open admiration.

The color scheme had turned out perfectly, inside and out. There was a definite retro feel to the design, while still seeming new and fresh. The real ornamentation of the shop, though, was the rows and rows of chocolate delicacies lined up in glass cases, each its own tiny work of art.

"They would have been so happy to see someone love this place again."

"So, the Castaldis were the florists?" I asked.

"Yeah. The DiMarcos and Castaldis have been connected for years. They're kind of all tangled up at this point—marriages between their kids and grandkids—but not in a weird way. It's kind of hard to keep straight, actually."

"Sylvia said something like that the other day."

"We're a little sensitive about it. If you'd grown up a Square in this town and heard all of the inbreeding jokes, you'd understand."

He smiled at my laugh, but in case it really was a sore spot, I moved on. "Your grandparents lived here. You really have a special interest in this place."

"Yeah, you could say that." The penetrating look in his eyes said his interest went beyond family ties. I smiled again and turned away. *You are so not ready for this, Kate.*

In the kitchen, container after aromatic container emerged from his seemingly bottomless bags. The third bag contained a laptop computer and other supplies.

"I can't tell you how thankful I am for your help," I said.

"We'll get it fixed. Don't worry about it." Gio began arranging the food between us.

These were no leftovers from today's deli business. Our dinner consisted of fresh, warm bread, a mouthwatering pasta dish and a colorful salad, along with the antipasto he knew I couldn't get enough of.

Dinner conversation was unpredictably fluid and easy. Even though we had things to get on with, it felt like the meal ended way too quickly.

"So this Henri guy convinced you that your life's calling was chocolate?"

"Yes . . . sort of . . . Well, eventually." I was clearing the table so we could work there. "It's a very long story."

"I'm listening. You can tell me about it while I get my geek on over here." He'd taken out his laptop and set it up next to mine. He appeared to instinctively know what to look for. "I worked my way through college doing this stuff. I could do it in my sleep." He began transferring files with a small flash drive, and my doubts slowly started to dissolve.

I filled the sink with hot water. "You could say it started with my mother. It was mostly just the two of us. In between a long series of her short relationships, that is." I swished the soap around to encourage more bubbles. "She always managed to have a steady day job, but her passion was food." I saw Gio nod with interest as he continued peering into the laptop. "She did a little catering and taught some basic cooking classes in whatever kitchen we had. Feeding people was how she expressed her love. I guess I inherited that from her."

"I can relate," Gio smiled.

"I bet you can," I said, picturing generations of Italian cooks and big family gatherings. I thought about the death of his wife and how moving her to the deli, and deciding to stay on, must be connected to the healing effect cooking can have for some of us.

"I was also an artistic soul." I washed the few dishes while I spoke. "From the time I was tiny, I wanted to create beautiful things. But then I got sidetracked. I started college as an art major, but came out a CPA."

"Very, uh, responsible of you," Gio laughed. "What happened?"

I sighed heavily. "The first boy who showed the slightest interest in me was in the accounting program and thought my choice of majors was 'a frivolous waste of time and resources,' so I switched."

"Don't tell me. You married that guy."

"I should have known it wasn't a match made in heaven. I'm a foodie to the core and he was lactose intolerant, gluten-avoiding, fat-phobic, sugar-sensitive, allergic to eggs, nuts, and shellfish, couldn't digest red meat . . . The list is endless." We both laughed.

"I changed everything about myself, hoping he would love me enough if I was more deserving." I began wiping down every inch of my already sparkling kitchen. "We opened an accounting firm together. I wanted to start a family right away, but he wanted us to focus on our careers."

"Of course," Gio scoffed, continuing his progress.

"Of course . . . Then he wanted to build the business, then get a bigger home, then a nicer one, and a better car, and a vacation home . . . I wanted children more than anything in the world, but Edward was never quite ready. In my mind, the money we were saving and investing was for when I started having babies. In his mind—well, who knows what was going on in his mind?" I pulled the plug from the drain, which responded with a loud sucking noise.

"So then what happened?"

"Well, Eddie never was very imaginative. He ended our story with the biggest cliché in the book." I was looking over Gio's shoulder now. "He knocked up the receptionist."

Gio swiveled in the tall stool and looked down into my eyes. "Oh, Kate, I'm so sorry. No wonder you—" He stopped himself.

"No wonder I what?"

"I mean," he shrugged. "I do feel like I've been chipping away at a brick wall for the past four months. I knew someone must have done a number on you, but . . . " he trailed off.

I didn't react. His description was accurate. The wall I'd built around me was thick and solid and safe. I hadn't realized until today, though, how much I'd welcomed his chipping, even if it had only barely scratched the surface.

I went on. "So, being accountants, it wasn't difficult for us to figure out how to divide everything equitably. I had plenty to live on and the only thing I was absolutely sure of was that I hated being a CPA. I was very good at it, but there was something inside that was scratching to get out. I'd allowed myself to be cast in a mold that never felt right." I went to the fridge, opened two bottles of juice, and brought one over to Gio. "After several months of wallowing in misery, I decided to spend the rest of my life in the place that made me happiest."

"In the kitchen." Gio was typing some kind of gibberish code now with lightning speed.

"In the kitchen." I nodded. "Once I enrolled in cooking school, they couldn't get rid of me. I took every program they offered while I licked my wounds." I crossed my arms over myself in a comforting way, recalling. "What a treat for the senses. The experience fed so much more than my body. I excelled. I got great job offers from top restaurants. I could have stayed and taught at the school if I'd wanted."

"And you met Henri there."

"Chef Leveque. Yes. Of everything I studied, his classes appealed the most to my artistic side. Henri is a world-class chocolatier. He's such a character. He would end each session with, 'And remember, *mes petits*, every day is a good one, as long as there is *chocolat*.' And I was so ready to start having some good days."

"So you decided to open a shop of your own."

"Right. After I came to terms with not having a baby— well, actually I'm still working on coming to terms, but that's another topic—I poured much of my savings and my whole heart and soul into this." I raised my hands like a game-show hostess highlighting the Showcase Showdown.

"Your baby."

"Yeah. This is where my 'baby money' went." I shook my fist in the air. "You can take that chunk of frivolity, Eddie, and you can stick it."

I watched this beautiful man in silence for a while, enjoying the ability to see him with new eyes. I'd always noticed the big, muscular body, the sparkling, thickly lashed dark eyes, and the disarming laugh and smile, but now that I finally allowed it, I was beginning to see beneath the surface. The person who'd been in plain sight all along was starting to peek out from behind the dark curtain of my prejudice. I was allowing myself to like him more, but trust would be slow in coming. Brick walls take a while to dismantle.

"Now that I'm the creepy stalker-woman, I feel like I'm

kind of at an advantage here. I feel like I know so much more about you than you do me"

"Oh, I wouldn't count on that." He didn't look up, engrossed in the computer work.

"What do you mean?"

"Well, I haven't read about you on the Internet or anything, but I feel like I know you better than you think I do."

I didn't know what to make of this, but I was sure he was mistaken. I chose a safe, less personal topic to discuss. "So, tell me about GDM."

He looked up and smiled, probably pleased I had pulled my head out of my own little world far enough to show an interest in his. "Ah. GDM. What would you like to know?"

This time his smile caught me off guard with straight, white teeth and a dimple I'd not noticed before. "I'm sorry, I shouldn't be interrupting you."

"No, you're fine. I'm just tweaking things a little here." His gaze returned to the screen. "GDM. Well, GDM is kind of my version of your accounting firm."

I took some flat candy boxes from a shelf on the far wall and brought them back to the table to fold. "You hate real estate like I hated accounting?"

"No. I love real estate. Well, I love this town, anyway." His brow creased slightly as he concentrated for a moment and continued on. "I love the history and the old buildings, the kind of craftsmanship you just don't see anymore." He laughed. "I love the 'old-world charm' the travel brochures brag about. My family built this town, you know, if you believe their version of the story. That's where the *old world* part comes from."

I loved that about Castle Springs too—the way the town had preserved so much of the European culture of its settlers. The fact that Gio's ancestors were part of that pleased me, maybe more than it should.

"So what don't you like about GDM?"

"I guess I just lost my fire for 'the art of the deal,' you know? Real life got in the way and put things into perspective for me." Gio worked quietly for a while.

I knew that for him, *real life* meant extended illness and the death of a loved one. There were worse kinds of loss than a failed marriage, though it would have been hard to convince me of it three years ago.

"I grew up in the deli, just like my dad and my grandfather. The smells and the sounds, the customers and my nieces and nephews who help me out, all of that makes me feel at home and warm and happy." He raked his fingers through his short, dark hair. "Sylvia runs GDM now. I made her CEO. She's better at it than I ever was. I just go in a few times a week, go over some papers, sign a few checks—stuff like that."

Yes, I could see Sylvia covering all the bases at GDM without breaking a sweat. She was smart, tough, driven, but I bet she was a fair and motivational boss. Everything you'd want in a CEO.

"All right. Go to your website and tell me what you think." Gio stood from his perch on the stool and reached for one of the dessert strawberries I'd laid out earlier. "*Mmmm* . . . ohhhh, Mama, that's good." He groaned in delight. "You're killing me, woman."

"Glad you like it," I giggled, feeling great satisfaction at his pleasure. Thinking the words *pleasure* and *satisfaction* in connection with Gio brought the heat back to my cheeks.

"It's pretty basic right now," Gio explained, hovering over my shoulder as I surfed to *monpetitchocolaterie.com*, "but I'll keep working on it for you if you'd like." He bit into another strawberry, with an encore of appreciative eruptions.

What Gio had created was masterful—at least compared to anything I could have done. He made the page feel like you'd wandered right in the front door of Mon Petit.

I felt his warmth as he looked over my shoulder at the

computer. "Once the store is moving along, we could set up online ordering—that is, if you want to—'cause that would be a great way to expand without a whole lot of added expense."

The "we" did not escape me. I spun around, jumped up, and threw my arms around his neck in excitement. "It's beautiful. Thank you so much."

He returned my embrace with a warm hug and only a hint of something more. I backed off, realizing how nutty my sudden change of attitude toward him must have made me look.

We talked effortlessly for the next two hours as Gio installed the shelf in its rightful place and helped me make sure everything was perfect for the opening. Working together felt natural—comfortable and exciting at the same time.

I liked him, I decided. I liked him a lot. That is, if he was really who he now seemed to be. Trusting my instincts was a muscle I hadn't exercised in a long time. I thought maybe I could allow Gio DiMarco to be my friend. It was going to take me a while to unpack all of my baggage, and I had too much to accomplish before I was ready to think of anything more than that.

We said goodnight with another quick embrace at the door. I felt Gio's forehead kiss all the way to my toes—and everywhere in between. Friends. It was an innocent, brotherly gesture of affection between friends. It wasn't his fault that his gesture weakened every joint in my body.

"Good luck, Kate," he said. "You're gonna knock 'em dead."

I stood and watched him as he crossed the street.

"And, Kate," Gio called, softly for a change, from the middle of the road, "don't give up on that baby just yet. You've got time." He continued on his way, whistling as he went.

Oh, he was good. He knew exactly which buttons to push to start the fluttering all over again.

I locked up for the night, watching the lights go on in the space above Mangia. I began turning off my shop lights. My face ached from the unfamiliar smiling I'd done all evening, and I couldn't stop. Happy was an emotion I hadn't felt in a really long time. I'd found my home in Castle Springs, was making new friends, and I was pretty sure this really cute guy kind of liked me. It was a little terrifying, and I wasn't sure what to make of it just yet, but I tried not to over-think it.

I popped the last berry in my mouth and laughed as I passed the picture of Henri, with his bushy eyebrows, pointy goatee and words of wisdom. Today had definitely been good.

My persistent smile carried on into the night. What the heck was wrong with me? If the memory of my evening wasn't continually looping in my brain, causing me to smile in the dark like a lunatic, then worry and anticipation about the shop's opening in the morning crept in.

If I started to briefly nod off, I dreamed of a woman's face I didn't know, though she seemed somehow familiar. I was never asleep long enough to see her clearly, but each time I saw her, it caused me to jerk awake with the same silly grin on my face. Such a strong sense of joy was strange and beautiful and amazing, but I knew that if I couldn't get some sleep soon I'd be sorry.

I thought I heard a whisper, but, of course, that was exhaustion talking. Had to be the wind. I covered my head with a pillow and squeezed my eyes shut, in a futile attempt to fall asleep.

5.

Opening Day & A Thing

A s I went through the card transactions at the end of opening day, what might have been the obvious became the ridiculous. Castaldi, Sarducci, Di Marco, Bendetti, Costanzo, Zarlingo —who were all these people? And who knew there were this many Italians in a town the size of Castle Springs, Colorado? Whoever they were, I was certain their appearance in my shop that day had been no coincidence. Mr. DiMarco had some explaining to do.

I had expected today to be chaotic; that was a given. First days are when you find out exactly what you didn't include in your contingency plan. But today had been crazy-pants-loony-tunes-bat-guano insane. I not only called in the reserves, but resorted to exploiting the kind nature of my mother.

I opened the drop safe under the counter and sorted a pile of cash while mentally cataloging the events of the day.

"K ate, another customer has a question for you," Alyssa, my new assistant manager, called through the kitchen door. I had promoted Alyssa from "assistant" to "assistant manager" within two hours of opening. That was the point at which it became obvious I needed to beg the second-wave of assistants to come in today, even though they weren't slated to start until sometime next month. I needed Alyssa to help get them trained, never mind that she pretty much had to wing her own training on the fly. Nothing seemed to rattle her, though, and she made her first real day on the job, with a line of customers out the door, look like a walk in the park. Forget the promotion; I wanted to adopt her.

By noon, the chocolates on the shelves had been replaced by half of the pantry's inventory, which I'd planned to last for at least a week. When my mother popped by to see how things were going, I put an apron on her and set her to work rolling fondant. My business plan was definitely going to require some re-working.

At first I thought it was odd how many times I got called out of the kitchen to answer questions. Then I started to get an eerie, exposed feeling, like these people were here to get a good look at me, and chocolate was an afterthought. A very generous afterthought. They all left weighed down by shopping bags full.

"Coming." On one such occasion, I removed my plastic gloves, wiping a splatter from my cheek with the back of my forearm, blew a stray curl out of the way with a loud puff of air, and remembered to smile as I entered the sales area. On the other side of the glass case stood Gio's gorgeous cousin, with two women who were unmistakably related.

"Sylvia. Thank you so much for stopping by."

"You didn't think I'd miss your opening day, did you?" Sylvia's presence, with her broad smile and throaty voice, filled the room. Her blonde highlights, carefully applied cosmetics, and form-fitting dress stood out in the crowd as usual. "Kate, the shop is gorgeous. I knew the first time I brought you here, you'd make it into something special."

"Why, thank you, ma'am." I smiled and bowed my head. "I hope the rest of the Castle Springs population thinks so." My eyes followed the line down the street. "It kind of looks like every one of them is waiting to come in."

"Word gets around, honey."

"I guess so." I glanced across the street at the deli. I had a clue as to just who I could thank for that. "What can I do for you?"

Sylvia nodded toward the other two. "This is my sister, Veronica and my sister, Angie." Although equally beautiful and well-groomed as their sister, they didn't possess Sylvia's command of the space around her.

Each smiled a polite "hello" and seemed to be taking inventory of me, from my crazy, curly ponytail—which had started out neatly this morning but was springing out everywhere now—to the dark brown smudge down the side of my chef's coat, where the whisk had gotten away from me.

"Nice to meet you," I smiled, trying hard to push past the self-consciousness.

Sylvia drew her sisters closer. "We want to get something nice for our grandmother's birthday."

"Grandmother?" This was getting pretty comical. "You're the third group this morning who wanted something for their grandmother."

Angie spoke up, "Well she is turning a hundred and two, you know." She looked at Sylvia and Veronica, suddenly appearing uncomfortable, and back to me. "I mean," she flustered, "that is, if we'd all been talking about the same grandmother. How funny would that be? It would be weird, wouldn't it?"

Sylvia interrupted, "We're having a big family party for our grandmother's birthday. Our great-grandmother. She specifically asked for nothing that needs to be stored, worn, maintained, fed, named or dusted."

"Good to know. Well, pretty much everything here fits that description. Would you like to sample something?"

"Not me, Kate, it would go straight to my thighs." Sylvia stood with one knee bent, toe pointing forward, a hand on her hip, just like a runway model. If she had an ounce of extra fat on her thighs, it would take an MRI to find it. I thought about all of my jiggly bits disguised under the white tube of chef's coat that made me look like an under-cooked cannoli. *Crème*-filled.

Angie looked around the shop. "Our grandmother has such a sweet tooth, you see, and she loves caramels and pecans. And, oh, she has a weakness for fruity things too."

"Well, let's see . . . " I showed them to a display against the far wall. "We could put together a little box with some caramel nut chews and cherry cordials . . . "

"Oh, no." Veronica chimed in. "We'll need enough for the whole family, won't we, ladies?"

"Ten pounds, at least," Angie said.

"Better make it thirty," Sylvia added, "and we'd like a variety of everything in the shop. I'm sure it's all delicious." Pointing, she added, "She will get such a kick out of the little animal-shaped truffles, so double up on those. And we want the fanciest boxes you have."

I took another look at these stylish, slender women, and knew that, with those tiny waists, they probably wouldn't indulge in a single truffle themselves, which was a shame. I did as I was told, however, knowing better than to second-guess paying customers. Especially when they were purchasing well over eleven hundred dollars' worth of product.

The women continued to roam the shop as Alyssa and her new crew filled tins and boxes, adding specialty items to the order at every turn.

Veronica took a bag in each hand as more were being filled. "You don't know how happy we are for someone like you to have this place. It's been rented out for so long, and no one in the family wanted it."

Angie chimed in, "What she means is that, it's always been in the family, but there were too many sad memories here."

"A lot of the properties around here have been owned by relatives of ours for generations," Sylvia interrupted. "You're one of the few people outside of family who has been able to buy one of them."

I handed Angie two more bags. "Outside of the family? Why is that?"

The longer I'd been in town, the more I'd felt like an object of the Sesame Street ditty, "One of These Things is Not Like the Others," and I hadn't been able to quite put my finger on the reason why. Could this be it? Was I the only non-relative in the whole neighborhood?

Sylvia added a pre-packed, heart-shaped box of pralines to the rest of the items waiting to be rung up and handed Alyssa her credit card. "It's all in the contract, honey."

As the staff finished the enormous transaction, I started to ask Sylvia to be more specific when she checked her watch. "Look at the time, ladies. We've got to get going." She gave me a quick hug. "Thank you so much, Kate. These are such special treats. Nonna will love them."

And so it went throughout the day, a shop full of curiosity-seekers queuing in and out, who acted as though they would die if they didn't purchase enough candy to put their whole neighborhood into a coma, and most of them wanted to be served personally by me. I would marvel at my stroke of good luck if I thought for a minute this circus was the result of my newspaper ad and placing a few samples around town. The fact that Mangia's business was also really hopping did not escape my attention. All day, customers left my shop and went directly across the street to the deli. I had no doubt that Mon Petit's opening had a little help from a friend.

I finished up the day's receipts, shaking my head. The haul was unimaginable. I didn't know whether I should think of it as a one-time fluke, or stay up all night in the kitchen to prepare for an equally crazy day two. Even with all of the extra help today, I was not able to replace even a third of what had been depleted from my inventory.

A familiar tapping brought my head up to see a handsome, smiling Italian man at the front door in a gray polo shirt and jeans. His biceps bulged as he held up two heavy sacks. I couldn't be annoyed with someone carrying a boatload of mouthwatering provisions, could I? Pretty embarrassing how well he already had me figured out. I smiled in return, shaking my head again at the crazy day, and unlocked the door to let him in.

The conversation with Sylvia and her sisters had been playing over and over in my mind all afternoon. I was confused by most of it, and I knew I'd be perusing my sales contract sometime soon with much more care than when I signed it.

Gio practically bounced into Mon Petit. "Hey. What a day, huh?"

I reached for one of his bags and headed for the kitchen silently, not knowing which degree of sarcasm to unleash.

"I mean, it was pretty wild, wasn't it?" Following me, Gio's cheerful tone went up in pitch by a full note.

I plunked the bag onto the hard steel table and went to the cupboard for plates and glasses, which I added to the setting with more resounding percussion.

"Can you believe it? Very first day? It was spectacular." He was beginning to lick his lips nervously now. "Congrats, Kate. I knew you'd knock it out of the park."

Of course you knew. One at a time I clanked ice cubes into the glasses, enjoying the harsh sound each made.

"So what do you think?"

I pulled up the same two stools we'd used last night and asked sweetly, "Oh, you're asking me what I think? Hmm . . . "

"What are you saying?" Gio had begun removing containers from the plastic sacks, arranging them on the table. "You're not mad at me or something, are you?"

Clang. Clang. Clang. Clink. Clink. Clink. Clink. Clink. Clink. I set out three serving spoons and two sets of flatware.

"Well, are you?"

I rubbed my nose with the back of my arm and sniffed.

"Kate, you're not crying, are you?"

I walked out of the kitchen and back in, door swinging both ways, and returned with a stack of paper napkins, setting all but one next to the other things. I used the one in my hand to blow my nose.

"Kate?" Gio put his hands on my shoulders. He gently tilted my head upward, but I kept my eyes averted. "What did I do? Aw, come on, Kate, look at me."

I slowly allowed my gaze to wander up to his face. It was too much. There was a fissure in the dike and I was trying hard to keep my finger in the hole that was beginning to form. A single tear escaped, sliding from the outside corner of my right eye.

Gio pulled me to his chest as I began to shake with silent, wracking sobs.

"Oh, *cara*." He cradled my head with one hand and wrapped the other arm around my shoulders. "*Carissima*." He softly whispered, "*Shhh*, it's all right," as I leaned against his chest. "*Bella*. Kate, what is it?"

The soothing sounds were all it took to crack the dam wide open. I was a blubbering fool now. "Oh, holy mother may I—" I choked out before taking a shuddering breath in. "I'm so sorry," I gasped. I grabbed a couple of the napkins and blew again, this time with disgusting gurgling noises. "Gio, I promise this is not like me." I took long, deep breaths, trying not to hyperventilate.

He wrapped both arms firmly around me, lifting me slightly from the floor. "Go ahead. It's all right. Let it go." Gio sat upon the tall stool, planting his feet firmly on the floor, and shifted my weight so that I was leaning against his leg, not quite sitting in his lap.

"It's just—" I tried the deep-breathing technique again. "I don't know—" I wiped my face with my sleeve. "Oh, boy, let me try to put this into words," I finally managed.

Gio settled in and silently waited for me to continue. And waited some more.

I closed my eyes and tried to picture a warm sun drying up the rain until I felt a little more in control. "Ah. Well, first of all, I didn't sleep last night—as in, not at all—and I am beyond exhausted, so I'm going to chalk some of this up to that." The flood waters were beginning to slow, but the disaster wasn't over yet.

"Me neither."

"I mean, I've been working toward this day for months—years, when you think about it—and there was just so much riding on it." I sniffed and took in another shaky breath. "And then there was whatever that thing was between us last night." I swallowed hard. "And all of those little noises upstairs. I've really got to call an exterminator tomorrow. They just kept reminding me that I wasn't asleep yet." I looked up, "Wait. What did you say?"

"Me neither."

"You had trouble sleeping?"

He looked skyward and exhaled before returning his gaze. "Yeah."

"Why?"

"That thing."

I blew hard into the next napkin and hiccoughed while considering. "Seriously?"

"Yeah."

"So I'm not going crazy."

"Well I wouldn't jump to any hasty conclusions." He braced for the punch I delivered to his arm. "But you're perfectly sane about . . . There was definitely a thing."

"I knew there was a thing! We shouldn't even be talking

about it. I can't have a thing right now."

"What's wrong with having a thing?"

"I don't know what to do with a thing." I shivered with another intake of breath. "I'm damaged and twisted, and my baggage is crammed way too full of crazy for a thing."

"Kate, the thing just is, whether you think you're ready for it or not. I, for one, plan to fully embrace the thing."

"Yeah, so there's this thing thrown at me out of left field—and maybe I should have seen it coming, but I'm a little dense where men are concerned—"

"No!" Gio mocked with an evil grin.

"Yeah, no kidding. Daddy issues. Mommy issues. Ex-husband issues. Blah, blah, blah." I tucked a curl behind my ear. "And then there were all these people. Thank you for that—really—but I was pretty sure I'd do all right on my own, and I didn't know whether to be happy about the business or ticked off at you for thinking I needed so much help—"

"Actually, I'm pretty sure you should save this topic for Sylvia."

"Really?"

"Well, it's not like I haven't talked you up to customers, but Sylvia's the big organizer." He rolled his eyes. "Of everything."

I laughed, picturing Sylvia putting a phone tree—or a bullhorn—into action.

"See why I let her handle everything? When she sets her mind to something . . . "

"So, there were all these people, which is great, but I guess I got a little overwhelmed." I snorted and rolled my now puffy eyes. "To say the least."

I stood and turned to look up at him, resting my hands on his arms. All of this close physical contact seemed normal, which, in and of itself, was so terrifyingly abnormal. "And then you show up, with your smile and your antipasto and your aftershave."

"That's a bad thing?"

"No, of course not."

"Then I don't understand."

"Well, that makes two of us." My chin jerked rhythmically as I cry-laughed, causing an odd guttural sound from the back of my throat.

Gio hugged me again, patting my back, as though I were an infant. "Ah, *cara mia*—"

"And your Italian words." I pushed away.

"Sorry, I—"

"No, no. I like them." I turned and crossed to the sink to splash my face. I certainly couldn't make my appearance any worse, and I welcomed the bracing, clarifying effect. Putting a little distance between me and the *stallone* didn't hurt the thought process either. "I wish I knew exactly what is happening here. I haven't got a clue."

"I think I understand." Gio began spooning out portions onto one of the plates he'd set close together in front of him. He pulled the other stool next to his and patted it in invitation. "First you've got to fuel up. When was the last time you ate, anyway?"

"My mother brought me something," I looked at my watch, "like, seven hours ago."

"Added to the no sleep, that's factor number two." He pulled a small bottle of oil from his bag and made a puddle on my plate. He tore a piece of bread, mopped at the oil and held it up, still warm, for me to try.

I took in the aroma of olives and rosemary and garlic before obediently taking a bite. "What is it about fresh bread that makes everything seem better?" I rudely asked while chewing.

"Big, important day, factor number three." He opened a carton and slid a serving of lasagna onto my plate.

I shoveled a huge forkful into my mouth. Forgetting my table manners again, I spoke more or less around it. "Mmmm.

Oh my goonness, thish ish de-lish-ush."

"Factor number four, the thing, but we'll talk about that later." He grinned wickedly."In great detail." He dished out a finely chopped salad, which included peppers, tomatoes, onions, olives and avocados.

I laughed, even though I was pretty sure I needed to be discouraging that train of thought. The food was already beginning to have a warming effect.

"But my theory about number four," only now did he begin dishing out his own meal, "is that emotions tend to get clumped together."

"Clumped."

"Yeah. Like, maybe you've been pushing down the bad stuff for a long time, and to keep it down, the good stuff kind of stays down there with it."

"In a clump."

"I'm sure there's a better way to put it, but that's how I think of it." He took the glasses to the sink and filled them with water. "So when the good stuff—like the thing between us—starts to surface, all sorts of other emotions bubble up with it." He handed me a glass and sipped from the other. "So, factor five would be dealing with the clump."

It sounded a lot like a fur ball, but at that moment, it made perfect sense. "How do you know this stuff?"

"Long story, but let's just say I've been examining my own clump for a while now."

I gaped at him momentarily. "Factor six would be that I keep discovering things about you, like, who knew you'd be Mister Sensitivity? I'm not self-conscious at all talking about us—and, oh, my sweet lard, there is an *us*—and we hardly know each other—"

"That sounds an awful lot like number four."

"Well, no, I'm trying to explain my reaction to the food and the smile and the aftershave—"

"And the Italian."

"Oh, holy crust. And the Italian! And you can wipe that smug look off your face. Is that your secret weapon or something? Do all the girls melt for the Italian?"

He looked at the floor and smiled. "The girl list is short, and I never thought about a secret weapon, but now that you mention it, I'll have to start—"

"And that darn . . . humbleness. You should package that and sell it—but then, that wouldn't be very humble of you, would it?" Up until yesterday, I'd thought the humility had been fake, a part of his shtick. Now I was just confused.

"Wait just a minute. Did you say your girl list was short?"

His chin dropped and he seemed to be inspecting his shoes. The tips of his ears turned red. "Yeah. Really short."

I pushed hard against his chest until he scrambled for balance. "Don't you dare tell me that! I've seen the bevy of baby dolls following you around."

"What?

"You know perfectly well 'what.' They stick to you like cat hair—maybe that's where your clump originated—and I've seen you kiss whole groups of them."

His mouth slackened and he scratched his jaw before running his hand through his hair. "Kate. What are you ta—"

"That day I fell on you. You were with three very young-looking girls and you kissed every one of them."

His brows came together and he stared blankly. Then his head came up and he bellowed in laughter.

"I'm glad you find this funny."

"Those girls looked young because they are. They're my nieces. Tonia's the oldest, and I think she's about sixteen."

"You kiss nieces on the mouth? Ew."

"We're a big bunch of emotional, demonstrative Italians. If you had been paying attention today, I'm sure you would have seen a lot of hugs and kisses. That's one Italian trait that seems to have stayed with us over the years."

"And you and Sylvia wonder why there are rumors about your family?"

I paced a figure-eight around the two work stations in silence until he blocked my way. "So all the women that buzz around you are related? Don't you have any male relatives?"

"Not all of them are related, but most. The rest—and I don't go around kissing them—are women other women keep trying to fix up with poor Gio, the widower. I try not to hurt their feelings, but I haven't met one I'm interested in. And as for male relatives, the truth is that right now the girls way outnumber the boys. I've got five older sisters myself."

The air was thick with silence until I finally made a tight circle with my lips. "Oh."

"So factor number six—or maybe we're on number seven now—is that you aren't comfortable with a nice guy paying attention to you."

"Well, that's something I always thought I wanted to be comfortable with—and a nice guy who can cook? I hear Barry White moaning in my head just thinking about it. But so far, my track record proves your point." I returned to my plate and dipped another bite of bread in the oil. "And just so you know, my track record is pretty short too. Pathetically short."

"Factor number—I think I've lost count now—you need more help over here."

Shaking my head, I said, "Once I get everyone trained, I think I'll be fine until tourist season."

Gio broke off more bread for me. "But for the next week or two, you need another set of hands."

"Well, come to think of it, my mother isn't exactly on the payroll, so you're probably right."

"I'll send Marco over. He really knows his way around the kitchen. He's a fast learner and he's got an eye for detail. I think you'll have him making truffles in no time."

Amused, I raised an eyebrow. "Marco DiMarco?"

"Costanzo." Gio smiled. "My sister's kid."

"But don't you need him?"

"I've always got a niece or nephew or third cousin twice removed wanting a few hours here and there. I'll be fine. Besides, as soon as there's a foot of powder on the mountain, Marco and his snowboard will disappear until late spring."

I hopped down from the stool, went to the cold-storage room and returned with the last three dipped berries for dessert. "I need to do a big batch of these tonight to fill the case for the morning. They have to be fresh, and they seem to fly off the shelf."

"I'm here to help," Gio hopped to his feet and began clearing away dishes. "That is, if you want me to."

"There you go, asking my opinion again," I sighed. I handed him an apron from the hook on the wall and watched as he lifted the strap over his head. Cue Barry White.

6.

Personal Space

I wasn't exactly sure how we wound up going to my apartment, but by the time we'd reached the top of the stairs, I knew I'd lost my mind. Not only was my place a disaster, it hadn't occurred to me until right then what inviting him up might imply to Gio. *Too soon, Kate.*

"Please excuse my mess. Now that the shop's open, I'll start figuring out where to put things up here. I haven't—"

I stopped short at the entrance. Was I at the wrong place? No, I recognized my things; I just hadn't seen them in this setting before. Not to mention, there *was* no other place. "Uh . . . " A nervous laugh was all I could summon while I tried to get my bearings.

Gio held the door for me and followed, searching for possible signs of danger. "What? Something wrong?"

I'd been surviving out of the commercial kitchen downstairs for the past four months. The apartment was only used as somewhere to crash when I was too exhausted to do anything else. Where there had been stacks of boxes, I now had a functioning living room and kitchen. Finally it dawned on me.

"My mom and Alyssa kind of vanished while I was counting the till and doing the books." I gaped in amazement. "The next time I noticed, they were saying goodbye."

The living room looked like something Martha Stewart would have whipped together—or about fifteen of her staff, more likely. I've always been fascinated by how familiar old things can transmute into *objets d'art* when arranged by someone other than yourself.

"They totally came up here and unpacked for me!"

Someone had organized my books in the twin oak cases. Alyssa's hand was at work there. My mother was most likely the one responsible for hanging artwork and placing tchotchkes in just the right spots. She had a natural gift for color and design, and no one understood my personal tastes and preferences better than she did.

Gio's face relaxed, but he stopped me to see how I was doing. "So I don't have to check for signs of forced entry or look for someone hiding in the closets?"

"No. I'm fine." I opened the coat closet and slammed it shut. "Thanks for putting that thought in my head, though." I took his outstretched hand. "And your concern is very se— attractive."

A large watercolor I'd completed after the divorce held a place of honor over the fireplace. The abstract was painted in the warm autumn hues I loved—and Eddie hated—with a loose representation of fabric blowing in the wind. I'd titled the piece "Freedom Flag." My easel stood in the bay window with an unfinished canvas resting there, as if I'd been working on it just this morning.

Gio's eyes lit brighter with each new discovery I came across. "You're like a little kid on Christmas morning."

I opened kitchen cabinets to see things neatly put away and organized. The oak tabletop had been securely reunited with its claw-foot pedestal, with four antique chairs tucked cozily in all around. Nowhere to be found was the gimpy card table.

Turning a full circle, arms out, I giggled in delight.

"Looks nice."

"Nice? It's like gnomes came in and made shoes while I was out." I left him there while I sauntered down the hallway—

without having to turn sideways at all. The bathroom revealed more of the same. I started to check my bedroom, but looked back at Gio and decided against it. *Way, way too soon.*

"It's elves, isn't it?"

"Hmm?" I was still thinking about the bedroom and wondering what was on Gio's mind as far as that went.

"The shoemaker had elves."

"Right. Elves." Looking in the spare room, I saw it was stacked floor to ceiling with sensibly arranged boxes, staged to make the rest of the move-in a breeze. I really would to have to start filing those adoption papers. Alyssa's parents might object, and she was technically an adult, but that girl was solid gold.

"I don't hear anything." Gio was getting to work with his ear close to the kitchen wall.

"Of course you don't. It's like taking your car to the mechanic. It never acts up when he's under the hood."

"Describe it again." He was running his palm along different spots on the wall, feeling for vibrations.

I sat down at my table, enjoying the luxury of finally feeling at home in my own apartment. "Sometimes it's a knocking sound and I think it's something wonky in the plumbing." I watched him methodically checking the entire surface. "Then it will be a scratching noise and I think there's a tree scraping against the window—but of course, there isn't a window or a tree there. And sometimes it sounds as though someone is moving around upstairs, but I'm the only resident—or only human resident, anyway. That's when I think I must have a raccoon or a possum or a herd of baby elephants living with me."

"Did you go up there and have a look?" He was tapping now, either trying to stir up varmints or locate pipes. I couldn't tell which.

"Up where? The attic?"

He raised an eyebrow and gave me a look that said, *where else would you go?*

"Don't laugh, but I didn't think of it."

He laughed. He laughed loudly.

"Hey. When I signed the sales contract, Sylvia said she'd have to do some searching for the key. I wanted to keep these old locks, because they're just so cool and unique. I was afraid a locksmith would tear up the doors.

"And you still don't have the key?"

"Yes. I do." I jumped up and began opening drawers. "Somewhere." Who knew where I might have put it? I couldn't recall seeing it since Sylvia dropped it by, weeks ago. "I'll have to search tomorrow. Those two did some major rearranging, you know." *Throwing your elves under the bus for your own forgetfulness. Nice, Kate.*

Joining Gio while he jiggled the glass knob, I said, "By the time Sylvia sent the key over, boxes were stacked all along here and I kind of got used to looking at them. With setting up the shop, this was not my most pressing issue."

"Looks like this thing is painted shut anyway. My family has had renters in here for over thirty years." He ran his fingers along the door's edges. "You find the key and I'll bring some tools by tomorrow."

What he did next took my breath away.

He clasped my hand and led me back downstairs to the front of the shop. I guess I needn't have worried about him looking at his visit as an engraved invitation for intimacy. As it turned out, Gio behaved like a (what was that archaic phrase?) perfect gentleman.

"Kate, I was wondering . . . " He continued to hold my hand and gazed down into my face, "And I totally understand if you are uncomfortable with the idea—" He brushed a curl out of my eyes.

The pulse at my temple began to throb, as I wondered what

question he was leading up to. I licked my lips as he went on.

"My family is having a big event out in the country this weekend—"

"Your grandmother's birthday."

"You heard."

I smiled at the understatement. Even though they'd pretended they weren't all one big family—as if today's flash mob of patronage wasn't clue enough—it didn't take a genealogist to get that most of my customers shared the same grandmother. "Yes, I heard."

"Would you like to go out there with me?"

Thinking of any type of crowd made my stomach churn, but a crowd of Gio's relatives further scrutinizing me? My sweat glands became tiny fountains of angst. I attempted a passive expression, but the terror must have shown.

"I'll maintain a safe zone around you, I promise."

Those eyes. Whatever this "thing" was between us, wherever it might be leading, I knew that sometime I would have to learn resistance to that pleading little boy look in his eyes. Right now was not that time. Who was I kidding? Despite whatever it was holding me back, if he was going to be away all day, I knew I wanted to be with him. Resistance was futile.

"Hmm. I'll have to give that some consideration." I encircled his waist with my arms, laying my cheekbone against his muscular chest, totally giving in to the "thing." "Maybe you should ask me again." Even the tips of my ears were feeling warm now. "In Italian?"

7.

Meeting Marco

The next morning, while I made to-do lists over my morning cocoa, a thundering grew increasingly louder until it came to rest near the screened alley door. A small pickup lurched to a stop with one final roar and a few sputters. It might once have been red. The best giveaway was a red driver's door that didn't match the puttied and primered body. It sported huge tires and wheels, and either a very large engine or a very large hole in the muffler was responsible for the racket. I guessed hole. A young man with curly, dark hair jumped out of the cab and climbed the steps.

"You Kate?"

"Hello," I replied, mildly bewildered.

"Gio told me to show up before seven."

Blankly, I eyed this shorter, younger, darker version of Gio. He was compact and scrappy-looking, with a cocky but kind face. The hair was different, but there was no mistaking this kid's genetics. I'd seen him somewhere before. I stood staring until the light of recognition came on. He worked at Mangia. "Oh. Marco." I shook his offered hand. "Thank you so much for coming."

"No problem." He flashed a bright smile. *Oh yeah. Gio all over.*

"Come on in. I'm just getting ready to start a batch of chocolate." I motioned him inside. "You should feel quite honored. This is my super top-secret, special recipe."

"You don't just melt chocolate and add other ingredients to it?"

"A lot of candymakers do that—they focus on the centers and mold the shell from commercially made product—but no." We entered the vault of secrets, otherwise known as the pantry. "I did not spend years in culinary school so I could just melt chocolate." The unmistakable aroma of raw cacao assaulted our senses from within the small, climate-controlled room. "I like to start as close to the beginning of the process as I can."

Marco wrinkled his nose and coughed. "Whoa. What is that?"

"What does it smell like to you?"

"Kinda disgusting."

"Keep breaking it down." Closing my eyes, I flared my nostrils and took a deep breath, raising my upturned palm for effect.

He breathed in and thought for a moment. "Well, there's a little bit of a sweet smell, I guess, but it mostly smells like dirt."

"Remember that smell—kind of like rich forest soil after a rain, with a hint of potato chips and peach wine and other things you wouldn't expect. If you detect a strong vinegar odor or if it has a 'hammy' smell, the fermentation is not right for my chocolate."

At my instruction, Marco loaded a cart with the sacks marked "*Cacao de Ecuador*" and some others filled with confectioner's sugar and brought them to the work area.

"Not right for *your* chocolate? What about everyone else's?" He opened sacks with a box knife.

I understood why Gio had confidence in the kid.

"The big manufacturers use a different variety of cacao, mostly from Africa. The beans produce more cocoa, but they also need to be fermented longer to make machine processing easier. Then to get rid of the rancid taste, they roast it at high temperatures, only to replace rancid with a bitter, burnt flavor. It's all about quantity and cheap production over quality."

Rolling a cooling rack over, I asked, "Would you please bring that food scale over here?"

He didn't need further instructions, locating the scale below the table as if he'd always worked at Mon Petit. "Then how do they make it taste all right?"

"If you throw in enough sugar, dried milk, lecithin, hydrogenated oils and other additives, you can mask just about any nasty taste." I handed him a scoop and pointed to the rack of aerated trays. "Put about seven hundred grams of beans on each roasting tray and spread them out evenly before you put the trays back."

"Why seven hundred?"

"Some things never change. I went from being a bean counter to counting beans. Pretty crazy, huh?"

He eyed me in confusion.

"Seven-hundred fits the tray."

"Oh, okay. Got it." He began measuring. "So if we roast these, won't it make them bitter too?"

"Good question. Glad you're paying attention." I pulled another rack from near the screened door, checking to make sure the trays were thoroughly cooled. "I use as little heat as I can get away with—barely enough to open the outer husks of the beans. I think the flavor is better if some of the enzymes are preserved. It's supposed to be healthier too, but honestly, anyone trying to wipe out an army of free-radicals with chocolate is fooling themselves."

We'd been in full production mode until nearly eight, when Alyssa arrived. As she opened the back door, she called something I couldn't quite catch over the sound of machinery. She came around to face me with a big grin and asked, "Kate. So, did you notice anything different last night?"

I turned off the food processor, but the sound from the winnowing room made it still difficult for conversation. I yelled, "Oh, my goodness. What an incredible surprise." I gave her a hug of appreciation, trying not to smear her with brown paste. "You must have been exhausted after yesterday, and yet you did that for me? I knew you were a keeper."

"Your mom's a hoot-and-a-half. We had a blast together. She wanted to do that for a long time but didn't know where to begin—and I have a thing for organization—so we decided to tackle it together." Alyssa looked over my shoulder. "So what's going on in there?"

"Marco is running the winnowing machine, removing the husks from the cacao beans. I think I'm going to make a chocolatier out of him if he's not careful. He's great."

"Who?" The color drained from Alyssa's face.

"Marco DiMarco. No, that's not right. He's from the deli across the street. Gio sent him to help for a couple of weeks." I mopped up splatters on the counter, watching her jaw drop. "Do you know him?"

Her eyes were as big as saucers. "Everyone knows Marco Costanzo."

The machine in the other room shut off just as the last two words were shouted. Alyssa's face went from alabaster to crimson in zero-point-two seconds when the subject of our conversation emerged.

"Marco, you probably know Alyssa then?"

"I've seen her around." He extended his hand to her, showing his good manners weren't reserved just for temporary employers. "Hi. How's it going?" That smile could probably turn any girl to jelly, but Alyssa—that confident young woman, who just yesterday was put in charge of everything—turned catatonic before my eyes. "Huh—hello," she stammered, and started paying particular attention to her shoes.

"Alyssa, I made a few fresh batches last night. If you'd put some of those in the cases and make a tasting display out front for the strawberries, that would be great."

She stood frozen, not showing noticeable signs of brain activity, looking as if she might drool. Maybe it was a good thing Marco was only on loan.

She rattled a nod and bumped her forehead on the swinging door as she left the kitchen.

Turning to Marco, I asked, "All done in there?"

"Yeah. How many buckets of, uh, nibs do you want done?"

"Let's just do one at a time." I smiled at his newfound vocabulary before adding one more word to it. "I'll show you how to use the *molcajete*."

"Mocha-head-day?"

"Close enough."

"Looks like a mortar and pestle to me."

"That's pretty much what it is, but you get extra nerd points for using the authentic Mesoamerican version." I laughed.

"Great . . . "

"I like its shape better for working chocolate, and I'm pretty much maxed out on nerd points, so it's no threat to me."

While there wasn't a line down the block, at least not continually, day two proved to be just as busy as day one. Alyssa and crew were refining the customer service process and herding the masses through the store at a higher rate of speed. I seemed to have fewer interruptions, so the kitchen was a tighter ship too. The vibe of the day was a more manageable degree of madness.

With Marco on board, I could see the possibility of production keeping up with demand. Zara and Emily, the second-wave assistants, managed to pop in and help in the back from time to time. We made large batches of some of our best-selling dipped goods. Overall, the day was looking brighter.

Alyssa was the queen of the sales area, but utterly worthless in the kitchen today. Every time she saw Marco, or even heard his name mentioned, she seemed to knock something over or trip on an invisible obstacle, and the sequence of her words became unintelligible. This girl had it bad. You'd have to be blind, or maybe one of the DiMarco men, to not see it.

When Marco returned from across the street with lunch I'd ordered for everyone, he was laughing and shaking his head. "I think Uncle G has gone crazy."

"Why's that?" I asked.

"He's whistling and singing over there and telling really bad jokes. I haven't seen him act that crazy since I was a little kid. He gets pretty close to it whenever you come into the shop, but not like this." He passed the sandwiches around. "My cousins are threatening to quit if he doesn't put a different CD in the player."

I opened the sandwich wrapper marked "Kate" and found a folded note inside.

It read, "The last park concert of the summer is tonight. Are you up for a picnic? I'll stop by at 7:30. Wear something warm."

With a smile I began devouring my food, not having the luxury of a leisurely lunch. "Oh? What CD was he playing?" I asked.

Marco's nostrils curled in obvious distaste. "Some old guy with a super deep voice. The thing was called *The Best of Barry White*."

8.

Saturday in the Park

Castle Springs' annual summer *Music in the Park* series extended through the end of September in an effort to squeeze in as much community bonding as possible before the explosion of tourism hit.

Midsummer sunset light against the golden rock face of The Keep was a show you could almost charge admission for. This late in the season, though, the sun was down long before the concert began. The trees in the town square and along its side streets were lit by a million tiny white lights. They stayed lit year-round, adding to the enchanted, idyllic character Castle Springs always held for me.

Gio's hand holding mine as he guided me along the streets gave me a similar feeling of warmth and brightness. Maybe the sensation from handholding was so monumental to me because Eddie and I had never done it. Never. He had a pronounced aversion to displays of affection, public or otherwise. It was a home run or nothing with Eddie, and he wasn't much of a team player, if you know what I mean.

By contrast, here was a man I'd not even kissed, who proudly let everyone in his inner circle know he was here with me. And it was his inner circle. There was not one person we passed who didn't call him by name and greet him warmly. This was his town. These were his people.

What an odd thought. Must be the fairy lights. Disneyland.

Castles. The prince waving to his subjects.

Through my summer of remodeling, I had gathered what I'd believed to be a pretty detailed history of the town from the contractors and laborers I'd worked alongside.

Castle Springs had originally been built around the square, which was still a source of great pride for the locals. There was a continual flow of organized activities going on here during the warm months, and other grand events conceived to draw tourists down the hill during ski season.

The shops and historic homes surrounding the square for blocks looked much the same as they must have in the late 1800s. Not, I might add, by coincidence. This very exclusive portion of Castle Springs was known as Oldtown and was practically an entity all its own. It was almost impossible to find a property for sale here, and those who lived and worked in the area took great pains to preserve its original beauty and historical qualities.

Like many small towns in the west, the focus for new businesses had shifted elsewhere when, in the nineteen-fifties, the interstate highway came through. Chain stores and fast food places sprang up along the highway's corridor, south of town. The sprawl had continued in that direction as the city grew.

The majority of the population in the southern part of town worked in Sunnyvail, the spendy, trendy vacation destination in the nearby mountains. They were employed as ski instructors, golf pros, massage therapists, domestic help, and other providers of service to the rich and famous. They earned their living on "the hill", but could only dream about someday living there.

As Sunnyvail had transformed into a chichi hotspot, Castle Springs grew proportionately out of necessity, to serve its needs. Oldtown had barely been touched by the expansion. It remained picture-postcard perfect. A little slice of Old Europe mixed with Old West Colorado.

A city within a city, Oldtown was bordered on the north by Castle Hill, named for The Keep atop it, with its resemblance to a crumbling medieval fortress. Its imposing presence only added to the town's European flavor.

The concert was already underway when we arrived. Tonight's act was a trio playing soft jazz, generating a soothing, romantic atmosphere. There was a brisk chill in the evening air with the aroma of a distant wood fire clinging to it, giving no doubt that autumn was in the wings, waiting to appear at any moment.

Gio led me to the spot with the best view of the log gazebo where the band played. He spread a denim quilt on the grass and set another folded blanket and his dinner-filled backpack on top. Gripping both my hands, he offered support as I sat. We ate in silence, enjoying the music and watching the park fill up with the familiar faces of the neighborhood.

The faces smiled and nodded, but kept a respectful distance. Maybe Gio's friends and family had been warned to back off a little. Regardless of the reason, I was happy for at least the illusion of privacy.

As the temperature gradually dropped, we found ourselves sitting close together, Gio's arm around my shoulders, sharing the warmth of the blanket wrapped around us. It was easier to carry on a conversation this way.

"You warm enough?"

"Mm-hmm." As if the awareness of Gio's breath near my ear and down my neck wasn't enough to raise my temperature, I sat a little closer and pulled the blanket tighter.

"I'm curious. What made you come to Castle Springs?" Gio rearranged himself so that he was behind me now and I could lean comfortably against his chest.

I bumped his chin when I looked up. "*Ooo*, sorry. Wouldn't anyone want to live here?"

"Maybe," he answered, "but there are easier places to make a living. You've got to be prepared to wait out the slower months, and not everyone thinks that far ahead. The snow crowd, with their big spending, has a way of distorting people's sense of success."

"I've taken that into account." I settled back in, where his massive biceps became my furnace. "I grew up near Denver. Well, actually, I grew up all over. Santa Fe, Las Vegas, San Diego, Seattle—my mom was a gypsy at heart—but we managed to stay in Denver through most of high school." I could feel Gio's heart beating and my own pulse trying to keep time. And, heaven help me, there was that clean, male scent again. "I went on a few of the school's ski trips to Sunnyvail, and I always loved it when we'd make a pit stop in Castle Springs. It was like a little hidden jewel, and everyone was so friendly, even to a bunch of rowdy city kids."

We began to sway slightly with the rhythm of the music. "Roots are something I really missed as a kid. I always dreamed of having a home in a place like this."

"And you found your way back."

"Believe it or not, my mother helped me out with that," I said. "She finally remarried—or married 'well' you might say—after I was out of college and in business back east. They retired to his vacation home near the slopes." I could feel Gio playing with a tight tendril of my hair. "During my divorce, I stayed with them for a few weeks, and that's when I decided where I wanted to end up, even if I wasn't sure yet how I'd get here."

"Well, I'm glad you figured it out."

I rested a hand on the knee that sat next to mine. "I am too."

After a short break, the trio was joined by three brass players.

"These guys are great." Gio leaned sideways to ask, "Do you like swing revival?"

"Do you? It was my favorite in college. I went to a Big Bad

Voodoo Daddy concert once and was hooked for life. Dancing was so fun until—"

"Well, let's go then." He nearly lifted me up in his arms when he stood.

"Go where? Here?" Couples were beginning to gravitate to a roped area near the gazebo as the band finished rechecking the sound.

"Sure! Come on, Kate." He waited with his hand out until I decided I'd make more of a scene by refusing than if I sucked it up and went with him.

The trumpet, trombone, and sax transformed the cool-jazz trio into a smoking hot little-big band. The gathering of couples was either of the Depends crowd or close to our age. Swing revival had been a big deal on college campuses during those few years we had been students. I couldn't imagine all the fun I would have missed without it—fun that had come to an abrupt stop after Eddie entered my life.

I could think of very few times when being little came as a distinct advantage. Swing dancing was one of them. Especially when you were a little woman being tossed around by a great big, handsome, delicious-smelling man, whose appreciation of the dance equaled your own. The guy had moves. On top of everything else he had going for him, he was a regular Maksim Chmerkovskiy.

The evening chill became a welcome guest to our exercise-heated bodies. The rosy glow I imagined having from the exertion was much preferred to self-conscious sweatiness I'd shared before, in dark clubs with smelly guys barely out of their teens. By the time the concert was over I was so energized, I practically skipped next to Gio on the way back home, in spite of sides and cheeks that ached from laughing so hard.

9.

Stripping

"I have a bad feeling about this." Gio held a stiff putty knife up to the indentation that was once a space between door and jamb but was now solidly filled in with an undetermined quantity of layered paint. "It's not going to be pretty."

After the concert, we'd swung by Mangia to get the tools he'd put out, and headed back to my place to address the problem, as promised.

"I know. I wish we could get to the hinge pins to take the door off, but they had to be on the other side, of course." I took a deep breath as he hesitated, mallet hovering over the knife. I loved these doors and wanted to restore them. I didn't want to risk damaging them any more than Gio, but there was no getting around it. "Go for it."

As the seal was broken, chips of paint fell to the floor, in some places peeling back patches of color. I examined the paint-equivalent of tree rings and counted at least twelve layers and probably more. This archaeological project revealed avocado green, burnt orange, turquoise, smoke blue, dusty rose, teal, burgundy, and hunter green among other colors more sedate.

"I remember this place being a happy yellow when my grandparents lived here, but it's amazing how bold people get when it's not their property," Gio muttered under his breath while tapping.

"Didn't you have painting restrictions? Most landlords I've had—"

"When I bought my parents out a few years ago, I updated all of the lease agreements. Up until then, renters could express their inner psycho with any putrid color they chose." Gio tossed the putty knife in the tool bucket with a clang and started using a sharp folding knife from his pocket to slice at the petrified paint. "There were very few restrictions, so tenants went a little crazy."

"I guess paint is easy enough to fix."

"No-paint would have been easier." He switched back to his hammer and chisel. "I think my parents wanted to give the renters a little feel of ownership, hoping they'd take better care of the place."

"Because this building was important to your family."

"*Is* important. This was my mother's childhood home. My parents grew up across the street from each other. This place will always mean something to them."

"So you bought it from them."

"I bought everything from them when they retired to the ranch."

"Everything? My building and the deli?" Intrigued now by the emerging deposits of many colors, I began following behind Gio's chipping to see what patterns I could make with the layers. This patch looked like an orange giraffe.

Gio worked on without speaking.

I waited for him to answer as a paint-layer rooster appeared. "How much is everything?"

"My family is full of traditions." He could work more quickly, now able to see what was what, and that no permanent damage was being done. "One of them is about property."

"Okay . . . "

"I grew up with the saying, 'Live poor, grow rich' pounded into my skull." He paused to turn to me. "It's sort of a family motto. You live frugally and you invest heavily. That's what they've always done."

I glared impatiently, wondering how this was leading to answering my question.

"And you use your blessings to help your family first." He stopped for a moment to look at me. "There are properties all over this valley, and particularly in Oldtown, that have been passed down in the family from generation to generation."

"They're all relatives?"

"It started out with one guy—one of the original settlers—and his descendants followed his example."

"So, one of your ancestors—"

"Aldo Castaldi. He was one of the last homesteaders in the valley and then he bought out other homesteaders and stipulated that the land couldn't ever leave the family."

"Like, *ever* ever?"

"Yeah. Like, ever. Perpetually."

"So you own—"

"A lot."

"Like," I gaped, "the whole town?"

"No. Of course not." He returned to the door.

"Well, then, how much?" I stared at his back.

He did not respond.

"Half?"

Gio dug around in his tools and found one that looked like it had a hook on the end. He tried using it to pull away the stubborn sheets from the slot.

I persisted. "It's not half is it?"

Finally he answered, "Probably more than half—of Oldtown, anyway."

I staggered around the corner to find a kitchen chair to sit on.

"And outlying properties too," he said.

"What about the other less-than-half places?" I stammered.

"The majority of this whole area is owned by direct descendants of either Aldo or the people he helped bring over from the old country—who were all somehow related to him too."

"Squares," I whispered.

"We just love that name." He shook his head and cleared his throat. "After the town square, because descendants have always owned the properties surrounding it."

I rose to put water in the kettle, returned it to the stove and bent over to adjust the gas flame. "So how does someone afford to buy over half a town?"

"Family discount," Gio shrugged.

I leaned against the hallway wall so I could see his face while he chipped away. "No, seriously. Sorry if I'm prying too much, I—"

"No. It's not that. I want you to ask. It's just, I don't talk about this stuff very often."

"Why? So that people don't try to take advantage of you? Ask too much of you?"

"That's not it. I can't help anyone if they don't ask, because how else would I know what their needs are? And I don't have a hard time turning people down when necessary. So, no."

"Well then, why?"

"People see money or success or whatever and they stop seeing who you really are," Gio patted his chest, "in here." He bent down to change tools again and came back up. "I'd rather people like me as the guy who wraps their cold cuts than for them to get all weird on me as the guy who owns a town."

"More than half. Don't go puffing yourself up."

He smiled at my not "getting all weird on him."

"So how did you do it?"

His brows knit together, and he worked silently for a few moments before finally answering. "GDM did really well up on the mountain during the real-estate bubble."

"Like, well enough to buy half a town?"

"Yeah." He was making noticeable progress now on the door. "I mean, some of it is just formality, really. I was going to inherit eventually, anyway. My sisters have never really been into all of this, so I bought out their portions of interest. I wanted to make sure that nothing changed financially for my parents when they retired—and that's the formality part."

"I imagine they weren't going to be hurting much, anyway," I offered.

He laughed. "No, but it's just the—well, the right thing to do, you know? I was taking over. I wanted to know they were taken care of and that everything was my responsibility now—a clean break."

Getting him to open up was like prying an egg open for an emerging chick. I knew I should be patient and let him tell it in his own way, but I couldn't help myself. "You still haven't told me how you could afford—"

"I financed a great big luxury condo project right before the market started going berserk. I made a killing on that, but the market hadn't peaked yet."

The kettle began to whistle, and I went to the kitchen. I took out two mugs and my own hot cocoa mix from the cupboards and began measuring and pouring.

Gio called around the corner, "I spent a very intense year of rehabbing properties—commercial and residential—but I had enough reserves to gamble on the timing of the sales. I kept an eye on things, and when I thought the prices weren't going to get any higher, I unloaded several vacation rentals near the slopes and a lot of the unrestricted parcels down on the south side." He tipped his head around the corner. "Do you have a dustpan?"

I opened cupboards until I found one under the sink, and he disappeared again with it.

"And it's not like I bought everything all at once. Or all of it from my folks either." He joined me in the kitchen, emptied the dustpan into the trash and sat down. "As the economy has gotten worse, I've been approached by a bunch of descendants who needed to move on."

I splashed some cold milk into the mugs and joined Gio with them at the table. "Why you?" I asked as I settled in. "Why do they approach you?"

He blew across the top of his mug, set it down, stirred it, blew again and took a cautious sip before answering. "One reason would be that I'm in the business." He slowly repeated the blowing and stirring process. "But it goes beyond that."

"What? Are you, like, the Godfather of Castle Springs or something?"

His laugh boomed. "No, nothing like that. Although," he put on his best Marlon Brando, "I would like to make you an offer you can't refuse."

"Tempting," I laughed, "but, again, why you?"

"There seems to be one of us in every generation. We're what my dad calls 'The Keepers' of the town. He was one. My mom's father was another, until he died."

"The Keepers." I drew my sweater tighter around me as goosebumps formed on my arms.

"That's what he calls us. Castaldi is a derivative of the Italian word for 'keeper of the castle.'"

"The one who sort of takes care of Aldo's legacy."

"Exactly. 'Legacy' is a perfect word for it."

I let the thought soak in until suddenly, the obvious question hit my brain like a frying pan. "Wait. So why would you sell this building if it were part of the legacy, and, more importantly, how could you sell it to me?"

"No one in the family wanted this building for themselves. There were sad memories here for them." He began rubbing his finger around the rim of his cup. "It got rented out for so many years and got into worse and worse shape—well, you saw how bad."

I nodded with widened eyes. I'd just gotten through months of fixing the worst of the mess.

"I wanted it to go to someone who would take care of it, but there was no getting around the family-only thing. Perpetuity clauses aren't as cut and dried as they were in Aldo's day. Legally there are ways of getting around them, but it's been a matter of honor. We've carried on the tradition and it's expected of us to adhere to the tradition. The perpetuity clause has been included in every transfer of title since Aldo was alive, including when I bought the place."

"How were you able to sell then?"

"Sylvia did some digging around in old documents at the courthouse. She found some kind of loophole."

We sat quietly looking at one another as this information began to sink in.

"And she found you." Gently stroking my face, the palm of his hand warm from the mug, he said, "It was like everything just sort of fell together—like it was meant to be."

My eyes closed at his touch, heightening the other senses. The now familiar scent, the slightly rough palm, the caressing sound of his whisper. There was no hope. I knew this could end badly. I'd stopped caring. I leaned closer to him in anticipation of the most epic first kiss ever, when a distinct knocking came on cue.

"See? That's it."

Gio sprang up to touch the wall, but . . . nothing. "You have that key?"

I reached under the three oranges in the bowl on my table and produced it. "Yes. I found it." I didn't tell him that I had found it, on of all places, the plaque next to my door with the word "keys" inscribed on it. I joined Gio by the attic door but discovered the key would not fit. "Ahh! Holy carp." I started trying other doors in the apartment and the key matched each of them. This keyhole, however had a unique shape. It was unusually large and formed the shape of a crescent moon or the letter "C." "You'd think I would have seen that before," I said in embarrassment. "I guess if I'd been able to actually look at the door all this time, I would have noticed."

Gio took a credit card out of his wallet and began fishing around the door's bolt, without success. "Usually these old locks are pretty easy to pick . . . but this . . . it's just not going to budge."

"Interesting." I took the card from him and tried wiggling it behind the bolt, thinking my smaller hands might be more nimble. Sure enough, there was no moving it. "I guess I'll have to get that locksmith after all."

"We'll ask Nonna about it when we're out at the ranch. Maybe she'll have some ideas."

"Nonna?"

"The birthday girl, my great-grandmother, Nonna."

"I feel like I'll be meeting a celebrity. I've been hearing so much about her for the past couple of days!"

"Better than a celebrity, I promise you that. We get celebrities through here all the time, and, believe me, they are nothing to get excited about. Now Nonna—she's something else, that's for sure!" Gio smiled.

"What is she like? I mean, I know she's very elderly. Is she an invalid? Does she speak any English?"

At that, Gio laughed, "Ha! Invalid? No. We finally convinced her that she couldn't go out to check the mail on icy days, but other than that, she's still going strong. And I speak more Italian than Nonna."

"Really? How's that possible?"

Gio was beginning to clean up his tools and I took the mugs to the sink to wash them.

"Nonna was born and raised in Castle Springs, as were her parents. She is the granddaughter of Aldo Castaldi."

I puzzled for a bit. "Wait, so your mother's father was a Castaldi and your great-grandmother on your father's side was a Castaldi—"

"I told you it was hard to keep straight." Gio came up to stand close behind me and I turned to face him.

"Before Nonna's time, the Italian community sort of kept to themselves. The square was originally a farm. Then, someone put a store there to serve the miners."

"Miners? There's a mine?"

I could just stand here all evening and look at him. I imagined how I would sketch him. Right now, I was concentrating on the lines of his face. I wasn't allowing myself to think for too long about his other lines just yet.

"There is a mine. Sort of. A lot of the Italian families—the non-Castaldis—migrated here because of the mine and the railroad. They heard of other settlers from the old country, so they weren't quite so afraid to make the trek. Most of them came from the agricultural regions of Italy and didn't want to stay in the big cities, like the bulk of them did. There were ads back east that promised free land and jobs. Of course, by the time most of them got here, the homesteading was long gone."

"Did the mine play out or something? I haven't seen anything in town about a mining industry."

"There was an accident in the mid eighteen-nineties—an explosion. It took about ten lives—a huge tragedy in a town like this."

I imagined what that must have been like. "How would you even handle an explosion with eighteen-ninety technology?"

"They couldn't. The explosion started a fire. A fire in a coal mine is not a good thing."

I became distracted by the realization that I was tracing the muscles of his upper arms. Even in their relaxed state, they were firm and well defined. "What did they do?"

"There wasn't anything they could do. There's still nothing they can do. That fire has been burning for about a hundred and twenty years."

I silently formed a "wow" as I tried to wrap my brain around such a thing.

"Anyway, that little farm—"

"Owned by Aldo Castaldi, of course," I said.

"Of course—one of his many farms—that little farm turned into a little town. It became sort of a 'Little Italy' at first, but by the time Nonna and Grandpa G opened the deli, the Italians had started assimilating into regular society. They were proud Americans, and wanted to play down being different from anyone else."

"So your great-grandmother was one of those who felt more American than Italian."

"Right. She speaks Italian like someone who learned it as a small child. She understands a lot but her vocabulary is pretty limited and her grammar is sometimes all wrong."

"And you?" I led him into the living room and we sat close together on the couch, Gio's arm around me.

"My parents sent me to live in Calabria for over a year when I was fifteen."

"They sent you? What? Was there a school there or something?"

"Uh, well, I'm sure there was one, but I didn't go there." His mouth formed a straight line before he continued. "They packed me up with a big pile of homeschool curriculum and a teach-yourself-Italian program and put me on a plane."

"What was in Calabria?"

"My oldest sister fell in love with a foreign student in college and, much to my parents' disappointment, she followed him to Italy and married him."

I snuggled into his warmth at his invitation, tucking my arm behind his back. "And why did they send you? Did you get in trouble or something?"

I could feel his nose and mouth against my hairline as he spoke softly, "There was a girl. We were only fifteen. My parents were afraid we were getting too serious, and they were right. We were. It took me a long time to figure that part out, though."

I looked up at him to see him gazing off into the distance.

"I mean, she and I had spent all those years in school with the nuns, so we were well aware of what was expected of us, but it was beginning to feel like we had our feet on the gas and the brakes at the same time, you know? I think our brake feet were beginning to wear out."

"How did you feel about going? About being packed off to your sister's?"

He encircled me tighter with his arms. "Oh, I was a very angry kid at first. I refused to speak to my parents for a full month. Finally, my sister got sick of it and refused to be go-between. I had to take their calls after that."

"And then?"

"I became less angry over time, but not by much." He ran his finger along my jaw line. "And somewhere in all of that I fell in love—with Italy."

I sat quietly and digested this information. "It sounds so romantic and sad," I said at last. "Whatever happened to the girl?"

Gio held me a little closer. "She died in my arms of ovarian cancer, five years ago, in our bed across the street."

Separating them at fifteen had given Gio and Susan time to grow up and gain a different perspective, but it had not severed their relationship. They were married at seventeen, with their parents' blessing, in the summer before going off to college together.

"Think what you want, but it was the wisest decision they

ever made as parents—that, and sending me to Italy." Gio mused.

He got a business degree with an emphasis in real estate law. She got a master's in social work, that she only got the chance to use on a volunteer basis, due to her illness.

After Gio turned daily operations of GDM over to Sylvia and bought the deli from his parents, he set up a special table in back for her to see the friends she'd made during long rounds of chemotherapy. Up until the time she could no longer leave her bed, she sat at that table, dispensing advice, counsel and a listening ear to those who came to her.

"I still have people come every day, just to talk—and she's been gone five years now," Gio said softly.

"They come to you?"

"Yeah. I used to be uncomfortable with it, like I'd turned into 'Dear Abby' or the local parish priest or something, and I didn't feel equipped for it at all—except for more or less feeling like a eunuch, so the priest thing—but I sort of got used to it. It kind of let me feel closer to her, you know? Like I was carrying on her work for her."

By the time Gio was done speaking, we were both crying. I got mascara all over his light blue shirt. I would have been embarrassed by that if I weren't more embarrassed by the contents of my dripping nose being deposited along with it.

"I'm sorry, *cara*, this was the last thing I wanted to do tonight, make you cry. I seem to be doing a lot of that lately." He kissed my temple, and both of my damp eyes.

I tilted my head upward to catch his lips with my own and, as anticipated, the kiss was nothing short of spectacular. It was the fourth of July in every nerve ending in my body. The kiss was gentle at first, and tentative. His breath was sweet and warm, his mouth soft and evaluating. Soon it became more hungry and insistent and I could almost hear my "brick wall" begin to crumble.

"Ah, Kate." He whispered. "If you only knew how long I've been wanting to do this."

So much for the eunuch, I thought, as the kissing became more intense and probing.

Bang, bang, bang, bang, bang. My noisy attic roommates brought us back to clarity. "Holy Hannah and her sisters," I muttered. Then I yelled across the room, "All right. I get it."

"I think the rats are jealous of me," Gio said, rising and pulling me to my feet.

"Uck. Don't say 'rats.' Anything but rats. And spiders? I've had a recurring nightmare after finding a gazillion of them behind that ugly ceiling downstairs."

"Rats, bats, squirrels, giant mutant ninja spiders—" Gio hoisted me over his shoulder and carried me, squealing, down the stairs to the front door where he gently set me down.

I reached up to encircle his neck. "Thank you for tonight," I whispered. "For the concert, the handyman work, for . . . everything."

He lifted me up off my feet and kissed me again, warmly, softly, sweetly. "My pleasure," he breathed. "Literally."

I laughed and kissed him again as he returned me to the floor.

"I'll come for you at noon tomorrow, okay?"

My forehead wrinkled as I asked, "Do you really think it will be all right to leave my baby so soon? I'm feeling like a really irresponsible parent."

"Kate, you've been working like a dog for months. You deserve a day off." He kissed the top of my head. "Besides, from what you've told me about Alyssa, I'm sure things will be fine."

I wasn't so sure. With Marco in-house to distract her, she was definitely off her game. But at the same time, I couldn't imagine the kitchen running smoothly without him. I needed him to keep up the ever-vanishing supply of fresh dipped strawberries. He was a natural at presentation.

Gio was right, though. I hadn't truly gotten out in months, and the thought of him being away most of the day made me antsy. I'd always thought the stories of people who were "in love" made them sound a little unbalanced—wanting to be together all the time, not being able to eat or sleep, thinking of little else but the object of their affection. I thought it was just a cheesy literary device, since my experience with love, up until now, had been quite different. I was beginning to get it. This separation anxiety thing was weird and unsettling and lovely all at the same time.

"I hope it will be fine," I said as I kissed him again, more slowly this time, savoring the moment. "Because," I continued, without removing my lips from his, "I'm going with you."

10.

Pink Ranch Dressing

"How far out is the ranch, anyway? How long until we get there?"

"Technically, we've been on it for the last five minutes."

The paved county road spanned by the occasional cattle guard gave no indication we were on private property. "What exactly do you mean by 'technically'?"

"What we call 'the old homestead' is one big contiguous piece of land—around sixty-four-hundred acres—but there are other sections scattered around it that aren't necessarily connected."

"Sixty-four . . . Oh, my freaking heck, that's ten square miles." At times my accountant-math-nerd superpowers came in handy. "How many acres altogether, when you add up the other pieces?"

He squinted, head at a tilt. "Hmm. It was always a lot, but my dad acquires more parcels all the time as they come available. We'll have to ask him."

Gio slowed when he came to a massive log structure extending over a private drive, red boulders flanking its sides. An iron, crescent-shaped "C" hung from chains at its center. The mailbox beside it was a miniature farmhouse, painted yellow and white with "DiMarco" handwritten in crisp black letters. I thought of Gio's great-grandmother checking the mail—only on non-icy days of course—and wondered how much of a hike it would be to reach it.

The driveway curved and twisted around rock outcroppings and pine trees for a good quarter of a mile. I gasped when we came to a low clearing. There sat a cheery yellow Victorian farmhouse, complete with bay windows, turrets, shingles, elaborate moldings, gingerbread trim, a weather vane and a generous wrap-around porch.

"Oh, a painted lady!" The yellow clapboard was trimmed in crisp white, two shades of green and gleaming copper. "It's right out of a storybook."

"I had it done for Nonna a couple of years ago, along with a remodel, when she turned a hundred. I wanted to do it in her favorite color, but she insisted on this. She didn't want people to hate it after she's gone."

A matching barn and silo across an expanse of lawn completed the picture. A white rail fence, which was now adorned in clusters of pink balloons, connected the house to the outbuildings on either side. Cars were parked around it all. A gargantuan white tent had been erected for the occasion, with more pink balloons secured at the openings.

"I bet I can guess her favorite color."

I took his offered arm when he helped me out of the car, and we plodded downhill toward the billowing tent.

Twin girls in matching pink outfits came running from the porch of the house shouting, "Uncle Gio." They rushed him and wrapped themselves around his legs until he picked them both up. They looked to be about five years old, but petite, as twins often are.

"Ah, bambini." He growled and rubbed his rough cheek against each of theirs, causing shrieks of laughter. "This is Giada and Gina. No. Excuse me. Gina and Giada. Did I tell you that multiple births run in our family?" He juggled them for a more secure hold. "Girls, this pretty lady is Miss Hannity."

"Nice to meet you, ladies." They giggled and Giada—or was it Gina?—reached for me to take her. I toted her on one hip until we got near more children, where they both squirmed down to play.

We were blasted inside the fluttering tent by a heat wave, caused by vents poking under the canvas walls. It must have been eighty degrees in there. "For Nonna," Gio said quietly. "She needs it pretty toasty."

Banquet tables wore crisp white cloths and pink explosions of floral arrangements with more balloons attached. A dance floor had been constructed in the center and a buffet table stretched the length of one wall. Dozens of platters and tiered trays, piled high with Mon Petit chocolates, commanded attention at the far end. I worried that the heat might make a big puddle out of them, but for the first time in my life, I felt a little like a rock star.

"Kate!" Sylvia hugged me warmly. "I'm glad this big moose was able to convince you to come."

"There wasn't too much arm-twisting," I smiled. "He just threatened to cut off my supply of artichoke hearts. I'm addicted, you know."

"This is your lucky day, then." She smiled as one of the nephews brought out heaping bowls of them.

It was only a few steps from the tent to the back porch and the enormous kitchen, abuzz with an army of cooks. The bustling family choreography went on without notice of Gio, but as soon as I entered behind him, a deafening hush filled the room.

It was a *Twilight Zone* episode—human statues, frozen in time, gawking in our direction. Sylvia broke the palpable silence with a brusque, "What's wrong with you people? You've seen me in this dress before."

The silent air thickened for a full five seconds until it was fragmented, at last, by laughter. The group went on as before amid introductions and welcoming smiles.

Recognizing some of them from the store made me remember to check in with the crew back home.

"Can you please get my phone to work? I don't know what the problem is this time. I will never figure this thing out."

Gio powered the phone down and returned it to me. "No cell service out here. I would have told you before, but you were being so worried and cute and head-chef-ish when we left. I couldn't spoil it for you."

I must have looked like a goldfish, opening and closing my silent mouth, when the topic changed.

"There you are." A dimpled woman with chin-length brown curls entered from beyond the workspace. Her dark slacks and crisp white shirt were embellished with a colorful beaded scarf and gold hoop earrings —simple, basic, with a flair for the dramatic.

"Hey, Mom." Gio grasped my hand and wove me through the maze of cooks. He bear-hugged the woman, whose head reached his chin. Someone once told me you could tell how a man would treat his woman by how he treated his mother. So far, we were on track, except I was hardly his woman.

She pushed away to smile graciously in my direction. "This must be Kate."

Gently squeezing my hand, she made a subtle evaluation with a flash of her light brown eyes.

"Mrs. DiMarco. It's so nice to meet you."

"Call me Cici," she said. "I'm so happy you are joining us today."

I had completely forgotten that his parents lived at the ranch with his great-grandmother. This was Cici's home and I was her guest at this special occasion. Her warm greeting put me at ease before I had a chance to get all weird and angsty.

"We'll be eating in a little while, but if you're hungry now, we can fix you something."

I recognized a fellow foodie at once. Like Gio, my mother, and, well, me, Cici expressed affection through food. "Thank you so much, but I think I'll wait."

Sylvia had assumed her place at the helm of the kitchen, directing everyone coming, going and staying, so Cici took over the tour. "Are you ready to meet Nonna? She's been asking for you."

Cici pointed the way toward a curving staircase, with more pink flowers and balloons tied along its carved balustrade. "Nonna is upstairs."

11.

Meeting Nonna

I expected to find someone of Sophia DiMarco's advanced years sitting in a big, soft chair—a recliner, maybe—hooked up to oxygen, covered in a quilt, prescription bottles on a table nearby. A happy surprise awaited me.

A cacophony of cheers and laughter blasted from a loft landing at the top of the stairs. I worried that such noise might upset a delicate elderly woman, until we found her standing amidst of a group of teenagers. She bent over a pool table in her frilly pink dress, lining up a complex shot that landed two balls into opposite corner pockets. The group erupted into shouts at her win. The boy with the other cue stick said, "Aw, Nonna, no fair."

"You guys are wasting your time," Gio boomed as we reached the landing. "Nonna always wins. I hope you didn't let her bet against you."

"Hey, Uncle G." Several of the kids called out and lined up for hugs and kisses. Now that I was looking for it, I did recognize a pattern of overtly affectionate displays. My stomach churned at the foreign nature of it.

"Giovanni, I've been waiting for you, boy." Sophia handed her stick over to one of the kids and reached up for Gio's embrace. "And who have you got there with you?" She was probably once at least as tall as me, which was not saying much, but now had to look up with her head cocked to one side from her bowed stance to smile into my face. Her white hair was freshly coiffed and lacquered and her eyes twinkled brightly.

Gio turned to me and laughed, "You'd think she hadn't already received intel from about a hundred people."

"I don't know what you are talking about, Gio. Now introduce me, please. Where are your manners?"

"Sorry, Nonna." He bowed his head slightly in submission, but the smile was still on his lips. "Sophia Maria Castaldi DiMarco, known to all as 'Nonna,' please meet Kathleen Fiona Hannity, otherwise known as Kate."

"How do you do, Kate," Nonna whispered as she formally took my hand to shake it. Somehow I got the feeling that this was probably as formal as she got. That look of mischief on her face said it all.

"You, my dear, are trying to fatten me up, I think," she winked.

"Just imagine how hard it is to smell melted chocolate all day long and not weigh a ton."

"You have a lovely figure, not too skinny like most of the girls these days."

"Um—thank you?"

"Yes, thank you, it was a compliment. Women are supposed to have a little wiggle when they walk—a little jiggle." She stepped back and looked me up and down. "Those skinny-hipped girls have a hard time pushing out babies."

If I'd had something in my mouth, I would have choked or sprayed. I felt my face flush as I looked up at Gio. He was holding back a laugh and wore an expression that told me I was on my own. I thought it a good time to change the subject.

"So, do you like Mon Petit chocolates as much as everyone hoped you would?"

"Ah, darling, let me tell you a little secret." She motioned me over, past the noisy group at the pool table, to an alcove in the windowed turret where two wingback chairs faced each other.

"Giovanni, could you please bring us something to drink?"

Gio shot me a quizzical glance, asking permission to abandon me. I nodded reluctant consent.

When he was safely out of earshot, Nonna leaned in with a low voice. "Honey, I pray you live as long and as happily as I have." She chuckled. "And when you do, I want you to remember one thing." She looked around to make sure no one was listening. "When you become a great-great-grandmother like me, never, never express a strong preference for anything." She pointed to the balloons and streamers. "You have a favorite color and the next thing you know, it's spread around until the whole place looks like an explosion in a Pepto-Bismol factory."

I laughed. "But—"

"You like a little sweetie now and then and—*poof*—an avalanche of gourmet chocolates appears." She put her hand on my knee. "They are delectable, by the way."

"Thank you. I'm glad you—"

"You say it would be nice if there was more elbow room in the kitchen and they add a wing to your house big enough for the White House staff." She rolled her eyes. "You smile at a pretty picture postcard from San Francisco and soon they've completely redone the outside of the house until you don't even recognize the place."

"It is beautiful, though—"

She interrupted again. "Oh, don't think my heart isn't overflowing with gratitude and love for the kindness of all my progeny." She patted my hand gently. "But I'm a very old woman, living on borrowed time, who has never needed fine things to feel the richness of life. That's not how I was raised, nor how I raised my children."

"Live poor, grow rich."

"Yes, my dear, that's always been our family motto. *Vivono poveri, diventano ricchi.*"

The children queued up to file down the stairs now that

their game of pool was done, and Nonna waited for them to clear out. "The younger generation is losing that."

"But Gio—"

"Oh, Gio lives a frugal life, but he gives too freely to the pleasure of an old woman who won't be around much longer to enjoy it."

Gio returned with two glasses of lemonade. "Are you ladies getting along all right?"

"Yes," I answered. "We only talked about you a little. Are your ears burning?"

"My ears are just fine." He set the drinks down and reached for Nonna's hand. "We need to go down now. They're ready to start serving."

When Sophia rose with Gio's help, she clapped her hands like a little girl and asked me, "Are you coming to the party?"

Gio helped me up as well, and I followed them, holding the drinks. Nonna pushed a button on the paneled wall and a door slid open, revealing a small elevator.

"Be careful what you admire," Nonna whispered to me as we entered. "You should have seen the remodeling mess for this little baby."

12.

Birthday Party

The tent was packed. When we entered, the guests rose and cheered for their beloved matriarch.

Sylvia called from a microphone in the corner. "And here is our birthday girl." She signaled to the deejay and "Moonlight Serenade" began playing softly.

"Aw, sit. Sit." Nonna waved and blushed at the fuss being made over her. She took a handkerchief from her pocket and dabbed at her nose, trying not to cry.

Gio walked Nonna toward the head table, but she stopped him halfway across the dance floor for a little spin. He gently twirled her and they continued on. As I followed close behind them, I was glad the attention was on her at the moment and not me. At least I hoped that it was.

Tears filled her eyes. "My Giovanni loved this song," she confided to me.

She sat in her place of prominence at the table most dripping in pink flowers and pink ribbons and soaring pink balloons. Cici and the man who was unmistakably Gio's father sat on one side of her while Gio and I took the other.

Sylvia motioned Father Michael to the microphone to offer a blessing on the food. It wasn't until then that I remembered he was also a member of the Castaldi clan. You really have to watch what you say in this town.

At Sylvia's prodding, a teen in a serving apron brought a

full plate and set it in front of Nonna, and everyone cheered before rising to form a line at the buffet.

"I'll stay and talk to Nonna while you get yours," I said to Gio.

"What are you girls conspiring about?" He laughed and gave us both wet kisses on our cheeks.

Nonna pointed a knobby finger at him and said, "Never you mind, boy," and winked at me, patting my hand again, before shooing Gio away. She quietly asked, "Is it hot in here, or is it just me?"

I suppressed a giggle. "I think they were afraid you'd get a chill."

She rolled her eyes and gave me a knowing look. "May you live as long and happily as I, my dear, and may you have as many people looking out for your comfort."

An involuntary sigh escaped me as Gio walked away.

"He is a handsome man, isn't he?" Nonna asked. "Just like a movie star."

"Better than a movie star," I looked at my lap and smiled shyly. "We haven't known each other long, but the more I see, the more I think the handsome starts way down on the inside."

"Just like *my* Giovanni."

We looked from Gio to one another and sighed once more. Never in a million years would I have imagined having "girl talk" with someone old enough to remember the World War I era, but here we were, just two giddy females with a shared experience.

Nonna unfolded her napkin swan thoughtfully. "I've been told that you've made your building beautiful again, dear." She poked around on her plate with her fork. "That makes me very pleased. I have a special fondness for that place."

"You will have to come see it," I said. "I'll give you the grand tour." I sipped at my lemonade. "I haven't even gotten started on the upstairs yet, though. I'd love for you to see it when it's all finished."

"I've lived for over a century, Kate. I think you'd better work quickly." She smiled.

"You shouldn't talk like that." I touched her shoulder, silently noting the truth of her words.

"Ah, honey, this is a beautiful life, but I have no aspirations to stay forever." She took a bite of the steamed vegetables and got a far-off look in her eyes. "Giovanni and my children have gone long before me. I'm ready to join them but," she chuckled, "I keep waking up every morning. I suppose God still has plans for me here."

"Well, the next time you are in town, please stop by. I'll brew you up some hot cocoa that's to die for." I gasped and put my fingers to my lips at my *faux pas*. "I mean, it's very good and I—"

Nonna cackled dryly at this. "I can think of worse ways to go, darling. On the day of my next doctor's appointment—at my age, those are the big events of my itinerary—I'll come and see you."

"That would be wonderful," I smiled.

Gio was back now with three heaping plates and two empty ones. His years at the deli had developed some mad balancing skills. "And maybe you can help us with a little door situation." He set the full plates in the center of the table and the empty ones before us, in effect bringing the buffet to us.

"And, what is *your* door situation?" Nonna asked, with a twinkle in her eye.

He ignored her teasing. "Kate's apartment has creepy-crawlies hiding somewhere. You should hear the thumps and rattles coming from her walls and ceiling. But we can't get into the attic to look because the door has a different key than the others. It's actually different than any keyhole I've seen in the States. That lock looks ancient."

"By seniority, I am the resident expert on antiquities, but an ancient lock doesn't ring any bells. The noises, however." She glanced at Cici, and back to him, lowering her voice. "That would be your grandmother, Juliana."

"Let's not go freaking Kate out with crazy ghost stories, Nonna."

I choked on a piece of ice. "Ghost stories?" I coughed. "I have a ghost?" I turned to face Gio squarely. "I have a ghost, and you didn't mention it?"

"My family's folklore is full of a bunch of, uh, weird traditions and, *hmm*." He shrugged in Nonna's direction and rolled his eyes. "Superstitious malarkey."

"Malarkey?" I laughed. "Thank you for the translation. It's my red hair, isn't it? It causes everyone to have fits of Irishness on my behalf."

"I was being polite in the presence of ladies. I could have said something colorful in *italiano*, but . . . " He nodded toward his great-grandmother, "She's still got a killer right cross."

Nonna tapped Gio in the middle of the chest. "It's not malarkey, boy, and I didn't exactly say the word 'ghost' now, did I?"

"Well, that's what you think, isn't it? You think my grandmother Juliana is a ghost in Kate's attic."

"Not a ghost, exactly. More of a 'presence.'" Nonna delicately dabbed at the corners of her mouth with her napkin. "We'll call her a very strong presence."

Gio grumbled unintelligibly, stabbing a mountain of beef and transferring it to his plate.

Nonna lowered her glasses and looked over them into his eyes. "Like Susan is a strong presence."

I started to ask, "You have a ghost too?" but thought better of it. Gio's body language spoke volumes of his desire to skip the subject.

Nonna went on. "Juliana and I were good friends. I had watched her grow up, of course, but ours was a friendship in which age was irrelevant."

"You were living across the street when they had their flower shop," I stated.

"Yes, and when Tony's parents ran the shop before him. Giovanni brought me a pink rose every day from that shop."

A similar gesture came to mind—Susan's table at the back of the deli, with the ever-present vase of fresh flowers.

Gio stared downward, brows knit together.

"Even if we were quarreling, I got a pink rose." Nonna smiled. "It was hard to stay mad at him for long."

"Yes, I can imagine." At last my eyes met Gio's, which responded with a twinkle.

"Juliana and Tony were a beautiful couple. So happy together." Nonna waved her fork around expressively as she spoke. "Tony and I were distantly related, you know."

"Castaldis," I said.

"Yes," she replied, "Castaldis. His father and I were . . . let's see . . . third cousins I believe."

"Why is Juliana living in my house?"

Gio's head snapped up. "There are not ghosts in—"

I reached over and touched his arm and he went back to eating with a glower.

"Why do *you* think Juliana is living in my house?" I repeated to Nonna.

"It was very tragic. They both died so suddenly. It was a shock to everyone. Gio was just a little boy, so he probably doesn't remember much, but it was really quite upsetting."

"They died together? Was it a car accident?"

"Not exactly together, but within days of one another." She sipped at her water. "Great loves often end that way, you know."

"How, then?"

"Tony had developed a sudden obsession with mountain climbing. More specifically, he focused on The Keep out at

Castle Hill." She narrowed her eyes, searching her memory. "He spent every afternoon out there, practicing with his mountaineering equipment, climbing the walls of The Keep."

"He went out there by himself?" I pictured the sheer vertical walls of the rock formation. "That seems awfully dangerous."

"Yes, it was terribly dangerous." Nonna's eyes misted. "Deadly, in fact, for Tony."

I started before asking, "Did he fall?"

"We can only assume, but they never found his body."

I ate in contemplation for a moment. "What do you think happened?"

Nonna glanced at Gio, heaved a sigh, and assumed an almost defiant expression before answering my question. "My family always spoke about The Keep with a sense of dread. They said it was cursed." The last bit was uttered with a final hiss.

Gio's spine stiffened. "All right, that's it," he said. "I'm sorry, Kate. You shouldn't have to listen to this—"

"What about Juliana?" I interrupted. "How did she die?"

"Oh, it was very sad, indeed," Nonna said, shaking her head and pursing her lips. "Juliana knew he was dead hours before a search party was ever called. She felt it. She was sure. She died of a broken heart, not two days later."

At this, Gio spoke with frustration and embarrassment, "She died of a heart attack, Kate, not a broken heart."

"Semantics, my boy. She was so distressed about Tony, she died." Nonna noted Gio's exasperation. "Of a heart attack," she conceded and returned to me, "there in the attic of the flower shop building."

Our conversation was interrupted by Sylvia's voice over the loudspeaker. "Please look at the list of questions on your tables. There are 102 of them, and they are all about Nonna. The table that has the most correct answers will win a prize."

Excitement spread throughout the room, particularly among the many children seated with their families.

"I would say I have an unfair advantage," Nonna laughed, "but with my memory, I'm not so sure."

"Don't believe her," Gio said. "The woman has more information stored up there than the library of congress."

"Oh, I have an excellent memory for the past, I'll give you that. Ask me what happened when I was seven years old and I might go on for hours." She smiled. "But ask me what day of the week it is, and I'll have to think about it for a very long time. That's the way it often is with older people."

"Don't be hard on yourself, Nonna." Gio dished up more food for himself. "I forget where I've put things all the time. Drives me nuts."

"How much do you remember about your grandfather, Aldo?" I asked.

Nonna took her time before asking, as though to assess whether I could be trusted, "Why do you ask?"

"No reason, really, it's just such a fascinating story. 'Italian immigrant starts a town.' You don't hear that every day." I looked to Gio for backup.

"I've been telling Kate about family history, Nonna. How the town came to be, stuff like that."

Gio's great-grandmother asked him something in Italian, which included the words *intenzione*, *sposare*, and *ragazza*.

To this, Gio answered, "*Presto, Bisnonna, presto.*"

"Molto buona. Mi piace questo," she replied.

My natural curiosity made me commit to memory as much of their conversation as possible for later research. And my memory was quite good.

"People didn't generally live as long back then, you know," Nonna began. "I was little when he passed away." She continued to eat in thought. "He built this house, part of it anyway. It is much bigger now. He built it for my grandmother after they began having grandchildren, so that the family could gather together more comfortably."

"Where did they live before?" I asked.

Gio became animated as he fielded this question. "There's an old cabin up in the hills. We use it during hunting season and sometimes for camping in the summer. You'd be amazed how well built some of those old log cabins were, and Aldo was a real craftsman, apparently. It seems like the older the wood gets, the tighter the joins become. It's still snug. Incredible."

"My grandmother gave birth to nine children in that little cabin and raised them there." Nonna shook her head. "It is amazing what a soul can endure. My father spoke with great fondness of that place, which proves that the best things in life aren't, well, things. And as far as he was concerned, his mother was a saint."

"But," I wondered, "wasn't Aldo buying up property during all that time his children were growing up?"

Nonna nodded, "Yes, but much of it was done very discreetly. Even my grandmother didn't know about the majority of it. And what little she became aware of, she believed it was worth sacrificing her present comfort for the future of her children."

I swallowed. "Do you think she ever knew the extent of it?"

Nonna thought a moment. "My father believed that this house was a peace offering of sorts. He always thought that it was a bit 'too little too late,' so to speak, once she learned how much information my grandfather had been withholding from her. She was one angry Italian." Nonna's lips pressed together in a smile. "Later in their lives he showered her with little luxuries, but it never quite made up for the years of deception by omission."

"What was she like, besides being a saint?" I asked as I helped myself to seconds of the most delicious risotto ever.

"I have some memories of both of them—early childhood memories, like being rocked and sung to in Italian—but there was always an air of mystery surrounding my grandparents. I don't think their children ever discovered all of the secrets, really. My personal sense, from an adult point of view based on childhood memories—for whatever that is worth—is that my grandmother came from a finer stock. The one luxury she had throughout those humble years was a lovely spinet piano. She played and sang beautifully. Her children were all very musically inclined because of her. It seemed to me that she had lived a privileged existence before coming to America."

"But she must have adapted to the pioneer life," I said, pushing food around my plate again.

"Oh, she was strong as steel, that is a fact, but I've always wondered about how lonely and isolated she must have felt up there in the cabin. She never really mastered English thoroughly, and it was years before the others came from Italy. I think that's why she insisted her children speak perfect English. She wanted them to be fully aware of what was going on around them and not feel left in the dark, as she often did." Nonna looked off into the distance. "Ironically, her sense of isolation only increased as English became the preferred language in the home."

Gio listened intently. It seemed that some of this information was as new to him as to me.

"My mother said that Aldo and Anna Maria were a very passionate couple. They loved fiercely and they fought, well, expressively. They were very much in love, right to the end, but she learned to ask more questions as they got older. She insisted on an accounting of their assets on a regular basis once her eyes were opened."

Sylvia rallied the group to sing for the birthday girl.

Nonna patted my hand. "We'll talk more about this later."

Her eyes glimmered with tears as more than two hundred voices were raised in tribute to her. "Ah. Too much. Too much." She shook her head and covered her smile with her hands.

A special program followed the cake cutting, honoring the life of Sophia Maria Castaldi DiMarco. I watched the love in

Gio's eyes as he laughed with the families and at the antics of the children. The winning table of the questionnaire competition received small individual gift boxes of chocolates from my shop. I smiled and nodded as they waved to me in appreciation.

There were songs and poems and jokes and favorite memories offered by Nonna's adoring family. She was presented with a memento that had been a group effort, a lovely brooch in the shape of a heart, encrusted with the birthstones of her many direct descendants. Tears streamed down her face as she touched her own heart with her fingertips and kissed the pin before Cici helped put it on. The pink silk of her dress puckered under the weight of it as she wiped at her eyes once more.

"And now, Nonna's favorite part." Sylvia gave the deejay the signal and the familiar refrain of *Moonlight Serenade* played once more. Gio's father, John, rose and offered Nonna his arm. She clapped her fingertips together softly before rising with his assistance and allowing him to escort her to the dance floor. She was still light on her feet for her age, and made sure to put on quite a show for the standing crowd, who hooted and clapped with her every move. The dance ended with a gentle dip, and the fans went wild. Nonna smiled and waved warmly to her progeny as John escorted her back to her table.

As the applause began to die down, Big Bad Voodoo Daddy boomed from the speakers. Gio and I perked up in unison and laughed. He stood, taking my hand, and bowed low. How do you refuse that? I jumped to my feet and we ran to the dance floor to swing to "Mr. Pinstripe Suit."

Gio shouted about the young deejay when I was close enough to hear, "He probably doesn't know Benny Goodman from Brian Setzer."

"That's okay. I like them both." I squealed as Gio hoisted me over his head and I kicked my feet rapidly in the air before he swung me between his feet and back up.

"Nonna will know the difference."

We glanced at her clapping in time to the music and laughing at our acrobatics. "I don't think she cares which decade it was recorded in," I yelled. Gio wound me in close and spun me out and back in, like a yo-yo. It felt almost as though we had shared the big-band revival obsession of our youth together, even though we'd been hundreds of miles apart at the time. I silently thanked Susan DiMarco for the bumps and bruises I was sure she sustained while he perfected his technique.

Children began to swarm around us, wanting to get in on all the fun. A few other couples joined in, and Nonna's face lit up with delight. It was easy to follow Gio's lead and we ended the number with a dizzying twirl.

A slow song followed and Gio pulled me in close. This time, he held me there.

"Your Nonna is great," I said.

"I hate to say 'I told you so,' but—"

"She's just so . . . so . . . "

"She's more alive than most people half her age." Gio held my hand to his chest and wrapped the other arm tighter behind my back.

I knew we were on display, but somehow it seemed as though we were dancing in our own isolated universe. It was just Gio and me, and everyone around us became the out-of-focus backdrop. His hand was warm and strong, and I could feel the tight muscles of his chest, now slightly damp from exertion. He hummed along with the music, which vibrated when I rested my cheek against him.

When a commotion of teenagers gathered around the deejay booth, the blur came back into focus. They chattered excitedly, laughing, no doubt up to something. As our dance ended and another song began, they broke into cheers and stomped their feet. An unmistakable, low-toned growl of a spoken lyric began with a disco beat, and as our dancing picked up the tempo, Barry White sang "I Can't Get Enough of Your Love." We could only laugh—without missing a beat—and adjusted our steps to the different style of music. The group of kids howled and shrieked and whistled and clapped. My face burned with embarrassment, but I kept a smile there, within the safe confines of Mr. DiMarco's arms.

When the song was over, Nonna was beginning to stand with the assistance of those around her. We returned to her as Sylvia's voice chimed over the sound system again. "Nonna wants everyone to stay and enjoy themselves, but she needs to have her afternoon lie-down. She'll be back later."

Nonna waved and called, "Stay. Stay."

"Are you all right?" I asked as I reached her, taking her knobby fingers in my hands.

"Yes, darling. My old bones are just used to a bit of a routine. That's all. I'll be back down in a while."

"But won't the noise bother you?"

"Not at all. I'll listen to the music for a while and then I'll remove my hearing aids and have a little nap." She smiled, giving my hands a gentle squeeze. "You and your Giovanni stay and enjoy yourselves."

Everyone applauded as the elderly woman shuffled toward the opening of the tent, paused to wave, and disappeared through it. When the music restarted, we followed her lead and went outside.

13.

The Devil's Maw

"Where are you taking me?" The coolness of the day refreshed my overheated face.

"I figured maybe you could use a breather from the mob about now. I want to show you something before Nonna gets back down."

There was a gate at the side of the barn. Gio held it open while I scooted through before he latched it behind us. I followed him along the steepest path, skirted by scrubby pines and sagebrush. A covey of quail formed a darting conga line ahead before disappearing into the brush.

I don't know why I had a fit of impracticality and wore the smooth-soled, pointy, spike-heeled numbers. Dating. Makes you go right to torture mode. "Just how far is this thing you want to show me?"

"Not too far. Maybe a half a mile further or so. You can handle it, can't you, short-shanks?"

"I can handle it, Lurch." I released his hand and pushed myself forward, determined to make him work to keep up with me.

He laughed. "Do you know where you are going there, squatty?"

"I'm counting on you to keep me on track, Sasquatch."

It only took two strides with his long legs to catch me. He tugged at the back of my sweater until I stopped. I turned around and looked up at him with a crooked sideways smirk. "Am I going too fast for you, Goliath?"

"Not at all, Tinkerbell, it's just that you have something on your mouth." He gently touched my lips with his fingertips.

"On my mouth? What is on my . . . Oh."

Gio bent down and placed his lips on mine, taking me into his massive arms and lifting me up to his height. "No, I was mistaken. There's nothing there but my lips."

Kissing him heightened senses I didn't know I possessed and completely dulled and confused others. My fingers touching his face and—oh merciful heaven—his touching mine was like a pleasant form of static electricity. The scent of his warm skin, combined with the smell of the Colorado autumn, filled my head in a deliciously dizzying way. But sound? All I could hear at this point was the drumline of pulse in my ears. I could swear the backs of my eyelids had been glitter-bombed. Taste, however, taste was the sense that was overpowering my good judgment at the moment. "I think whatever it was is on *your* mouth now." I'm not sure when it happened, but somehow during the enounter my legs managed to encircle his waist.

Gio finally came up for air and, with strength of will evidently greater than mine, set me down on my feet, turning his back to me. "Come on, spider monkey. Hop up," he groaned, lowering himself slightly. "Your feet won't hold up with your princess shoes on."

I climbed up on his back with my arms around his shoulders and he piggy-backed me a few steps up the hill. "Just let me clear my head a little and we'll be on our way. Whew." To emphasize his point, he tilted it from side to side with a pop of his neck and cleared his throat before slowly picking up the pace.

I giggled when he started singing his best Mick Jagger rendition of "Beast of Burden."

"All right, *cara*. Open them."

At Gio's instruction, I had closed my eyes for the last little bit of the hike, still clinging to his back. I squeezed them tighter as he climbed what seemed to be a nearly vertical surface, stretching my trust to its outer limits. As he set me on my feet, I pictured Gibraltar. Kilimanjaro. Everest. When I saw the reality of it, I was sure getting back down from there would require anesthesia and a rescue helicopter. "Maybe I should have mentioned my fear of heights."

Though it was solid as a—well, as a rock—the hard, flat surface we stood upon seemed to sway and grow smaller as vertigo engulfed me. My legs trembled and I struggled to gain my balance. I couldn't seem to catch my breath and the harder I tried, the more impossible it got.

"Kate, you're hyperventilating. Here, sit down." Gio grabbed my arms and pulled me down with him until we both sat squarely on the stone, our feet almost to the edge of the overhang. "I'm so sorry. I didn't connect your ladder thing with . . . I'm an idiot. Just breathe, Kate. OK?"

I could feel the great abyss below sucking me downward. I pictured my broken body at the floor of the canyon, a tasty coyote snack. "What . . . was . . . I . . . thinking . . . ?" I wasn't thinking. I had been enjoying the ride with the boy, not thinking about the destination. That was how girls always got into trouble, wasn't it?

"Put your knees up and your head down." He put his arm around me as I clutched his other hand. "You're fine. You're not going anywhere. Breathe slowly. Come on, *cara*, breathe slow."

"I can't. I'm trying, but I can't." The ironic thought hit me that someday he'd make a fine labor coach—for some other woman, of course, because I knew I would be long dead, just an unrecovered pile of bleached bones. "Why . . . exactly . . . are . . . we . . . up . . . here . . . again?" I managed to huff out while willing my respiration to slow, my eyes squeezed shut.

"I wanted to show you the view. No, you don't have to look yet. Just close your eyes and take a slow breath. That's it. S-l-o-w. In . . . and out . . . " His voice became as soothing as a hypnotherapist's while he demonstrated relaxed, steady breathing.

"You're sitting on solid granite, Kate. There's not a whisper of a breeze," he cooed while rubbing my shoulders. "You are completely safe. It's only a couple of steps down from the rock to the trail behind us. We can go back any time."

"Really?" With my eyes closed, the swaying had stopped and his voice was beginning to calm my nerves. "Just a couple of steps?"

"Yes, that's right. Don't open your eyes until I turn you around and you can see for yourself." He wrapped both arms around me, held me tight and turned us both to face the opposite direction. "All right. This time when I tell you to open your eyes, it won't be a shock at all, just a few trees and, hey, there's a little squirrel up there. Hear him carrying on? You can look up and see him when you're ready. And he's throwing things down on the ground right there. Whenever you're ready, Kate, open your eyes."

I tried to zone in on the squirrel. It was obvious by the chirping that he or she was ticked off by our invasion of his turf. I cautiously squinted and looked through my lashes, then with one full eye, and finally both of them. I followed the squirrel down the pine tree with my gaze and saw that it was just as Gio described. The way down was an easy hop to the trail from here.

"Good. See? You're safe, right?"

"Right."

"Okay. I won't force you or anything, but if you want to, you can turn back around when you're ready and see The Keep from the Castaldi side. It's the best view of it. It'll knock your socks off. But only when you're ready. Okay?"

I was being such a baby. What was wrong with me anyway? Of course I wouldn't fall off a cliff just because it existed. Millions of people managed to appreciate the beauty of a lofty view without plunging to their horrifying, skull-shattering death. This had been a time of facing my fears—my fear of being alone, my fear of the unknown, my fear of failure. What was one more fear? And an irrational fear, at that. "Okay," I breathed, clutching Gio's hand. "I think I'm ready now."

"Good." A broad smile slowly eclipsed Gio's look of worry. "All right, *cara*, hold on tight and we'll just scoot around in a half-circle. You can keep sitting. Less wobbly that way."

"Thank you for refraining from mocking me. I know this is silly. I have always been this way—or at least since my father took me for the first of only three visits I ever had with him. We went to a park with a rope bridge that swayed in the breeze, and we had our first ever standoff, our war of wills. He wouldn't come up and save me and I couldn't move without him. I was paralyzed with fear and he was trying to toughen me up, I guess. That was his great first attempt at parental interaction. He left me up there crying for an hour. Eventually, a big kid took pity on me and carried me across." I shook my head, embarrassed. "Sorry. For a minute, I mistook you for my 'Adult Children of Pathological Liars' group."

"They have that?"

"Yes. Of course." I shook my head. "No. I made it up." Shrugging, I said, "The apple doesn't fall far from the tree, I guess. At least when I'm really scared."

We began our bottom-scooting circle, with my grip on Gio's hand, tourniquet tight. Sitting down really did make it seem less frightening, more stable. My breathing was steadier now.

My first sight was my feet with a blurred backdrop of red and green behind it. Next, there was the rock we were sitting on, which protruded out from the mountainside in a triangular knife shape. Once I thoroughly inspected it for solidness, I panned out to see that it was actually one of five jutting stone projections, arranged around a semicircle of mountainside, tips pointing toward one another.

"They look like teeth."

"Yeah, Aldo named this place the Devil's Maw, *Trappola del Diavolo*. Pretty impressive, huh? It drops off sharply here, but each tooth sticks out a good twenty feet. This was obviously some sort of volcanic formation that split apart and has weathered away to this."

"The Devil's Maw. That's really fitting." I pictured a scary red devil, opening up his jaws to swallow me down into the canyon. I squeezed Gio's thick, solid bicep for support.

"You can see part of the town from here, off to the side of Castle Hill. If we had binoculars, you could see Mon Petit, right over there.

I gazed in the direction he was pointing. Looking off into the distance was not nearly as stressful as looking down. "I think I might see it. Cute little red brick building."

"I would agree with you, because it is a cute building, but the town's full of them, and if you think one of those little red dots is yours—well, never mind. Yes, Kate. I see it too."

"Wise man. We wouldn't want the hysterical acrophobic woman to get all riled up, now would we?"

"That's what I was thinking."

His lighthearted banter was starting to work on me. I was relaxing some now.

"Now look at The Keep. Can't you see better from up here why they call it that?"

My gaze turned from the town up to the red rock formation springing proudly from the top of Castle Hill. From this angle, it looked like something built in the Middle Ages to keep the Huns at bay.

I admired all I surveyed. "Look at the way the light is hitting it. I love autumn light. It's lower in the sky than summer light, and it casts this golden glow, which I have always thought was a good design choice on God's part. It goes with the pretty leaves, and pumpkins, and harvest . . . "

"And big volcanic red rocks that look like a medieval fortress."

"Yes, those too. Although I've seen The Keep in all kinds of light, and it's stunning in all of them. I am so going to paint it someday."

"Is that what you had on your easel in your apartment?"

"Oh, gosh no. I haven't had time to paint. I've been too busy with getting the business off the ground since I rolled into town. My mother put that painting up. It was going to be an abstract, but you are right, it does have some of that rich, almost vermillion red in it."

"You should make time for that, Kate. It's an important part of who you are."

Honey to my heart. A man who actually valued something that was not only important to me, it was an intrinsic genetic code I was born with. Holy Helen Back! I'd forgotten how much I once craved that, before I was made to believe that creating something beautiful was a silly self-indulgence.

"Maybe I will, once I get over the new-shop growing pains."

I wished I had some charcoal and paper to sketch with right then. The sight of the formation was so spectacular from up here. You could actually see turret-shaped projections on either corner. They weren't quite symmetrical, but because of that, it only gave it a skewed perspective, as though we were looking at it from an impossible angle. And very close to dead center of the hulking rock was a deep impression of the approximate size and shape of an oversized entry. There was even a line, more or less vertical, that you could imagine was where the doors met and locked shut.

Gio pointed to the foot of the hill. "I always liked to think of the little pond down there as the moat, although it's not really close enough to the castle to be one."

"But it does sort of give that vibe, doesn't it? Beautiful."

"And if you look down there, right at the surface of the water, you can see a cave tucked in there. Just the top of it is showing."

I squinted and shielded my eyes with my hand to see it. There appeared to be the top of two arches, joined together in the middle. "Yeah. It's that dark curved spot. Very intriguing. Have you ever explored it?"

"We all wanted to when we were kids—every kid in the family for generations, I'm sure—but we were threatened within an inch of our lives not to ever try. Some guy drowned there once a long time ago, or something like that." He put his arm around me and squeezed. "Besides, in the middle of the summer, the water is too high to even see the cave, and the rest of the time it's too cold. It's spring fed. They say the pond appeared after a miner dynamited way down deep. It fractured a water vein." He nuzzled his nose into my hair and inhaled deeply, then kissed my temple. "And now there's a little pool that never existed before."

"We should probably start heading back, don't you think? How long does your great-grandmother usually nap?"

"An hour, maybe. Not much longer than that."

He stood and jumped down to the trail behind me, and I scooted around to look below at him. He held out his arms and smiled. "Jump."

I thought of my father on that day in the park. I thought about how all he would have needed to do that day, to make it right, was reach up and utter that one magic word. I stood and positioned myself.

"Jump," Gio repeated.

"I can't."

"Come on, Kate, I've got you covered."

I wanted to. I screwed up my courage twice, and growled and shook out my hands each time I failed to take the leap.

Rather than belabor the point, Gio came closer. "Sit down, *bella*. That will be easier."

I followed his instruction. He put his hands at my waist and lifted me to the ground. "There you go. Safe and sound."

I smiled up at him and silently agreed.

I pointed to a tall tree on our way down the hill. "That heart there on the big pine . . ."

"Yeah. What about it?" The force of gravity was making his steps lurch forward in a quick, jerking motion as he continued to pack me on his back.

"That's the second one I've seen. There are no initials in it."

"Yep. No initials."

I arranged my weight on his back as he held me with his forearms tucked under my thighs.

"Well, isn't a heart carved in a tree a little empty without initials?"

"There are hearts hidden all over the place up here. We used to play a treasure hunt sort of game on the ranch, us cousins, when we were kids. 'How many hearts can you find?' Whoever found the most, won. It was better than Easter."

I tightened my grip around his shoulders. "So, who do you think put them there?"

"I don't know. They're not just on the trees. There's one up at the old cabin. A couple scratched into rocks. Somebody just liked hearts, I guess."

"You think they've been here a long time?"

"Yeah. That one we just passed has a lot of bark all built up around it, and the tree has got to be around three feet in diameter or maybe more. I'm thinking the heart could have been there for over a hundred years."

I laid my cheek against the long muscle bulging on his back.

I'd never been piggybacked by anyone before. It was an odd sort of thing, to be toted like a child by a tower of a man, but it made me smile that he was worried about my feet. What kind of guy would think of such a small and thoughtful thing? I'd say I was more worried about the shoes getting destroyed than I was my feet. They cost me a fortune when I'd gotten them for a wedding a couple of years before, and I hadn't had much opportunity to wear them since. But, yes, I'm sure they would have torn my feet to shreds if I'd walked the entire way.

"Do you think all the hearts were made by the same person?"

He made a little hop with his feet and hoisted me up higher. "Probably. They all have a fairly uniform size and shape, although the ones carved into trees have changed over the years."

"What do you think they mean?"

"They could mean any number of things. The obvious, of course, would be that they're like little love letters scattered around by some twitterpated kid."

"Aww. That's sweet."

"But it's probably not that romantic. The Castaldi brand has a heart shape in it. It's carved into the logs at the main gateway. I always imagined it was like mirror images of the letter 'C'. Did you notice the hearts carved into the stair railings in the house?"

"No. The house is so beautiful. There's so much to take in. I didn't spot them."

"There are hearts all over this property; all over town too. We'll have to take a little tour together someday. I'll point them out."

"Do you think it was Aldo who made the hearts? Maybe they were for Anna Maria."

"Could have been. Maybe. It's hard to think of him as being particularly romantic, though. Shrewd, yes. Romantic? I doubt it."

I knew he was wrong. This guy who carried me down the hill on his back, to spare my feet, could not have sprung from an ancestor with no romance in his soul.

The party was going strong when we returned. The yard was filled with children playing and dancing to the music that still rang throughout the rolling glen of the ranch.

Gio and I entered the house through the back door, where I found an adorable little powder room. Now that we had discussed it, I saw hearts everywhere, even in this tiny room. They were in the motif of the wallpaper, embroidered on the guest towels, embossed in the faucet handles, and there was a large glass vase filled with heart-shaped scented soaps.

Besides needing to use the facilities, I had to take some time to work on my decidedly grubby state after our little expedition. My hair, as always, needed some taming. One of the very few perks of having curly hair was that water functioned as a reasonably effective styling product in a pinch. As I ran damp fingers through it, I stopped to look at myself. Really look. For the first time in I don't know how long, the face looking back at me wore a truly contented expression. Deep down contentment. I applied lip balm from the tube I carried in my pocket and rubbed my lips together with a kissing motion. Yes, she looked happy. And a little sunburnt.

It didn't take a private investigator to locate Gio. His voice bounced off the walls as he joked with his mother and a group of other women in the kitchen. "There she is."

I took his offered hand, and he pulled me in close to him. "My mom has something for you."

"Oh, really? It's not more birthday cake, is it? It's wonderful, but—"

Cici reached into her pocket and held out her down-facing fist until I reached up for whatever it was she was offering. "You can have more cake whenever you're ready, but that's not what I have for you."

The object was unrecognizable for a few seconds. I puzzled over the large, rusted metal object, so unlike the modern-day versions.

"I heard you talking with Nonna about a key, and about the attic door in your apartment. Then I remembered that I probably had it in my cedar chest with some other things that belonged to my parents. I used to love this key when I was little. I pretended it was from an enchanted castle."

The key. It did look like it could have come from an ancient castle or a dungeon door, great fodder for a child's imagination. It was almost as long as my hand, from the base of the palm to the tip of my middle finger. It looked like it was forged from iron, with a large and ornate heart shape at the gripping end. A metal tag was attached to the heart with words etched on it. I moved to the kitchen windows to get a better look. The writing seemed to be written in Italian.

"'*La chiave per il mio cuore.*' I'm probably slaughtering the pronunciation. What does it mean?"

Gio came up behind me to see the tag. "*Cuore* means 'heart.' It basically means, 'the key to my heart.'"

"More hearts." I turned to look up at Cici. "Was this a gift to your mother?"

"I don't think so. My dad grew the most beautiful roses for her. He named several varieties for her. That was his biggest romantic gesture. But I'm pretty sure he used this key for the attic, just like you'd use any other key."

Tipping the key to look directly at its end revealed a crescent shape that very clearly matched the "c" of my keyhole at home.

"This is incredible. It seems so exotic and foreign. I've never seen anything like it. It's got to be much older than turn-of-the-century."

"Yes," Cici confirmed. "I think you are right. My father had that lock removed from some old antique and installed there. He loved treasures he'd find in farm auctions and sales, particularly from the old Italian homestead farms in the area. He had quite a collection at one point. I would guess this came from something that was brought over from Europe, way back when."

"Thank you so much for finding this," I smiled. "I will take good care of your castle key."

Sylvia's voice echoed over the speaker system again, and Nonna's name was mentioned.

Gio tugged my hand toward the tent. "Let's go see what's happening. I might have to save Nonna from Syl's over-enthusiasm. She's probably pretty worn out. Even after her nap."

14.

Mr. Sandman, Bring Me A Dream

"Thanks for coming with me, Kate. You looked right at home with all us crazies." Gio unlocked my shop door and handed the keys back to me.

"Just what are you saying?"

"You know what I mean." He held me close and kissed my forehead.

I tilted my head upward and stood on my toes for the real thing—if only briefly. "Thank you for taking me there. I love your Nonna, and your parents, and all of those cute little kids, and . . . " I kissed him again.

"Get some sleep, *cara*. I'll see you in the morning."

I locked up and studied him striding away into the darkness until he popped up under the street light on the other side.

The shop had been put to bed perfectly without me, clean and shiny, product ready for tomorrow's business day. I looked back toward Mangia and got a silly idea. Giggling, I ran up the steps and into my dark apartment, turning on a lamp near the bedroom window. In perfect synchronicity, a window lit across the street. My heart pounding from the run, I stood close to the glass and saw Gio looking out from the other side.

I began tapping his number into my phone as planned, but he had beaten me to it. I answered his ring instead. "Hi."

"Hi. Just wanted to say goodnight one more time."

"Good night. I had so much fun."

"Me too. Good night, *bella.*"

Sleep came easy for a change that night until it took a decidedly odd turn.

My nose touched a yellow rose with coral at the tip of each petal. The sweet, earthy fragrance filled my senses as I inhaled. "Mm. This is lovely."

Gio feathered my face with light kisses. "I'm calling this one '*Bella*' for you."

"For me?"

"Of course, my darling."

I inspected and sniffed the bloom again. "It is a beautiful variety, love, and the fragrance is unbelievable."

I kissed him tenderly on the cheek. "You are too good to me."

"Only because you are so good."

He sat me down at the kitchen table. "You rest now. You've been on your feet all day."

"But," I protested, "so have you."

"I will rest after I clean up the kitchen."

The setting was familiar; it was my apartment, yet different in so many ways. The kitchen sported wallpaper, covered with happy clocks and kettles. The cupboards and other woodwork were painted a bright, sunny yellow.

Gio wore cuffed jeans and a tucked-in blue shirt. His hair glistened with some sort of hair product, which held it in an elaborate style, high on top and combed into a sort of seam in back. Like an Elvis impersonator.

I picked up my knitting from the basket on the table and listened to him sing while he did the washing up. His voice crooned a Frank Sinatra song along with the radio. I tried to hum the harmony, but my voice seemed hoarse, and keeping up with the tempo proved impossible. I couldn't believe my good fortune to have a man like him in my life, a man who wasn't too proud to do women's work. I set my knitting down for a moment to put both hands on my expanded belly.

Gio came to me with dripping hands. "Are you all right?"

I grinned and returned to my knitting. "Your son is going to be an athlete, a football kicker, I bet."

"If he is my *son*, why are you knitting a tiny pink dress?"

"Just covering my bases. I've knit tiny blue things, and tiny white things and tiny yellow things too."

Gio dried the last pot and hung it on a rack over the shiny new turquoise gas range.

"Come on, I want you to see something." He pulled me to my feet and led me toward the attic door, where he pulled the string switch and stood for me to pass. "Ladies first."

"Oh! You painted it to match the kitchen. How pretty."

I climbed the yellow stairs with my slightly swollen feet and Gio patted my bottom from behind. "Watch your step, Mama, those treads can be slick if you don't hit them just right."

"Isn't that just funny? I'm going to be someone's mama."

"You were made to be someone's mama. You're going

be great at it."

The whole upstairs room lit up with the color of bright, pure sunshine. Gio had worked all summer on this room, changing it from a dingy storage space to something we could use together. With the baby coming, he wanted a space just for us. His desk stood under the window, and my sewing machine rested right beside it. He'd built in shelves for supplies and fabrics, with a fancy keeper for my spools of thread.

"This way, the kids can have the run of the house, and we won't ever have to get after them for bothering our things. The stuff will all be up here safe and out of the way. And when the kids are asleep, we can work together up here without waking them."

"Kids?" I laughed. "Let me finish working on this one first, OK?" I arched my back and cupped my abdomen to highlight my point.

"OK. But, you know, sometime in the future there'll be more than this one." He kissed my temple. "And I promise to do my part. I'll practice every night until I get it right, if that's what it takes."

"You are nothing if not vigilant." I hugged him tightly. "This is wonderful. You've done a beautiful job."

I looked at the items on his desk. "What is this one?"

"I found it out at the old Zarlingo place. It's a diary, I think, written in Italian. Someday, I'm going to translate all of these old things."

"You will. And the people in Castle Springs will know of their heritage because you'll write that book you've got inside you." I kissed him.

He spun me in a circle and I giggled when he started singing Rosemary Clooney's "Come On-A My House" as we danced there in the attic.

Then I got a glimpse of us in the mirror on the wall and pulled Gio over to it. I gaped at the realization that Gio wasn't Gio at all. The eyes were different. My hair wasn't red. My eyes weren't green. No, this person I thought had been me had rich, olive-toned skin and nearly black-colored eyes that hid behind thick, curly lashes when she smiled.

"You have the key, silly," she said to herself, but there was no doubt in my mind that her message was intended only for me.

I woke with a jerking start, my heart racing at a full sprint. I put my hands on my flat stomach and, for no logical reason, began to cry.

15.

Surprise (Attic) Attack

"So, let me get this straight." Gio chopped celery like a Benihana chainsaw.

This was the first time I'd been in his apartment, which looked an awful lot like mine, if you could mentally strip them both back to bare walls. I had expected dark furniture and a masculine, sleek, ultra-modern look. I suspected instead, by what I found, that nothing much had changed up here since he'd shared it with Susan.

There were a number of exposed nails where pictures had hung, until probably very recently, with faint outlines of discoloration. Had he removed old photos for my sake?

Once again, he did the cooking, but at least I brought a killer *crème brûlée* for dessert.

"You actually thought it was good I did 'women's work'?" He chuckled and shook his head. "That doesn't really sound like you, Kate."

"That's what I'm saying. It wasn't me. Well, it was sort of me, but it wasn't."

I peeled and cleaned a bowl of shrimp and arranged them artfully on a plate, then began to carve hot radishes into rosettes for a garnish in the center.

"It was as though I looked out of someone else's eyes, but on the inside, it was me. Except I thought her thoughts. Juliana's thoughts."

Gio rolled his eyes and shook his head once more.

"Hey, it was my dream." I wiped up my mess on the counter and dumped the shrimp shells into the waste bin. "Just listen to the story."

"I *am* listening. You were sitting at the table knitting. Still doesn't sound like you."

"I knit once in a while. I'm not nearly as skilled as she was . . . but that's not the point. It was me, but it was also her."

He threw the chopped celery into a bowl with other vegetables and dumped the whole thing into a hot wok. I checked the steamer to make sure a steady cloud still rose from it. I didn't want to overcook the rice.

Gio lifted the pan and tossed its contents to stir. "And I was doing 'the women's work' over at the sink."

"And singing Sinatra."

He snapped his fingers jazzily and crooned out, "Luck be a lay-dee to-night."

"Yeah. Different song, but you get the picture."

He added his special tamari sauce to the cooking vegetables. The aroma of soy and garlic wafted from the pan.

With hand on abdomen, I expounded. "She feels her baby move and that's when I realize I—she—is pregnant. They were so happy. It was their first child."

"Uncle Al."

"Did I meet him at the party?"

"No. He's passed on."

"Oh. I'm so sorry."

"It's all right. I'm sure he's taking care of business up in Heaven. He was their first child. That is, if we were really talking about Tony and Juliana."

"Did he play football in high school?"

"I think so. Why?"

"Nothing." I pulled the dessert from the broiler. The topping was caramelized to perfection. Taking a dishcloth from the counter, I carried the two warm ramekins to the table. "It's just that I mentioned, I mean, Juliana thought he was a good kicker, that's all."

Gio laughed at that and shook his head.

"Anyway, we went upstairs, so you could show me that the attic was all bright and shiny and freshly painted. We did the swing to a Rosemary Clooney song. And you had a thing for my bottom."

"This is sounding familiar." He popped a stray piece of green pepper in his mouth. "Wait. Are we still talking about my grandparents?"

"So there we—they—are dancing and I look over in the mirror at us—them—because it was definitely them and not us. He was tall like you, but your eyes, your real eyes, look just like hers."

"Did Nonna tell you that?"

"Tell me what?"

"That I got my eyes from my grandmother?"

"I'm telling you, this is just what I saw in my dream. Your great-grandmother didn't describe either of them physically."

"Well, not that I believe all this stuff, but I've been told I favor my Grandma Juliana, especially around the eyes. I just thought you'd want to know that."

Gio handed me a serving bowl, which I filled with steaming rice. He ladled stir-fried vegetables into the other.

"See? I didn't know that, but that's what I saw."

"You are making a lot of assumptions, you know. You are, first of all, assuming this dream actually means something. You've been a little stressed out, you know. You could have had indigestion or something. There could be any number of reasons for a nightmare."

"The dream was beautiful." I put my hand reflexively on my stomach, before catching myself and returning it to my lap. "I was just a little startled at the end."

We set dinner at his cozy little table and sat down.

Gio motioned for me to begin serving myself. "So my grandma tells you to use your key."

"Yeah. Your mom's 'enchanted castle' key."

Gio piled his own plate. "Did you see the key?"

"Mm. The shrimp came out perfectly." I took a sip of water before answering, "I didn't have to *see* the key to know it was the enchanted castle key. It doesn't matter. Let's just try it after dinner and see how it works."

He held my hand as we crossed the street later. By the time we'd reached my front door, three cars had honked at us. It felt for a moment like New York, until I realized these were friendly honks, with friendly little waves of recognition. They used considerably more fingers than most New Yorkers, too.

His following me up the stairs to my apartment felt very familiar after my dream, except this Gio kept his hands to himself.

The surface of the brown, hand-forged key was rough against my palm. I could imagine a locksmith or a blacksmith heating and pounding the metal until it was formed into just the right shape. It was probably smooth once, but time and elements had oxidized and pitted the metal over the years. It wouldn't be a surprise if it truly had come from a castle in Italy, as Cici had imagined when she was a child.

"So, are you going to do it?" Gio stood beside me, anticipation plain on his face.

"Yes. Just a second." I took his hand and sighed.

Intrigued by the tag attached to the heart-shaped base of the key, I puzzled over what was meant by the Italian words written there. *The key to my heart*. What was the connection between those words and the door to my attic? What was it, anyway, with these Castaldis and their hearts? Maybe it was true what they said about Italians being more passionate than the average bear.

I handed the key over to Gio. "Here. You do it."

"Okay." He shrugged and accepted it. "Chicken."

The lock turned with a solid clunk and the door made a crack of complaint when Gio pushed it open. The escaping air from the stairwell was cool, a little musty, and had just a hint of roses in the mix.

"Roses, just like in my dream," I muttered.

"Hmm?"

"Don't you smell it?"

Gio shook his head. "Smells like an attic to me."

When he couldn't find a switch on either side of the door, he waved his hand overhead to grasp a cord and pull. The stairway brightened to show sunny yellow walls and stair risers, with dark hardwood steps.

"My grandfather grew roses. He had a big hothouse out back. He supplied his own for the shop; they were his specialty." He tugged at my hand and we began our ascent. "Of course, he's been dead for thirty-something years. If there are any roses up there now, they probably smell like worm dirt."

The stairway was narrow, so Gio gestured ahead. "Ladies first."

My eyebrows lifted and my lip curled with trepidation.

He nodded upward once more and grinned. "I'm right behind you."

"All right," I exhaled. It was time to rip off the metaphorical Band-Aid and get it over with. I took a big breath and clattered up the steps. Gio followed, taking the stairs two at a time and chuckling under his breath.

I called over my shoulder. "You know, I'm not so sure it will be *me* screaming like a little girl if there are bats up here."

When I reached the top, I screamed like a banshee.

"Ahhhhh!" Gio echoed my chorus and ran the rest of the way up. "What is it?"

"Look at all of this dust," I spat. "This is disgusting. It will take me a week with a shop vac to get it all up."

Seeing his pale face, I laughed. "Told you you'd scream."

"*Cavolo*! Don't do that. It sounded like you'd tripped over a bloody corpse up here."

There was a stack of boxes over to one side and drop cloths over furniture pieces. The mystery lump closest to the solitary, grubby window was vaguely recognizable. I tiptoed to it and gingerly raised a corner of the cloth. Yes, it was a desk. Trying not to stir motes into the air, we carefully removed the tarp. Just as I did, the lights started to flicker.

The solid oak roll-top had to be a century old, at least. It was sturdy and built to last. It had all those lovely pigeonholes and card file drawers that made old desks so intriguing.

I ran my hand along its stout edge. "I wonder how they hauled this thing up here."

"Guido power. I'm sure my grandfather had a half-dozen big, strong Italian relatives to help. I bet this was one of his farmhouse finds."

What was remarkable about the contents we found was that they appeared to have been left untouched for all this time. A few bills marked "paid" were skewered onto a paper spindle.

Gio flicked through the stack. "September 1984. That's about the time they died."

I pulled out a long, narrow drawer to find a scrolled piece of paper inside. "Looks like a map."

"This could be really old," he said with an earnest expression. He tried to carefully open it and see what might be on it, but thought better of it. "I better take this to someone I know who deals in old documents."

"A cousin?"

Gio smiled. "But, of course."

He opened another desk drawer and pulled out a parcel wrapped in brown paper, apparently a book.

I challenged, "I'll bet you a million dollars that is a diary, written in Italian."

"Only a million?" Gio unwrapped and opened the book, then laughed. "If I'd taken your bet, you'd be a million dollars wealthier right now."

Scrawled inside the cover were the words, "*Il Mio Diario: Aldo Castaldo di Calabria*."

"No way." Gio turned pages gently. "No freaking way."

"What is it?"

"It's a diary, all right." Gio looked down into my face with a huge grin. "It's *his*." He kissed me quickly in excitement. "It's Aldo Castaldi's diary."

His kiss and his excitement sent a sizzling little spark through me. I reached up for another serving of that and basked in pure sensation. "Mm."

The lights flickered again until the room darkened, lit only by the glow from the door at the foot of the stairs.

"Great. She just had to have the last word, as if finding Aldo Castaldi's journal wasn't dramatic enough." I laughed as I felt in the dark for Gio's hand.

"It's probably just a breaker or something, Kate. I'll see what I can find out."

"Bring the book downstairs. We'll look at it together. I think Juliana has just told us to get a room."

Gio draped his arm around me and made ghost noises as we clomped down the stairs together. "G'night, Grandma," he laughed, and made another high-pitched moan.

16.

Lost in Translation

We sat close on the sofa, my body tucked under Gio's arm as we examined the leather-bound book together. Given its age, it was in astonishingly good condition.

"The Zarlingos probably had it packed away in some old trunk when my grandfather found it, and it looks like he took pretty good care of it himself."

I caressed the brittle edges of its yellowed pages. "Most of the town would want a copy of this, you would think. Why would he just hoard it upstairs?"

"Maybe he planned to write out the history himself before sharing it."

"And you know about his being a writer and historian . . . how?" I poked Gio's ribs for effect.

"Well, you said—"

"Oh, now I remember. I told you about my dream involving your grandparents. Those grandparents who are not ghosts. That dream where they talked about Tony writing the family's history—and the Zarlingo farm, for that matter."

"Well, I—"

"Welcome to the dark side, young Jedi."

Gio's chin lowered to his chest, his eyes peering sideways from beneath dark lashes. "I'm playing along for harmony's sake. Let's just go forward with the assumption your dream was accurate."

"Oh, I see. That's kind of a copout, but I'll take it. Yes. Let's assume."

"You are a very aggravating woman, Kate." He smiled.

Smiling back, I kissed him. "I know."

Gio's initial stabs at translating the calligraphic text were faltering. "There are multiple ways you can go with some of these words, and my Italian is a little rusty. Conversationally, I'm pretty fluent, thanks to my sister and brother-in-law. They still won't talk to me on the phone unless I use *lingua Italiana*, for precisely that reason. Translating 100-year-old texts exercises a different part of the brain, I think. The phrasing is different sometimes, a lot more formal—and I know fancy penmanship was part of their education back then, but his sure isn't making this any easier."

Pointing to the wording on the front page, I asked, "So it was Castaldo, not Castaldi?"

"The last name most likely got changed when he came over from the old country. That happened a lot. This is definitely the same guy, though."

Rather than daily diary entries, the book was written as a memoir of Aldo's earlier years. It began with stories of when he was a child in a village named Ruscello, in the region of Calabria, Italy. By his account, the name Castaldo had some connection with the aristocracy in his region.

"I've heard *that* one before. Every Italian I know claims nobility in their lineage. If you go back far enough, you'll be connected to someone. Even you and I could be distant cousins."

"Well, maybe if you go back to Noah's ark." My arm— freckles over frog-belly white—held next to his dark, olive-toned one made me giggle.

The first portion of the memoir went roughly like this:

"The Castaldo name goes back in time to the days of kings and queens when Castaldos served as keepers of the castle. In

Calabria, we served the Duke and his line, for as long as such existed."

Aldo described his early childhood as being one of privilege and great wealth. Although not directly in line to the duchy, his family had inherited fortune and property from them over the centuries, through close association and loose familial ties. The Castaldos had a summer villa by the sea as well as an abundant vineyard in the provinces. Their household supported many servants and *contadini*, or farmers, who were generously compensated and happy to live and work among one another. Aldo's father, Jovanni, protected and provided for a vast network of distant relatives, who lived in the nearby village. According to Aldo, this system of feudalism existed in pure harmony and bliss from as far back as the Middle Ages.

Gio interjected, "If any of this is true, I'm sure the servants' and peasants' version wouldn't include singing "Zippity-Doo-Dah" while slaving away for the rich family."

By Aldo's account, unification of Italy and the complete breakdown of feudality didn't happen until after he was settled in the states.

When Aldo reached the age of ten, things began to change for them all. In the mid-nineteenth century, age-old clan and village rivalries began to transform from Capulet-Montague-like skirmishes into the early stages of organized crime. Those establishments coalesced into what would eventually come to be known as the 'Ndrangheta organization.

"That's what they call their version of the Mafia in Calabria. It's got its fingers into everything." Gio's eyes became filled with animation as he spoke. "When I was there as a kid, I wasn't allowed to go to certain areas because my sister was afraid I'd get iced. 'Ndrangheta is separate from La Costa Nostra—those guys are mostly Sicilian. The two have some ties, though, because they're geographically close. I had no idea it's been around so long."

As Aldo reached his early teens, much of the family fortune had been lost to various forms of extortion and outright theft by the sinister brotherhood. It was when he turned fourteen, he recounted, that he vowed to reclaim his family fortunes from those who had taken them.

Gio's voice reading the Italian sentences and then repeating them in English to the best of his ability was entrancing. It took me a few seconds each time he did so before I could mentally process it.

"Interesting. How did he think he would go about doing that?"

"Fourteen-year-old boys have way more guts than brains. They're like those little dogs that don't know they're just a tasty snack for the Rottweiler they're yapping at. Boys that age are invincible, as far as they're concerned, and their body mass never equals their audacity."

Despite all of this being enthralling, my own body was beginning to run down. My eyelids had become heavy and I stifled a yawn.

"I'll tell you what. Why don't we do this again tomorrow night, only more efficiently? I can type this stuff up as you're reading it. I'll set up the laptop over here and transcribe your translation as it happens. I can look up any words you might have problems with, and I think it will go much more quickly. Plus, we'll have the copy of the information to share with your family."

I sat in a comfortable chair next to a lamp with a scalloped, ivory-colored shade. With a silver thimble, I adeptly slid a needle through a patch on the knee of a child's pair of trousers, shaking my head and frowning. "With as fast as they grow out of them, you'd think they wouldn't have time to wear holes in their clothes."

"Boy's gotta use his knees. It's the law," Gio defended. "How's he gonna play marbles or dig up worms without using his knees?" He was sitting at the attic's desk with two books open. One was Aldo's diary and the other was a thick reference book with index indentations at the edge of its pages. He pointed down a long column of words and said, "The name of the village, *Ruscello*, means 'stream' or 'brook.'"

"Well, I wish he could learn to do those things without ruining his clothes. These will have to be his marble-playing pants now, and he's down to two pairs that are acceptable for school. Sister sent a note home yesterday about uniforms being kept in good repair." After tying a secure knot, I snipped the thread with small swan-shaped scissors Gio, I mean Tony, had given me for Christmas.

That's right, I remembered, this is a dream and I'm not me, I'm her. "Brook. That's a lovely name for a town. And Ruscello is pretty too."

Tony wrote down the word and frowned as he figured out a few more from memory, adding them to the sentence. "This whole process is so slow, but the tortoise won the race, right?"

"Slow and steady, honey. You're doing an excellent job." Juliana and I picked up another garment from the mending basket. This one needed a button. She and I shuffled over to the shelf in our fuzzy slippers to rattle the red-and-green fruitcake tin full of buttons down onto the sewing table. We selected a spool of thread from the spindle rack on the wall and opened the tin. As I was sorting through to find the perfect button, I caught her face in the mirror again. This time Juliana looked at herself but was staring intensely into her eyes, staring right through, as though she knew she was looking at me on the inside.

"You don't have to reinvent the wheel, you know," she whispered pointedly.

Tony looked up from the Italian-English dictionary. "Hmm?"

She stared into her eyes once more and then smiled and winked at me. "Nothing, sweetheart. Just thinking out loud."

Under the lamp by the chair, I got a better look at the buttons. Choosing a small, white, pearlescent one, I returned the rest to the shelf and sat back down.

Tony puzzled over another word. "This one's not in the dictionary. It's a name of something and I can't even pronounce it." He attempted it anyway. "'Ndrangheta."

"What do you think it is?"

"We'll have to find out. Maybe we could ask around town."

Then I was no longer in the attic looking out from Juliana's eyes. Instead, I saw Marlon Brando, cheeks stuffed for his most famous role.

He spoke, "Now you come and say 'Don Corleone, give me justice.' But you don't ask with respect. You don't offer friendship. You don't even think to call me 'Godfather.'"

Waking with a jerking kick of my feet and quick intake of breath, I had no illusions about going back to sleep. Staring at the glowing numbers of the alarm clock, I went over the details of the dream and attempted to make sense of them. The movie scene at the end obviously came about because of learning about Aldo's connection to 'Ndrangheta. My brain must have been trying to give Tony and Juliana a clue about the meaning of the word. Even in my still-groggy state, that made me smile. It was like holding up pictures with circles and arrows for them. *Hello! Mafia!*

But the real point of the dream, if there was a real point, wasn't about what I was trying to tell them. It was about what Juliana was attempting to show me.

"You don't have to reinvent the wheel, you know." That's what she'd said.

17.

Long, Long Night

I couldn't get back to sleep. That was nothing new, but tonight Juliana's noises seemed more persistent than ever—or maybe having seen the attic with my own eyes made me hyper-aware. It wasn't her who made me stare at the ceiling, though, but the thoughts ping-ponging around my head. The past few days had flown by with too many new people and experiences to neatly classify in my brain.

One thought kept bouncing back to front and center. What was it that Sylvia had said about my building? "It's all in the contract, honey."

I gave up and began pillaging around until I found the tidy package presented by the escrow officer. His Italian surname was no surprise. A Square, no doubt. Taking the packet back to bed, I settled in for a rendezvous with a stack of dry documents. Better than a tryptophan-melatonin sleep bomb, for sure.

Slumber seemed in the bag. My head snapped up once or twice from nodding off, but curiosity pushed me forward. Sorting through the stack, I came to a photocopy of an old courthouse ledger page, handwritten. The penmanship was impeccable, but it took effort to make out each word. I scanned through to an entry for a deed of transfer between two parties with the last name of Castaldi and a reference to another record.

Licking my fingers, I tabbed down until I came to it: a

homesteader's land grant, issued to Aldo Castaldi in 1865.

Another record struck me with the words "In Perpetuity." Perpetual. Forever. This had to be what I was looking for.

Wading through page after page of cursive writing that had been photocopied innumerable times, I longed for a Rosetta stone. By the time my eyes started crossing, I'd figured out that my building was protected by a clause, keeping it within the Castaldi family for over 150 years. I knew very little about perpetuity clauses, but I was pretty sure modern law put a limit on them. Hadn't Gio said something about it being a family tradition to renew the clause with each transfer of property?

More digging, more reading, until I found another scan of a handwritten file with lettering so pale, I had to make it out, syllable by syllable.

I wrote each deciphered piece of the puzzle until a string of words strobed in my vision to the rhythm of the jackhammer at my temple. The words read, "Exemption for Courtship With The Intention of Marriage."

Twenty minutes of transcribing later, I thought I'd either faint or throw up from hyperventilation.

The original document had been drawn up in the 1880s, when an influx of settlers migrated to the area. This "exemption" was created by Aldo Castaldi himself. Although not expressly stated, I could read his intent between the lines. The *exemption* to the perpetuity clause wasn't one at all, but a means to *guarantee* perpetuity.

Aldo could lure suitors for his daughters with the promise of land, test them for a year while they worked to prove themselves. If they didn't make the cut, he could take everything back. (The daughter's preference in the matter was conspicuously unmentioned.)

If the marriage did not take place during the prescribed year, the purchaser's financial investment would be refunded. There was evidently no such compensation for blood, sweat, and emotional distress.

Castaldi had no risks. Test out some poor schlub for a year. The schlub thinks he's there for the girl and to make a new life in America. He works hard to show he can provide for her, builds a livelihood on property he thinks he owns. At the end of a year, Castaldi either marries off the poor girl to Mr. Schlub, or puts the land and enterprise back into his own possession. A total win/win for *him*. Either way, the land with a farm or business he didn't build himself stayed in the family.

Just how, I wondered, did this exemption apply to me? No one would dream of using such a thing in this day and age. At least not out in the open.

But then, it wouldn't be in the open, would it, if I was just now finding out about it?

When I'd asked Gio how I—the non-Square—could buy the building, he'd said, "Sylvia found some sort of loophole at the courthouse." *Mister Wide-Eyed Innocence!*

He didn't just fall off the real-estate truck. He owned the building and the company that sold it. He had to have been in on whatever this was from the start. But to what end? He already owned half the town. Why would one little falling-down brick building make a big difference to him?

There are sadistic people in the world who get sick pleasure from giving someone false hope, so they can knock them down and take away their toys. Was that who Gio DiMarco was, down deep inside?

Maybe the Godfather dream meant something else. Maybe it was a warning not to get in any deeper with someone with that kind of dark place in his soul. Holy Mother of . . . invention—what if Gio really was the don of Castle Springs? Keeper of the Castle, my white Irish Aster! Of course that's how the Castaldi clan had successfully kept Oldtown in their control for this long! They had their own little mob right here in Podunk, Colorado.

Then I remembered the conversation between Gio and his great-grandmother at the party. The one spoken in Italian to exclude me.

I brought my laptop to bed to try to translate words I'd written on a party napkin. "*Intenzione . . . sposare . . . ragazza . . . presto, bisnonna . . . mi piace questo . . . voglio . . . ballare vostre . . . nozze.*"

My jaw hit my chest and I began emitting guttural noises when I guessed what had been said. The conversation went roughly like this:

"When are you going to marry this girl?"

"Soon, great-grandmother, soon."

"Good. I like this one. I want to dance at your wedding. Soon is good."

No, this was no accident or oversight. It looked like I was the victim of a scam perpetrated by an entire family, including that sweet old woman.

And Gio, all personable and charming, pretending to be Dudley Do-Right to my face. What kind of expert at deception would he have to be, to pull off a plot like this?

I didn't believe for a minute, though, that he was planning to marry me. He hardly knew me. Of course not. There had to be a courtship going on, I suspected, in order to make the "loophole" legit. Then, bam! At the end of the year, he says, "Oh, by the way, *cara, carissima, bella*—pack up your stuff and vacate. You've been punked. You shoulda read the fine print." It was all there in black and white. He could do just that.

"That snake! Humble, tortured widower, my left . . . ovary!" He would not be getting away with this. I didn't care if I had to call in the FBI, the CIA, and DHS. He was not getting his slimy hands on Mon Petit . . . or me. "In perpetuity."

After three previous attempts to wake him without letting the call go to voicemail, I held the phone to my ear for another four rings. As I was about to hang up and redial for the next chorus, Gio finally answered.

"Kate?" His voice was hoarse and disoriented.

Now that I had him on the other end, I froze in silence.

"Is that you?"

What the heck was I thinking, calling him at nearly two o'clock in the morning? Oh, Helena Bucket, was sleep deprivation making me get all *Fatal Attraction*? I opened my mouth, but nothing came out.

"Are you all right, Kate?

"You'll be hearing from my attorney in the morning." My shaking voice matched my hands as they dropped the phone and picked it up to power down.

"So what you're telling me is that you signed these papers, right?" Eloise, my best friend, and the attorney who helped me with my "no-fault" divorce, wasn't giving me the sympathy and solutions I'd hoped for. "And nobody duct taped you or held a pistol to your head?"

I stood in the shop's kitchen, hand-whisking a batch of dark chocolate. "Of course I signed them . . . technically . . . but I was so happy to be getting this building in this location, at that price, I guess I got a little sloppy."

"Sloppy is a good word for it." I could hear Elle tap a pencil, something she did when she was thinking a problem through. "It's going to take hazmat gear to clean up this mess."

"The contract is legal, then? They can pull this kind of crap, in this century, and get away with it?"

"If crap is what you signed up for, Katy, crap is what you get—a whole dump-truck full."

I growled and hurled the whisk, splashing dark brown goo all over my freshly painted wall. I was half inclined to leave it there for the next owner—or previous owner, as it were—to clean up himself. "Are you saying I'm stuck with this deal?"

"Well, it's not likely to hold up in court, I'm pretty sure of that, but it will take a long time to get sorted out. A fully cognizant adult, a highly trained chef, former CPA, signs her rights away . . . an attorney might have a hard time proving you were conned into this. That's all I'm saying."

Grabbing a wet rag to clean the wall, inspiration struck instead. Chocolate graffiti, a new art form. I got as far as "R-A-T-B-A-S-" before running out of chocolate.

"You do think I'll be able to keep my place, though, don't you?" I licked my finger before sighing and washing the sticky wall and floor.

"Katy, I'm not going to blow rainbow unicorn kisses in your ear. This is going to take time." I could swear she was playing a drum solo now, but I couldn't quite make out the song.

"How much time will it take?"

"There are serial killers and rapists in the world, my friend. Getting this thing on the docket could take years. Not to mention—if this guy owns half a town—"

"More than half—of Oldtown, anyway."

"If this guy is as powerful as you say he is, I can assure you he has a legal team that would make me look like a bucket of chum at the shark exhibit—that is, if I were licensed in the State of Colorado, which I am not. He could just starve you out, you know, counter-sue and just keep filing more papers that you and your attorney have to respond to, at great expense, until you've exhausted your resources."

"Great. Wonderful. I finally figure out what I want to be when I grow up, and for the first time in my life, I take a risk. I put all my chips on this one spot, only to let myself get taken in by some sleazy, slumlord, Mafioso don, in western small-town America."

"Just a minute, Katy, I've got to change over to the other

breast."

Eloise had always been an early riser, but even the two-hour time difference would not have found her awake to see my text if it weren't for an early-morning feeding.

Elle had been so driven in her career, not particularly fond of kids, and now here she was, totally in love with her newborn son and taking a year off from practicing law. While I was ecstatic for her, there was still that familiar sting.

"Doesn't the tapping keep him awake?

"You heard that?" She laughed. "I've found it soothes him back to sleep. Weird, huh? Do you think he got used to it while he was on the inside?"

I was trying to picture the physical logistics of breastfeeding while talking on the phone and tapping a pencil. Eloise always had been a woman of many talents.

"That's OK, Elle, go ahead and feed Max. I think you've answered my questions. Love you."

"Love you too, Katy. Let me know if you need anything else. Good night . . . or good morning. Whatever."

I wiped the wall down again with a fresh cloth, wondering if I'd ever get a chance to sleep. It was now four.

My mind went into rewind mode, going over everything that had transpired.

Not long after my dial-and-ditch call to Gio, there'd been a gentle tapping at my front door, followed by more insistent tapping. And then it got so bad, I was afraid he'd shatter a window.

"Aw, come on, Kate. Open up." He wasn't exactly yelling, but at two o'clock in the morning, his customarily loud voice echoed in the quiet street. He looked upward. "I'm going to start singing in a minute."

I knew he would, too. The man had no shame. I shoved open the old sash window and leaned my head out.

"I've got 911 on speed dial," I stage-whispered. "I suggest

you leave. Now."

Gio backed up a few steps to see me better.

"*Cara*, what's going on? At least tell me what this is all about."

I leaned inside and started to push the window back down. I didn't owe him an explanation.

"Kate, wait. What did I do?"

I'm not sure what made me pause. Maybe something in his voice got to me for a split second. I didn't owe him *anything*, but his hurt tone, fake or not, made me go against my resolve.

"You're not getting Mon Petit back. Not when the year is up. Not ever." I pulled the window closed again. The lock made a satisfyingly loud click when I shut it.

Gio stood gawking at me for a moment before sticking his hands in his pockets and turning to go. With hunched shoulders, he padded across the silent street.

His lights stayed on the rest of the night, along with mine.

18.

Tent of Truth

Sleep was out of the question. I had no choice but to begin my day—or further extend yesterday, really.

I made the mistake of turning on my phone mid-morning. There were twenty-seven messages, twenty-two of them from Gio and three from Sylvia. I deleted those without regret. "Sorry. Wrong number."

The other messages were from my mother.

There were plenty of good days to talk to her. This was not one of them. I wouldn't be able to keep it light and get off the phone. She had a sixth sense when something was wrong, and her worrying made me worry about her worrying.

Still, I knew if I didn't get back to her soon, she'd show up on my doorstep, and then I'd be obligated to admit my stupidity to her face. To the woman whose labor had, by many, many accounts, lasted thirty hours. Back labor. Excruciating sciatic pain. No drugs. I'd have to tell her how I'd allowed a dazzling, despicable man to slither into my heart—

Oh, Helen Keller. It was true. Gio DiMarco, the disgusting ooze of a human, made me love him. Of all the diabolical deeds I suspected, that was the one I could never forgive.

No, I absolutely needed to talk to my mother. There weren't many topics for which I sought her counsel. After all, she was too often a leaper and not a looker, while I was the logical, pragmatic one. But in matters of the heart I was completely out of my element, and no one had more experience in matters of the heart than my mother. She got it wrong most of the time, but she was nothing if not experienced. I punched the call button only to hear her ringtone at the alleyway door.

"Kathleen Fiona, you look like death on a Ritz. What is wrong with you?"

No matter the time of day or location, Marilyn O'Brian-Hannity-Schultz-Epstein-Montoya-Evans was the perfect picture of bohemian chic, with an emphasis on chic. It took a lot of time and effort to put together this much casual sophistication, but she gave the impression she rolled out of bed looking that way. Her shoulder-length honey-blond hair, the shade of the moment, enhanced the youthful veneer. Even with skin that was beginning to loosen around the eyes and under her chin, she couldn't pass for my mother without flashing her driver's license. The vertical line between her perfectly shaped brows gave her away as she stared at me, fists on hips.

I'd sent all three girls up front to deal with the store and Marco out to run errands. I didn't need them to know about my distress and broadcast it all over town. And every time I looked into Marco's dark eyes, I was reminded of the other pair they resembled, and I wanted to strangle him. The crime of looking like his uncle, the ooze, did not fit the punishment hatched by my insomnia-addled brain.

Having the kitchen to myself when my mother arrived was a mixed blessing. If I'd had witnesses, I would have had to hold myself together, keep a stiff upper lip and all that. As it was, when I saw her worried look, all I could do was run to her in a heap of hysteria.

"Ah, Katybug, it's all right. Just let it go. Mama's here." She clucked and shushed softly. "Just let it all out."

She opened the swinging door a few inches and whispered to Alyssa, "Hi, honey, we'll be upstairs for a little bit. Just call if you need us." Leading me by the hand up to my apartment, she put the kettle on to boil, deposited me in my unmade bed, plumped up the pillows and leaned me against the headboard. Then she climbed in beside me and pulled the sheet over both of our heads.

"Oh, for the love . . . Mother, we don't need the Tent of Truth. I'm thirty-four years old. I am well educated—an entrepreneur. I've been married and divorced. I've—"

"You're never too old for the Tent of Truth, Kathleen. It's ageless. Now tell me what is going on."

"I'm fine. I haven't been sleeping well for the past several days is all, and—" I reverted back to human-puddle mode and couldn't go on. It was an ugly cry. My mouth opened, and my eyes squeezed shut while still producing enough salt water for the Shamu tank. I knew from experience that my nose looked like a cherry tomato. Nothing but the sound of air escaped as I convulsed in wracking sobs.

Marilyn moved around to face me, legs crossed, Maharishi style, with the white sheet held aloft by her head. "Tent of Truth, Kathleen. What's his name?"

"Only you would assume this is about a man, Mother," I choked out between pitiful, shuddering breaths.

"It's always a man. I know that look, sweetheart. That's the look you had when you caught Pencil Man doing more than tax returns late at night."

"Mother."

"I can just imagine the *spreadsheets* those two were working on."

"Stop it, Marilyn. I've moved on."

"What's this one's name?"

"I don't want to talk about it." I wriggled down and away into the fetal position to continue my cry in peace.

The kettle whistled.

"You stay here and cry it out for a minute, Katybug. I'll

go make us some nice cocoa. You're not allowed to leave the tent until you've talked it through with your mama, you hear me?" She jostled the bed, uncrossed her legs with a groan, and disappeared into the kitchen.

I knew it was ridiculous, letting her turn me into the child and her the parent—I thought we'd established our reversed roles when I was about ten—but the Tent of Truth was the only place I granted her maternal authority. I needed nurturing and advice enough to cede control. I lay there letting toxic emotions escape onto my pillow and accumulate in the growing pile of soggy tissues on the floor.

"All right, here we go. I couldn't find marshmallows, but I did find your Fluff. I added some of that."

She wasn't kidding, either. I reluctantly sat up and stirred my mug, which seemed to be half marshmallow cream—just the way I liked it when I was little. My breathing calmed enough to blow on the mug and take a sip.

Mother resumed her position as tent pole and sipped her own cocoa, grimacing at the sickening sweetness. "Ah. Sugar bomb. Just right."

She placed her hand on my knee and sipped in silence for a while. "Tell me when you're ready to talk, Kathleen. We're not going anywhere until you do."

Using the last thread of rebellion left in me, I took my sweet time drinking the concoction, staring at my mother and blowing my dripping nose from time to time. Tent of Truth or not, she couldn't force me to spill the goods until I darn well wanted to.

"All right," I exhaled when the spasms in my throat finally relaxed.

"That's a good girl. Tell Mama all about it."

I laughed at the absurdity, which made her laugh, but I did start talking. I told her the entire story. About how much I loved this building at first sight. About how I couldn't stop looking at the big, beautiful, soulless man across the street. About how he deceived me with his sad stories into trusting him. About his big, crazy Italian family, who made me want to be part of something so solid and loving—despite my suspicions about their code of ethics. I talked about Nonna, and Juliana, the ghost—or presence, or whatever—who apparently lived in my attic, and was occupying my dreams. I recounted my sketchy translation of the Italian words Nonna and Gio spoke to one another. I brought the pile of papers from the floor into the tent to show her what I'd found. I talked about my call to Gio in the middle of the night and how he'd looked when he went away later, and how I felt guilty, which was ridiculous, because he didn't deserve my guilt. I told her about my phone call with Elle, and about the unheard messages on my phone that I was beginning to wish I could retrieve.

"How do you know?" Marilyn wiped goo from my cheek with a clean tissue.

"How do I know what?"

"How do you know he's the one responsible for this?"

"How could he not be, mother? That makes no sense."

"You put a very high premium on 'sense,' Kathleen. Sometimes the truth makes no sense at all." She gave up on the liquid candy and lifted the sheet to set the mug on the bedside table.

"I don't understand."

"Put your conjectures aside for a minute. It's obvious this Sylvia found a way to sell you the building whether she should or not—and maybe her motives were honorable—even if she acted in a, hmm, an unconventional way. You can't assume the worst about the man, without even discussing it with him. That's unfair."

I let my empty sticky mug *clunk* to the floor. "How could he not know?"

"You said he isn't very involved in that business anymore.

That's a lot of trust he's placed in his cousin, you know. Is it possible she told him everything was in order, and he signed the contract the same way you did—with his eyes half closed?"

I trumpeted into a new tissue and thought for a moment. "Theoretically, I suppose . . . "

"Kathleen, I know it's difficult for you to approach things in a non-analytical way, to trust your feelings, but I'm a pretty good judge of character—"

A snort erupted from the back of my throat, causing a sweet-dairy coughing fit.

"My former taste in men aside." She slapped at my thigh and shook her head. "I always was a sucker for a pretty face."

She winced and untwisted her legs to dangle one off the side of the bed. "I mean, sweetie, if someone strikes me as an honest, decent human being, and an overwhelming amount of evidence supports that feeling, I can almost certainly depend on that person. Heaven knows we needed a lot of help along the way. Our lives could have been so much worse without those people."

There was that. We'd had no extended family to speak of, but my mother made friends easily and always had them to fall back on in her many times of need. I guess she *was* a good judge of character—when her ovaries weren't involved.

"But—"

"Here are my thoughts. Maybe you need to give Geno a chance to explain. Maybe things aren't as bad as they seem. Maybe there's good reason to be in love with him. And maybe if you got a good night's sleep things would look a whole lot brighter."

Why did she make so much sense in the Tent of Truth, when I could depend on her to be airy-fairy the rest of the time? I hated when that happened. And I loved it.

"Gio," I whispered. "His name is Gio."

"Give me a squeeze, honey. You need a lot more human

contact in your life, if you ask me."

I laid my head on her generous chest and held her tight. "But what if I got my judgment about men from you? I didn't do so well the first time, you know."

"Oh, that," she spat. "Honey, Eddie was not the love of your life. He represented a lot of things to you, but I don't think true love was one of them."

I stiffened at her assessment. How could she possibly know a thing about 'true love'? It seemed she'd found security with Doug—Daddy number whatever—and it looked like this one might be in for the long haul. But someone with five marriages and countless other entanglements couldn't claim to be an expert on true love.

"And precisely what is it you think Eddie represented?"

She touched her index finger to my temple. "That's something you need to figure out. You would never accept it from me."

The Tent of Truth was getting plain spooky now. My mother was starting to sound almost wise.

"Well . . . let's see . . . " I closed my eyes for a moment to concentrate. "Eddie came from a nuclear family with parents who are still married, and his mother stayed home and baked cookies like June Cleaver. He represented a stable family background."

"Good. That one's too easy."

I settled back against the pillows and began twisting an errant ringlet. "Eddie had a plan, a vision. He was outcome-oriented. I recognized some of myself in him. I found security in what I perceived as the steadiness I lacked from my upbringing."

"Ouch—but also true. Go on." The sheet was flattening the carefully cultivated windswept look of her hair.

"He was good-looking." I pushed a throw pillow at her when she made a face. "He was. Not the way Gio is good-looking, but he had a safe, sort of wholesome look."

"Totally sexless, if you ask me."

"I'm not. Ew. This is getting weird."

"We're sitting under The Tent of Truth and it's just now getting weird for you? I call that a win." She started massaging my feet. "Come on, Honey, what else?"

"There's more?"

"I think so."

"Well, he showed an interest before I did. He didn't ever say it in words, but he found me attractive. At first."

"It's a crying shame he never said it in words. Every woman needs to hear those words."

She was right. I desperately needed those words from him and he had never given them.

"He was smart and ambitious."

"Those are good qualities, but do these things add up to him being your soul mate? The love of your life?"

"Forgive my rudeness, Marilyn, but I'm not sure you are qualified to pontificate about soul mates."

"I had one. I did. Stop rolling your eyes."

"Seriously? You had a soul mate? Who?"

"Kathleen, you really *are* being rude. Don't sound so shocked. I'm not as superficial as you seem to think I am."

"Can I have your cocoa?"

She smiled with a hint of disapproval and retrieved her mug. "Sure, sweetie."

It was the perfect temperature. I noisily gulped down a gooey mouthful. "I'll tell you one thing. I never had all of these . . . mm . . . physical sensations with Eddie. And, we were, you know, married and," I cleared my throat, "intimate and everything."

"Well, I certainly hope so!" Mother looked heavenward before nudging me. "And you haven't, you know, with this man . . . Gio?"

"I'm not like you, mother. I actually pay attention when the priest is talking. And to be honest, I'm kind of impressed he hasn't tried to seduce me. Gio. Not the priest. But, oh my lard, that man can kiss. Like, hummingbird-in-the-belly-turn-me-to-jelly kind of kiss."

"Now we're getting somewhere."

"Great. Can we get out of here now?"

"Nice try." She stared me down and I knew I wouldn't be making a break for it until I'd come to whatever epiphany she thought she was leading me to. "Keep going, pumpkin."

"Gosh, Mom. That's one you haven't used in a while." I had hated "pumpkin" because it likely had something to do with the color of my hair, the bane of my childhood existence.

"You are stalling, my darling."

I closed my eyes and released my breath. "OK. Hmm. Well, I just don't think that being physically attracted—even like, really, really . . . really attracted—is something you can base a long-term relationship on."

"Oh, honey. Without that part, I don't think you can really even call it love."

"Don't take this the wrong way, Mom, but I never wanted to be led around by my lady parts."

"Like me. That's what you're thinking. Go ahead and say it."

"It's the example I was given. I'm sorry, but it's true." I hugged her. "And sometimes bad examples are good motivation to take a different path in life. So don't beat yourself up about it. Everything worked out just fine."

She didn't let go when I started to pull back, but clutched me tighter. "Kathleen, I think you understand that my worst choices were somewhat out of my control. Those things mostly happened during the raging manic phases, and then I'd come to my senses and find myself sleeping next to a virtual stranger."

I tightened the embrace. "I know. You don't need to explain, but I did learn from your mistakes. That's all."

"Here's the thing, though, sweetheart. Sexual attraction is a beautiful thing. It is this wonderful gift that can make your very best friend into your one true love. I know this with every ounce of my being."

I considered for a moment. Could I call Gio "my very best friend?" I recalled how we talked over dinner that first evening, how easy it was, and how I'd told him things I never would have told Eddie—or anyone—so early on. And he had opened up to me too. I woke up in the morning thinking of things I wanted to tell him, inconsequential things and big things. He had become, in just a few short days, someone I wanted to share everything with. Was that a very best friend?

"He really is a good man. I think so, anyway." I sat up and pulled my knees to my chest, wrapping my arms around them. "I think I may have screwed things up."

"Well, you won't know until you talk to him. Give him a chance to explain, Kathleen. You owe him that much." She pulled the sheet off of us both, fluffed her hair and got up off of the bed. "I'd make you lay here and take a nap, but I don't think you'll be able to sleep until you get this thing ironed out, do you?"

No kidding.

"Thanks, Mama. I love you."

"I love you too, Katybug. Let's go downstairs and finish your batch of candy, and you can figure out how you want to handle the next step."

19.

Abduction

My mother and I had always felt closest in the kitchen, where we had a long-practiced choreography and could anticipate each other's next move. Today was no exception. We turned out enough ganache pieces to store for a few weeks and made the kitchen sparkle after a batch of Crème de la Crème truffles was completed.

Absorbed in our work and thinking about how I would approach Gio, I didn't hear Marco pull up behind the store.

The screen door screeched open and slapped shut. "Hey, Kate."

"Hey, there you are. Did you find the restaurant supply place all right?"

Marco's eyes darted from my mother to the swinging doorway to the shop, and back to me. "Uh, yeah, sure."

"Well, where is everything?" Something about his body language seemed off.

"About that . . . " He contemplated his shuffling feet.

"Were you able to find the trays and pastry tubes I need?" He cleared his throat, rubbing his nose with the back of his sleeve.

"Marco, are you okay?"

"Yeah. Sure, Kate." He glanced again toward the door.

"Where is the stuff?"

A squeak made me peek backward to see who was coming

in, but the door swung closed again as soon as I turned.

"Is something the matter?"

"Uh, well, Kate, I need to show you something out back."

"What is it? You didn't get into an accident with the van, did you?"

His eyes lit for a split second before he shook his head and frowned. "Well, you'd better come check it out."

"You can tell me. I'm sure you drove carefully . . . and I've got excellent insurance. Don't worry, Marco. I won't be angry." Removing my plastic gloves, I followed him out into the alley.

My big, beautifully restored, vintage panel delivery truck, with its rich brown paint and Mon Petit graphics, had not a scratch on it. "What's wrong with it? It looks fine to me."

"Maybe you should come to the back."

I inspected the van thoroughly. No dent, no ding. It appeared the same as this morning. The back doors stood open and I scanned the interior to find the items I had requested tied down securely at one side.

"See that thing up toward the front?"

It was dark inside except for what little alley sunlight penetrated the glass in the front seat area, creating a glaring backlit effect. "Where? What thing?"

"Why don't you climb in and I'll get into the driver's seat and I'll show you from up there."

I gaped at him as he strode around and hopped in behind the wheel. Shrugging, I grabbed onto the looped leather strap near the back door and used it to help hoist my short legs up and inside. As soon as I got all of me in and regained my balance, the doors behind me slammed shut. Alyssa's face, pink and contorted with guilt, grimaced at me from the other side of the window. Bungee cord in hand and mouthing the word "sorry," she lashed the doors together by the handles.

I whirled frantically. "Marco, what is going on?"

He started the engine and began to back out of the parking

spot.

"Sorry, Kate, but I had to do this. It's for your own good. You'll thank me later."

The expanded steel mesh between us kept me from carrying out my earlier wish to strangle him.

"You had to do what?"

Alyssa stood with an expression of despair next to my mother, who laughed hysterically in her chocolate-splattered apron.

"What is this about?" I searched for a way to escape, or at least join him in the front of the vehicle, but it was futile. I didn't feel threatened, but I sure as Helm's Deep wasn't going to let him get away with this. "Are you going to answer me?"

"Gio wants to talk to you." Marco's nervous eyes met mine in the rearview mirror.

"Gio instructed you to abduct me?" If my doubts about the man had subsided since the Tent of Truth ritual, they now spiraled out into the stratosphere. Only a thug would send a kid to throw a woman into a van and speed off. "You do realize there's a long sentence for kidnapping, don't you?"

His jaw dropped. "It's not what you're thinking, Kate." As he tightened his hands on the wheel, the color drained from his cheeks. "I told Gio I'd try to convince you to come talk to him. You haven't answered his calls and—"

"This is how the Castaldis convince people? Am I going to find a horse's head in my bed later? Is this an offer I can't refuse?"

"What? No! He agreed to let me encourage you, like with words. What are you talking about, Kate?" His face began to dampen with perspiration. "Alyssa said you were upset, and I thought I couldn't talk you into coming with me, so I—"

Now here was a new development. My mind shifted gears. "Alyssa is talking to you now? The last I noticed, she was slamming her fingers in the cash register when you walked in."

I evaluated him through narrowed slits. "What did you do to her?"

"Ah . . . " He laughed nervously and returned his gaze to the road. "We kind of, uh, smoothed all of that stuff out."

How in the world did Alyssa go from Manager McKlutzy around him to being his accessory to a crime? "Smoothed it out? How, exactly, did you *smooth it out?*"

"Well, I kind of figured all the, uh, awkwardness wouldn't go away on its own." That big, seductive Castaldi grin flashed across his face as he wiggled his eyebrows. "So I kissed her."

My breath caught like a hiccup. "You what? When did this happen?"

"While you were out at the ranch."

I frowned. "You're not messing with her, Marco, are you? You know you could hurt her if—"

"No, Kate, nothing like that. Kissing Alyssa has been on my to-do list for a long time."

"To-do—"

"Since, like, seventh grade."

"Wha . . . You didn't seem . . . I mean, you sure didn't act nervous. If anything—"

"Isn't she cute when she does that? Yeah, nervous isn't my style." Straightening his posture, he ran fingers through his hair. "It takes nerves of steel to be this cool."

Up on my knees and clutching the cage between us for balance, I peered ahead. We were winding our way to GDM Enterprises at the northeast corner of the town square.

"Wait until you let me out of here and we'll see how cool you are, you little dipstick." I growled in frustration, but seeing there was nothing to do about it—for the moment—I sat on my haunches and practiced yoga breathing before speaking again. "You didn't need to do this. I was already planning to call him."

"Gio?" Marco evaluated my reflection with narrowed eyes.

"You're not just saying that so you can make a break for it, are you?"

"No. I was going to call as soon as my mother left." Now that the office was closer, though, my stomach began knotting. Was there a logical explanation? Or did Gio DiMarco have a spot in his soul dark enough to commit fraud with that unnerving smile on his face?

When Marco pulled up to the curb at GDM, I could only sit and wait.

The passenger's side door opened and Gio's tired voice asked, "No luck, huh?"

Marco's eyes met mine in the mirror. "I wouldn't exactly say that."

"Hmm?" Gio's tone lightened. "She agreed to see me? When?"

"Now!" I fumed from my cage, smacking the mesh barrier with my palms.

Gio's dark head and massive shoulders leaned into the truck. He squinted rearward, finding my face. "*Cara*? Is that you?"

"You'd probably better skip the Italian endearments, at least until we iron a few things out. Do you think you can manage that?"

"Kate, what are you doing in the back of the van?"

"You should ask Marco about it, but please don't hit him. I'd like the honor, if you don't mind."

Gio glared at Marco. "Wha—?"

"I'm sorry, Uncle G. Sweet-talking her into coming on her own wouldn't have worked. I heard she was pretty hacked off so—"

"How did you manage this?" He palmed his forehead and let out a long sigh. There were dark circles under his eyes. "Never mind. I don't want to know. Just get her out." Exhaling, he whispered, "*stupido*." With contrition, Gio's gaze locked onto mine. "I'm so sorry, Kate."

The two met in back and the uncle smacked away the hands of his mini-me. "Get back, I'll do it."

Marco skulked backward with hands in pockets, while Gio freed the damsel in distress.

No, Kate. No shining armor. Just the deli guy . . . who owns half a town.

Gio reached out his arms for an embrace, but I only took his hand to help me over the bulky bumper and down.

"Kate, I—"

"Is Sylvia in there?"

"Yes. We both want to have a chat with you."

"What we are going to have, sir, is more than a little chat. You'd best be thankful my attorney is in Connecticut right now . . . and . . . on maternity leave." And couldn't practice law on my behalf if she wanted to. But he didn't need to know that.

Marco's head bowed now in abject humility. "Sorry, Kate."

Socking him squarely on his upper arm was worth the pain it cost my hand. "You should be. That was a pretty bone-headed thing to do. You're lucky I like you."

"I know I am." His face brightened. "But you're here, aren't you?"

Some people's nephews. My attempted stern glower didn't seem to penetrate his adorable, thick skull. "Yes, I'm here," I sighed.

20.

The 411

The sleek glass and stainless steel doors of GDM swung open and Sylvia emerged, lips held in a tight line, eyes downcast. Finally, she spoke. "Kate, let's go inside to the conference room. Would you like some coffee?"

Standing next to Sylvia in my tent-rumpled chef's coat—a sticky mess all down its front—and fiery, wild ringlets springing out everywhere, I had to fight off acute inferioritis. Not only hadn't I had a good deal of sleep in days, I'd cried all of my makeup off and hadn't bothered to look in a mirror or brush my mop before returning to work and being kidnapped. Add to that, feeling like a chihuahua just released from a carry-on bag; this was not a winning moment for me.

Her willowy frame was draped in a silver satin shirt and narrow black skirt. Long, blonde-streaked hair was ironed sleek and perfectly in place. She would tower over me in bare feet, but today she wore three-inch red heels. Maybe she chose them for the intimidation factor. Or maybe it was because of the way they accentuated her killer calves. Either way, it took great effort for me to stride wordlessly inside the building, head up, shoulders back, with every bit of dignity I could summon.

The conference room was upstairs. Its enormous picture windows looked out over Castaldi Square in all its autumnal glory. A long glass table top, supported by more shiny metal, sat in the center, complementing its gleaming surroundings.

I wonder who gets to wipe the fingerprints off that thing every day?

I sat in the offered chair at the far end of the table, where neat stacks of files were lined up. Gio sat near me on one side and Sylvia the other.

Gio pierced the silence by clearing his throat. "Kate, I'm glad you came. There is a lot of ground to cover, so why don't we let Sylvia begin."

I'd never seen him perform his duties as president. The voice was different, official, commanding. I tried to shoo away the hummingbird in my heart.

Raising my eyebrow toward the sophisticated woman, I said. "Yes, Sylvia, let's. Let us let you begin."

"Well, um, first, Kate, uh, hello."

"Hello." Seeing her squirm was delicious. It showed a side of her I hadn't thought existed.

"First off, I want you to know that this is not Gio's fault in the least. I take full responsibility for my actions."

I looked squarely from one to the other. Gio had a pained expression on his face. I wanted to believe it was genuine. "It's very convenient to have a town full of character witnesses."

Gio's head dropped. "Kate. I owned the building and the company that sold it to you. I am legally responsible for anything my staff may have done—"

"May have?"

Sylvia put her hand on mine and eyed me with remorse. "What I did, Kate. I did it, and I did it intentionally. I hope you will give me a chance to explain why."

"An explanation would be nice, but I can't promise it will change anything. I clearly have been deceived. What I can't figure out is why? Is this another Castaldi tradition? Bait and switch?"

Gio reached out for my other hand before I pulled away both and set them in my lap. "Kate, I promise you that I'll do everything I can to make it right."

"You say that, but you can't fix this by throwing your money at me. I can't think of any solution which doesn't end in a lawsuit, or me walking away from all of my hard work. Neither option sounds particularly enticing, you know." I cleared my throat to keep my voice from quavering. "I've spent the past few years pulling myself up out of a bad situation, and I swore I'd never tie my self-worth, success or failure to a man ever again. Yet here I sit, at the mercy of another one. Look up 'fool' in the dictionary and you'll see a picture of Kate Hannity."

Sylvia went on. "Honey, it was all me. That's what I'm trying to tell you. When you came to me inquiring about that building, I knew I couldn't sell it to you, but I liked you so much, right off the bat. I figured we'd go take a look—and seeing as it was in such rough condition, I could show you some better places—and you'd forget all about the florist building. There were quite a few that made much more sense for you, you know."

"Financial sense, maybe. And normally I would have chosen one of them based on numbers alone. But none of those properties was the one that called to me. I can't explain it. I knew the florist building was where Mon Petit belonged. It was where *I* belonged."

"And I tried to talk you into a long-term lease, but—"

"And I told *you* that wouldn't do. I came to Castle Springs to settle for good. I *had* to have my *own* place, a tangible symbol of my achievements and a permanent place to call home. Permanence is something I've wanted and lacked my entire life. I intentionally chose Castle Springs for Mon Petit, because it represents everything I've craved since I was a little girl."

Gio broke in, "And Sylvia told me she had a client who was willing to pay cash for the place, without so much as an inspection. But—"

"Well, and like I said, I really liked you—like you— and I

wanted to make you happy and wished there was something I could do about the situation."

"But there was the perpetuity clause, and you couldn't." I noticed a sticky spot on my arm and returned my hands to my lap.

"Yes." Sylvia went to the sink in the corner of the room and returned with a wet napkin for me.

Adjusting the height of the office chair so my legs were no longer dangling like a six-year-old's, I asked, "So what in the name of—what possibly made you do it anyway?"

"After we spent the morning looking at properties, where did we go?"

My face grew warm as I looked from her to Gio. "We had lunch at Mangia."

"Exactly. We had lunch at Mangia." She said it as if it were a revelation.

I stared at her as the clock ticked loudly on the wall.

"Do you remember anything *special* about that lunch meeting?"

"Not particularly. The food was good." I darted a glance at Gio and away.

"Well, I do." Sylvia clacked her heels over stone tiles to look down into the park. She exhaled audibly and turned to face us both. "You two couldn't take your eyes off each other. It was like flipping on the Christmas lights—pure, bright electricity."

Gio's eyes glittered. His head nodded ever-so-slightly in recognition.

"My cousin had been grieving for five years. Five. That's a long time, Kate. The whole family has tried all this time to fix him up, and he showed no interest whatsoever."

"Yes. Gio said that."

"And then you walked in, and suddenly there was something in his eye I hadn't seen in a very, very long time."

Gio folded his arms across his chest and looked down at

the table.

"And you." She gestured wildly in my direction. "I thought you were going to need a drool bib."

"Now, that's just an . . . outright . . . exaggeration. I thought he was cute. How could I not? But—"

"But, nothing. You hardly heard a word I said throughout the entire meal."

She laid her hand on Gio's shoulder and then on mine, and I could swear I actually felt a current of energy pass through her as a conduit.

And the clock ticked.

I leaned back, breaking the connection. "And because you saw that we were attracted to one another, you decided that perpetrating a fraud would be a marvelous idea?"

Sylvia came closer and leaned her hands on the table. "That's not exactly the way I would put it, but it got my wheels turning, that's for sure. After you left, I went across the street and walked around your apartment. That's how I think of it. It *is* yours." She went to the small refrigerator and pulled out three small bottles of water and returned. Opening one and sipping, she said, "I've always liked going up there to think. You know, there's a story in our family about Juliana and Tony. About how she still lives there, waiting for him to come home. Anyway, while I was in the apartment, wishing I could find a way to get you in there, I got this really strong impression that I should go to the courthouse and sniff around."

Gio snorted loudly.

"I'm not saying I heard the voice of a ghost or anything, but all I can say is that this idea came to me while I was up there."

I eyed her with suspicion. "You're saying Juliana wanted you to look for an answer at the courthouse?"

She looked at the ceiling and back. "I don't know what I'm saying. I just know that until then the idea would never have occurred to me."

I stared at the stacks of papers before me. "And the courthouse is where you discovered your 'loophole.'"

Sylvia began reorganizing the piles. "Kate. You know how you were able to find the information in your closing papers?"

I nodded.

"Well, let me just tell you right now, that is not standard practice. All you would normally get is a statement from the title company that the property was free and clear, and the contract itself. I had all of those documents included in the contract for your information. If you had taken the time to read them before signing them—"

"So we're trying to blame me now, for trusting you?"

"No, of course not." She opened a file. "I just wanted to make sure all of the pertinent information was there for you to find, whenever the time was right. But here's more stuff, if you want to have a look. I wasn't going to hide the facts from you completely."

All of this made a nice little story, but it failed to answer too many questions.

"So, what made you think the intended spouse provision applied to me? How was this going to benefit me long-term? You knew I couldn't keep the building forever."

"I was hoping it would become a moot point."

The clock's ticking continued.

With exasperation on her face, Sylvia said, "I was hoping I wouldn't have to spell this part out for you. My cousin never responded to *anyone* in his life the way he did you that first day."

Gio's head came up, his mouth poised to speak.

"Anyone, G, including Susan." She paced the width of the room and back, like a nervous tiger in a glass enclosure. "And your response to him . . . I saw that spark—no, it was more than just a spark—I saw magic right before my eyes. And I hoped with everything I have inside that before a year was up, the two of you would be married."

My ears filled with the rhythmic sound of coursing blood. "That's insane! We hardly know each other. And what makes you think I even *want* to get married again?"

Gio spoke this time. "Our family has a very long history of falling fast and hard. Short courtships, shorter engagements, and happy marriages that last a lifetime."

I spun my chair forcefully in his direction. "And speaking of your family . . . Is 'Ndrangheta a family tradition after all these years? And what was all of that *'sposare'* and *'matrimonio'* stuff with your grandmother? Please don't tell me that sweet little old woman is in on this too."

He puzzled for a moment before showing signs of recognition. "Nonna? You think Nonna is in collusion with some master plot to defraud you?" He and Sylvia looked at one another and broke into hysterics. "Oh, wow, Kate. Wait 'til you get to know her better, God willing. If she even thought we were doing something dishonest, that 'sweet little old woman' would have both our hides." He chuckled some more and shook his head. "I can still taste the soap from the first— and last—lie she ever caught me telling." He licked his lips in distaste. "And I didn't know about any of this until about two hours after you did, when I decided this had something to do with Syl."

Sylvia nodded in corroboration.

"Then what—"

"Nonna wants to see me settled, that's all. She's healthy as a horse, but let's be real. One of these mornings she's not going to wake up. It's hard to believe sometimes, but that's just life. She'd like to see me married before she dies."

"But you told her *'presto.'* You led her to believe . . . "

"Because that's what I believe, Kate." Those chocolate-brown eyes softened. "I believe—no, I know. I know without a doubt, we will be married. *Presto.* Soon. And that has absolutely nothing to do with a neatly stacked pile of bricks my grandparents once owned."

Unintelligible noises began erupting, in rapid succession, from the mouth of the person sitting at the head of the glass table. The short woman in the sticky-fronted chef's coat. The one with wild red hair. The one who looked like she hadn't slept in days. The woman who looked an awful lot like me. She jumped out of her chair and headed for the door.

Gio followed her. "Kate. Wait."

She spun around. "No, you wait!"

"Kate, I—"

The sleep deprived, sticky, crazy-haired woman placed her small hands firmly on Gio's chest and pushed hard, though the effort didn't move him more than an inch.

"You just hold it right there, *boyo*." I took a few deep breaths, trying to clear my head and feel like myself again—and not this disconnected observer. I held up my hand when Gio reached for me.

"You cannot just haul me over here, kicking and screaming, and smooth everything over with pretty words."

"I'm trying to—"

"Just wait."

Gio stood patiently and watched while I did nothing more than breathe. Every time he thought it was safe to speak again, I held up my hand and closed my eyes.

Sylvia began inching her way around us to leave.

"Stay where you are," I snarled. Then more softly added, "Just give me a minute. I want you here. I'm not done with you yet."

Anyone looking in would have found a window-dressing of mannequins, standing still in time, one trying to gather her sanity, the others frozen by their fear of setting her off.

At long, long last I regained my composure enough to say, "I'm going to give you the benefit of the doubt and take you at your word. I know that's two clichés in one sentence, but

I'm a little too exhausted for witty conversation right now. I think I'm just starting to babble." I tilted my head to see into Gio's face for the truth. "How could you possibly know we are going to be married, *presto* or otherwise? Haven't we only been on a few real dates? I thought you were a relatively rational, intelligent human being, but this is certainly no indication of that."

"Kate. Just bear with me here. You know how I have been a widower for a while."

Sylvia chimed in, "For *five* years."

"Yeah. Five years." He rubbed the stubble on his chin. "And the reason I haven't much felt like dating all this time is that, deep down, I haven't ever stopped feeling married. Every time I'd see a beautiful woman, I'd get this guilt thing—"

Sylvia put her palms up in front of her. "Well it doesn't help that your wife has never left the deli."

Gio's right eyebrow lifted in annoyance at his cousin's accusation. "Oh, and now we're talking about ghosts again." He turned away and muttered, "This family. *Madre Santa.*"

"You can deny it all you want, G, but you know you feel her there. You bring her flowers every day."

"I do not bring her flowers. I keep her table for the people— her people—who come to talk."

Fists on hips, Sylvia disagreed. "Well, if that isn't bringing flowers to the ghost of Susan DiMarco, I don't know what is."

"Excuse me. I think we're getting a little off track here." I'd never had real siblings, only the occasional, short-lived, step-this-or-that, and no cousins to speak of. No matter how good-natured in intent, this kind of family bickering always made me uncomfortable.

"Sorry, *bella*—sorry, Kate." Gio gestured away from the door. "Can we all just sit back down and discuss this? Please don't run away until you've heard me out, OK?"

"All right. Of course." I settled back in and opened my

bottle of water, ready to listen. Ready to defend.

"Like I said, I just couldn't look at women that way after Susan died. I knew everyone was looking out for me, wanted me to find happiness and all that, but it just wasn't happening for me. After that first year or so, I felt like I could function as a person. I was able to run the businesses just fine. Actually, I probably would have closed GDM without Sylvia's help."

She reached across the table and squeezed his hand.

"But I was okay with my life the way it was. I just kind of figured you only get one shot in life at something like that, and I'd already gotten mine. I kept busy and put all those feelings on the back burner."

"In the deep freeze, more like it, G." Sylvia's acrylic nails tapped the glass table for emphasis.

"Whatever. I was so long like that, I guess I thought it was better to not stir anything up, because it was just easier that way."

"Like a parish priest," I whispered, remembering our conversation about how he continued to see Susan's cancer patients and their families.

"Exactly. I imagine pushing away that part of myself was a lot like what a priest has to do, to be able to focus on his duties. Only there wasn't a real logical or spiritual reason for me. I just couldn't—or didn't want to—see anyone in that way anymore."

"And then I brought you into Mangia for lunch." Sylvia tried to hold my gaze, but I wouldn't give her that much just yet.

"Kate, I can't explain it any other way than this. You walked in and I heard myself think, 'Oh, *there* she is.' Just exactly like that. 'There she is,' as though I'd just found something that had been misplaced for so long I'd forgotten I was looking for it. I saw you and I knew, and it felt right, and that guilt thing disappeared. Poof."

I scrutinized the two of them. The sincerity was plain on his face, while Sylvia wore a look of smug satisfaction.

"But I wasn't even nice to you. I barely even gave you the time of day."

"I knew you weren't ready. Every day I would make small talk, joke, do everything I could to get your attention, but I'm a little rusty in that department. I didn't want to scare you off with too much too soon. And, hey, the last time I had to try to impress a girl, it usually involved putting something squiggly down her back. I knew I wasn't exactly smooth about it, but I tried, and every day you'd go away and I'd think, 'Ooooooh. Shut down again."

"Shut down? I didn't think I shut you down . . . exactly."

"You weren't ready—and still aren't ready—but I've waited a long time, Kate. I can afford to be patient, because I know what the outcome is going to be."

He reached for my hand, and, this time, I didn't pull away.

"So this is not a proposal." I sighed in relief.

"This is not a proposal, *cara*, it's just a statement of fact. When it is a proposal, you'll know it. I'm not going to push you. You've got to know it's right too."

"Let's not confuse the issues." I removed the elastic from my hair, stood and bent forward, running my fingers through it. Returning to a standing position, I twisted it loosely into a bun at the top, replaced the band and returned my attention to Gio. "You said once that there are ways to get around perpetuity clauses. What are they, besides marrying into the family—that's pretty crappy, by the way. 'You can have this, just as long as it is community property and can never actually leave the family.' Just crappy."

Sylvia chimed in. "Aldo's intent has been carried out by the family, and they've always, with a few exceptions, only sold to other Squares. There are layers upon layers of restrictions, piled on by each succeeding generation." She shuffled files to find a large book on real estate law. She opened to a marked page. "Modern laws limit perpetuity clauses. No matter the intent of all of those Castaldis, a perpetuity clause can't legally stand forever. They can, however prevent the new owner from fully vesting in the property for a period of time."

Gio reached for the book and read. He closed his eyes, tilting his head back. "*Abbi pietà.*"

"How long is this period of time?" I looked at the line Gio pointed out. "No way. No freaking way! This says the property can be all mine—as, let me remind you, it is supposed to presently be—when it fully vests to me in *twenty-one* years? What about Gio? He wouldn't have been vested when he sold to me, right?"

Gio looked skyward. "It wouldn't have applied to me. I'm a descendant."

"Correct." Sylvia rolled her seat backward when I leaned toward her menacingly. "Twenty-one years is nothing in the scheme of things. Aldo's original request took perpetuity very literally. The law wouldn't enforce that, even back then, but no one wanted to tick off the ghost."

"Enough with ghosts." Gio held his palm to his forehead while shaking his head, and mumbling, "*Famiglia di pazzi.*"

"Aldo too?" I looked to Sylvia, who smiled and nodded.

"That's what Nonna says. She says she sees him out at the ranch sometimes." She turned to her cousin, "And, no, your '*famiglia*' is not crazy, Gio. Some of us just have a little more sensitivity to these things than others."

"Tell me about Aldo. How many poor guys did he con with this matrimony thing anyway?

Gio and Sylvia looked baffled.

"And what about the daughters? I just imagine them having to marry some poor guy their father picked out—for them being stuck forever. Talk about perpetuity! This was the United States of America, for Peter, Paul and Mary's sake. Didn't he realize that? I was beginning to like Aldo, too, from his memoir, but he must have been a real piece of work."

"I think you'll have to ask Nonna," Gio answered. "I don't think it was like that at all, but she would know. Those daughters were her aunts, after all."

I looked at the mountain of papers. "Can I take this stuff home to look at? I've got to process the data and my body's seriously in need of a reboot."

"Of course." Sylvia looked much more at ease.

I thought maybe I had let her off the hook too easily. I was just too tired to fight any longer. I needed to go home and sleep. Now.

Gio looked like I felt. I asked him, "Can you please take me home? This is a lot to carry."

"Yes, *bella*. Absolutely. You have a lot to think about. Take your time."

Sylvia stood up and crossed to the door. "I'll go get a box for these things."

I called after her, "Don't get too comfortable. This isn't over yet."

I eyed the pile of papers with dread and said to Gio, "I need to talk to Elle—I mean, my lawyer—about all this. But not right now."

21.

It's All In The Delivery

Gio's SUV lumbered over the last of the cattle guards before winding its way to his family's ranch house. He'd been uncharacteristically quiet on the drive—quiet for him, anyway—as if he'd been paying particular attention to minding his manners. "Thanks, Kate."

"For what?"

"With all of the . . . with the real estate issue, I thought—I sort of figured you were done—that you'd be 'needing space,' you know?" He glanced from the corner of his eye without turning. "Kinda awkward, considering we can pretty much see into each other's bedrooms."

My pulse surged, having just been outed as a peeping tom . . . and wondering how many times I'd forgotten to close my own blinds.

Cici, surrounded by an assortment of sheep and a gangling alpaca, waved from the barn. She called to an Australian shepherd, who raced wildly away from her to beat us to the house.

"That's Chuck. You didn't get to meet him at the party."

Taking his offered hand, I smiled. "I wasn't sure if I would talk to you either, until I went home and my mother made me have nap time." I laughed. "This parenting thing has got to stop. I wouldn't want her to make a habit of it."

I grabbed the dashboard for balance when Gio gunned the

engine, bumping over the winding driveway to win the race with the dog. "Anyway, she manned the troops downstairs while I crashed and burned for over four hours. When I woke up, the shop was shiny and bright, there was a boatload of new product made, and a pot of my mother's good-for-what-ails-you chicken soup in the fridge."

"And your opinion about me—about the real estate deal—had magically changed?"

"Magically is an appropriate word, but I'm still figuring out my opinion."

The dog was now jumping straight up and down next to the vehicle with a heavy piece of firewood in his mouth.

Gio looked from him to me and back again. "So she talked to you when you slept. Juliana did."

I laughed at Chuck's antics and his comical face with one silver eye and one brown one bugging wide with excitement. "You're really coming around about the dream thing, aren't you?"

I hopped down from the high seat and waved to Cici. "Yes. I'll tell you about it later, but basically, Juliana put me at ease about a few things. I still have a lot to think about," I added at his hopeful expression. "But I'm pretty sure no one's sleeping with the fishes in Castle Springs because of Squares—at least not current Squares."

"Where is all that stuff even coming from, Kate? You don't strike me as one of those people who automatically equates *Italian* with *the Mob*."

"Of course I'm not. It's just that Juliana said—no, that's not entirely true. In one of my dreams I saw Marlon Brando."

Gio's uproar of laughter made the dog bark with equal enthusiasm.

"Anyway, I'm perfectly all right sharing 'my space' while I'm working things out in my head. Besides, you're not getting off the hook so easily about Juliana's request—and we're not even sure what she *does* want yet."

"We've got to find my grandfather's notes, I guess. That's what you said, right?"

"Right. No reinventing the wheel. Tony spent years translating. Juliana wants us to honor that."

The hyperactive dog had returned the "stick" to Gio for the third time before Cici got halfway to us. Deeming me an acceptable alternative, he dropped the log at my feet for the fourth go-round. I cupped his chin, scratching his ear while talking to that tongue-lolling, eye-popping, lunatic face. "You are a clown, aren't you, Chuck? It's a silly name for you, but you don't seem to mind at all, do you? Do you, happy boy?"

He wiggled away and picked up the log to put in my hand. I tossed it as far as I could, and he ran to try and beat it to its destination.

"Chuck is his middle name." Gio laughed.

"Your dog has a middle name? What's his first name?"

"Wood." Gio stared at me until I connected the dots. "Wood Chuck. He brings it. I chuck it."

Noticing the large stack of firewood lined along the side of the house I said, "Looks like he's been entertained a lot lately."

"We both have." Gio sent the slobbery chunk sailing. "I come out here two or three times a week and do some of the heavy work. Keeps me sane, and Dad won't admit it, but his back can't take it like it used to."

"Ah, so that's how you maintain your . . . I thought maybe you went to the gym."

"Firewood, bucking hay bales, herding cattle, mending fences, tilling, planting. 'Honest sweat and toil,' as my dad would say. Way more satisfying than faking it on a machine with some guy checking out your abs."

"Some guy?"

"It's always a guy. Whether he's spreading his scent, proving he can lift more, or one who is *actually* checking you out—and there are plenty of those at the gym. Guys look at women, but women usually ignore them back." He cleared his throat with a growl. "It's always a guy."

"Oh, I'm sure it's women too." *Very sure.* "We're just stealthier about it. Do you wear a cowboy hat and ride a horse when you go herding?"

"Sometimes. Why?" Gio waited for my answer. And waited. "Kate?"

"Sorry. I was just taking a moment of silence to picture that."

Cici squeezed through the barely opened gate, carrying a basket of eggs and making sure the procession of animals didn't escape. "Hello," she called, bypassing her son to enfold me in a welcoming embrace. "It's so nice to see you again when we can actually talk. I love them dearly, but the family—well, you saw them."

"Kate brought you a surprise, Mom."

"A surprise? What kind of—for me?"

Gio opened the back of the SUV to reveal stacks of cardboard boxes and, poking up from behind them, the top of a treadle sewing machine.

"Your enchanted castle key worked," I announced. "Gio and I found so many things in the attic, and we're not even done yet. These are some things I thought you'd like to have."

Cici's hands came up to her startled face. "My mother's Singer. I can't believe it. She loved that thing." She stood back while her son set boxes on the porch, revealing more of the sewing machine's intricately carved cabinet. "It was one of Daddy's found treasures. She had a very nice modern machine, of course, she was such a seamstress, but my mother swore this was the best for certain things."

"I hoped you'd be happy to see it." I hugged her once more.

"But Kate, everything left on that property belongs to you, not me."

"Your mother wants—would want you to have it."

Gio lifted the antique down to a flat furniture dolly he'd set on the porch, rolled his eyes without comment, and shoved the whole thing into the house. He turned around. "You'll have to go visit your father's desk, Mom, 'cause it's not coming down those stairs. I think they built the apartment around that thing."

Nonna stood in the foyer waiting for us and reached her knobbed, blue-veined, but meticulously manicured hands out to me. "Oh, my dear, how wonderful it was to hear you were coming to visit us today!"

Gio stopped his progress to wrap his arms around her and gently lift her for a kiss. "What am I, chopped liver?"

"No, boy," she cackled, "You are always a treat, but Kate is an honored guest."

He didn't set her down right away but carried her to the other side of the room and her pink walker. "You forgot your dancing partner again, Nonna. You know what the doctor says."

She waved at it with derision, "Oh, that. Pfft. She said I need to have it with me. She didn't specifically say I was required to use it."

"Nice try. You know we want to make sure you don't fall." Gio looked to his nodding mother for support and back to Nonna. "Could you humor us, please?"

Cici chimed in. "And it's so convenient to have the nice little seat with you so you can sit whenever you feel like it."

"I'm old, dear; I'm not lazy."

I walked beside her to the elevator. "Don't you look adorable today, with your pink slacks and pink polka dots?"

She paused, patting the blush-colored Gerber daisy pinned in her hair. "Did you know pink is my favorite color?" Then she hooted with laughter. It would be impossible for me to have guessed otherwise.

Gio wheeled the sewing machine into the elevator and guided Nonna in beside it. "We'll meet you on the topside, *Bisnonna*. Don't get lost."

"Don't you either, boy." She wiggled her fingers at me in a wave.

At the top of the stairs, the door slid open and there was Nonna, pretending to swim upward, blowing imaginary bubbles. Gio assisted her out of the elevator. "Always the life of the party, aren't you, *animatore*?"

"You know it, sweetheart!" She told him, then winked in my direction.

Cici cleared space in her craft room by pushing a table a few inches to the right. "Why don't you put it here under the shelves?" The old Singer slid perfectly into place. The shelves contained rows of brightly colored thread cones and labeled, see-through boxes of fabrics, patterns, laces, trims, buttons and the like. An entire wall looked like it was taken from a yarn shop and set here, with a spinning wheel off to one side. That explained her ovine herd outside.

I touched her hand. "This looks a lot like the way your mother arranged things. She loved having everything close by."

Cici dabbed at her eyes with a tissue and blew her nose. "Yes, she did." Then she laughed. "But she only kept what she needed. I, on the other hand, need to buy stock in every fabric and craft store in Colorado. They see me coming a mile away."

"But you keep everything nice and organized like she did."

Cici and Gio stood side by side, arms around one another with identically tilting heads, as they assessed the position of the new acquisition. "Yes, well, I suppose I've tried to recreate a bit of her favorite place right here."

Gio nudged her playfully. "Only yours has a serious case of *roid rage*."

She nudged back and sighed. "The heart wants what it wants."

"Well, do you want to open it up?" I ran my hand along the detail of the cabinet's carving.

She lifted the flat wooden cover, which folded out to create an extended work surface on the left, then pulled another hinged piece of wood forward to make way for the machine to swivel upward from inside. She struggled to lift the heavy steel relic. "Oh, I might need some help here. It's not moving."

Gio pulled at the bulky machine. "It's been sitting a long time. There could be rust. Let me have a look." He got a tighter grip. "It's catching on something."

Awkwardly bending over and holding it up as far as it would go, Gio attempted to slide his other hand underneath to feel for the obstruction. He regarded his mother's hands and then mine. "Kate, can you feel around under there?"

I moved to my post, sighing at the attention drawn to my small stature once again. As I snaked an arm toward the back of the cabinet, the space opened slightly, but only enough for my fingertips to graze the back panel. "Something's been taped behind it. A large envelope, I think. Don't push too hard, but if you could give me a little more space . . . There. I'm easing the edge down a bit. Okay, now try it."

Gio swung the black and gold sewing machine out of its compartment to the full range of its sturdy hinges. Sure enough, there was an envelope attached in place with masking tape.

Dry and stiff, the age-darkened tape gave way easily as I pried it loose. I handed the envelope to Cici. "An owner's manual, do you think?"

Gio pivoted the cabinet's front wood piece back into place and settled the Singer on top of it. We all stood back to admire the intricate gold design and lettering emblazoned on the black enameled steel.

Running my hand over the design, I hummed in pleasure. "I love how they mixed form and function back then. I guess if it was going to be in the house, it had to be a work of art, as well as a useful piece of equipment."

Nonna agreed. "Oh, yes. Yes, indeed. This has got to be older than I am, if you can imagine such a thing, and I remember many useful objects of that era being embellished just so."

Cici unwound the figure-eight of string that held the manila envelope closed and looked inside. "It's not a manual." She emptied the contents onto the wooden work surface.

Gio picked up one of several school composition notebooks, separated by an assortment of loose notes and drawings. He thumbed through a book before lighting up like a gas burner. "What the . . . " He checked inside another notebook. "No freaking way!"

"What?" I opened another book and echoed his enthusiasm. "No way!" I jumped up to throw my arms around his neck and he caught me in a kiss of excitement before we both remembered our audience, and he set me down. Too thrilled for embarrassment, I said, "Well I never would have found it in the attic, that's for sure. My sewing is atrocious."

Opening another of the books, Cici seemed confused. "This is my dad's writing, but . . . what is it?"

Gio hugged his mother. "It's Aldo's story. Why don't you get settled and we'll join you in a minute." He motioned for me to follow him down the stairs to the porch.

Helping arrange boxes on the furniture dolly gave me time to make a strategic plan. "What do you think? Should I be selective about what I tell them? I wouldn't want to upset Nonna."

"That's something to consider—"

"But then again, why would I have the dreams if I were supposed to keep them a secret?"

Gio grunted softly as he eased a heavy box down. "Well, there is that, but—"

"But if she wanted them to know, Juliana's had thirty years to make her point."

"Maybe—"

"Of course, you said the family sort of avoided my place. Maybe she was trying to tell them something, and would have if they'd hung around once in a while."

Gio closed the back of the vehicle and pushed the stack forward without comment.

"Aren't you going to tell me what I should do?"

He stopped, silent for a count of three and turned to face me. "Come here a minute."

"What?"

"Come on." He waved me toward him.

I hesitantly narrowed the distance in increments, until he held up his hand when we were toe to toe, never taking his gaze from my face. "What is it?"

He tilted my chin up and eyed me appraisingly. "You've got something on your mouth."

"I do?" I touched my upper lip, expecting a milk mustache or something.

He removed my hand, bent and placed a lingering kiss on my mouth, putting my current dilemma and everything else completely out of my mind.

I laid my cheek against his chest and sighed before jerking my face upward and narrowing my eyes. "I'm such a sucker for that one."

He chuckled. "Yeah. I really like that about you." He kissed me again before adding. "Just play it by ear, *cara*. No need to clench just yet."

Inside, Gio called, "Ma, you still up there?"

Across the formal dining room, Cici poked her head out from the kitchen. "Go ahead and take those up to the landing. I'll be there in a minute."

We kissed again in the elevator and were surprised to find

Nonna standing just outside the opening doors on the second floor.

"Oh, don't mind me," she said. "You go right ahead."

Rather than returning to our previous activity for her entertainment, we moved the stack of boxes out with flushed faces.

With Nonna comfortably settled in the sitting alcove, we placed boxes around the chairs for easy access. Cici brought a tray with warm chocolate chip cookies and a pitcher of ice cold raw milk.

Gio used his pocket knife to break the seal on a carton marked "photographs" and put it on the coffee table in front of his mother. She opened it gingerly, honoring the precious nature of what might lay inside.

"I don't know why I'm nervous. I'm sure I've seen every picture in here. It's just . . . "

Gio sat down next to her and put his arm around her. "It's just that you haven't seen them since before your parents died. It's time you did."

"Yes. Of course it is. When they died, no one had the heart to go through the things in the attic. It was their special place, you know, and being there poked at our raw feelings. We decided to leave everything to tackle another day and locked the attic door. And then not one of us ever got the desire to go back to it." She took another tissue from a box on the table. "It wasn't from lack of interest. Maybe we were leery of what we'd stir up, emotion-wise, once we got started. After so much time we stopped thinking about it at all, as though that room never existed."

Nonna patted her hand. "Maybe she wanted you to forget about it."

Cici blew her nose. "Maybe."

"Maybe she is ready, now that Kate is here." Nonna took a tissue of her own. "It could be, she was waiting for someone like her all along."

"I saw her," I blurted. "I saw them both. Your parents. They were very happy, and she was pregnant with your brother, Al, and they danced together in the attic. And then again, a few years later she was sewing on buttons." I announced it all like someone with Tourette Syndrome and then wanted to rip my tongue out and stomp on it with both heels. But it was too late now. So much for worrying about what I was supposed to say and how it would affect Nonna, who nodded her smiling face to urge me on.

Cici laid a stack of photos on the table to stare at me. On top was a picture that caught my eye and I picked it up by its scalloped edges.

There was a toddler sitting on a kitchen table in front of a cake with one lit candle. She wore a beautifully hand-knit dress. Five older children gathered around, lips pursed, ready to help blow out the candle. Her two doting parents, with hands placed protectively on her back, bookended her face with their own..

Cici leaned in. "That's my first birthday. Al is the tall one on the left."

Cici's parents looked different here than in my dreams. Juliana was a little fuller in the face, but those lush, curly lashes were unmistakable. A Jackie Kennedy bob replaced the pin curls I had seen. Tony's hair was cut in a simple flattop rather than the greased pompadour he'd worn when he sang at the kitchen sink, and his eyes sported the beginnings of a few laugh lines.

I looked up to the expectant faces of Cici and Nonna.

"That's them," I confirmed. "These are the people I've been dreaming about.

22.

Feather in the Wind

Aldo Castaldo had always been good with numbers. When he was a boy, the Sisters often drew attention to his gift, which, just as often, resulted in brutal schoolyard confrontations afterward. To give him, the eldest son, a better understanding of the family business, Aldo's father had regularly put the vineyard ledgers before him to study. When his father died suddenly during the year Aldo turned sixteen, he used his grasp of numbers to wheedle his way into the employ of Massimo Santelli. It was also during the year he turned sixteen that Aldo revised his vow to return his family's fortunes to include avenging his father's death.

Santelli was the man now in charge of the village, the one who had been primarily responsible for the undoing of Aldo's family fortune and, it was rumored, the architect of the 'tragic accident' that had taken Jovanni Castaldo's life.

All of his mother's pleading, threats, and tears could not stop Aldo from his chosen course. "They will turn your heart cold, black, and evil as their own. And failing that, they will grind you into dust as they did your father."

But being a wise and invincible man of sixteen, Aldo could not be swayed by the tears of his mother. He knew his own heart. He knew nothing would mend its deep fissure until Santelli received the pain and humiliation the villain once heaped upon his father. Yes, the Brotherhood had broken his

192

father, made him less than a man, and discarded the empty vessel of him like garbage to the pigs. Aldo would make them pay, in his own time and his own way.

He was not so much a half-wit as to believe he could beat them openly through a show of force. No, this would be a slow and exacting process, one in which he would need to employ cunning, patience, and perfect timing. Unlike most men of sixteen, Aldo possessed more than his share of patience. He was willing to take whatever time necessary to put his pieces into place before reclaiming the fortunes and honor of his family.

The Brotherhood was no more than a ragtag assembly of thugs, who took what they wanted and used fear and intimidation to control the populace of the village. Aldo would use the gift his God gave him to win out over them. He would use his mind.

Because of his reputed talent for figures, his youth, and presumed innocence, Massimo took Aldo on as an assistant to the *ragioniere*, the accountant.

Aldo writes: "Santelli—sitting at my father's former desk in my ancestral home— looked me in the eye and with an open face told me it was a shame I was left fatherless, with a poor widowed mother to support. He clenched my hand from across that desk, and said he would be my father now and would protect me from the bad people of the world."

Within the organization, the *ragioniere* oversaw the collection of gambling, lending, and protection revenues. Massimo employed Aldo to check the work of the accountant, tallying the money that had just been tallied, checking the figures just entered into the ledgers. Both the accountant and his assistant were threatened daily that dishonesty with the Brotherhood's funds would never be tolerated. Massimo believed that, with the death of his father so fresh in Aldo's mind, he would take the threats quite seriously. And he did.

Next to me on the couch in my living room, Gio stopped translating to look over my shoulder. "I like what you're doing there. You're making it more like a story."

"The language is so beautiful, but the literal translation sounds a little jumbled up. As long as I'm sorting it out, I might as well have some fun with it. Right?"

"You're good at it. I think Nonna will love it."

I lifted an eyebrow. "Aldo became a mobster?"

"Yeah. That's what it looks like, huh?"

"Do you think we should edit that part? It might upset Nonna. It could be a big embarrassment to your family."

"Nonna's tough. She's more likely to get a kick out of it. I don't think we need to add saccharine to any of this stuff. It's about time my family stopped canonizing this guy and started realizing he put his *pantaloni* on one leg at a time, like everyone else."

"I wonder if this is what Juliana was trying to tell me with the Godfather dream." I reached up for his kiss. It was meant to be a quick brush of the lips, a momentary reconnection that seemed to be happening with more and more frequency, but the taste of him and heat of his mouth against mine turned it into something more urgent.

"Mm." He pulled me closer and began planting a row of kisses from my earlobe along the jawline and back to my mouth. "*Cara.*"

Then he wrenched away with a look of pure torture on his face. "Gotta stop, whew, or . . . " He kissed me one more time before rising to his feet. "*Le porte dell'Inferno.* I thought it was tough when I was a teenager—at least back then I didn't know what I was missing. Now I do, and well, you know . . . Five years . . . "

He ran his fingers through his hair at the top of his skull and rasped out a low groan.

"Keep translating," I snapped, like a cold splash of water. I straightened up and returned focus to my laptop, pulse racing, my entire body still warm from his embrace.

I loved that he desperately wanted to hold off from more intimate contact. I knew marriage was what he was aiming for. I understood the reasons. I was a practicing Catholic myself, but I couldn't help but think my resolve was weaker than his. Maybe it was because my faith wasn't instilled in me from birth like his. Maybe it was because I'd married outside the church and divorced. I was a refurbished model. Things didn't turn out right the first time. I was mostly repaired, but I'd likely always feel like a scratch-and-dent bargain. I didn't know when—or if—I'd risk my heart to marriage again. Being abstinent, waiting for a wedding that, as far as I was concerned, might never take place, seemed cruel to us both. But his lofty ideals, those I strove to possess myself with his level of conviction, were part of what was wearing down my resistance toward him. The irony burned.

Gio paced while comparing Aldo's text to Tony's, lasering his focus away from the thickening sensual tension in the room.

Tony had done a fairly decent job of decoding the language, but there were many misinterpretations throughout. I barely kept up with my task of transcription. Hearing Gio speak Aldo's words in Italian first, then Tony's English version, and his own tweaks here and there, made my fingers pause, allowing my ears to drink in its delicious resonance.

In all of Aldo's planning, there was one contingency he had failed to foresee. Aldo did not know he would encounter, in the home of Massimo Santelli, an angel sent from above to forever transform his life.

Anna Maria Santelli floated through Aldo's childhood home like a feather on the warm summer breeze. She was the loveliest creature he had ever beheld in his short life and, indeed, ever would. Her tinkling voice captivated him with its cultured accent and well-read vocabulary. Her beguiling feminine scent, creamy golden skin, and shimmering black hair made her impossible to disregard. She was refined and perfect and filled every measure of womanhood in its purest form. Every element of her multiplied into one continual, excruciating distraction for Aldo. And distractions were something he could not afford.

Blessedly, she was utterly unconscious of her power over him. Indeed, she seemed unaware of his very existence. Her notice of his daily presence in her father's study was no more than that given the elegant clock on the mantle. He and the clock were useful items that were looked at for their function, but rarely admired for their unique appeal.

I finished transcribing the latest sentence. "Aw. He fell in love with the don's daughter. How sweet."

"Sweet? My great-great-great grandmother was the nineteenth century Victoria Gotti of Ruscello, Italy?"

I squeezed my eyes shut and wrinkled my nose. "Stop it. Now instead of a tinkling-voiced floating feather in the warm summer breeze, I'll think of a Jersey accent and big, over-bleached hair. Bubble burst."

Gio flipped the book shut. "I'm ready to quit this for the evening, how about you?"

"I think so too, but I wish we could get to the part Juliana wants us to see.

"Maybe this is only part of it. There could be other stuff we're overlooking."

"Would you like to do some more poking around upstairs?" I blushed. "Sorry. I mean looking."

He narrowed his eyes at my inadvertent innuendo and chuckled in a guttural tone. "Sounds great." He helped me up off the sofa and hugged me, shaking his head. "You are going to be the most frustrating wait of my life."

I tapped his chest. "You've got this all figured out, don't you? Like the outcome of our . . . our thing . . . is a foregone conclusion."

"I already told you what I know, Kate. I'm just waiting for you to get up to speed." He kissed me again. "Just don't take too long, *bellissima*." He moaned, shrugging tension from his shoulders, then growled before swooping in for another short kiss. "Killing me."

Fingers intertwined, we assessed the piles in the attic, wondering what to tackle next.

"Why don't we work from left to right, and we can use that corner for sorting."

Gio kissed the tender spot on my temple that seemed to have a direct connection to every nerve in my body. "That's why I love you so much. You are so smart."

It was the first time he'd said the words. He'd admitted pretty much the same, but the words "I love you" spoken simply, without embellishment, shot point-blank to my center mass. I should have protested or let it slide by as a casual phrase people use without profound meaning. But I knew it wasn't the case with Gio. Instead, I found my mouth, of its own volition, whispering the words, "I love you too."

The silence became thick enough to bounce on. Gio looked at me wordlessly for an eon and opened his mouth to say something, blinked, and stared some more.

He took both of my hands, looked deeply into my eyes and finally found his words. "I need to go."

Not exactly what I'd anticipated. "You need to go?"

"Yep. I do. I need to go."

Without warning, he lifted me up into his arms and started down the stairs.

"What are you doing? I can walk, you know! From your perspective, you might not realize these squatty legs go all the way down to functional feet, but they— "

"I want to say goodbye downstairs."

I laughed. "Okay . . . why down—"

"Because if I kiss you up here right now, I'll never go home." He took two stairs at a time and nearly ran to deposit me near the glass door, just out of sight of the street. "And, Kate, I want everything that happens with us to be done right, you know?"

I caught my breath and smiled sympathetically at his expression of anguish. "I never knew *not* being kissed could be so romantic. You make me feel, I don't know, adored, cherished."

He pulled me up again to his height, placing his lips tenderly on mine and mumbled, "And probably as frustrated as me."

My extremities began dissolving as the core of my consciousness zeroed in on just his lips, then his strong arms around my waist, squeezing the breath out of me. Or maybe my racing heart was to blame for the breathlessness.

Gio's dark eyes shined with what appeared to be unshed tears, which made my own eyes start to leak. Again.

"I think I may be coughing up another clump," I sniffed.

If this was love, it was very unpredictable and, well, inconvenient.

Loving him did not change one thing, though. Emotional fur balls aside, I would sue his firm and his firm behind if he didn't find a way to make my home legally mine. Fair was fair, after all, no matter what the hummingbird flutters in my gut were telling me.

23.

The Hike

After sharing Sunday brunch with his family, Gio and I closed the back door of the ranch house behind us to begin our reconnaissance walk.

"I told you. He kissed Juliana goodbye and she told him to be careful, and that's all I got. But I knew Tony was coming out here. It was unspoken, but I knew."

The nights were beginning to bring frost, but the days remained sunny—perfect conditions to incite a riot of fall color. The chill in the air made me glad for my wool pea coat with deep, hand-warming pockets. We stopped to talk to the animals at the barn—or at least I spoke to them while Gio smiled indulgently—and then proceeded out the back gate and up the trail.

"Do you think I can get cell service at the top of the hill? I really need to check in with my staff. The shop's barely open, and I—"

"You know you've done an amazing job training them. Alyssa is a natural manager. Marco is a whiz in the kitchen. And, the answer is no. We don't want no stinkin' cell tower up here."

"But I—"

"They will be fine for a few hours. We'll be back this afternoon. You do get to have time off for good behavior once in a while, you know."

At the fork, we took the branch going off to the right, rather than the steeper one leading to the Devil's Maw. Around a curve, a twelve-point buck silently posed, contemplating whether or not to bolt. We stood equally still, taking in his magnificence before his inevitable escape.

"Yeah," Gio whispered to the retreating white tail. "You show yourself now, but where are you during bow season? Nowhere."

"Run, Bambi," I murmured as he paused to once more assess us, then disappear.

A squirrel climbed onto a stump and loudly chirped a scolding litany in our direction.

"Oh. There you are, little guy. What are you doing way down here? You're a long way from home."

Gio detonated his explosive laugh, causing the poor creature to scamper up a nearby tree with blinding speed. "Kate. There is no way that is the same squirrel."

My hands went to my hips. "You don't know that. He could be the same one. I think he is. Aren't you, Mr. Squirrel?"

"We're at least a mile from the Maw, Kate. I'm pretty sure that's a different squirrel."

I peered at my new fuzzy-tailed friend conspiratorially. "It's okay. People are always underestimating me too."

The squirrel hurled a pinecone, hitting Gio on the side of his face.

This time it was me who laughed.

Mr. Squirrel jumped from branch to branch, skittering back down and away.

"See that tree?"

"Where?" Gio rubbed the scratch on his face, smearing a few drops of blood left by the prickly pinecone.

Pulling a tissue from my pocket, I dabbed at his face. "On the twisty tree, right under the lowest branch on the right. Another heart."

Climbing on the squirrel's recently vacated stump pedestal, I stood as tall as Gio.

The heart bore no initials. Upon closer inspection the possibility that the hearts were mirrored, intersecting letters 'C' was evident.

"Maybe they are a way of marking off acreage?" I traced the rough surface with my fingertip.

"Possibly." Gio did the same with his thumb in quiet thought. "But I saw plat maps when I bought this place. This isn't a section marker. I know that." He turned to envelop me with his muscled arms and kissed me tenderly. "You're right, though, they must mark something."

I enjoyed looking him straight in the eye for a change and thought I could get used to kissing him from this angle, so I took the opportunity to put it to a test. And then another. And then . . . I jerked away. "You bought the ranch too?"

Gio's kisses had moved to the spot below my ear. "Hmm?"

I lost my train of thought again until I remembered something. "You said before, you'd show me all of the hearts. Why don't we look for them today?"

His eyes unglazed enough to comprehend my question. "They're everywhere, Kate. It will take more than an afternoon."

I jumped down with his hands at my waist, for a soft landing. "There must be a pattern or a purpose for them. I think this must have something to do with Juliana and Tony."

He guided me back toward the trail. "Showing you the old cabin was something I wanted to do today, and there are several heart markings between here and there."

The further into the hills we rose, the more vibrant the fall colors. "I should have brought a sketchpad. I've been itching to paint some of this scenery."

He squeezed my hand and pulled me to a stop. "Oh, yeah, definitely bring it next time. Don't lose that gift, Kate. It was given to you for a reason."

Take that, Eddie, you soul-sucker.

Gio nudged his head toward the trail. "There's one up around this next part. It's not along the main path but scratched into a rock, kind of behind some bushes."

As we got closer, an unmistakable chirping returned.

"Here's my friend." Softly padding up to a scraggly pine I asked, "How did you beat us here, Mr. Nuttycheeks?"

"Not the same squirrel, Kate."

"Sure it's the same one, aren't you, little guy?"

"And if it were the same one, I think I would owe him a payback for the blood. Have you ever tasted squirrel stew?"

"Oh, no you wouldn't."

"Just like chicken. It's delicious."

I crooned to the agitated rodent. "He's just mean, isn't he, Mr. Nuttycheeks?"

The animal responded by gyrating and using its back legs to push pine needles onto us out of the crook of the tree before scampering upward, serving us a mouthful of squirrel smack talk.

Gio's blast of laughter sent the sassy creature skittering on his way once more before we continued on our own. "The marking is this way."

We wound our way through a narrow opening between the thick sagebrush and pinyon-junipers on the rocky terrain.

"This was our fort. The cousins would all come and spend the night and tell ghost stories—about Aldo, of course—and get sick on hot dogs and burnt marshmallows."

Climbing over a jagged boulder revealed another pile of stones. When viewed from the backside, however, a gap exposed an inside space large enough for a group of kids in sleeping bags. Near the entrance, sure enough, a heart was scratched into the stone with the words "*Nel cuore dell'anello di fata*" written below.

Two of the larger stones balanced against each other at the

top of the stack, forming a roof over most of the little fortress.

"Holy Shinola, this is awesome!" I climbed into the interior, which was warmer than I expected. "What does the inscription say?"

"*Cuore* means 'heart' or 'core,' of course." He scratched his afternoon stubble. "And *anello* means 'ring.' *Fata* is used like the word 'fairy.' I would think it means, "In the heart of the fairy ring.""

"*Cuore*. Like on the key to my attic."

"That's right. Like on your key."

"Do you think they are related? I rubbed my finger along the words.

"Could be, but, I mean, heart means heart. Whoever marked everything might have just liked them."

"He named this circle of rocks the 'fairy ring'?""

He inspected the etching more carefully. "I remember the words being here, but I didn't know the language yet. Unknown words only made the place more mysterious."

"The name reminds me of Celtic folklore, you know, like stone circles in the British Isles with fairies and little people. Only this group appears naturally formed."

Gio nodded. "Yeah. These rocks fell like this. Just a freak occurrence." He rubbed the back of his neck. "There is a stone circle in Italy, you know. A long way from Calabria, but I've seen it. They're not only found in Great Britain."

The climb along the trail became steeper. Gio navigated obstacles without much of a struggle. I, who didn't possess his advantage of height and strength, gratefully accepted assistance around and over rocks and fallen logs.

Gio said, "At one time this trail was broad and smooth enough to get a wagon up and down, but spring wash-outs over time have made it pretty gnarly."

The sky showed signs of darkening. "This morning was so beautiful. Do those look like rain clouds to you?"

Gio protectively rested an arm across my shoulders. "Yeah. But they're heading south. I don't think there's anything to worry about. The cabin's not too much further."

The next stretch of road was segmented by deep, snaking, rain-washed crevasses. We found ourselves needing to repeatedly jump across from one side to the other of the gouges to pick our way up the hill. Or rather, Gio jumped across; I jumped in his direction and he pulled me the remaining distance into his arms. As it turned out, a big, strong, Italian, sandwich-making, land-baron cowboy was a very handy thing to have on a hike.

24.

Cabin

The trail crested to reveal a hidden meadow, fortified by a sheer rock wall to the east and rimmed all around by a stand of quaking aspens. Tucked within stood a charming log cabin and barn. What remained of a decayed split-rail fence sprouted here and there amid tall grasses, while both weathered log structures stood solidly intact. The music of a nearby stream pierced the silent calm of this Castaldi hallowed ground.

The massive front door, engraved with a motif of interlaced hearts, would have looked more at home on a European palace. The absurdity of its presence in a pioneer cabin was an intriguing new piece of a puzzle that grew more complex at every turn.

"I wish I knew what I was supposed to be looking for." Grasping at straws, I jumped down to check under and around the porch. "Why did Juliana pick me? Other people have lived and worked at my place. I mean, I know I have my quirks, but being some kind of medium isn't one of them. If anything, I'd be a medium petite. Wouldn't I have presented extrasensory behaviors before now if I were supposed to be one?" Seeing nothing out of the ordinary, I rejoined Gio at the door. "Sure! The one time in my life I get picked first for a team, and it's the freak squad."

If I were going to discover anything new, I had to embrace

the crazy and harness its power.

I examined the door more carefully, running the pads of my fingertips along the scrolls and curly queues. "The hearts have got to mean something."

Gio scooped away a spider web. "Maybe they meant something once, but they don't mean a whole lot now."

The more I contemplated, the more I was certain. "They were *meant* to mean something now. Someone left them for posterity. That much, I know."

The door took a firm push to open, even with Gio's bulk. A chilly draft escaped from within. Hints of ash from the fireplace, pine, and the mustiness of a seldom-used room assaulted my senses. I shivered when I recognized a more familiar scent overpowering the rest.

"Do you smell that?"

Gio's blank expression answered my question.

"Roses. Juliana is telling me we're getting warmer. No, wait. These roses smell different."

Without so much as an eye roll, Gio offered, "Juliana died in town. Maybe this has something to do with Grandpa Tony. He was the rose grower. Maybe he's the one being smelly."

"Fragrant, not smelly. It feels like I'm learning a new piece of software here. I know the program can make colorful boxes with numbers in them, but I have a long way to go before learning how to make the boxes do the math."

The corner of Gio's mouth curled as he brushed hair out of my eyes. "You really are an accountant, aren't you?"

"That software was easy to master by comparison."

Inside, the floor was of solid oak planks with a fine-sanded smoothness that bespoke great care. Gio ran his hands over a log in the wall. "Each one of these is custom fit to the one below. It's an old Scandinavian method. That's always been a mystery to me, how an Italian immigrant made a Swedish cope structure in the American frontier. It's not like he had YouTube to show him how." He shook his head in amazement. "As the wood aged, it just clamped down tighter. Not a bit of chinking anywhere."

Low ceilings had Gio ducking to avoid hitting his head on support rafters for the floor above. They evidently were growing bigger Castaldis these days than when the place was built. The room we occupied was a sort of great room, with a central hearth and a kitchen area off to one side. This had a considerable amount of built-in workspace with a hand pump and basin sink. A mammoth wood range stood proudly at its core.

"Castaldis do love a good kitchen," I said. "It must be in the DNA."

I tried to picture a family sitting together around the fireplace, maybe reading or singing. Again, the scent of roses permeated the air.

Gio started to say something, but I held up my hand to quiet him. I closed my eyes.

Aldo and Anna Maria sat side-by-side at a piano—the piano that now sat at the foot of the grand staircase in the ranch house. He waited patiently for her nod, before turning page of the sheet music in front of them. The piece she played could have been Verdi, but I honestly wasn't up on my late nineteenth-century classics. A toddler slept in her lap as she played, its head resting on her ample bosom. Four, no five, children sat on the floor in a semi-circle listening to the concert. The two oldest girls sat closest to the fire, the bigger one brushing the hair of the other to dry. Three boys quietly commanded tin soldiers—one from the vantage point of his belly and another sitting like an Indian chief in a B-Western movie.

When the music came to an end, the children clapped their hands and begged for one more song.

"No, my dears, it is time to go to bed. Daylight comes all too soon," Aldo said.

The children responded in unison with a resounding, "*Awwwww.*"

Anna Maria scolded, "No '*aww*.' You go like Papa say. Give me kiss and go."

All five children lined up to receive an abundance of hugs and kisses from their beautiful mother and adoring father.

The girls' long nightgowns were clean and white and fresh. I wondered what it must have taken to keep them that way, and what it might have been like to sew them by hand with a needle and thread by lantern light. I also felt sad for the girls, knowing their father would force them to marry someone of his choosing someday.

The children filed up the narrow staircase, the youngest being carried by his big sister.

Anna Maria spoke in Italian to Aldo, but I understood every word.

"I will join them for prayers. Will you be up soon to tuck them in?"

"Yes, my angel," he responded.

Anna Maria checked on the infant sleeping in a cradle next to the double bed in the corner of the room, pulled a curtain closed around it all, and disappeared up the stairs.

Aldo stoked the fire and slowly paced the room, listening for the sound of prayers from above. He padded to the southwest corner of the structure and rolled back the rug. He stuck his index finger in a small knothole and pulled a section of the floor up on its hinges. Quietly, he stepped down into the hole, patting his pockets as he went.

I opened my eyes.

"Whoa! Ghost Whisperer moment," I breathed. "Big time."

"Just now? I didn't—"

"Yeah." I rubbed my eyes with the heels of my hands. "Now if I could just have Jennifer Love Hewitt's killer bod—"

"You had, like, a vision?"

"How am I supposed to know? I closed my eyes and it was like my attic dreams, only even more vivid. And it wasn't Juliana this time." I raised my arms out into a wide semi-circle. "It was them. These people."

Gio apparently had decided to go with the flow. "Aldo's family? And what did they tell you?"

"Have you ever seen the cellar?"

"You kidding me? Boys out camping, they see a secret dungeon and they're not going to go down there? Yeah. I've spent plenty of time in the cellar."

"There's something down there."

I sent Gio down as my first line of defense. I wasn't afraid of the "ghosts." So far, the only things I'd experienced were thoughts or feelings—a sense of their presence as little scenarios played out in my mind. So many scary feelings I'd long suppressed had bubbled up since meeting Gio, this was a snap by comparison. My fear surrounded the thought of going down a rather rickety-looking stairway into a dark hole, with potential creatures of a more tangible nature. Shuddering at the remembrance of my spider dream, I followed the man down, hands on his shoulders.

"Why do you carry a lighter? Just curious."

"Are you wondering if I smoke? Do I look stupid?" He held the flame high above his head and bumped into a rafter, dousing the fire. "Don't answer that."

"Then why—."

"The stove at the deli is older than my dad. It's my favorite place to cook, but there's no pilot light. I keep it in my pocket out of habit."

Rather than the dank odor one would expect in an ancient cellar, the place smelled of the fresh wood shavings lining the dirt floor. "Someone's been here recently," I said.

"We put shavings on the dirt floor every year before hunting season. Makes it easier to clean up afterward."

At first I didn't understand why cleaning up would be necessary after hunting season. Then I realized that a temperature-controlled interior space, like a root cellar, would be an ideal place to skin and field dress a hanging, dripping carcass. Leave it to a man to think dragging it through the main part of the cabin was perfectly all right. My nose curled involuntarily. "Ew."

Gio pulled me in close to him when he reached the bottom step. "I don't want to lose you in the dark."

And then the flame went out.

"The lighter gets too hot to hold after a while." Powerful arms pulled me to a hard chest with its own pleasant scent. His lips grazed my temple. "Can you think of anything to do while it cools off?"

The darkness was so thick you could almost taste it, almost feel it pressing against you like the weight of water in the depths of the ocean. There was nothing left to do but reach up my hands until I caught him by the hair and pulled his face closer to taste and feel sensations roll over me, wave after wave. Of all his many talents, kissing had to be highest on the list.

He squeezed tighter until a low moan escaped his throat and he broke away.

The light came on. His upstretched arm held the lighter over our heads. "Did you see that?"

I couldn't see anything but the stars behind my lids, and feel the buzz in the tips of my fingers and toes. "Hmm? In the dark?"

"I was just minding my own business—and getting all up into yours too, I guess—and boom! I saw him.

"Aldo?"

"I'm guessing, yes." The darkness returned as Gio gave his hand another rest from the heat. "I thought it might be some sort of osmosis process, you know? Like, maybe because you saw it, I was able to see it too. Not a bad theory, considering the proximity of my tongue to your tonsils at that particular moment."

"You saw Aldo." I restated.

"I saw this guy in a black suit with a funny looking tie, coming down the stairs."

It was comforting knowing I apparently wasn't the only pick for the squad, but I needed a moment to think. "Is there somewhere to sit?"

Gio pulled me down onto his lap on the steps, where I burrowed into his warmth.

"It's like you picked up where I left off. At least, I think so. He started to go down the stairs for me to see, and he finished going down the stairs for you. Like two different shots of the same scene of a movie."

"I didn't sign up to be a Ghostbuster, Kate. Why would I start seeing stuff like this now?"

"Oh, and I did? I don't know these people. I don't even particularly believe in this nonsense. I really didn't before I met Juliana in my sleep. All I know is that ever since I moved in, your dead relatives have been trying to tell me something—and they are getting better at it. Maybe they are losing patience and want to get you in on the act. And why shouldn't they? You're the posterity, not me."

"You'll help produce further posterity when you marry me. Just sayin'." Gio reached for my hand as I started to move away. "But I still think it's superstitious malarkey."

"Fine. Malarkey. But now you see it too." I clamped down on his hand. "And don't think getting my juices flowing down here in the dark will iron out your legal woes, sir. There's still a little matter of real estate fraud that needs to be cleared up before I'll even consider entering into any further binding contracts with you."

"As if I needed an incentive to—"

"Look, why don't we both just sit here quietly for a few minutes. I don't have the hang of this mumbo jumbo at all, but I think part of the trick—if there is a trick—is to not think about it too much. Let's just sit here and be still and listen."

I listened. There was my own breathing. And Gio's. My pulse sounded in my ears. I felt Gio's own pulse in the palm of my hand. I heard a faint breeze above us. And then I stopped thinking about what I was hearing and feeling. And saw him.

Burlap sacks full of turnips and potatoes, and garlic and onion braids hung from hooks on the ceiling. Barrels lined two walls while shelves of preserves occupied the others. Pumpkins, squash, and gourds filled baskets in the corner.

Aldo, carrying a lantern and still patting his vest pocket, moved a basket and felt along the stone foundation wall until he was satisfied he'd found the right place.

And that was the end.

Gio's startled face appeared, relit by the flame. I jumped to my feet, pulling him to the basket corner. He moved the lighter around the surface until he came to the exact place Aldo had touched and, much as I expected, one of the stones had a very familiar marking.

I applied pressure to the stone inscribed with a heart, and it gave way a millimeter or two. Adjusting my grip, I wiggled until the stone eased into my hand.

"Ahhhhh!" The room darkened again and I heard the lighter drop to the floor. "I may have just been branded. I'll be right back."

Gio eased to the bottom of the stairs, now alive with noises of his fumbling. A sheepish expression was illuminated by the light of a camping lantern as he returned. "I remembered my dad probably left this during elk season for anyone who might need it."

Suppressed sarcasm scalded my throat as I smiled. "Nice."

It seemed as if someone had plastered inside the wall's

cavity, making it a sealed container. At first I thought the hiding spot was empty, but at the almost unreachable back, I touched a small pouch, raked at it until it was close enough to grasp, and pulled it out.

Lantern light, though an improvement over our first alternative, had its limitations. After drawing close to it, only to become frustrated by deep shadows and not much else, I gave up. "Let's get out of here. I think we have what we came for."

Did I actually, physically smell roses, or did this crazy sixth sense borrow one or two of the others to make its point? Either way, I knew I was onto something because Tony made his presence known.

On the cold stone hearth of the main level, I sat next to Gio. Inside the pouch was a packet wrapped in waxed paper. Did they have waxed paper in Aldo's time? I carefully removed its contents.

I unfolded one sheet at a time and looked each over before passing them to Gio. A new puzzle piece lay before us. "This is Tony's handwriting."

I opened another small bundle that contained several gold foil wrapped pieces of chocolate—or whatever disgusting substance it becomes after over thirty years—and a note that said, "$500 in gold coins, 1890 and older, found here in 1975. Stored for safe keeping."

There was a crude map with hearts all over it. Gio studied it. "Haha. You wanted to know where all the hearts were? Tony had it all figured out."

"Do you think he's the one who put them everywhere?"

"No. By the way the heart trees look, the hearts came way before my grandpa." He walked to a window for a better view and pointed to a spot on the map. "Here's the rock fort, or I guess it's called the fairy ring, although no self-respecting eleven-year-old boy would have been caught dead camping in something called a fairy ring. Here's where your squirrel tried to take my eye out."

"It was a pinecone. Did the big squirrel hurt you, Princess?" I stood on my tiptoes and waited for him to bend so I could kiss his owie.

"And here's that first one you saw out by the cliffs where I showed you the Devil's Maw."

I took the map from him. "So what is this great big heart on the map by the mountain?"

"Good question."

As we studied the papers, a blast of wind came through the open door, scattering everything. Gio got up to collect them and glanced at his watch. "We'd better start heading back."

He put the packet of refolded papers into the inside chest pocket of his jacket as we left.

I pushed closed the ornate door, feeling as though I were abandoning the family who once lived there.

"*Porca miseria*! I was wrong about the rainclouds. We'd better move fast." Gio took my hand and I had to run to keep up with his pace.

Just as we got to the circle of rocks, the skies opened up and poured.

"We should duck into here and see if it dies down."

"And if it doesn't?"

"Well, we'll need to get wet, I guess. We shouldn't try to make it in the dark, but I'm hoping it's just a shower." He waited for me to enter before following.

Snickering under my breath at the obvious omission of another option—that of spending the night here together—I followed him to the ring's opening. There was no question about when, and under what circumstances, he wanted those possible descendants to be created, and he'd made it clear that even his restraint had its limits.

25.

Inside the Ring

The stone fort's floor was layered in pine needles. Despite the downpour, I froze just inside the entrance. "If you wouldn't mind, would you do me a huge favor and kick around in there for crawly little surprises?"

"As you wish." Gio kissed my forehead before sifting every cubic inch of the bedding, and finding it rodent, reptile and giant arachnid free, waved me inside. "Looks safe to me, Buttercup."

"You mock my pain." I grimaced and hesitantly entered.

A thick tree limb spanned the portion of the fairy ring not sheltered by stone. Overlying the limb were green, needle-covered branches. This, I assumed, was the handiwork of the latest batch of young Castaldi campers. The makeshift roof was only marginally successful at deflecting rain; I knew we couldn't stay here forever under present conditions. The stone-roofed section sat higher up, providing a dry, cozy island, should the downpour engulf the semi-exposed area, but it was by no means a long-term solution. Gio leaned against a flat spot and patted his thigh in invitation.

His warmth helped quell the quaking that had overtaken my body from the cold rain. I tucked my arm behind his unsupported lower back and rested the side of my face against his shoulder, feeling the rhythm of his beating heart.

"I can't figure out why it's important for us to know that Aldo hid money in his cellar, or that Tony apparently found it." Gio's distinctive scent, atomized by the warm dampness of his shirt, derailed my train of thought for a moment before I continued on. "The chocolate coins he left are a fun touch. I almost want to use them for shelf-life research, but it's probably more like concrete than chocolate under the foil by now, or some poisonous strain of bacteria. He could have just left the note by itself, but he left something for someone else to find. And chocolate, *hello*! I knew I liked him."

Gio held me closer when I shook again. "What makes you think it *is* important—knowing about the hiding spot?"

I could almost hear the *Jeopardy!* Final Round jingle playing in my head while I translated my weird hoodoo experience into actual words. "Well . . . Tony was directing the show back there at the cabin. I'm pretty sure of it."

"But we know my grandfather didn't die at the cabin. Aren't ghosts supposed to, you know, stay put or something?"

I sat up straight. "I never called them ghosts—not since seeing them, anyway. That's all you, skippy. They are more like thoughts and images and feelings. Who makes up the rules, anyway? Aldo and Anna Maria's family didn't die in the cabin either, and yet, there they were." I snuggled back down against my personal human furnace. "All I know is that Juliana seemed to be playing a wicked game of hot and cold back there. Every time I got an idea she approved of, she let me know."

A crash of thunder made me jump, only to resume shivering.

Gio ran his finger along my jawline and repositioned his back against the stone. "*Cara*, why don't you try to get some rest? I know you're still not sleeping. Looks like we'll be here a while."

Being cradled like a baby in the arms of a big man should have felt odd and, well, should have chafed against my determination to be strong and independent. Instead, it was simply safe and warm and easy. "Okay. I'll try. I really am kind of tired." I looked up. "But if anyone asks, I did not sleep with you."

"If anyone asks, you slept on me. Got it."

The sound of the rain outside, and the slow, steady breathing of the man on the inside, lulled me into the depths of slumber.

Aldo ducked hastily into the ring of the fairies, fighting to calm his wracking breaths brought on by a mad retreat up the hill. A hound bayed, too close for comfort, and the voices of the drunken men in pursuit called out in the dark.

"Where'd that slippery little dago go? I told you, you can't trust 'em. Sneaky beggars."

"I don't know, but that fat little bag he was carryin' looked awful heavy. Wouldn't want him to go and hurt himself, toting the weight of it all over these hills."

"Yeah, 'do unto others,' as my mama used to say. We're just gonna help him out, bein' neighborly and all."

The raucous laughter and calls of the men trailed off as, blessedly, they and the dogs moved on in another direction.

With bare hands, Aldo scraped up soft earth at the base of the stone. Fumbling in the dark, he found a fist-sized chip of rock and used it to help dig further. When the hole was deep enough to place his entire forearm into, Aldo removed a leather pouch from his breast pocket and buried it before standing to tamp down the dirt.

"I think it's safe for us to go now, *cara*. The worst of it seems to have passed."

I lurched awake with a quick intake of breath and realized that the warm spot I was cozied into was the luscious smelling man who wanted to marry me. "Gio."

"Yes, *bella*?" He kissed my temple.

"We're supposed to find something here."

"Like, *here* here?"

"Yeah. Like, exactly right *here* here. Scoot over." I disentangled myself to make room.

"We need to dig a hole . . . hm . . . " I pushed him to scoot some more, "here."

Gio stuck his hands in his pockets. "Gee, Kate, I didn't have room for a shovel in here with the lighter, car keys and . . . hey, would you like some gum?"

I gratefully unwrapped the proffered stick and popped it in my mouth. "Aldo didn't need a shovel. We might want to look for something to gouge with, though."

While he went in search of a makeshift implement, I drew my hand over the general area in which Aldo had buried his pouch. It was fascinating that I knew the spot, considering he had worked in complete darkness, but there was no question in my mind about where it was. While there was no physical pull, drawing my hand back and forth was similar to dangling a tethered screw over a magnet to zone in on the sweet spot. By the time Gio returned with a sharp stick, I knew my first impression had been correct. "This is it."

We worked as a team, Gio using the stick to break up the ground while I scooped the soil out with my hands. After a few minutes, the wood found resistance against something rigid and Gio paused. I touched all around the object, and was confused.

"That's not right," I said. "He buried a sack, not this."

Gio used the stick to scrape dirt from around the container. "It's a coffee can."

I knew what I'd experienced in the dream, and Aldo had not buried a can. Then it dawned on me. "Tony."

Gio took care to dislodge the can without damaging it, and our artifact came up completely intact. Rust covered the surface, but the label was plainly visible, "Chock Full O'Nuts," and no spots of the metal were eaten completely through. He brushed off the bulk of the clinging dirt and opened the plastic lid, holding it for me to look into.

"Another of Tony's notes," I muttered, "and . . . Ha! More chocolate coins."

The note read, "$250 in gold coins found here, 1898 and older. Stored for safekeeping."

"Oh, no, he didn't." I shook my head at Gio.

"Looks like he did."

A sudden dawning made me laugh. "This is like geocaching, isn't it? Only in this case, I guess it would be G-I-O-caching."

Gio put the note with the other inside his jacket. "My nieces and nephews love that joke, but I'll give you a C+ for originality because you didn't know that, and I like you. It's too bad geocaching wasn't a thing in the eighties."

Deciding the outside patch pocket of my coat was the place least warmed by body heat, I stowed all of the candy coins there. I doubted they would melt from their semi-petrified state, but you never knew. "Right? Map coordinates and a cellphone would be a lot more efficient than waiting for your deceased ancestors to draw us pictures, except for the no cell reception out here."

"Actually, you can use GPS without cell, but . . . Never mind. Not pertinent." Gio scratched his emerging five-o'clock shadow. "So you think there are more spots like this?"

"I guess two isn't exactly a pattern, but they're marked on Tony's map, and both are at places with the heart marking. I'm not sure if that's enough data to go on, but if I shut out all logic, I get a good case of the feels about it. I think I'm supposed to follow the feels."

The rain was now downgraded to just a mist.

"All right, *cara mia*, we'd better go before it starts getting dark. The temperature is dropping pretty quickly now."

We shoved everything back into the coffee can and made

our way out of the fairy ring onto the path, only to hear a familiar call of the wild.

"Mister Nuttycheeks! Are you being our guide home?"

"Not the same—Oh, never mind." Gio kept striding forward, and so I was forced to end my conversation with the squirrel.

26.

Song of an Angel

I held a clipboard with the photocopies of Tony's notebook fastened to it, as I walked around my living room and read aloud. Gio read along from the original diary of Aldo Castaldo, who later changed his last name to Castaldi.

Torture. Pure torture. Nothing less could describe what I endured while laboring in the home of Massimo Santelli—or rather, the home he had stolen from my father. Daily I entered through the kitchen to the back stairway en route to the office at the end of a hall. In this room—the very room in which I had studied estate accounts with my father—I verified journal entries of the *ragioniere* against the receipts stacked neatly on the dark oak desk. Boring and tedious, to be sure, but boredom was not the source of my agony.

Each morning I would follow up the stairs, the ethereal sounds of an angel playing the piano. Her scent filled the air, and I would slow my pace as I passed, trying to catch a trace of it. The long, graceful line of her back, swaying in time, always beckoned a furtive glance. With the morning halo cast from a window beyond her, it was no wonder I feared being stricken with a flaming sword for daring to cast my eyes upon the heavenly being.

Anna Maria had finished her studies at boarding school six months before my final days in my ancestral home. She was charged with running the household of an important but infamous man, as was her daughterly duty. Once the drone of full daily activity began, practicing would be considered a frivolity. Yet her talents would be often called upon to entertain guests, and she must work at preserving her skill.

The profound ache in my heart grew incrementally as time wore on, knowing she would never be mine. I prayed with all my soul to keep a clear mind for the purpose of attaining my ultimate goal. I would avenge the death of my father and reclaim the fortune that belonged to my family and the once-happy village we had supported.

Notwithstanding my prayers, my goal became less and less focused, hearing the angel's song daily, sending my heart to my throat and wrenching them both.

She was far too preoccupied to notice a drudge such as myself, working for her father. How could she notice? When one was in the service of sending sweet refrains toward heaven, she could not be troubled with the mundane things of this world.

"How's Tony doing so far on the translating?" I asked.

Gio flipped pages back and forth, rescanning portions of the text. "Actually, pretty well. A few little things, but the gist of it is close."

"Poor guy. Aldo, I mean. He had it bad. He adored her." Reading out loud was turning the inside of my mouth to kindergarten paste. I gulped bottled water while contemplating. "This is going to kill me. I want to read all the juicy tidbits, but I think we're supposed to skip ahead." A creaking from the floor above made me laugh. "See? Juliana agrees."

"You do whatever the voices in your head are telling you, *bambolina*."

"*Bambolina*? What does that one mean?"

Gio tilted his head and looked at me with one eye closed. "Little doll."

I twisted my mouth at his use of the diminutive form, even though I knew it was simply an expression of affection. "It's not voices." I stopped for a second to make sure that was really true. No voices. "I just get this really urgent sense that there's something we need to know, further along."

I came up behind him and squeezed the tight muscles of his shoulders. "Thanks for not making me feel any weirder than I already do about this."

"I'm running to keep up, Kate, but I can't exactly give you grief after, well, you know, I've had a little woo-woo experience myself." At my blank stare, he shook his hands and slowly raised his arms, moaning, "Woooooooooooo! Woooooooooooo!"

After rolling them to their full range of motion, I closed my eyes and began touching each page of the copies with my flattened palm until I came to one that "felt" right.

"This is an important one."

"'The time had come . . . '" Gio read the opening sentence of my copy, then flipped through Aldo's diary until he came to the corresponding section. "'*Era giunto il momento*.'"

I began reading aloud again.

The time had come. Two years of working for Santelli had passed, and during that time, I had seen and heard of more evil than a man of eighteen—or eighty, for that matter—should ever have had to bear. A carefully plotted course had, over time, provided more and more admittance to the man's trust and confidence. I knew that the longer I stayed, the more likely that I should be compelled to do more dishonorable acts than merely counting the brotherhood's currency. I feared for my eternal soul and the relentless fires of hell. The warnings of my mother became abundantly clear as time trudged forward.

Although Massimo Santelli never acknowledged his part in my father's death, my belief of it was fortified during my tenure in his home. There had been other fatal "accidents" in and around the village, far too similar in nature for it not to have been so. Accusations were whispered, but the murders went unchecked. If they could have been traced back to the brotherhood—and they could not—the blind eyes of local authorities would have easily been purchased or gained through fear and intimidation.

Men with soulless eyes came and went from the now garishly opulent home of Santelli. When she was not in sight of her father, the eyes became animated with unveiled lust toward Anna Maria. The lust was clearly not limited to carnality but included a quest for the status they would gain, should she become their prize. Or possibly, they calculated what ransom they might command if they were to take her unwillingly away. I feared for her safety, in the event they ever found her unguarded.

Santelli would wed Anna Maria to one of these soulless men, for the purpose of his own gain. Anna Maria's opinion would never have been consulted on the matter. She was esteemed by Massimo Santelli as a pet, tethered to him or traded away as he saw fit.

I knew that I must open the gilded cage and free her from the prison of her father—and the one she would soon find herself in.

"Wait. Had he even spoken to her yet at this point? Do you think they were secret lovers?" I began to skim back through the previous pages.

"I doubt that. Why would he risk becoming the next accident?"

"And what about *his own* daughters? Didn't he do exactly the same thing to them? Choose their husbands based on financial gain? Hypocrite!"

Gio patted the seat next to him in invitation. "Just keep reading, Kate. That's what you're supposed to do, right?"

"Right."

I chose a date on which to act, and aligned my game pieces for the checkmate against Massimo Santelli.

My sainted mother was on a ship destined for America, along with my three younger siblings, where they would be welcomed by her sister. My instructions were implicit, but out of necessity for their safety, her knowledge of the details was limited. She was to arrive in New York City, change their names and move on to another city immediately. This was most important. She was to take the family as far west as she could and await further instructions.

In the duration of my employment, there was much talk of the Sicilians, our cousins to the south, forming an organization in New York City. If even a breath of my family's true identity was made known to them, no distance would be far enough to shield them from danger.

Only my mother and I knew that they were not embarking on a pilgrimage to Rome to pray for the eternal soul of my father, as reported. Only she and I knew that I, too, readied my belongings for a long journey.

Because I had planted subtle seeds of doubt about the

ragioniere, Massimo allowed ever more personal financial information to fall from his lips to my ears only. His revelations increased, of course, according to the severity of his drunkenness. I became very dedicated indeed to my work, staying later in the evenings in which his drinking began early. I was entrusted with the key to a large trunk in the wine cellar, where I would go to hide money away for him. He often sent me to the safe in his bedroom for important papers and gave instructions about what to do with them should he meet an untimely death. On an evening so drunk he would never remember doing so, Massimo informed me about a store of gold coin, cleverly concealed in a long-abandoned water duct in the garden.

Santelli pronounced that there was to be a huge celebration on Friday, the eve of the feast of Saint Anthony di Padua. An important announcement was to be made concerning his daughter. Suitors came and went over the preceding weeks, young and old, handsome and hideous, educated and imbecilic—all of questionable character. Anna Maria played hostess to dinners that included scores of men deemed strategically suitable by her father. One of them would be chosen, and would be announced as her betrothed at the feast.

As the day approached, I came across her as she sat at her piano, playing but not singing. The sweet melody ended abruptly with a loud, discordant blare. Seeing no one about, no one to come to her aid or comfort—and no one to witness me entering her private space—I edged my way to her.

"Excuse me, *signorina*," I said in low tones.

She looked up from her slumped position at the instrument, then burst into sobs against it.

"Excuse me," I repeated, not knowing what one in my station should say. "May I help you?"

Emboldened by the fact that she did not send me away with a scream, I sat down beside her on the bench. I cautiously patted her hand. "Excuse me," I said for the third time.

She took a handkerchief from her pocket and wiped at her eyes. "I'm sorry, Aldo—Mr. Castaldo—you should not have to see me so."

Stunned to be so directly addressed, a moment passed before my tongue became unbound. "I apologize for my awkwardness, *signorina*. I was not aware that you knew my name."

"Of course I know it, sir." Her red-rimmed eyes gazed tentatively into mine. "You are the one bright spot of good in this house. You are the one who rightfully belongs here, not I. It is the sound of your feet on the stairs of a morning that brings a small bit of peace to my day. But if anyone finds you in this room or sees me speaking with you, you will be in grave danger." The emphasis she placed on the word "grave" did not deter me. Could I dare conclude she might have spoken to me before, had she not feared for my safety?

"Miss, may I ask you something?"

She sniffed and shuddered with an intake of breath.

"Yes, Mr. Castaldo?"

"I know that there is to be an announcement regarding your future."

Her eyes welled and she cried again in earnest.

"I'm sorry, miss, but if I may be so bold . . . "

She whispered urgently. "I must play or my maid will come to inquire about me." She returned to the sonata she had been practicing.

I whispered as loudly as I could, to be heard over her playing, but quietly enough that I would not be detected by servants milling about. "What would you be willing to do to escape your father's plan for your future?"

Her hands stopped, hovering above the keys, aghast at my suggestion. I motioned for her to continue, and after two false starts, she resumed the sonata.

"Mr. Castaldo, there is no escaping my father and his plans for me. I have no say in the matter while I reside in his home, and I would get no further than the butcher's shop before being retrieved by one of his henchmen. If I did go beyond, one of his rivals' men would spirit me away and return me one piece at a time until his leader's demands were met."

She played on and nodded toward the page for me to turn it.

"Forgive me, *signorina*, but what if someone could get you far beyond the butcher's shop? Far beyond Ruscello? Beyond Calabria?"

The dynamics of the music softened and slowed as she closed her eyes to consider. "My father's influence is far-reaching, Mr. Castaldo. He has many associates in Sicily. He has contacts in Roma and beyond. It would be just a matter of time before—"

"But what if this person could take you away from Italia, from Europe? What if this person would vow to protect you with his whole might, mind and strength—and more importantly, with his whole heart?"

The music crescendoed into quick, bold notes. "I would not want for that heart to be served on a silver platter, along with a tongue that speaks so boldly and freely with the daughter of the Don. I could not bear it if that someone were to die while I lived on to marry a vile man I could not possibly love."

At the coda, I turned the music back to the first page. "Either way, a vile man would be the groom, whether I— whether the person died fighting, or allowed the lamb to go peacefully to the slaughter. At least with one scenario, there is a possibility for a different outcome."

She played a staccato series of notes and went back to a softer, gentler pace.

"They will bring me breakfast on a tray soon. You must go."

"But, miss, you must—"

"Meet me in the south garden this evening at seven-thirty. Dinner will be over and my father will be having cigars with his *compari* in his office. I will think about the question you have posed. I will consider what you ask, and answer you then."

I quietly exited to the balcony. The garden was empty below and it was a short hop to the balcony of Santelli's study. He would be out in the village taking his morning walk, as he did every day before breakfast.

I slapped the table. "I told you this was a good place to start. Just think how many pages of him mooning over her we skipped."

"Yeah. It's starting to get good. Funny there isn't a 'how I met your mother' story still floating around in my family. You would think . . . "

I went on reading.

A t the appointed hour, I waited in the shadows of the walled south garden, near the climbing bougainvillea vine. I will never forget the scent of jasmine in the air that evening. And how I waited for her, pulling the watch from my pocket every few seconds, until her scent mixed with that of the flowers. And then she was there with a look of fear and excitement upon her face.

"Mr. Castaldo, I have a question to ask before I answer yours."

"Yes, Miss?"

"What is meant by this person vowing his might, mind, strength and heart to my protection? What, specifically, would that mean?"

At that, I lowered myself down to both knees. Surprised to see that the feet of the angel did, after all, rest on the ground, I reached for her hand. "It would mean, Miss Santelli, my beloved Anna Maria, that this person would ask you to be his wife and love you with every breath he was given the privilege of taking afterward. He would ask you to make a new life in a new country and never look back. He would ask you to trust him to do everything in his power to make you happy as long as you live."

Anna Maria's eyes glistened with tears as she said, "That is what I hoped you would say, Mr. Castaldo."

The seconds seemed years while I awaited the answer I sought, the silence piercing my heart, the stone I knelt upon digging mercilessly into my knees.

"Would I have time to visit the grave of my mother?"

Hope returned, but I dared not give way to it yet. "Yes, but it must be tomorrow. We will leave the night of your engagement announcement—or the night of your father's celebration, for I fear the announcement may be overshadowed by something else. It will also be the night of your father's grief, for you are to leave no note. You are to say nothing to anyone, even your most trusted confidante."

Anna Maria squeezed my hands tightly. "Then this brave and beloved person may rise and kiss me, because my answer is yes. I will also endeavor to bring him the joy he has given me, every day that I live."

And that is how I proposed to Anna Maria Santelli, and she did me the honor of making me the happiest man on earth.

I stopped reading and rested my hand on Gio's shoulder. "Well, there's your story. I guess the only family members who knew were Tony and Juliana. Aldo and Anna Maria must have never told their children the truth of how they left Italy."

27.

What a (Dead) Woman Wants

Juliana sat in her comfortable chair, once more knitting little things, reading glasses perched at the end of her nose. Her hair was styled big, shorter at the crown but reaching just past her shoulders in length. Still thick and glossy, it was accentuated by a few glittering white strands at the temples. Judging by the smooth texture of her still beautiful face, she could have passed for her early forties, but if I had the time period right, she would have been more like in her late fifties. "I'm almost done with this part. I can stitch the pieces together just in time for the shower tomorrow." She sighed. "So many grandbabies this year, I've gotten behind."

As thick brows pushed a vertical furrow in his forehead, Tony held a large sheet of paper to the light. From the back, the marker bleed-through of circles and crossed lines formed a winning tic-tac-toe pattern.

Juliana scooted down in her seat, stretching out her leg to poke Tony's knee with her toe. "What are you thinking so hard about?"

"Mm? Oh, just planning out my trip for tomorrow. I'm running out of places to look."

Juliana moved a stitch marker ring from one knitting

needle to the other before ending a row and turning her work to begin a new one. "'Once you eliminate the impossible, whatever remains, no matter how improbable, must be the truth.' You're going to find it soon."

"Quoting Sherlock Holmes?" He crossed to the tall file cabinet on the other side of the stairwell. "You have got to be the most positive woman on Planet Earth. Anyone else would have put her foot down about this baloney years ago."

"Have you ever given me a reason to complain? Never! We all have our passions, sweetheart. At least I know you're out doing something you love and something that will be significant for the family one day."

"You are my passion, Jules. Always have been. This is just something I have to see through, that's all. I—"

"It's your calling. That's what it is. You are The Keeper now. You are the one who cares the most. It will be someone else someday, but for now, it's you, and protecting what Aldo worked so hard to build for his family is your job."

Tony set the map on the desk, put his hands on either side of the easy chair and nuzzled Juliana's neck just behind her ear until she squealed.

"If you make me drop a stitch, I will be forced to skewer you." She set her work in her lap and grabbed his ears to plant a lingering kiss on his lips.

Tony raised an eyebrow in the exact same way his grandson did when turning on the charm. "You don't have to finish that right now, do you?"

"I do, or I'll be giving a box of sleeves and a collar

tomorrow instead of a sweater. Hold that thought, though." She *tsk*ed when she picked up her knitting again. "Darn it! Can you hand me that crochet hook, please? You did make me drop a stitch, you bad man."

"You're not going to stab me?"

"I'll let you live this time because I might need you later." Her eyes gleamed into his.

Tony played keep-away with the hook until she paid for it with another kiss. "Need me later? Is that a promise?"

Then all at once the room grew dark and Juliana's face became lit, as if by a spotlight.

"You have to find him. He's tired and wants to come home. Follow his steps. Please, find Tony."

I rolled over and looked at the clock. Three o'clock a.m. A perfect time to wake the neighbor, I figured. If I didn't know it before, I was relatively certain now that Juliana considered this a joint venture with her grandson.

"*Ciao, bella.*" Gio's voice was almost a whisper but clear and free of annoyance or concern. Was it sad that getting a call from me in the middle of the night was becoming standard procedure?

"Top o' the mornin' to ye, *boyo*. Sorry. That's the best I can do for my representing my lineage." I twisted a curl around my finger and yawned loudly. "So, it looks like we're going on a treasure hunt."

To find out what happened to Tony, we needed to fully understand what it was he was looking for and why. To do this, we had to retrace his journey from the beginning, and that had started with Aldo Castaldo's diary.

Over the next few weeks, we systematically searched for

hearts and treasures, in what we hoped was close to the order in which Tony had discovered them. We also continued studying the written works of both Aldo and Tony himself. Not only was there his translation of the diary, but his own thoughts and discoveries about Aldo.

Our trove of Tony's offerings was expanding exponentially and becoming more colorful and creative with each new acquisition.

We sorted our newly excavated archeological artifacts into labeled laundry baskets on the floor of Ancestor Central, otherwise known as my attic. So far, our categories included 'Toys,' 'Antiques,' 'Memorabilia,' 'Hypothetically Edible,' 'UBOs (Unidentified Buried Objects)' and 'Other.'

'Other' included the skull of an animal—which Gio dubbed a pack rat because I refused to believe it was a squirrel—and a note decrying the futility of materialism. "Set not your heart upon the things of this world." This category also included springy snakes that popped out of a can, with no note at all, but chocolate coins and a smiley-face badge at the bottom. Clearly his message here was to not take yourself too seriously.

An entire wall of the attic was covered in notes, maps, diagrams and illustrations, all rendered in Tony's hand.

"Now this is a metaphor if I ever saw one. Pretty clever." I lifted the latest finding from the toy basket and posed him in a running stance. I used my low movie-trailer voice. "Steve Austen, The Six Million Dollar Man." Steve ran—which was really more of a crow hop if you were imagination impaired— across the table as I made whooshing sounds. "I wonder how much six million would be in today's economy." I removed his sweatshirt before tugging at the waistband of his matching pants. "This is the best doll ever."

"It's an action figure, Kate, not a doll. What are you doing? Don't take his clothes off. He's not a Barbie. Give the guy some dignity."

I pulled off Steve's tank top to find a black-marker heart in the middle of his chest. "If you never take off his clothes, how are you supposed to attach the bionic arm and leg?" I clucked and shook my head. "Boys."

"Yeah, well that's different. That's what is referred to as 'performing surgery,' but you don't just strip him for no reason. Poor guy doesn't want you to see how flat and smooth he is down there." Gio snatched the doll—the action figure—from my hand. "Humiliating. Right, Steve?"

I read aloud the note pinned to the sweatpants, which I still held away from naked Steve. "Great-Grandfather said the family fortune is hidden in the heart."

"Great," Gio said. "Is that another metaphor or is it meant to be literal?"

"Maybe both," I answered after consideration. "I mean, Aldo took back what had belonged to his family and used it to relocate them. He 'lived poor and grew rich' so he could afford to help more and more of his people get set up in their new homes. That's a treasure in the heart." I touched the center of my chest to illustrate.

"And Tony burying little stashes and marking the spots with hearts is literal, but metaphorical too. It represents how important his family responsibility was to him."

What we had discovered about Aldo and the family's fortune he had stolen back from the criminal, Massimo Santelli, shed an entirely new light on the man. He truly meant what he said about bringing the fortune back for his family and the village, and he managed to do it from across the ocean. There were so many things I wanted to share with Gio's family about all we had found, but something—or someone—inside me said we had to wait for now.

28.

The Heart of the Matter

While tackling a new quadrant of Tony's map out at the ranch, and unearthing more stores of booty, we took a break to eat our picnic lunch. I pointed out a heart on the map that looked like it must be near the top of the hill.

"Do you think we can get there today?" I asked.

"Yeah. If we veer off the path and cut through the trees, we'll be on the right trail. Then it will be another mile or so from there. We'll need to go as soon as we're done eating, though, so we have enough time to work up there."

Breathing hard, we rested at the summit, the place where I had noticed the first tree with a heart carved on it. It was here that I first saw my squirrel. It didn't matter how many times Gio tried to convince me otherwise, I was sure Mr. Nuttycheeks was my little guide on behalf of Aldo. Either that, or he thought I was one of his tribe. I'd been called worse things than a squirrel, or a nut, for that matter.

We dug around with our little folding camping shovels at the base of this tree until we found what we were looking for. Here we discovered a fruitcake tin, much like the one Juliana had used to hold her button collection in.

I handed it to Gio to open because the edges seemed to be fused together, and I couldn't wait to see what was inside.

He unfolded the knife from his pocket and began using it as

a prying tool, and growled. "I hate this, I'll be sharpening this baby tonight. Man's gotta have a sharp knife, just in case . . . Sheesh, this thing is stuck tighter than my cousin Lolita in her Spanx after a buffet!"

At last the rust seal popped loose and the tin opened at the hinges. There was a soft flannel drawstring bag inside, a dark, rich purple. Gio handed it to me to do the honors. I stuck my index finger inside and wiggled it to loosen the strings until my entire hand fit. The object it held was cold and smooth and rounded, with a point on one end. I pulled it out of the bag and held it up where the sun glistened on it. It was a heart-shaped locket, solid gold, its front embossed with curls and leaves with a smaller heart in the center. Two intertwined A's were carved there. The back curved gently and was polished to a sparkling sheen. The chain of the locket was most unusual. It was made up of flat, elongated hexagons, embellished with tiny hearts and held together by miniature circle links.

"There are the initials you wanted, Kate. They weren't on the trees, but Aldo gave Anna Maria a heart with initials, after all."

I opened the latch to find a miniature photograph inside of Aldo and Anna Maria when they were very young, maybe at about the time of their marriage. A tiny scroll floated loosely in the interior of the locket. I removed and unrolled it.

"Look deep inside your heart," it read. In the tin was another map of the Maw with the one great big heart where the pond now lay at the foot of The Keep.

"Promise me you won't tease me about this," I said to Gio.

"What? Do you have to pee again? Really?"

"No. Not this time—although I might have to in a minute after we do what I know we need to do next."

Gio squinted his eyes at me, awaiting my explanation.

"I need for you and me to get back up on that rock to see what this big heart is all about."

I was prepared for the thundering laugh, but I was happy that was the only humiliation I had to suffer at his hand.

"Of course, *cara*." He stooped down and motioned for me to hop on his back, just where I had been the first time he took me to the ledge.

I laughed and did as he invited me to do. I even closed my eyes for a reenactment. I held tight around his shoulders and waist, begrudgingly trusting him to keep me from sailing off the end of the earth.

"Okay, Kate. I'm setting you down. This rock isn't going anywhere." He lowered me to my feet and pulled me around to sit close to him on the stone. "All settled in? Good." He took my hand. "Go ahead and open them when you're ready, *bella*."

After a cleansing breath, I opened my lids, being sure to focus outward rather than downward. Golden autumn light glimmered against the red stone of the mountain, seeming to draw out the red hues from the iron infused surface. Indeed, you could almost see the fingerprints of the Creator in the shadows of its surface, as Gio had once described. A mist clung in a circle at the base of The Keep, which perched atop the hill. The rich warm hues of the aspens and oak trees in the canyon sang brightly in harmony with the red of the castle-like formation. I removed my pack to retrieve the sketchpad and charcoal pencils Gio had insisted I bring. I needed to capture this view now, the lines brought out in strong relief by the light.

Gio shuffled through the notes he'd collected along Tony's little scavenger hunt. "We've checked all of the hearts on the right side of the map. I wonder if we're going to find The Bionic Woman in one of them to go with the Six Million Dollar Man? Geez, I wish I knew what he was trying to say. He was having way too much fun."

I roughed out the lines of The Keep, then began superimposing a fairy tale castle over them, with arched windows, pointed roofs over the turrets, banners floating in the wind. I drew a great massive door and a bridge. I visually shortened the distance between the pond in the valley and The Keep, turning it into the moat the bridge crossed. The two curved arcs that barely peeked out from the surface of the water became the arched support of the bridge.

Gio stopped what he was doing to admire my sketch. "Kate, that's beautiful. What's it like to be gorgeous, smart, kind and talented?" He kissed the top of my head. "I always said they named this place right because, from this side, that thing looks more like a castle than any rock formation I've ever seen."

Then he pulled in a little closer and reached for the pad. "Can I look at this?"

I held the charcoal away from the paper and eased my grip.

Gio studied the drawing. "*Cara*, are you familiar with Italian castles?"

I rubbed the black charcoal dust from my hands onto the rock surface. "I've seen pictures of castles, but I don't know if they were Italian or not. Why?"

"Because this is dead-on like one in Calabria." He returned the pad. "I swear. It's exactly like the one my sister took me to when I was living with her. You know, one of those tour things. Except it wasn't all Disneyed up with pointy roofs and flags. Nice touch, though."

I looked at The Keep and back to my castle drawing. When I had begun sketching, I only wanted to catch the way the light and shadow played on the face of the rock formation. While I worked, the mountain drawing seemed to take on a life of its own and became a representation of a castle. I stared agape until Gio nudged me to continue. The details began filling in quickly. My muscles remembered something my mind did not. Stones and climbing vines that were not native to our surroundings appeared in the picture as though I were merely an observer of the moving pencil.

And then the oddest thing of all happened. As my hand was filling in details of the moat, it suddenly connected the two bridge arches with a curving point down into the water. The two arches of the bridge now formed a heart on my page.

Gio held up the map next to my drawing. The map showed the jutting 'teeth' of the Devil's Maw, curved in a semi-circle, with a heart centered amidst them. A castle—or The Keep, which looked like one—sat behind the heart. "They chose to live on this piece of land because it reminded them of home."

And then another image came to mind. I flipped the page and began a new drawing. This time I started with a framework—a horizontal line at the base, long vertical lines at each side, and a pointed arch at the top. I roughed in the triangular 'teeth' of the Maw, arranged in a curve, points reaching toward one another. Above that, rather than drawing The Keep, my hand began to portray a figure, a portrait, a woman's face, draped in a veil. Her hands were steepled in front of her. As a final flourish, I inserted a large heart shape on her chest, with rays of light emanating outward.

Gio said, "*Bella*, it's the Immaculate Heart of Mary."

"The window in the church," I confirmed.

"Do you think there's something hidden there too?"

"There's got to be, right?

"And you thought Grandpa Tony was clever. Aldo put a clue right above everyone's heads, over a hundred years ago."

A squirrel chirped maniacally from the tree behind us.

I shut my eyes and pressed my fingers to my temples to try and ease the sharp pain that was beginning to form there. "So what is he telling us?" I asked.

Gio cleaned charcoal from my face with the hem of his shirt. "Kate, remember I said there's an underwater cave there, where the two connected humps stick out above the water."

His eyes lit up in recognition. "One summer—I think I was about thirteen—my cousins and I camped out up here. It was the brightest full moon I had ever seen that night. I couldn't sleep after everyone else was snoring like chainsaws, so I took my flashlight and climbed up here on the rock to see what the mountain looked like in the moonlight."

"I bet it was spectacular," I said.

"It was. The town lights off in the distance were pretty, but far enough away they didn't interfere with the moon and the stars. I remember wishing I had a telescope. The stars were so bright, and the moon seemed huge in the sky. But that's not the amazing part."

"Sounds pretty amazing to me," I said.

"Well, all of that was pretty amazing, but the part that blew me away was that the cave sort of glowed in the moonlight."

I tried to imagine the cave glowing. "Like the water reflected light around it? It glittered?"

"No. I'm saying it glowed. From the inside."

"From the inside?" I tried to remember what he had told me before about the mining history in Castle Springs, and about the story his family passed down of the dangers of the underwater cave. They'd told him that someone had exploded the inside of it. And then there was that mine explosion in the 1890s that had left a perpetual underground inferno. "Do you think it's burning in there?

"No. It wasn't that kind of a glow." The look of excitement on Gio's face made him look like that thirteen-year-old boy who'd seen the sight all those years ago. "It was as though the moonlight was shining down there from up above."

"Do you think there's an opening on top? You'd think someone would have figured that out before now if that were the case."

"I'm telling you, Kate, that's what it looked like." He rubbed my knee as his face took on a look of contemplation. "I'm thinking maybe the moon has to be just right to cast that much light in just the right spot. Maybe something like a super moon? Aldo could have seen it before and I was just lucky enough to be in the right place at the right time."

"What about the opening at the top? Do you think there's a mine shaft or something like that?"

"There could be, but I doubt it." He put his upper body in close behind me and outstretched his arm, pointing in a line from the pond's cave to The Keep above it. "Look up at the top. No vehicle can really get up there. You have to use mountaineering equipment, and this rock is pretty soft; that would be suicidal. I don't think many people would be aware of an opening. And if they ever did see it, they probably wouldn't know it has a connection to down here. This half of the mountain has been Castaldi property for generations."

"That's where Tony died, wasn't it? Using mountaineering equipment out at The Keep?"

"Yeah, that's the story, anyway." Gio put his arm around the back of my shoulders and squeezed. "Kate, Aldo hid something in that mountain and Tony was trying to get to it."

I looked at my window drawing and flipped back to the one of the castle. "But what is the connection with the big heart?"

"Oh. I forgot to tell you that part." He kissed my temple and quietly said, "The cave isn't two arches. It connects to a point at the bottom."

"It's a heart."

"Yeah," he smiled, "it's a heart."

I burrowed up against his solid body behind me while we stared wordlessly at the puzzle before us for a good long while. Gio watched as I sketched—just me drawing this time—and tried to capture the perfect lighting conditions while they lasted. The rising and falling of his chest as his breath grazed the side of my face, his strong heartbeat on my back, and the protective power of his arms barely out of the way of my work, broke my concentration from time to time in a pleasantly vexing way.

When it was time to head back, Gio stood and offered his hand. I faced him and that tree of safety with the reassuring squirrel singing from it. Rising with barely a thought for the devil and his maw behind me, I gasped when Gio jumped high in the air before landing with both feet on the solid ground near the rock.

"Jump, Kate. I'll catch you. I promise."

I inhaled, positioned myself for the launch, swung my arms for momentum . . . and stopped against an invisible wall of terror.

"Okay. That was for practice. You can do it, sweetheart."

I repeated the process two more times. "Sorry. I just can't."

"That's okay, *cara*." The look in Gio's eyes spoke not a word of reproach or mocking, only pure love and reassurance. "I'll help you down."

29.

Father Mikey

"I promise you, Mikey. We won't have it torn up for more than two days, three tops. I've got the best subcontractors in the area. They'll drop everything at a moment's notice for me. I'll pay them double to do it quickly and the chapel will look better than ever when they're done."

Father Michael looked at Gio with uncertainty. "I don't know, G., the parishioners shouldn't have to come in for early morning mass with it all torn up, even for a couple of days. Besides, this building is such an icon in town, I'd hate to see it altered."

"What are you talking about, Father? When this church was built, it would have been stone all the way through. I spoke with Nonna, and she thinks the interior walls were put in sometime in the thirties. She remembers men in town being happy to have the work." He patted the young priest on the back. "I bet you there's sawdust or newspaper for insulation in there. We could install good R-15 fiberglass batts and plasterboard, then I can put some beautiful stone tiles over that. It will look a hundred times better and this place will be toasty. It will save the parish a ton in heating bills, and I'll cover all the costs."

I persuaded, "Oh, Father, it would be so beautiful. Can't you just imagine? I was looking at marble for my candy kitchen and there are some slabs that have a little of that greenish color in the Immaculate Heart window, and that one over there too. It would be stunning."

Gio glared at me from behind the priest. "Marble. Well I

don't—"

I interrupted. "Yes. Marble would be lovely. It would cost more, of course, but I think it would be perfect."

Father Michael's eyes lit at the idea. "I've had a particular interest in this place. I've read through the history of the building. The Squares kept excellent records. They were proud of their church. As the story goes, marble was one of the things the founders wanted for this chapel. Old Aldo Castaldi promised marble for in here. But, unfortunately, he passed away before he could make it happen."

Gio shrugged, "OK. Marble it is, then."

"All right, but I'll have to get permission, and that could take some time." Father Michael put his hands in his pockets.

"I'll call the Monsignor myself," Gio replied. "The last time I visited Uncle Paul, he was needing a donation for the school. I think he'd be just fine with some improvements in here." He patted Father Michael on the back again. "We'll start on Monday."

"But, the Monsignor," Father Michael sputtered.

"I'm telling you, he'll be okay with it."

As we walked down the steps outside to the sidewalk below, I asked, "New marble walls and a donation to the school? Boy, you got generous in a hurry."

"You know, this church wouldn't be here in the first place if it weren't for Aldo. I wouldn't have the success that I have if not for the property handed down through the family. I figure if he hid something under that window, or in the wall, he wanted us to find it someday. It's all tied together." He stopped me and kissed me firmly on the lips. "Besides, someday our kids will go to that school."

I stared at him with my mouth open for a moment, before catching up with him. After sputtering for at least twenty steps, I sighed and took his offered hand. Who was I kidding? I wanted children. I loved Gio. Of course we'd have kids someday. Of course we would.

I imagined them playing in the square after school before doing their homework on the corner table in the candy kitchen. Gio would pop by from across the street and kiss them all, and . . .

"So what do you think is in there?" Gio asked.

"Hm?" I blinked my eyes to return my thoughts to the present. "I'm not sure, but I think Tony didn't know about this part.

Gio hadn't been fooling about his crew. An army descended into the church right after early morning mass and had the dark mahogany pews covered in tarps, protection over the stained glass windows and the interior lath-and-plaster walls torn out by noon. It was better than those extreme home shows, because of the anticipation of what we would find. Gio told the men as little as possible about why we were replacing the walls. He only told them that we were increasing the insulative value and that we wouldn't be framing in for sheet rock right away. He said he and I would be inspecting the bare stonework and marking places that needed to be patched, and that they should return at two-thirty sharp.

"Are you sure that's enough time, *cara*? There's a lot of square footage to cover."

"I think so." I carefully inspected each stone and the surrounding mortar. "I hope so."

This church had not been built with cut stone blocks. A building of this size could have taken decades to construct if each stone were cut with hand tools, as they would have had to be during that era. Castle Springs would have been little more than wilderness. Rather, these walls were built from stacked natural stone, squarish and angular, but not perfect. The walls resembled the old stacked walls that divided properties in Scotland and England, and I suspected Italy as well. The only difference was that in these walls, mortar had been included to seal out any potential drafts. Some of the patches of mortar were less than a half inch in width while others were as much as three or four inches across. The potential for hiding places was endless. I went to the window with the Immaculate Heart of Mary first. It was the obvious choice. Of course, it was possible that what Aldo was trying to tell me was more of a generalization. The window in my drawing could have been merely an easily identifiable image to point us to the church in general. But it couldn't hurt to start here. I decided to employ the tactic I had used to find the right pages of the diary to translate. I closed my eyes and held my hand out just slightly away from the surface of the wall and moved it in small circles, covering an entire section about the width of my body before moving on to another one.

I looked up at Gio. "Maybe it doesn't work with rocks. Paper covers rock, after all."

"Take a big breath, close your eyes, clear your mind. Try it again, *bella*."

"How do you know that will help?" I asked.

"I'm not a psychic, but I've seen them on TV," he said, kissing me on the cheek.

"I'm not a psychic either."

He tilted his head to one side and stared at me in disbelief.

"I was not a psychic before I moved into my apartment, and I plan to not be a psychic after all of this is done."

"That sounds more like it." He rubbed my shoulders until I rotated my neck and shook out my arms. "Okay. Deep breath."

I did as requested before closing my eyes and holding my palm next to the wall again in the same pattern I had used before.

Then, I leaned in and supported myself against the stone as I saw Aldo.

The church was a big empty space with only the sky above. There were openings where the windows would eventually be placed. Aldo walked in just before sunset, by the looks of the light in the sky. He turned and looked back out the door to make sure no one could see what he was doing. When he was satisfied that was the case, he came here to the spot I was leaning against. The mortar was already in place; I imagine that was something they did as they stacked the stones. Aldo took a small hammer and chisel from his coat pocket and began tapping away at the triangular space between three stones. When the mortar gave way, he pulled a chunk of it out. I knew that he was one of the volunteers who had helped erect these walls and that he personally had added this mortar in this particular spot. I wasn't sure how I knew it. I guess I saw it through Aldo's own memory. I could see now that the space was filled with two clay roof shingles, laid in such a way as to form a tube.

He'd made a little chamber and then filled it in and covered it up. But now he was here to actually put something in. Again he looked around and out into the street. He reached into the breast pocket of his coat, removed a leather pouch, and laid it inside the tile tube. From another pocket, he took a wooden disk and smiled when it fit the hole snugly. Good, he'd measured correctly.

Against the wall that was in the least state of completion stood a bucket half filled with water and a wheelbarrow with a dry gray powdery substance. I guessed it was whatever it was they used at the time for mortar. He took a shovel and added some of the dry mix to the water and mixed it with a stick until it was the proper consistency. He grabbed a nearby trowel and came back to the secret hiding place and covered over the wooden disk, taking great care to make it look as it had before.

I took a chilling breath of air and jolted upward and away from the wall.

"You okay, Kate?" Gio had his hand at the small of my back and looked at me with concern.

"I'm all right," I answered and pointed to a large triangular patch of gray material. "It's here."

Gio put his hands on his hips. "Easy as that?"

I shivered and crossed my arms over my chest. "Apparently so."

"You're sure it's only one place in this whole building? Maybe you should keep checking."

"I'm sure."

"You mean, I could have punched a little hole and patched?"

"What are you complaining about, Mister 'I own a little more than half a town'? I'm sure the church needed it anyway. Your great-great-great-grandfather would be proud."

"Yeah, but I'm sure we could have done it without bringing in a SWAT team of carpenters at double pay and lining the place with marble slabs. *Le cose che faccio per questa donna.*" He groaned, took a deep breath, and held up his palms in surrender. "You're right. You're right. It will look beautiful."

Gio stared at me in anticipation. I stared back, and at the wall, and back to him again.

What if we'd gone to all of this trouble for nothing? What if I was having some psychotic episode? Maybe all of this was a severe manic phase, like I'd seen my mother have during the worst of her bipolar disorder—before she'd finally sought help.

Gio nudged me hard enough that I had to reposition my feet to stay balanced. He handed me a screwdriver and a ball peen hammer from his coat. "You ready to do this thing?"

"I think you should do it. He was your ancestor. Just start close to the rocks and go around roughly in a circle."

After a few minutes of tapping, Gio exposed parts of the

red clay roof tile as he broke the cement seal away from the rocks. He turned to me. "It's ready to pull out. Your fingers are smaller. Can you get them in there?"

I squeezed three fingers mostly in and around the mortar plug. I tried to wiggle it, but it was not budging. Looking at Gio I said. "I think you need to pound the screwdriver into the center of the patch of mortar."

He started to protest, then shrugged. "Okay, chief. Whatever you say."

With one solid blow, he drove the shaft of the screwdriver through the mortar and into the wood behind it. In so doing, he knocked it loose and was able to pull outward and remove it.

I took a small flashlight from the pocket of my jeans and shined it into the tube. "There you are, little pouch. I wonder what is inside of you."

Gio kissed my temple. "Kate. Having conversations with inanimate objects. I worry about you sometimes."

If he only knew how much I worried too. I was trusting that when we found whatever it was we were supposed to find, this would all go away. But there were no guarantees.

The leather of the pouch was dry and stiff and crumbling in places, but it was, for the most part, in one piece. The cord that held it closed was knotted firmly and so stiff, I couldn't move it with my bare fingers. I felt the bag, but because there was no suppleness left, I might as well have been holding a flattened football. I could only vaguely discern that there were probably coins and a longer hard object inside.

Gio touched my upper back with his hand as he moved in for a better look. "Why don't we take this outside and find a nice park bench to sit on. The dust is too bad in here."

He stopped at the door. "Just a minute." Taking a piece of chalk out of his pocket, he went around the chapel, marking spots that needed work. "Almost forgot."

The sun was out and the town was bustling around the square. Trees were adorned with autumn finery. We went to the log gazebo in the center of the park, next to the water feature that was still running this late in the year. Gio waited for me to sit before he joined me on the bench. Just over there was where we'd had our first official date, not that many weeks ago, though it seemed like it had to be years, considering all that had happened.

He got out his pocketknife, freshly re-sharpened, and handed it to me. I had to love that about him. Rather than being the big man doing the "man stuff" he always let me have a go at it first.

I cut through the leather thong drawstring and the bag fell open easily. I reached in and came up with five gold coins, a small portion of what the bag contained. I handed two of them over for Gio's inspection as I looked at the others in my hand. These were very old. They were Italian. They were solid gold.

"Holy Mary Tyler Moore. I wonder what these are worth. They're heavy."

"I don't have a clue. But with what gold is going for per ounce right now—plus if you figure in historical value, collectible value—I think it's safe to say we're not talking peanuts."

I didn't want to dump everything out right there in the park. We'd have to give it a thorough inspection later. I felt inside once more for the longer object and realized it was a key.

Gio took it from my offering hand. He turned it over and examined it from all angles. "It's just like the one to your attic."

I took it from him and did exactly as he had done. "All right. Now I'm really confused. Your mother said she thought the lock on my door came from one of her father's antique finds. How could this match it if it has been walled up since the church was built sometime in the Gay Nineties. Scott Joplin Nineties, not Ricky Martin Nineties. What could the connection be?"

"I think we're going to have to do some more digging in Tony's stuff, or you're going to have to have one of your voodoo mamba vision things. I have no idea."

"Wait. There's something else in here." I pulled out another piece of leather, rolled up like a scroll. This leather was softer and more pliable than the bag that held it had been. I unrolled the scroll to find Italian writing in the now familiar hand of Aldo Castaldi.

A group of young mothers pushing jogging strollers were running our way. I collected the plunder and stashed it back in the pouch. I stuffed the pouch into my handbag before they got close enough to identify anything. "I think it's time to consult your mother and Nonna."

Gio helped me up and lifted me to his height to kiss me. I blushed as the women ran by, but I was starting to like this emotional, demonstrative Italian thing very much.

30.

Chez Kate

Gio's assignment for the afternoon was to take his parents and Nonna on a long drive while I worked in the ranch's kitchen with Marco and Alyssa. I had allowed Gio to feed me so often, it was high time I reciprocated. And since I was also feeding his family, the meal had to be perfect. I was going French cuisine all the way, and what would a French gourmet menu be without snails? We'd start off with *Escargots à la Bourguignonne* and a cold-smoked French herring with warm potato salad and greens. Then for the main course, there'd be Salmon *Dijonnaise* and colorful *Ratatouille* for the vegetable dish. If the diners could take one more bite, there was Raspberry *Brûlée* for dessert. Of course, I also came packing an assortment of chocolates because, well, chocolates.

Marco served as *sous-chef* and Alyssa as *chef de partie*. Marco's familiarity with the huge, magnificent kitchen saved me the steps of hunting for things. The two were excited to learn something new and help out, but mostly, I think, they were happy to spend time together and have gourmet dishes to carry off for their own romantic dinner.

Before we descended upon the kitchen, the two helped me carry boxes and baskets up to Nonna's favorite landing. Everything was ready for Gio and me to show the family later.

Just as Marco and Alyssa gathered their takeout cartons to leave, the sound of big tires on gravel announced Gio's return.

I peeked out the kitchen door to see him carrying Nonna's walker over one arm and guiding the lady herself with the other. She began to head my way until Gio made a growling noise and pointed to her bright pink "dancing partner," which Nonna grudgingly consented to use. Cici and John came in behind them, and the three grandparents fussed over the departing young couple long enough for Gio to slip away.

"Mmmm, *cara*, something smells delicious." When the door swung closed behind him, he kissed me, encircling my waist and pulling me up to my toes to nuzzle my neck. "And the food smells good too."

I kicked my feet behind me and squeaked when his stubble tickled my ear. As I slid to the floor, I frowned nervously and whispered. "I hope they like it. I have some soup in the fridge in case the food is too rich for Nonna."

"She'll love whatever you serve. Nonna has a very sophisticated palate, and she's a heck of a cook herself, you know."

"Well, chocolate is my favorite, but it's high time I put some of my other training to use. I've always wanted to entertain. You know, without actually having to interact with, like, real people and stuff."

"Kate, there is no escaping being around people in this town, especially after we're married. The family is like a creature itself, needing constant tending, but they're all pretty fun as individuals too."

"Haven't proposed. Haven't accepted. I see what you did there, just breezing right past the 'after we're married' part."

He went on as though he hadn't heard. "You'll get used to them, though. It's nice to know that someone's always got your back. We may not get along all the time, but nobody else, no one outside the family, better start something with one of us."

My stomach twisted. "I'm not so sure I'm resilient enough to be the outsider under those circumstances."

"That's the thing. We're also a very inclusive family. It's pretty hard to tell the difference between the born-intos and the married-intos. I mean, look at my mom. She's Nonna's granddaughter-in-law, and they are thick as thieves."

"Well, from what I can tell, the married-intos are all distant born-intos, so that doesn't really count, does it?"

He poked me in the ribs until I squealed again, just as John pushed the door open and held it for Nonna and Cici.

Nonna's hair was freshly tinted with a light blue rinse, teased, combed and sprayed. Today had been her "do day." There was a sparkly butterfly pinned over her left ear. She wore a soft pullover sweater with sparkles and butterflies on it and a jaunty, bright lime green pashmina wrap. Cici smiled broadly and embraced me after Nonna had had her turn.

"Everything's ready, if you'd like to come into the dining room."

Marco had insisted on setting up the silver chafing dishes on the beautiful antique sideboard, with a promise to come out here the next day to polish them. His eye for presentation shone as he brought out all of his favorite special serving pieces. He had created a beautiful, enchanted atmosphere. "Nonna will love it, Kate," he'd said.

I suspected he was motivated by a desire to show Alyssa that he was more than a snowboarding prep cook, and could be civilized when he wanted. If he could only have seen what I saw in Alyssa's eyes, he would know that it was too late to try to impress her. He'd had her way before "Hey. How you doin'?"

Nonna took a seat at the head of the table where Gio led her. "I love a nicely set table."

"I do too." I nodded. "The more beautiful the presentation, the better the food tastes. At least that's what we were taught in cooking school."

Cici ran her hand along the crocheted lace tablecloth. "Oh, absolutely. And using treasured pieces makes you think of happy gatherings from the past. It's like getting the cumulative effect of all the delicious meals before."

Gio and his father just looked at each other and shrugged. At least neither of them said, "How about those Broncos?"

"I could have had the kids stay to serve, but I'd hoped to have a more intimate meal tonight. I'll dish up the first round. I'm a bit out of practice on my plating, but I'd like for you to have the full *haute cuisine* experience."

The silence during the meal was interrupted only by occasional groans of pleasure and exclamations of appreciation.

"*Carissima. Adoro questo*! You've been holding back. You'll be sorry now. What's for dinner tomorrow and the next day?" Gio kissed me in front of everyone, making my tummy buzz and my face redden.

John, who was normally very quiet, said, "We don't get anything this fancy in Castle Springs. You should open a restaurant, Kate."

"It's something I thought I wanted to do someday," I admitted. "Right now my plan is to make sure the chocolate shop is running profitably and then begin teaching gourmet cuisine in the evenings. I'm not sure I'm up for running two full-time businesses. The chocolaterie was always my first choice."

Cici chimed in. "A cooking school here in Castle Springs? That would be wonderful. Think of all the potential job opportunities that would create for the young people who work up the hill."

"My mother taught cooking in our kitchen at home, so it's just a natural progression for me."

Nonna ate everything and even had seconds of some of it. My fears about the state of her delicate digestion were put to rest.

As John loosened his belt and Cici gave him a disapproving look, I quickly ran to the kitchen and torched the *brûlée*, returning to the murmurs of protest. The murmurs didn't stop them, though, from each taking a ramekin of the dessert to try.

Nonna smiled. "The meal was divine, my dear. You could definitely have a wildly successful restaurant, but I understand that your joy is in the chocolate. It shows with each beautiful, tasty morsel."

Gio cleared his throat in his 'now it's time to get down to business' way. "Kate and I came out tonight because there's something we wanted to share with you."

Nonna interrupted by smiling at me and patting my hand. "Finally! You've agreed to marry little Giovanni. Now I can die a happy woman."

While I responded with unintelligible syllables, "little Giovanni" went on.

"She hasn't agreed yet, Nonna, but I'm wearing her down. I do that. I'm very wearing." He bent over and kissed me on the cheek loudly. "Sorry, Nonna, that's not why we're here."

"Well, you'd better wear faster, boy. I really want to be at the wedding, you know."

31.

All About Aldo

Deciding it was better for them to draw their own conclusions from what I didn't say about matrimony, rather than what I did, I began clearing the table.

"Why don't we clean up later, *cara*? We probably need to get on with it, so Nonna won't be up too late."

"I would whine about my bedtime, my dear, but unfortunately, this old body is in charge of those decisions. You wouldn't want me to fall asleep right at the peak of the party. I'm sorry to be such a fuddy duddy."

Climbing the stairs knowing there was a mess left behind made my eye twitch a little, but I followed obediently.

Nonna was assisted into the elevator by John. She asked him, "What is an elephant that doesn't matter?" Before the doors closed she cackled and answered, "An irrelephant!"

Gio laughed and shook his head as he offered me his hand. "She loves that one."

We settled into the cozy sitting area surrounded by an assortment of boxes, bins and baskets, fresh from Ancestor Central.

I presented each of our hosts with a spiral-bound book with *The Castaldis of Castle Springs* printed on the front.

Gio called the official meeting to order. "Kate and I have been working on this book together. We're going to do a nice printing for everyone in the family once we've settled everything."

John feathered through the pages. "Settled? What is it?"

"The original Italian version of Aldo Castaldi's diary is in the back, but the front part is a collaborative translation by Grandpa Tony and me—with Kate's narrative style thrown in. That was a trip and a half." Gio looked his mother in the eye. "I'll have to tell you all about the experience sometime."

He rested his hand on my knee. "The English version was a little choppy—I really only corrected the major issues, not the syntax—so Kate did her magic and made it read like a story. This woman, I'm telling you. She surprises me every day." He put his arms around me and kissed my forehead.

"Don't be silly. You did the hard work. I only—"

Nonna patted my hand. "Take it, darling. We all know he's right." She pointed her finger at me. "Keep the surprises coming. It drives them crazy, but they'll spend the rest of their lives trying to figure you out. Men love a challenge."

I held up my own copy of the book and looked to Cici, steering the conversation clear of that subject. "Anyway . . . In doing all of this, and with a little help from a number of your forebears, we discovered a lot of interesting information."

"*My* forebears?" Cici asked.

"Well, some of them are only yours and Gio's, I mean, of those of us in the room. The rest of them belong to all of you."

"Yeah," Gio said. "Kate told you she was having those dreams."

Nonna's eyes sparkled. "Ah, yes. She's got the gift. She fits right into the family. Besides the fact that we love her so much."

"I don't have the gift," I blurted, then took a breath, counted slowly to three, and smoothed out my book from where I'd scrunched it. "I think . . . I don't know . . . I think Juliana wanted a neutral person—one who is not so closely connected—to tell the story to. She is sorry that everyone was hurt by Tony's death and her own." I took a sip of water. "I keep thinking, or at least hoping, that everything will go back to a level of normalcy at some point."

Gio rose and walked to and fro, his voice increasing in volume. "But now it's not just dreams about Grandma Juliana and Grandpa. Kate has seen—we both have seen—well, now there's Aldo and his wife, Anna Maria, doing their thing too."

The discussion became lively as Gio and I told them everything we had discovered. They stopped us to ask questions now and then, but mostly they listened with curiosity.

We gave them the Reader's Digest version of Aldo's story and how he came to Castle Springs in the first place.

"My grandfather was part of the Mafia? Well, that's going to stir up the community. Mercy, mercy me." Nonna was shaking her head but didn't seem in any kind of distress. That was a relief.

Gio clarified. "Well, I like to think he sort of did undercover work, like he infiltrated the organization so he could put them out of business. At least for a while. And it wasn't quite the Mafia yet. It was a forerunner of 'Ndrangheta. You've heard me talk about how they have their fingers in everything in Calabria—or did when I was there. But organized crime, as we now know it, was in its infancy back in Aldo's day."

I spoke up. "His real name was Aldo Castaldo, which is a funny story in itself. Anyway, his intention was to work there long enough to get the goods on the leader, Massimo Santelli, and then take him down. He was only sixteen when he got in, but bright enough that he was made second in command of the money."

"And then there was a little wrench thrown into the works. He fell in love with the don's daughter, Anna Maria." Gio laughed. "So we are all descendants of the big mob guy. I think it's safe to say we Squares can get off our high horses now."

I started to gush. "And it's so sweet how he cherished Anna

Maria, but she wouldn't even look at him. He thought it was because he wasn't worth her notice, but all along it was because she feared for his life if she allowed him to show any interest in her."

"Yes," Nonna said. "He was always very much in love with her until the day he died. My mother always told me that."

I spoke again. "Finally, he had all of his plans in place but couldn't stand the thought of leaving her. As it turned out, she didn't want to stay to marry someone of her father's choosing. So he proposed to her and whisked her away secretly. They got married in Switzerland before going into France and eventually got on a boat for America."

"But that's not the best part." Gio tapped his copy of the diary.

"I think it's the best part." I pressed mine to my chest and sighed.

"You're a girl." He rolled his eyes. "The best part is that he'd been slowly sneaking out gold coins and hiding them in barrels for his planned escape. Then he gave information about Santelli's organization to a rival. When Aldo and Anna Maria left, the Don's fortune went with them, and the don was left with hiding places full of rocks. The other gangs took care of the rest, and Santelli lived out the rest of his short life in shame and poverty."

John was really interested now. "So our founding father was a thief, too?" He burst into laughter, showing where Gio's most defining habit came from. "When I think of all the stories we've heard over the years about what a pillar of decency he was—"

"Well, yes and no," Gio explained. "He did wipe the Don's fortune out, but it was Castaldi money to begin with. Or Castaldo. He wasn't very creative about changing his identity."

I jumped in. "Castaldo mean's 'keeper of the castle,' and the way Aldo told it, his family had been tied to the duke's for many generations. He sent his mother and siblings ahead of him with instructions for her to change their names. And when it came to it, she couldn't stand to let go of such a prestigious label, so she changed it by one letter. Way to go incognito, Granny. High five!"

Gio's hands waived in animation. "Santelli and his goons had stolen everything the Castaldos had, even took over the family home, which had been granted to them by the duchy a couple of centuries before."

I rose to fill everyone's glasses while I spoke. "They left Aldo's father a broken man, and then they killed him as a message to show who was in charge of the village now."

Gio touched my cheek and smiled in thanks for the drink. "So, anyway, he manages to run off with Santelli's daughter—which might sound like revenge, but he really did love her. And he takes all of his money and eventually gets a homestead in what is now Castle Springs."

I stood next to Gio, feeding off his excitement. "But it was at the very tail end of the homesteading era. He buys this piece with a great big rock on it that was entirely useless to farm or run animals on." I looked at my guests, who were enthralled at this point. "But the rock on Castle Hill looks a lot like the old Duke's castle in Ruscello. He took the place because it reminded him of where he came from."

"Not to mention, no one else wanted it." Gio began pacing. "But a lot of homesteaders didn't make it, and as they gave up, Aldo would buy them out. That's how he ended up owning most of this valley."

I smiled. "Anna Maria never knew that among all of the barrels brought over from Italy, Aldo had stashed the gold he'd taken back from her father. How he pulled that off, we'll probably never know."

Cici said, "Surely she would have suspected something."

"All she knew was that they had to live very frugally and

not draw attention to themselves, in case her father would somehow be able to track her. That's why she was willing to stay in the cabin for so long." I brushed away a strand of hair that tickled my nose. "I'm sure she knew they weren't penniless, but I doubt she had a clue about the extent of their wealth."

"But here's the kicker." Gio ran his fingers through his hair. "He didn't bring all of that money with him so he could live high on the hog. As you know, he didn't. He used it, little by little, to invest in the town. The village of Ruscello was made up of family members, a lot like Castle Springs is today. He quietly sent money and instructions to the priest there, who arranged for the passage of families, one at a time, until half of the population had been transported here. Eventually, Aldo brought the priest, too, and built the church in town."

"He set them up in trade, farming, ranching. It's like he recreated the Ruscello of his childhood right here in Colorado. Except he didn't live as the wealthy young man with ancient ties to the royal family. He lived among them as an equal and relative, because they never knew about the money. He managed to get them off to a good start without them even knowing it was him."

Nonna spoke for the first time since we began the story. "By the time I came along, the farmhouse had been built and I never saw them live quite as meagerly, but something my father told me always stuck with me." Her eyes were bright as she recalled. "He said that his parents never had many material possessions, but the things they did have were always of the finest quality and workmanship. They had nothing fancy, but things were always made to last and they kept them forever." She pulled her wrap up higher on her neck. "Now I understand. Aldo did not want to appear to have much, but what he did have was the best that money could buy."

John said. "But the townspeople knew he owned everything. He collected rents and his ranch was huge."

Cici nodded thoughtfully. "But he didn't flaunt their good fortune."

"Aldo and Anna Maria taught my father and his siblings to manage their resources with wisdom," Nonna said. "They believed the love of money led one down a forbidden path. This is a tradition that has, for the most part, continued through the generations."

"He was a Keeper, like Gio," I said.

"Yes. And like my Giovanni, and Tony as well," Nonna said. "The Keepers of Castle Springs."

I looked into her clear, dark eyes. "But I have a question that has been eating away at me about Aldo, Nonna."

"And what is that, my dear?"

"Do you remember your family ever talking about their arranged marriages? About property grants to suitors on a conditional basis?"

"Ah, yes! Grandmother's rule." Nonna smiled. "My aunt Sophia, for whom I was named, told me all about how she and her husband fell in love. She lived to be almost as old as I, you know."

My eyes widened. "Your *Grandmother's* rule? The courtship exemption was Anna Maria's idea? Why would she—?

"My grandmother was almost forced to marry someone she didn't love for the benefit of her father. Grandfather brought potential suitors here. Once a daughter showed an interest in one of them, the man would be given the opportunity to prove he could make a livelihood—but the daughter got to decide what she wanted." The old woman cackled. "Aunt Sophia's husband failed miserably that first year, but she loved him. Her parents accepted him into the family and guided him down a path to success. Uncle Guido built many of the buildings around Castaldi Square. Maybe even your building."

"So, it wasn't really about the property at all?"

"The clause gave a suitor an opportunity at a life here, but if the daughter didn't love him, he had to forfeit his interest. He would likely leave angry, but he would go away as he came—without land—but maybe richer for his efforts."

32.

Talking Tony

Cici asked, "But where do my parents come into all of this?"
I fielded this one. "Your father was The Keeper of his
time. He had a love for the history of the place and a curiosity
about Aldo. When he found Aldo's diary, he discovered that
there was a hidden treasure out there somewhere."

Gio put his arm around me. "We think that Aldo was so good
at managing his wealth, and the town became so profitable,
that he eventually didn't have to access the bulk of what he
took from Italy. The town became self-sufficient, and Aldo
could finance new ventures out of his own profits. He wanted
to save the treasure for hard times or emergencies. He'd seen
by what had happened to his own family that fortunes can
come and go. He wanted to make sure that if Castle Springs
ever fell into the hands of an evil force like Ruscello had, his
people wouldn't lose everything. Because he'd grown rich in
his own right, he stashed a portion of that wealth in sites all
over the property. There was no FDIC in those days, and he
wasn't entirely trustful of banks. So he had all of these little
caches of money hidden, but the motherlode, the old gold
from Italy, seems to be in one place. A place that Tony was
never able to locate."

I laced my fingers with his. "Or that's what we think. In any
case, at a farm sale, Tony found an old trunk that had once
belonged to Aldo. Inside was the diary and other documents

that were, of course, written in Italian. Once he was able to decipher it all—and it took years, looking up words in a dictionary—he started seeking out Aldo's buried treasure."

Cici laughed. "That's why we had 'Italian word of the day' at the dinner table every night. There were never any conversations in the language, but we'd get that one word. We'd groan and complain, and not one of those words comes to mind, but he was trying to share his newfound knowledge with his family." A corner of her mouth rose and she shook her head.

Gio looked from his parents to his great-grandmother. "You really have to have the context of the whole sentence, I think, to make the words stick. I could study all I wanted, but it wasn't until I was immersed in the language in Calabria that it began to make sense."

Nonna nodded. "I heard snippets of Italian growing up, but as the town filled with others, it became important in my generation to downplay that which made us different, and we lost the language. We were still very proud of our heritage, mind you, but the language died away."

Gio gave the go-ahead and we arranged containers on the coffee table for the others to see.

"This is where it gets weird. I'm guessing Tony was fun to be around, because it's clear he had a well-developed sense of humor." I blew a curl off of my nose.

Cici, Nonna, and John all looked at each other and smiled.

Cici's eyes sparkled. "My dad was a real prankster. April first was like Christmas for him. No matter how hard we tried to avoid it, he got every one of us by the end of the day."

Nonna chuckled and nodded. "Giovanni and I used to get together with them on Saturday nights and play games. Tony would have us all in stitches every time." She stared off into the distance and sighed. "It was nice having such good friends right across the street."

It is nice. My face warmed as Gio and I exchanged knowing glances.

"Well, he must have had a blast with these shenanigans." Gio laughed when my eyes lit up. "Yes, Kate, more Irish for you."

"Wow. Malarkey and shenanigans. You're practically tri-lingual now, sir."

Gio tugged our linked hands upward to kiss mine. "He found all of Aldo's hiding places we know of, but we think he must have wanted to preserve the history and the experience for those who came after him. For every treasure he retrieved, he left something interesting behind for the next guy to find. We took Tony's treasures and left some of our own, to keep the tradition going."

I pulled my favorite antique wicker basket out from under the coffee table and placed it on top. Reaching in and sifting through the hundreds of chocolate coins, I asked, "Do these mean anything to you?"

Cici laughed and then her eyes misted. "Daddy made sure every birthday, every holiday, every good report card included chocolate coins. He loved them because they made something mundane into something magical."

Gio held one of the coins up. "Whenever I saw one of these as a kid, I thought of him, but I couldn't remember why. They were probably at celebrations when I was little. I guess you didn't carry on with them after your parents died."

Cici dabbed at her nose and spoke wistfully. "They weren't magic for me after that, and the chocolate inside is really kind of gross."

"Now there's a woman who knows chocolate!" I snorted and nodded vigorously. "But nevertheless, he used them as a replacement for the real coins he took, and left them for others to find, so they could experience the quest for themselves. Maybe he meant for them to be found while they were still edible. Maybe he planned a fun scavenger hunt for his grandchildren, which is a theory I'm leaning toward. He turned it into a fun game for someone, but he died before he could share it."

We went from one container to another, beginning with the more sentimental items. There was, of course, the locket, which I handed to Nonna. She wept when she opened it to see the faces of her grandparents, so young and happy and full of hope. There were other little trinkets that Tony had found in his antiquing adventures, like a set of old spectacles wrapped in cloth. The note that accompanied them read, "Trust in God to see things clearly." There was an old draw knife, the tool used to skin a log of its bark. With this, Tony left a note that read, "Grandfather used this to help build his house on a firm foundation, always hoping his family would be strong and safe within its confines."

"Each place Gio and I visited was left with a word of wisdom like this to go with the item. And also a note describing what he had taken 'for safe keeping.' I think the message he was trying to convey was that, while Aldo had wealth, the greatest treasure he left his family was their deep-seated values of hard work, humble living, and acts of kindness."

Cici said, "My dad believed that being rich could be a curse rather than a blessing, unless what you had was used to help others. I think he might have not left the real thing for fear that an obsession with money could ruin the life of someone he cared about."

She made a tall stack of the foil-wrapped disks on the table in front of her. "He believed in protecting what you earned, and doing whatever was necessary to expand it, by investing wisely and saving. He knew that the more you had, the more you had to give. They lived in the flower shop building until they died, although they could have retired early and lived anywhere they wanted."

"Did you know that?" Gio asked. "Did you know they had money when you were growing up?"

"I knew that we never wanted for anything important. We had everything we needed, but anything extra, we had to work and save for—the same as we taught you and your sisters. You are very much like him, you know."

"And my Giovanni too," Nonna added. "All of this can be traced back to my grandfather and the things he taught those he helped."

"Here are some of his more clever additions to the treasure hunt." I shifted containers until I found the Bionic Man action figure, once again fully clothed. "This one made me laugh."

There were game pieces and colorful paper money from a Monopoly game, which were found in several places at the ranch. Gio said, "Obviously referring to Aldo's wealth and owning property all over the area."

I held up a yellow card. "Actually, he used some of these to direct us to other places. It took us days to figure out that, 'Go directly to jail. Do not collect $200.' meant that there had been two hundred dollars in the next cache, but he had, of course, taken the money—"

Nonna said, "And I'll bet you found the coins in the jail in the old barn."

I asked, "It wasn't really a jail, was it?"

"Oh, heavens no. We used to pretend that big stable door with the bars in it was a jail, though, when we were children. Now that you bring all of these other things up, however, maybe my grandfather made the stable extra secure, just in case there were any uninvited guests. They were quite far from town, especially considering all they had for transportation was a horse and buggy."

I recounted my dream about the men and hounds near the fairy ring. "Maybe you're right about the jail."

"Then there were these." I handed Nonna a miniature

treasure chest with springing snakes that jumped out and made her laugh so hard she started to cough.

"I remember those," Cici said. "That was his favorite trick. I still open drawers and cupboards very slowly. And unmarked boxes, too."

"I nearly wet myself out on the trail with that one," I said, and blushed when Nonna laughed some more.

John asked, "But what about Aldo's big treasure that Tony couldn't find?"

"We think he had caught on to where it was but didn't know quite how to get to it. That's why he was spending so much time out at The Keep. We're certain it's inside the mountain, unless someone over the years has just happened upon it, but you'd think we'd have heard about something like that."

Then came the part where I divulged the details of my dreams and whatever you would call the strange little movie clips in my head. Luckily, they listened intently and reserved judgment about my sanity.

"I knew I had seen Grandfather!" Nonna tapped the tips of her fingers together in excitement. "But it was always so fleeting, I had a difficult time believing my eyes."

"That's how we found the first treasure in the basement of the cabin," Gio said, "and it wasn't just Kate who saw that; I saw him too."

"Yeah," I said. "Mister 'Ghost Malarkey' got onboard the crazy train with me after that."

"It's a shame my dad never found the last piece to the puzzle," Cici said with a frown. "If he couldn't find the treasure, do you think it's lost forever?"

"Wait until you go to Sunday mass." Gio nudged me and rolled his eyes.

Cici tilted her head quizzically. "Sunday mass? Tomorrow? What does that have to do with—"

I smiled. "I think you'll like the new renovations."

"Renov . . . ? I was just there last Sunday. I didn't see any—"

"You're gonna love the new marble in the chapel. Marble was Kate's idea. It is beautiful. She has excellent taste." He bent over and licked my cheek. "Mm-mm good."

"Ew!" I wiped my face on his shoulder. "Can you please behave yourself in front of your family? Such a twelve-year-old."

"They all are, sweetheart." Cici patted John's knee. "They just slow down a little, over time."

John's face piqued with curiosity. "So, what does the church have to do with Tony and Aldo?"

Gio looked for my okay before jumping into the weirdest part of all. "Kate figured the church part out, but she had help from somebody." He pulled my sketchpad from a folder under the table and opened it to show the picture of the stained glass window. "Kate drew this, only it was like someone was doing it with her."

I surveyed our audience, trying to gauge their reaction. Their faces were placid. "Aldo hid something at the church. He put this big fat clue under everyone's noses, and no one figured it out until now."

"And you demolished the church so you could look for Aldo's final clue," John said. "Nice!"

Cici's eyebrows lifted. "And you found what you were looking for?

"We found something, that's for sure," Gio said. "There were detailed instructions on how to get inside the mountain from the top."

"Tony had been trying, but as far as we can tell, he'd never been successful." I passed the plate of chocolates we'd carried up after dinner.

"Hence his sudden interest in rock climbing." Gio threw a truffle in the air and caught it in his mouth. "Yes! Score."

"We found this with the instructions." I passed the key to

Cici. "At first we thought it was an exact match for the key to my attic, your enchanted-castle key. But if you look inside the crevices, you can see there's another tiny ridge in there."

"And," Gio said, "It came with a note that said '*Cuore*.'"

"Heart," Nonna said.

"We think that Tony read about the key and thought he'd found the right one. There's gotta be something up in the mountain that opens with this key."

John circled the rim of his glass with his finger in thought. "So what are you going to do?"

Gio smiled broadly. "I'm going in, of course."

I put my hand on his. "*We're* going in."

33.

Come Fly With Me

I was afraid of falling. I was not afraid of flying. Encapsulate me in metal, strap me to a seat that doubles as a flotation device, give me peanuts, and I'll willingly ignore my violated personal space for two to three hours without screaming. My first helicopter ride, on the other hand, was terrifyingly new territory. It had no flight attendant pointing two fingers at emergency exits. No one instructed me to elbow the oxygen mask away from small children and take care of myself—or whatever. All I could think about while levitating choppily into the air was smashing into mountains, electrical wires, and giant gorillas clinging to tall buildings. I discovered a barf bag in the seat pocket and clutched it to my chest.

My hair was tucked under a green beanie with the headset over that. Gio held my hand on the console between us and tried to distract me by tugging ringlets free and tickling my nose and cheeks with them. Why was I in love with a seventh grader?

The pilot's voice in my headphones startled me to attention. "We're getting close to Castle Springs now. You can see The Keep up ahead."

Booking the helicopter hadn't been difficult. Ski season wouldn't start for a while yet. When it did, Gio's cousin, Jason, would be busy flying rich heli-skiers to remote mountaintop locations.

On our flight from Sunnyvail, he'd given us a rundown of some of his more famous clientele. "A few of the entertainment people have been really nice, you know, regular people. But I gotta tell ya, some are such arrogant, pretentious, entitled— well, anyway—there are days flying them around almost makes me miss Afghanistan."

Following a week of intense after-work training at a climbing gym, Gio pronounced me rock-worthy. Already an experienced climber, he had been very patient and reassuring while talking me through climb after climb. The false security of a Clydesdale-strength safety harness and squishy floor mats, along with a handsome man cheering me on with every foothold, seduced me into believing I was ready for the real thing. I had been like a seal getting a fish for clapping my flippers together. Climb a little higher without passing out, get an 'atta-girl' from the Italian Stallion. Pretty soon all he had to do was utter the word "good," and my mouth watered. He was Pavlov and I was his barking sea lion.

If it hadn't been for Gio joking about needing a helicopter to get to the top of The Keep, we probably would have tried to climb up from the canyon floor. Because of how Tony had likely died, Gio spared no expense for the best equipment possible, but if there was a safer way in, we intended to find it.

"You, sir, are putting a lot of faith in a woman who can't climb a ladder without falling on random strangers."

"And I thought I was the only one." Gio put fingertips to his rounded lips in feigned shock. "Your problem is that you think too much."

I narrowed my eyes. "Because a thinking woman is a bad thing?"

"I happen to like brainy redheads." He squeezed my knee. "But you talk yourself into being scared, Kate, you know? You did fantastic at the gym. You're a natural." He moved the microphone booms away from our faces and kissed me. (More positive reinforcement? Clap, clap, clap.) "Besides, I earned my rappelling badge way before I was an Eagle Scout. I've got enough experience to make sure you're all right."

"Why does it not surprise me you were an Eagle Scout?"

"Oldtown troop 405. The Square Pegs." He looked over my shoulder at a flat spot on top of The Keep. "How's that for a place to land, Jason?"

"That's what I was thinking. I've always wanted to set down up here and just have a look around. Never have, though."

"Come back in about four hours," Gio told him. "We're going to have a little picnic and take pictures."

"That's an awful lot of stuff in your packs. Kate must be quite the cook or quite the photographer."

We didn't want to advertise what we were doing to the whole family, which was as good as telling the entire county. Gio looked into my eyes and smiled. "Oh, she's good at many things." He kissed my hand and leaned toward Jason. "We want to take a look around up here. We brought some climbing gear too, just in case we find some tricky spots."

With the aircraft landed, Jason said, "You guys be careful. It's a long drop and the stone of The Keep isn't very stable. Or that's what they say. I don't want to have to come out here with a recovery team."

Gio hopped out and took our backpacks as I passed them, before helping me down onto the rock surface. The helicopter was a lawn blower, trying to dislodge a quivering leaf—that would be me—from the mesa. Gio held my hand firmly until Jason lifted the bird gracefully into the sky.

I walked with bowed knees, trying beyond reason to increase the contact area of boot soles to stone.

The view was stunning. The Devil's Maw on the other side of the canyon had a comparatively benign appearance from this vantage point. The rock from which I had sketched the castle lay far below our current location. The "teeth" of the maw were a series of long wedges reaching all the way to the canyon floor. Once a prehistoric cylinder of molten rock, it had split like firewood and portions had crumbled away to rubble at its foot.

I was still shaky, but the herbal anti-anxiety tincture I'd used was helping steady my nerves to a certain degree.

"I've got you, Kate, and you have so got this." He put his arm around me protectively.

Every so often I flailed my arms for balance, sure I was walking on a moving surface. But he was right, with him by my side, I was steadier than I ever would have imagined.

The top of The Keep had little in the way of vegetation. Here and there, tufts of grass or small cedars and an occasional scrubby pine grabbed hold of what soil they found inside narrow crevices. They would not provide a sturdy anchoring point for our gear.

We kept to the center of the plateau as we systematically checked for a way to enter The Keep.

"What did he say?" I pulled the leather scroll from my pocket. "*Scale*. Scale?"

"Skah-lay. It means stair steps."

I butchered the next group of words, knowing I hadn't even come close.

"*Buco della serratura*. It means keyhole. We need to search for something that looks like stair steps and a keyhole."

"Great. Stairs to a keyhole. A keyhole would be on a vertical surface. How are we supposed to see a keyhole on the castle if we're on its roof?"

Gio turned in a circle and then pointed across the chasm. "The *Trappola del Diavolo*, the Devil's Maw. Think about your drawing, Kate. The keyhole would probably be visible from over there. You couldn't see it with your physical eyes, but your mind's eye. What did your mind see on The Keep that looked like it might be a keyhole?"

I closed my eyes to picture The Keep from the perspective of the Devil's Maw, and my drawing of the castle I'd been guided to create. "It's on the right side of the sketch. One of the arrow slits has a roundish hole connected to the top. That would put it roughly over there." I aligned my arm in a southwest direction.

"Okay. Let's get our stuff and head that way."

The closer we got to the ledge, the more my gut felt like I'd chugged a pound of clarified butter. Where was that barf bag now?

Gio took one look at me and soothed, "Deep breaths, Kate. It's not getting less scary than it is right now."

Did I say soothed? "Thanks for that," I muttered, clutching my stomach.

"Feel the fear and do it anyway—or you can always just wait it out up here while I go in. It's up to you."

"You know I can't do that. Your people came to me. I don't understand why, or even how, something so loose-lug-nuts crazy could happen in the first place, but I think they chose me for more than waiting it out up here." I clutched his arm to steady my vertigo-dizzy sway. "Besides, who's going to keep me from falling off of this thing if you're down there?"

"All right, then. Think about finding Tony for Juliana, and stop thinking about everything else."

"Okay." I took the tincture from the pocket of my puffy vest and squirted a dropperful under my tongue.

"I love you," he said, and kissed me.

"I wuff oo too." I had to hold the vile tasting stuff in my mouth for thirty seconds and hadn't swallowed yet, but he understood what I meant. At least I was given one more chance to tell him before—

"Nothing bad is going to happen."

"I'm sure Tony thought that too." At Gio's scowl, I did as I had been instructed and started breathing slowly and deeply.

When we arrived at what looked like the edge of the universe, the place I had imagined the keyhole to be beneath, I sat down. Gio lay flat on his stomach, head jutting into space off the ledge looking down. His laugh echoed from the canyon walls. "*Bella*, you've got to see this."

"Have you lost your freaking mind? You want me to dangle part of my body over that?" Sweat surged from every pore.

"Seriously. Lay down like me and scoot over here. It'll be all right. Really." He patted the earth beside him with a come hither expression. "And, sweetheart, you'll be dangling a lot more than that in a minute."

I glared at him in suspicion while I gingerly moved from my seat to my belly. "You really do learn a lot about a person in life or death situations. You are enjoying this entirely too much." I could have crushed the protrusions I gripped, if they weren't, well, part of a big herking rock. I felt lucky to be wearing the special gloves Gio got for me, because I was sure my hands were wet and slippery—like a seal's. Centimeter by centimeter, I slid into position, brushing Gio's shoulder, and peeked over the edge. I figured if nothing else, I might find a convenient place to vomit.

But it wasn't a sheer drop-off at all. It actually did look like steps here, almost as if they had been chiseled for the sole purpose of leisurely walking down the face of the cliff. The puzzling part was that, from the other side of the valley, or presumably from down below, you couldn't make out the stairs at all. The rock face above them had so many angles and crags, it must have somehow disguised the pathway.

The 'stairs' were only about two feet wide. Plenty of space to walk on, if you were a ram.

Despite my ninety-proof Celtic blood, I'd never heard actual keening, but I was pretty sure I keened at the sight.

"Don't worry, *cara*. I saw some perfect anchor points up here. You get a harness on you and it'll be just like the climbing wall at the gym. I promise."

"And there's a big, squishy cloud to break my fall down at the bottom too, I bet."

"Whatever makes you feel better, Kate. We'll get you ice cream when we're done, too."

I swallowed hard, scooting backward at Gio's lead, and sat upright again. "With sprinkles?"

"And a cherry on top."

There were three boulders, each nearly the size of a Smart Car, about twenty feet from the ledge. They snugged together like a puzzle. One of them was a rounded triangle, with a top point that jutted slightly outward, while the other rocks leaned their weight downward against it. Gio took a length of wide nylon webbing out of his pack and wedged a loop of it between two of the rocks and over the protruding part. He did the same with another strap and tied them both at the bottom of the anchor rock. Each strap had a metal ring firmly attached.

"This thing is rooted to the magma layer, Kate. The straps are sturdy enough for a grand piano, and I've doubled them just for you."

"Just what are you trying to say, Giovanni DiMarco?"

"Funny, Kate. No, they're doubled so you feel safer, that's all. And I got my knots badge, you know, so this baby isn't moving."

"They have that? A knots badge?"

"I don't think they let you out of Boy Scouts without it." His arm compressed me in his embrace, easing my jitters. "There's no better anchor than this setup. Okay?"

My head against his chest, him holding me together once more, I was lulled into agreeing to the unthinkable. "Okay."

I had expected The Keep to be solid on top, with some sort of shaft in the middle channeling light to the pond's cave below, but that wasn't it at all. Like the boulders Gio had anchored to,

The Keep was actually a network of stones fit together tightly like a free-form Rubik's Cube. But some of the blocks didn't fit so neatly. It was volcanic in nature—what had once been a core of cooled lava—but countless centuries had allowed cracks to form. With seismic activity over eons, a spider web of fissures opened in places, so deep you could see several feet down. There was no magic portal inside from the top, however, that I could see. I wondered if all of the light Gio saw that night somehow filtered through these cracks. "Are you sure it's safe to go inside? What if the mountain decides it doesn't want people crawling around in its bowels and caves in on us?"

"Thinking too much, Kate. Why don't you sing a song or something while we sort out the gear?"

I cleared my throat and tentatively sang, "Nobody knows the trouble I've seen . . . "

Gio and I continued unpacking our equipment. Between our two jumbo-sized backpacks, we had enough ropes and devices to reach well beyond the floor of the canyon. More than sufficient, we hoped, to support us on the inside.

Gio asked, "Are you sure about this? We could wait until Jason gets back and have him belay us down."

"Aldo and Tony kept it quiet for a reason. I wanted to tell your parents and Nonna because it just felt like Juliana wanted them to know. But the fewer people involved, family or not, the better, I think."

A cloud in the sky was almost heart-shaped. I smiled. "There was a reason Aldo didn't want to establish himself as the local deep-pockets, and it wasn't greed. He wanted for people to stand on their own feet, but he helped them get off to a good start. He didn't mean to become an important man, or have some charity named after him. He wanted to teach a town to fish, not open a Red Lobster food bank. If you think people come to you for help now, think what it would be like if everyone in town knew about his fortune? As The Keeper of the castle, and the legal owner of this property, you would have control. You and I and your parents can see that it will be used to help the lives of others in the best way, just like Aldo did."

"I can pretty much picture a mess of lawsuits from descendants laying claim to whatever is in there"

"I think your family is pretty perfect. They get along so well. That probably wouldn't happen, would it?"

"Yeah, well, you've met the nice ones," Gio's roar of a laugh echoed through the canyon and called back from the other side.

"Holy crust! You mean I haven't met all of them?"

"Not by a long shot." Gio held my harness for me to slide into. "Just like all family trees, we have our share of nuts and bad apples."

He checked and rechecked all of the equipment before letting out cable a little at a time as we returned to the edge. Resuming our belly-crawling position, we looked over to plan our descent.

"It looks like we don't even have to belay down." He looked at our legs side-by-side. "Or at least I don't, but, of course, I will. My legs will almost reach if I go feet first from my stomach."

I felt sick again. "You'd do that? Dropping down there without seeing what you're doing? I can't watch you do that."

"Kate, I need you to watch, to make sure my foot is aiming for the right place."

"Oh, Hell O'Kitty." I closed my eyes, inhaled deeply, and released my breath slowly. "At times I really hate when you're right."

Humming "Hakuna Matata," I clutched tighter to whatever rock protrusion I could find—as if that would make him safer—and watched with one eye closed as he eased over the side.

"Okay, you're there. You need to slide straight down another foot or so."

He slid, grasping the cable that was way too slack for my comfort, until his foot reached the solid surface. "It's nice and wide, Kate. You could roller skate on this patch right here."

I felt my pockets. "Sorry. Must have left my skates at home." Without further drama, I got into belay position and Gio stepped down one level to make room, holding my rope to guide me into place. Our disparity in height made my descent seem longer, but because I faced the rock with him guiding me down, it was oddly less heart-stopping than watching him had been.

I kept my line of sight ahead, taking cues from Gio, trying not to focus on the route to my imminent, skeleton-smashing death.

The steps were uneven, and not what you could really call a stairway, because, more than once we had to rely on our equipment to lower us slowly down to the next level. As long as I didn't obsess, I was able to keep my breakfast down and not launch—poor choice of words—into an emotional tailspin. There were three such drops in a row, and a series of levels we could walk down before we got to what I had sketched as an arrow slit. Aldo's description had been more accurate, though. Its merged shapes of circle above and narrowing rectangle below really fit his term for it.

The area of the steps that aligned best to it was about six feet below the slit. Gio cinched up the slack in his rope so that it held him securely. Every time I got a solid foothold up toward the opening, he winched my cable tight to hold my position for the next one. He pushed upward on the bottom of my boot to provide the final bit of leverage. I fit comfortably inside the hole, which was low enough for Gio to barely look into. "Do you see anything to anchor to in there?"

34.

Inside Job

Iwas a hamster in a tube, crawling with determination and stubby limbs to an unknown destination. The lamp on my helmet lit the way like a colonoscopy camera until I came to a sharp turn.

I mentally ticked down Gio's checklist of specifications for anchoring. The fissure at the bend was clean, uninterrupted by adjoining cracks, and separated otherwise solid, stable stone. I inserted cam anchors loosely into two separate spots for added strength and made sure they fit snugly, but not too tight. Only what was necessary for them to grip the stone firmly when resistance was applied.

"Are you sure about letting me do this?" A choir of soprano echoes assaulted my ears as I called to Gio. After attaching a carabiner and rope, I placed my boots on either side and leveraged against the wall, yanking and twisting with all my strength to test its hold. It would support me; that I knew. Now all it had to do was carry the weight of the big dude loitering out on the Express Stairway to Heaven.

"Well have I taught you, young Padawan." Gio's Yoda voice breathed in my ear, amplified by the long, stone conduit separating us. "*Know* you what you are doing."

By the time he cleared his throat from the screechy recitation, I popped my head out and fed the cable to him. "Much fear do you sense in me?"

"Nah. You're not afraid, Kate. Besides, it's me out here on the ledge." He clamped the new cable to his harness and clicked the winching apparatus to tighten it, then sprang into the hole under his own power, like a striking snake. "And, seriously, you can't fall anywhere with me here. I'm like a cork plugging this thing up."

Our headlamps clanked together when I stretched forward for a kiss, and the light dimmed until we separated. "Why do you look so—I don't know—so uncomfortable?"

"I'm all right."

I scowled in skepticism.

"Really. I'm good. I'm just reminding myself there's plenty of oxygen for both of us."

"Gio, what's the matter? You're having trouble breathing?"

"I was breathing just fine till you said that." He gulped in a series of short breaths. "Did I mention I'm a little nervous in tight spaces?

I gripped his shoulder. "I'd think this was hilarious, if I didn't need you to get me out of here later, Mr. 'feel the fear and do it anyway.'"

"I'm doing it, aren't I? Lead the way, already. Okay? I'll be fine once we start moving. At least from this end, I'll be the first one out."

Leading required crawling backward about ten feet to where the tunnel opened up enough for turning. With the expanse between us lengthened now, Gio's breathing became less labored. I went on solo and waited at the wall on which I'd placed the anchor. "This turn is going to be a little tricky. See if you can take your pack off. You're going to have to pass it around to me on the other side and then come through."

Pure torture filled his eyes.

"Don't worry. I know there's room. You might have to finesse it a bit, but you can do it."

His deep baritone reverberated through the stone amplifier

as he sang. "Nobody knows the trouble I've seen . . . " He wriggled out of his pack and slapped my bottom as I shimmied through the turn.

First a pack, then one arm, a tilted head, and finally the other broad shoulder presented on my side of the narrow passage. Gio's beet-red face turned upward with a grimace. "Push! Bear down! No wonder women make such a big deal out of having a baby." At last a torso, legs, and size 13 boots slithered their way out of the canal. "Can't be Disneyworld for the kid either."

I touched the racing pulse at his neck. "You made it through the worst part. I hope so, anyway." I shrugged at his rolling eyes. "There's a slight breeze coming through here, so plenty of air, okay?"

"Yeah. Got it." He unclenched his jaw and took a long, slow, meditative breath. "I'll be way behind you."

The tunnel seemed to go downward in a jaggedly spiral pattern, gaining breadth as we descended.

"Hey. Do you see that?" I stopped to allow him to catch up again.

"About all I can see now is a view of one fine caboose."

Turning off my lamp, I rotated to face him. "You're such a man."

He tucked a dangling curl from in front of my eye into my helmet. "Woman, I hope so. I was beginning to wonder for a while there, before this hot little redhead moved in across the street."

We clanked our heads together for another kiss.

"And I thought I was destined to be a man-hating cat lady for the rest of my life. Except for that dander allergy thing." I clicked off his headlamp and touched his heated cheek. "Do you see it now?"

A dim light filtered into the area from somewhere ahead.

"Does that help the claustrophobia at all?"

"I'm not afraid of the dark, Kate. I just don't like closed-in spaces, that's all. I still feel like an intestinal blockage in here."

I wrinkled my nose. "Ew."

"Yeah, well, let's go for some forward movement. Now, please, *bella*."

"Ha. You said 'movement.'" I snickered like an eleven-year-old boy and continued ahead.

The light grew brighter and the space opened up gradually as we forged on, until we came to a brightly lit cavern. Our tunnel overlooked its floor from high above, yet the room vaulted even higher to a canopy of mottled stone.

Gio sat on the edge, his shoulders relaxing at the sight of the immensity. "*Grande sala da ballo.* The grand ballroom." He pulled Aldo's map from my pack and unrolled it. "See? He's got it right here."

The domed ceiling overhead streamed light through gaps of varied width amid the mammoth stone.

Interlacing my fingers with Gio's, I took in the amazing view, comparing the setting to Aldo's crude drawing. "Kind of like being in a capitol building, isn't it? With little windows in the dome that brighten everything."

Gio lifted my hand to point upward. "And there are the chandeliers." White stalactites draped elegantly from the ceiling, brightening the space even more with their reflective properties.

All around the large cavity was a series of openings, leading off in different directions. "This reminds me of an old black-and-white movie I saw when I was a kid, about Christians, lions, and gladiators." I looked from one opening to another. "In the film, danger lurked behind every door that opened onto the arena." I giggled. "With my limited understanding, I thought of it as the ancient Rome version of *Let's Make a Deal.* Would the Christian get the lion behind door number one or the team of stampeding horses behind door number two? But wait, he could trade them both for a chance to fight the gladiator!"

"Game Show Network?"

"Yeah. I had a sitter one summer who watched that stuff all day, every day. She took up almost the entire loveseat in front of the TV." I shook my head. "I think my mom kept her because Ms. Sally was willing to take her cooking as payment."

Gio made a series of whistles, chirps and maniacal laughs, just to hear the echoes. He looked around the cavern with its numerous passages. "Are we supposed to search each one? What now, O gifted one?"

"I don't think I'll know until we're down there." My boots, reaching only about halfway down the length of Gio's calves, swung back and forth over the ledge while we contemplated our next move. "I know you're thinking you can jump down there and catch me, but you can just scrub that thought from your head right now."

He put an arm protectively around me. "You know I'd do it, don't you? I'll catch you every time."

I leaned the helmet on his shoulder. "This is something I thought I'd never say to a man. 'It's not you. It's me.'"

"I promised we'd take every safety precaution, Kate. I'll set another anchor and we'll belay. Seems stupid to waste the rope when we don't know how much we'll need further on, but I'm not going to push you to do something you don't feel ready for."

"You keep saying that, and yet I find myself hanging off the side of The Keep, crawling through bat holes, and—most frightening of all—spending every free non-life-threatening, waking minute with you." I sailed a smooth oval rock out into the void, where it made a satisfying crack at the bottom. "No, you haven't pushed me at all, sir."

"I gave you the option of—"

"Yes, you did. You said I could let you do this alone. But you knew I wouldn't back down." I clicked my tongue on the roof of my mouth, then sighed in resignation. "And that's okay. Being pushed is good sometimes. Especially when you don't realize it's been done." I poked him in the ribs. "And you can wipe that cocky expression off your face. I take at least some credit for stretching my own boundaries."

Gio spoke in Italian with a clear tone of adoration.

"I don't know what you said, but it kind of makes me weak in the knees. We'd better get moving before I melt into a puddle of goo."

Red-gold rock debris littered the floor of the ballroom. Picking our way through it required attention and coordination. While my stature was a benefit for scooting through narrow spaces, I was at my usual disadvantage for this part of the journey.

Gio guided me by the hand while I stepped over a teetering stone. "Getting any feels yet?"

I shook my head without breaking concentration.

Stepping around the perimeter of the chamber was slow going. At each opening we came to, I waited for inspiration to hit me, but nothing so far.

Abruptly, Gio jerked and grasped my shoulders, spinning me to point toward the center of the room. "There's something over there."

"What kind of something?"

"On the flat, pedestal-looking rock. I thought I saw— yeah—it's metallic."

To save time, if not my dignity, I hopped on Gio's offered back before he waded through the rubble to the object in question. How he had even spotted it was beyond me. Literally, beyond me, with the two feet of elevation between us.

Billowing dust engulfed us when Gio's forceful breath exposed a mound of gold-foil-wrapped chocolate coins, topped by a Spiderman action figure.

"He did it. Your Grandpa Tony got this far!"

Under the pile of petrified chocolate, waiting patiently for this moment, sat an envelope. Gio opened it and read aloud. "Good for you, bambino! You've defied gravity like Spiderman to get inside The Keep. If I were a betting man, I'd say the person reading this note is little Giovanni DiMarco, all grown up."

Chills bloomed all over my body. "But how in the world would he . . . Gio, you were so little when he disappeared."

"I loved Spiderman." His mouth fell open and his face grew pale with a far off expression. "Grandpa gave me his old stack of comic books before I learned to sound out words, and so I'd sit on his lap and he'd read them to me. Every Christmas morning photo, until I was eight or nine, has me in a brand new set of Spiderman pajamas. There's even a picture of us both with matching PJs the year before he went missing."

The note continued. "Of all my grandchildren, and others in the family, you are the most curious and determined to find answers. Like me, you have a great love of our home. You will be The Keeper someday if I'm not mistaken. If I am in error, congratulations to whomever has made it to this point. You are much closer to finding the treasure of Aldo Castaldi. I know it is here somewhere. If I don't find it myself, I give my blessings to you and wish you luck. Use Aldo's fortune—or, rather, the Castaldi family's fortune—wisely, for doing the most good."

Tears washed tracks clean of the dust on Gio's face.

My time with him so far had revealed many things. There was heart-stoppingly handsome Gio, the goofy singing waiter Gio, the sensitive widower, serious businessman and devoted family man Gio. All of those things and more had slowly drawn me in, fighting like a fish on a line. None of that could have prepared me for seeing the vulnerable little boy in huge man form standing before me. Like the Grinch on Christmas morning, seeing him so moved by his grandfather's note, written with hopes of his reading it at this time of his life, made my heart grow three sizes that day. "Are you all right, *mon amour?*"

"I'm fine." He stood in silence for what seemed an eternity. "I don't know what to say. Wow. I mean, I don't understand. He hoped it would be me. Brings more questions than answers, doesn't it?" He hugged me tightly, squeezing my pack and its contents painfully against my back, then cleared his throat. "Did you just use an endearment? And in French?"

I sniffed loudly and wiped my wet face against his chest. "Surprised the holy heck out of me too. Could you find the bandana in my pack?" I blew my nose hard and took in a hiccoughing breath. "I only know kitchen French."

"Kate, you rarely even use my first name. This is a milestone and should be celebrated, don't you think? It's huge. What you said . . . It means, 'my love,' right?"

I lifted my chin in embarrassed defiance. "Actually, it does."

He emitted a low growl and pulled me in even tighter, placing a series of long, lingering kisses on my lips with the accompanying clank of our helmets. Then he paused to ask, "Who called you 'my love' in the kitchen?"

"That's not important, *chéri.*"

Groaning, he returned to the business of kissing, interrupted by interspersed words. "Seriously . . . Kate . . . Who—"

"Shh." I backed away suddenly, palm toward him, and closed my eyes. After a moment to clear my head, I spun in a counter-clockwise direction and pointed to a dark passageway, tall enough for Gio to walk through without hunching. "That one feels right. I think we're supposed to go that way."

He switched on my headlamp and did the same to his own before following me to the tunnel, mocking me in a high-pitched voice. "That's not important, *chéri.*" He laughed and murmured. "Speak French to me, Morticia. I love it when you speak French."

35.

Getting Deep

The dark tunnel pitched steeply downward and the wet stone floor was as slippery as ice. I was grateful for the aggressive tread on my climbing shoes. "I can't imagine your great-great-however-many-grandfather getting through this mountain with nineteenth-century equipment. He must have been made of cast iron." I ran my hand along the slick wall for balance.

"Parts of him, anyway," Gio muttered, slowing to give more space between us. "I guess if you beat the village bad guy and take his daughter when you're still a kid, you figure you can do pretty much anything."

He took the lead when the slope became more treacherous. "Be careful. A super slide could be fun—except we don't know what's down there."

I shuddered. For all we knew, this slide could send us sailing out to the open air for the rest of our short lives.

What we did find at the bottom was another chamber, sunlit through crevices overhead. This was no ballroom, but open enough to put Gio at ease and cozy enough, with the rich red of the rock glowing like fire, to be a comfortable place to rest.

I sat on Gio's proffered knee and opened the map. "*L'Inferno*. This must be it." I wiggled around so I could see him, the clunky headwear having blocked most of my peripheral vision. "I don't like it when things go too smoothly. I'm waiting for an Indiana Jones moment to happen."

"Booby traps? That would be awesome!" Gio rubbed my back. "Maybe you should rethink your stance that 'going smoothly' equals 'bad.' For instance, the thing between us has gone pretty smoothly—"

"Smoothly? What about—"

"Except for a little misunderstanding about property ownership, which we will find a solution to—and my dead relatives climbing into your head—it's gone beautifully, don't you think?" Gio brushed an escaping tendril away at my neck and placed a series of light kisses there, with a minimum of helmet-tapping.

"Except for that, yes." I closed my eyes, trying to concentrate through the pleasant distraction. "Just your average, every day fraud with a large side-order of poltergeists. No biggie."

"My point is that, for once in your life, I think you need to let go of *the worst that could happen* and open yourself up to the possibilities of what is meant to be."

"Trust me. Acknowledging all of this—a man in my life, which is oddly more terrifying than the weirdo hocus-pocus that comes with it— is about as open as my neurotic little mind can get. Any more open, and my brain will fall out."

Gio squeezed me in an enveloping embrace and changed the subject. "I don't see any signs of Tony, do you? He wasn't lucky enough to have Aldo in his head—or at least, as far as we know. He would have had to search by trial and error."

I nodded. "And Nonna said his fascination with rock climbing came as a sort of mid-life crisis. Maybe it took him a long time to figure out something might be here, and longer to find the way in."

"We know where he intended to go, at least. I think we should continue moving toward the treasure. That's all we've got to go on." Gio drank deeply from his water bottle and handed it to me, perusing the map further. "So it looks like the next stop is the *cuore di fuoco*. Heart of fire."

"It's close." I took a gulp of water and rubbed the coolness of the bottle against my warm cheek. "He did have a flair for naming things, didn't he? This place looks just like the inside of a furnace. The heart of fire can't be too far off, right?"

"You're asking me?

My eyes narrowed at him before I closed them to clear away everything but the 'vibes'. Aldo was holding back. I felt a tiny tug in a general direction, but he wasn't going to lead us with the big picture. Maybe that wasn't even in his wheelhouse. Every other time he played a 'scene' in my head, we'd already been at the location in question. The 'tug' pointed toward the only outlet from the inferno. "Thanks, Aldo. You're a flipping worldwide web of information."

Gio assisted me to my feet as he stood and stretched. "What's great-great-whatever-grandpa saying now?"

"His lips are sealed, but he's getting anxious for us to keep it moving."

The passage was tall and narrow but well lit, a crevice that went all the way to the upper reaches of the mountain. No sky was visible through the undulating lines of the crack, but the bright oranges and reds were afire, illuminated by the sun somewhere above. Because of the tight fit, navigating could only be accomplished by sidestepping.

The cleft narrowed dramatically at the six-foot mark—face-level for Gio—while I had a much wider margin down in the toddler section.

"Sure! Of course the way had to be through here." Gio attempted various bent-leg stances to get his head in a more phobia-friendly position, but ultimately, he had to sidle through with his nose inches away from stone. "How . . . much . . . more . . . of . . . this do you . . . think?" His words wheezed their way out.

"I don't really know. Shouldn't be too long, right?"

"You're the one on the psychic hotline. Dial him up and see

what he says."

"It doesn't work that way and you know it." I held fast to his hand and whispered. "Slow, deep breaths, Gio. You're doing fine."

Fortunately, our journey through the gash in the rock was over before Gio lost it completely.

His face froze when we entered a small alcove; clearly he had been wishing for something more commodious. He paced laps around the outer edge of the area. "Nothing here looks like the heart of fire to me. What do you think?"

I strode along with him, getting my ancestor bearings in order. "Yeah. We definitely need to keep going. I'm just not sure if we should take that way, which means more of the tight-squeeze, or there. That one looks better."

"You know what my opinion is on the matter, but I'll suck it up either way."

"I'm kind of enjoying your struggle."

He leaned over with his hands on his knees, catching his breath, and gave me some serious side-eye.

"That didn't sound right. I mean, I wouldn't wish that kind of angst on anyone, because I so get it, but at least I know I'm not the only one. We kind of go together like Almond Joy"

"What? Like a couple of nutty bars in a wrapper?" He raised up enough to kiss me. "See what I've been telling you? We go together like New Year's Day and Jenny Craig."

I couldn't help giggling. "Like a T-Rex and tiny arms. You're Rex. I'm the arms."

He walked some more, his movements loosening with each step. "Like a Nicholas Sparks movie and every other Nicholas Sparks movie."

"But *The Notebook* was really good. Stop rolling your eyes. It was." I walked back and forth between the two alternate routes. "Like Mario and Luigi."

"Looking for the princess in the dungeon. Nice." Gio

laughed. "Now I'll have the game music stuck in my head for a week."

The laughter visibly eased Gio's tension until he finally stopped to ask, "Anything yet?"

"Yeah, you're in luck. We get to go on the super highway, not the little slice of hell. That way."

Gio sighed in relief. "There is a God, and He loves me."

Not long after entering the chosen track, we came to a fork. Both choices reflected the same warm orange hues caused by the streaming sun overhead. From where we stood, there was no physical advantage to either. I leaned against the stone between them, a hand placed near each one. I pictured Aldo in my mind, trying to decide himself. Still not in the mood to help, my little Italian hallucination left me stranded there without so much as a *buongiorno*.

I attempted to clear my mind of all thought and waited for a sign. Still nothing.

"How could we have taken a wrong turn? I was sure we were supposed to come the way we did."

"Maybe they join, and it doesn't matter which way we take."

"That's a possibility." I concentrated, willing a movie to show me the way. Crickets. "Holy Cranapple! Thanks a lot, Godfather. You couldn't make it easy, could you?" I rolled my eyes in impatience. "All entitled, right? Now that I've had his help, it's suddenly become my *right*."

A warm sensation filled my chest and I had the answer. "He wants us to figure out this part ourselves. He wants us to find the heartburn and it's in one of these tunnels.

"You go right and I'll go left. Let's call out to each other and keep going until we can't hear anymore. If we haven't found anything by then, we'll come back and regroup."

"Got it!" Whistling the Mario Brothers' theme, he disappeared into the void.

"Halloo!" There was that chipmunk voice of mine again, piercing my ears like a tattoo artist. "Can you hear me now?"

"Yes, *cara*. You hear me?" Gio's voice was still strong. Of course, I'd probably be able to hear him all the way from town.

"Do you see anything?"

"Not yet. How about you?" He was further away than before, but was in no danger of fading out. "Wait! Problem solved, Dead end."

"What?"

His voice bellowed as it drew closer. "The tunnel ends. There's no way to go forward."

I stopped in place and waited.

I covered my ears as he approached. "Inside voice, please. I hear you."

The high-pitched sound of the game's tune expanded until he popped his head around a bend in the tunnel. "No heartburns there."

"One down. It's got to be this way, then."

We twisted back and forth through the serpentine pathway, finally arriving at another fork. "All right, Aldo, I could use a little help here, if you don't mind." Again, one way looked pretty much like the other, more of the rich russets, burning bright with highlight and shadow.

Gio slipped his hand into his pocket. "Let's flip for it."

"No. Sorry. That's not going to—I know there's something we're supposed to be seeing, like, hiding in plain sight." Furrowing my brow in concentration, I tried to force an impression to come to the forefront of my brain.

"*Cara*, you're going to pop a blood vessel that way."

"I don't know what to do." I looked from one tunnel to the other one more time. Still nothing.

Gio followed me in circles as I grasped for anything that might be even close to one of Aldo's little scenes. "All right. It's either one of these paths. But you've gotta decide."

I whirled on him. "I know! I thought having ghosts in my head was hard, but not having them right now is . . . is . . . I think I'm having abandonment issues."

We continued to pace as I considered each choice before me. And then I saw it.

"Right there. No, come over here to look."

Gio crossed to me and crouched to my eye level to look down the tunnel on the left. The protruding ridges within the opening curved in graceful lines from high above to the floor of the cave. On one side of the tunnel, a brilliant orange ridge swooped in a lopsided arc. The other wall arched a darker red in the opposite direction. From other perspectives, this path only looked like a zig-zaggy route through the crevices. But standing right here, the two arcs appeared to meet gracefully at the bottom, forming Aldo's favorite shape.

"Cuore."

"Heart of Fire." The warm feeling in my own heart returned, confirming what I knew to be true.

Gio pulled me in front to lead the way. "Let's get a move on, boss. I think you've got your mojo working again."

Once past the illusion of the *cuore*, through a series of switchbacks, the pull grew stronger. "We're getting warmer. We're almost there. I can tell."

I stopped short.

"What is it, *bella*?"

"We're almost there."

"You said that."

"Yes, I did." My knees locked and I was frozen still.

"Then, what? What is it, Kate?"

"Oh, holy . . . Here we go again." Tears welled and spilled out in torrents. "What is *wrong* with me?"

"I'm pretty sure this is one of those 'does this make my butt look big?' moments. Maybe you should tell me what's wrong."

I sucked in a shuddering breath before blubbering, "I think I'm coughing up another fur ball!"

36.

Stirring the Hive

Gio's theory about long-suppressed emotions, good and bad, coughing up together in one big, uncomfortable clump, was starting to make sense. This chunk was big enough to choke a moose. These sensations couldn't all be mine, could they? All I knew was that I was swamped, overcome, completely engulfed by a huge case of the feels.

"Talk to me, *cara*." Gio leaned me away with a gentle shake.

I convulsed in a sob. "I'm trying." I rested the top of my helmeted head against his chest, swallowing hard, inspecting my shoelaces. "I know we have to go forward, that we're at the point of no return. Once we find Aldo's stash, everything will change."

"Agreed. So what's the problem?

"I'm not sure there *is* a problem." I broke free and lurched toward what I knew to be it. Aldo's legacy. After a few steps, I snapped to a halt and returned, shifting from foot to foot. "There's a hive stirring around in me, and each honeybee represents a unique emotional response. I wish there were a way to better articulate it, but how do you describe something so bizarre? Bees are the only thing I've got."

"All right. Name me one bee."

I walked forward again and then back, stretched my neck from side to side, and shook out my arms. "Excitement. See? I told you they're all kinds of things. Not all bad."

"Excitement. Good. I'm excited too."

I took Gio's hand and inched ahead slowly. "Fear. No, terror."

Gio's voice soothed, "More terror than you had on top of The Keep?"

I considered that. "No. And yes. I'm not nearly as afraid of what lies ahead as I am of falling. I know that." I propelled him a few inches and stopped. "But there is a definite fear of the unknown screaming in there somewhere with the volume cranked up."

He nudged me another three steps toward our goal. "So that's not so bad, then, right? What else?"

I looked away as my cheeks flushed. "Well, the thing, the thing between us, is just about killing me right now. I mean, not in a physical way—although, now that I think of it, the physical way is, well . . . "

"I like that," he said.

"I'm not saying the physical thing is bad, but it's not the stronger of the two, you know?"

Gio laughed. "No, Kate. I'm a guy. The physical is always strong. You have to tell me."

I sighed. "Since you must know, I thought I loved you before—quit gloating—but right now I love you so much, I want to laugh and cry and dance. And I kind of want to make out too. All at the same time."

"Now you know how it's been for me since I first laid eyes on you!"

"Seriously?" Each footstep I advanced, taking Gio with me by the hand, cranked up the chaos level of the bees. "I don't know how you stand it. It's pretty horrible."

He pulled me up and kissed me forcefully. "Does that make it any better?"

I grabbed the straps of his helmet and kissed him back with as much enthusiasm. "What were we talking about?" The kissing resumed for a moment before I remembered. "Right. The bees. There is this gargantuan anxiety, a killer bee, that's nearly drowning out the others. I know anxiety, but this is completely unfamiliar. Like, of an African or Brazilian strain."

"I think the Brazilian ones are technically Africanized European bees." Gio shook his head. "Entomology badge. Never mind. *Bella*, do you think the bees will quiet down once we get to where we're going?"

"I don't know, but not moving doesn't seem to be working."

Gio loosened his grip, letting me slide to my feet, and gently tugged me along.

"Shame. Humiliation. I feel like I'm standing in front of my second grade class and I've just wet my pants."

"Aw, Kate. Did that actually happen to you?"

I stuck my chin up. "Maybe."

"I'm so sorry, sweetheart."

"It was my first day at a new school. Third new school that year alone. I always wanted a nickname, but Tinkle Toes wasn't one I would have chosen."

I held my breath and squeezed my eyes shut as he guided me around a tight angle for about thirty steps, where he stopped and snorted in frustration.

"Oh, *bella*. You gotta see this."

The way was blocked by a mound of rocks and debris that must have been blasted into place.

"No!" I shook my fist and shouted. "Really, Aldo? Seriously? You really are a sick little son of a Sicilian aren't you?"

"Calabrian," Gio corrected.

"Whatever." I sat on a stone and swayed back and forth to the rhythm of the bees. Kicking a bowling-ball-sized rock, I said, "Anger. Distrust. Grief. Those are all *my* bees, for sure, and have my father written all over them. And Aldo too, at the moment."

"*Cara!*" Gio snatched me away from the blockage and

shielded me with his body. "Did you see that?"

"See what? I kicked a rock and it rolled. That's all."

He pulled the back of my shirt when I went to investigate. "Not that rock. Did you see the big one move?"

"Big one? What are you talking about?" The pile of rocks looked the same as it had before, minus one.

"You stay put, Kate. Aldo did not bring you all this way to squash you like a bug." Gio held up his hand and edged back to the pile of rubble.

Knocking the hand away, I fumed, "What about you? He brought you too. Do you plan to be buried without me? Because I don't think I'm all right with that."

"*Cara*. Didn't I just say to—"

"Do you see what I see?" I pushed past Gio and bent down to the place I had been sitting. With the smaller stone kicked away, a larger one was freed to roll in a controlled way. It was almost disk-shaped, rounded on the edges to roll back and forth.

Gio kneeled beside me. "An explosion didn't cause this. There's a ton of engineering involved here.

"It's like the door of a sepulcher." I applied the slightest pressure and it rolled to expose a solidly supported threshold of an entrance, barely large enough for us to crawl through. I gave a double thumbs up to the air. "Way to go, Godfather! All is forgiven."

"I can't even . . . " Gio ran his hand along the load-bearing structure. "I pictured Aldo hiding his stash and never coming back. This took serious man-hours to accomplish."

I clutched my fists. "I guess this means we have to go through it now."

He gave my shoulder a squeeze. "I guess it does. Ladies first."

"Right."

We could smell it before we could see it. A rich bouquet of earth and moss saturated the moist air. An echo of trickling water punctuated the silence from someplace beyond. I waited as Gio extruded his way through the secret door. When he stood and we both turned away from the passage, our headlamps revealed the holy grail, the hiding place for Aldo's legacy. A stout oak set of doors displayed faceplates that formed a heart when closed. There was no mistaking the keyhole shape; it was fashioned into a crescent "C".

I reached for Gio's hand. "I think I hear harp music and choirs of angels singing."

Gio grabbed my hands and searched my face. "For real?"

"No. Of course not. What are you thinking?" I gaped at the doors, almost afraid to ruin the moment of triumph. At least I hoped the moment was triumphant. "I just can't believe getting here was this easy."

He stared at the worm hole he'd just come through. "Yeah. Easy."

"Helicopters, ledges and suffocating mazes notwithstanding, I'd say it was relatively straightforward."

"How are your bees doing?" Gio kissed the spot above the ridge of my nose, the closest thing to my forehead he could reach at the time.

I assessed before answering. "They're quiet."

"Good."

"No. I mean they are totally mute. More silent than before I knew they were there.

"What do you think that means?" Gio asked.

"I'm not sure, but I feel like—I don't know—like I've been through some sort of emotional cleanse." I interlaced my fingers with his.

"Exorcism by bee? *Bella*, this thing just gets weirder all the time."

"I'm not oblivious to the weirdness. And exorcism is the

wrong word. It's not like I'm an authority on paranormal activity or anything—I'm winging it all the way—but coming through that door felt more like a healing. No, not that either. A reset button being pressed? If I were to get really poetic, I guess I'd call it a rebirth. That's the closest I can come to it."

"Come here." Gio held me to his chest. "Happy birthday, *cara mia*."

"Thank you for being so accepting. You're a good man, Mr. DiMarco." His arms were home and I basked in their comfort and peace awhile before returning to the problem at hand. "Where did we put that key?"

"I thought you had it." Gio patted his pockets in wide-eyed panic until he got the reaction he sought from me. "Just messing with you. It's right here."

It was rough with rust and heated from having been held near Gio's heart. The touch of it in my hand brought a warm, reassuring sensation to my own core. The one that told me when something was good. "All right, Aldo, let's do this thing."

The key slid into place with ease, but it took Gio's muscle to rotate it to the open position with a resounding ca-chunk. The hinges—attached to beams that had been bolted to solid stone—resisted before shrieking open in disapproval.

Kegs, loads of them, lined the walls of the vault, stacked five high and an undeterminable quantity deep.

Gio hefted one down to the floor with a groan. "Man! What an anchor." He inserted a flat screwdriver tip, from his pocket multi-tool, under the lid and pried the top off. "*Che diamine*! Kate—"

"It's gold. Oh my gosh, Gio! These are Italian gold coins!" I scooped out a handful for inspection. "Twenty-lire pieces, solid gold, and they're old!" I laughed. "Of course they're old. Aldo hid them here himself."

Gio's massive hands scooped out a larger sampling. "1855, 1862, 1849. Kate, not only are they solid gold, and old, they've been sitting in a hole for over a hundred years. They're in excellent shape."

I sprang into his arms and he threw me into the air in our best jitterbug lift while I squealed and kicked my feet.

Back on the ground, I asked, "What must they be worth?" I turned over each coin in my hand for more careful inspection.

"Think about it, Kate. I have no idea how much each is worth, but do the math about how many there could be."

It was unfathomable to me. "We'd have to count, of course, but let's just say there's 500 coins in each—"

"There'd have to be more than that, Kate. These are close to the size of a quarter. There's forty quarters in a roll and each roll weighs a half a pound. That keg must weigh one-twenty-five or more, and when you subtract the weight of the wood, let's say it's a hundred pounds of coins in each keg."

Gio's brows knit in concentration. "I haven't checked gold prices lately. But for collectors? You know that's got to bring the value way up."

I put my knuckles to my temples. "How many kegs are here? Oh, good gourd, my head hurts!"

Our view into the vault was limited with the small barrels crammed in, but our best guess was five high, five deep and five wide, or one-hundred-twenty-five casks altogether.

I pulled another one down to see if we could assume all barrels held the same thing. Gio reached to help me but was too late, I let the heavy container slide down onto my foot. "Gah! Holy shh . . . shin splints, that hurts like . . . Ow!"

Gio sat me down and removed my shoe and sock. "Can you wiggle your toes, *cara*?

I gingerly gave it a try. "Yes. It's not pleasant, but I can."

He pushed against the ball of my foot, toward my ankle. "How about this. Does it hurt?"

"No. I think I just got my toes."

"Oh, yeah, *bella*." Gio got closer. "You're gonna lose that toenail. It's already turning pretty colors." He brought it to his lips and kissed it.

"That is the weirdest thing anyone has done to my foot since I was a toddler." I pulled my foot away and snatched the sock from him. "And I think I like it."

"Just kissing it better. Don't worry. I'm not one of those foot guys." He pried the top of the offending barrel, which, as anticipated, was also laden with gold coins. "How the heck did he do this?

I shook my head. "He obviously came in from the top at some point. He led the way for us, after all. But that is not how he got in here over and over again. No way."

We walked in silent circles, pondering the mystery, the tinkling water providing a musical score in the background.

"Oh, no!" It finally occurred to me. I bounded back to the vault. "There's no note from Tony."

Gio ran his hands between the cylindrical stacks to look for anything that might be wedged in. "He didn't make it here, then. You know there'd be a note if he had."

"And chocolate coins, of course."

"Yeah, and those." He looked around the dark edges and frowned. "That really stinks."

"It's so sad." I wiped my eyes, before another flood could erupt, and sighed.

Again, we stood in thought, with nothing but the sound of cascading water filling the void.

Shoulders slumped, Gio shook his head. "The key. Even if he got all the way here, he would have had the wrong key."

"The one that almost fit, but wouldn't have done the job." I carefully put pressure on my foot, testing the pain level. "Now there's a whole new conundrum, isn't there? Exactly what did your mom's enchanted castle key go to, other than the attic?"

"Maybe it doesn't go to anything else. Maybe it was only wishful thinking on my grandpa's part."

I looked at my watch and fidgeted.

"What's the matter, Kate?"

"It's nothing."

Gio squinted an eye and raised his brow in skepticism.

"I was just estimating how long it would be before we're supposed to meet Jason."

"We've got plenty of time. Why?"

I shrugged.

"You have to go to the bathroom, don't you?" He folded his arms across his chest.

"Doesn't the water noise make you . . . You'd think that with five sisters, you'd be a little more under—"

"Shh!" Gio cocked his head to one side. "The water."

"That's what I've been telling you. The water sound is—"

"Do you hear where the sound is coming from?"

With an ear turned toward the tinkling, I moved my way past the vault to the other side of the cave, where another pile of rocks stood. "This isn't a dead end. There's more on the other side. That's where the water is."

We inspected and gently prodded the newfound pile, but, unfortunately, there was no sepulcher door here.

"Rats!" I clenched my fists, stomped, and groaned. "I'm so tired of this! Why does there have to be a puzzle at every turn? Can we go now?"

Massaging my shoulders, Gio wasn't about to let me quit yet. "Calm down. Why would there be a blockage here in the first place?"

When my tantrum blew over, I considered. "It could be nothing but a natural phenomenon. Just a cave-in."

"That's true. It could be." He took my hand and began to pace. "But, Kate, there's nowhere else to go but out the way we came, which brings us back to how the heck did Aldo carry all of this gold in by himself? He didn't have a helicopter, and if he did figure out how to climb The Keep, and then get to the keyhole without killing himself, he wouldn't want to make a regular habit of it."

"I don't know. I can't figure it out."

"Do that thing with your hand. See if it tells you anything. We're not done here yet."

The only thing I wanted to do with my hand right then was put my fist to his nose. "Why won't you just believe me when I say I'm done? I'm so done! I've never been more done in my—"

My hand lifted of its own accord, drawn to the wall like steel to a magnet. My feet had to follow or I was sure to be dragged along like a clumsy water-skier. I was pulled directly to the middle of the heap of stones, to an orb shape, larger than a foot in diameter, which was smoother and lighter in color than the other rocks. I touched it and sensed rather than felt a vibration emanating from it.

"Correct me if I'm wrong, but I'd say Aldo doesn't want you to be done either, *cara*."

"It's this one." I nudged the spherical stone and shot backward as it came tumbling down, fearing its rock buddies would follow. But they remained in place.

We got close enough to see that this opening, too, was soundly braced.

Gio slipped out of his pack, ready to blaze ahead into the new chamber.

I visually measured his broad shoulders against the opening. "You're not serious, right?

"I think I can—" He ran his palm around the inner perimeter of the opening then shook his head.

"*I'll* do it."

"But if something happens to you, Kate, I can't come through to help you."

An unseen brightening radiated outward from my center, confirming the truth of my thoughts, and I knew I had no choice but to go in alone.

"I think it's supposed to be just me. That's what he wants. And face it. We didn't bring any jackhammers to open that thing up any wider."

I finessed my way, barely making it through with my hips, and set my boots on solid ground. I winced at the pain in my foot, but didn't make a noise that might alarm Gio.

His baritone blasted through the hole. "Well? What do you see?"

"It's a grotto with a pool of water down below here. There's water coming down the face of a rock, but it also looks like there's some bubbling up from underneath."

"You can see all that with just the light on your head?"

"No. There's a light source down in the water." I stretched up on my toes and poked my head through to look at him with a grin.

"What do you mean, *cara*?"

"I mean, there's light coming in from outside, down in the water." I squealed and laughed in excitement. "The light shines in from a double-arched opening that meets below in a point!"

Gio's forehead furrowed before he put the pieces together in his head. "*Cuore*. You're on the inside of the cave that the pond goes into."

"I am. The moat to the castle in the drawing. I'm in the cave that Castaldi children for generations were warned to never, ever go near, for fear of their lives."

Gio found his phone and passed it through to me.

"Who am I supposed to call without cell service?"

"That's not what I had in mind." Gio laughed. "Take lots of pictures, sweetheart. We've got a lot of planning to do."

37.

Ins & Outs

Knowing the owner of half a town had its advantages, especially if part of his holdings included the historical Castle Springs Day Spa. Gio gave the staff three days off with pay, and closed the facility "for maintenance."

"The manager has been asking for a new filtering system for months anyway. We'll do what we need to do and then the pool company is scheduled to make the changes on Thursday after we leave."

What we needed to do was use the pool to conduct a series of experiments on how two people alone could best extract thousands of gold coins through an underwater cave without attracting attention.

On Tuesday, when Gio picked up the huge box of "equipment" from the back of my van and discovered it weighed almost nothing at all, he raised an eyebrow.

"Just wait until we get inside. I'll tell you all about it. Why don't you take my scuba gear? It's heavier. I'm so glad I hung on to it when I moved from my San Diego days. I knew I'd need it someday. I'm still certified too."

Once inside, he opened the box and hooted with laughter. "Pool noodles? You brought pool noodles?"

"I know it seems weird, but after considering all of our options—the challenges we've discussed—this seemed the best solution." I threw ten noodles into the pool. "They were easy to find on the internet and lightweight to ship. I get several packages every day anyway, so a few more aren't going to put anyone on alert." I stripped down to my bathing suit and took the stairs into the pool. The hot-spring-warmed water soothed the ache in my sore, but not broken, foot.

"They are hollow, and the coins will fit perfectly inside. Each one supports the weight of an adult, but we don't want it to float on the surface, we want neutral buoyancy. We need them to float a few feet underwater and not get hung up on the rocks above or below. We can attach them end to end, so we can feed them in a long chain, instead of carrying in a bunch of heavy, bulky equipment. And, the best part is, they come in lots of fun colors."

"Well, as long as they come in colors, then of course they'll work." Gio rolled his eyes dramatically.

"You brought the quarters?"

Gio pointed to a plastic bin in the corner. "I called the bank a few days ago to make sure they'd have enough. I told Jenny— you met Jenny at Nonna's party—I told her I had a plan for some awesome stocking-stuffers this Christmas."

"And she didn't think it was out of the ordinary?"

"Not at all. You've seen how many kids there are in the family. We all have to get creative." He dragged the bin over near the other containers. "Now you have to help me figure out what my awesome stocking-stuffer project is going to be."

We spent the next two and a half days working out the logistics of the retrieval process, but once perfected, we would need to work quickly. The colder weather would be coming soon, which would not only make going inside The Keep more difficult, it would also bring ski season, and the bulk of our year's livelihood. We both needed to be present when the onslaught hit.

On the eve of the big day, we spent much of our time on the phone, looking at one another through our apartment windows, as we thought of more details to discuss.

"You're sure your big, shiny SUV can get into the canyon in the morning, right?"

Gio sighed. "She may look too pretty on the outside, but Jolene can handle it. I haven't had her in there yet, but I used to take my old jeep down all the time."

"Your car's name is Jolene?" I waved my hand in the air in an exaggerated gesture, so he could see it. "Don't tell me. The jeep's name was Dolly Parton."

He laughed sheepishly. "It had very large headlights."

"Is there anything we're missing? I keep running through the routine in my head and I can't think of another item we might need."

"Everything's packed up and ready to go at daylight, *cara*. Get some sleep, okay?

There was only one way to get into the valley floor beneath The Devil's Maw, but to my way of thinking, it was more like *not quite* one way. After dropping some things off at the cabin, Gio bounced Jolene over rutted deer trails, cow pastures, fallen logs, and boulders until we came to rest at the pond's edge.

The amount of flotation tubes we needed to do the job weighed very little, but filled every available space in the vehicle. Gold, on the other hand, was dense and heavy. Several trips to the cabin would be necessary to transport its weight safely.

Gio had devised a system of large spools on which the noodles, strung on fine rope like a first-grade macaroni necklace, were wound. He talked me through the procedure one last time until all of the equipment was set and ready to go.

"Kate, I still don't know about leaving you here to do this by yourself. I know I'm abandoning you."

"No other way makes sense. We agreed about this, right?" I checked my scuba tanks. "You can't do the swim in, because you can't fit through the entrance, and there's no way to safely open it up without knowing more about the structure. And who knows what kind of tools it would take? You've done everything in your power to make my part easy. I've got this."

He fixed his gaze into my eyes. "Are you sure?"

I touched his cheek. "I'm sure, but can you hold me for just a minute?"

"Always."

On the day we found the treasure, we'd had the foresight to run a secured line down into the canyon for later use. I blew out my breath in relief. The climb would be much less dangerous than if Gio had had to start from scratch at the bottom, and would take a fraction of the time.

I was awed by his strength and agility as he made his ascent up the sheer cliff. Each time Gio found a foothold, I would secure the cable from below to support his weight. It hardly seemed necessary, though. You'd think the man had been bitten by a radioactive spider, the way he scaled the wall with ease. Still, I knew that many a skilled climber had made a fatal last move.

I swallowed hard, remembering that, likely, Tony had met his end like this. I whispered, "Don't worry. We haven't given up on you yet."

When Gio reached the keyhole, he called, "Hey, pretty lady, want to meet me downstairs in about an hour?"

"Let me check my calendar." I blew a kiss and he caught it in his hand. "See you there, Sir!"

I had no time to lose. I got into my wetsuit quickly, shivering in the chilly air. I tested the scuba gear once more, strapped it in place, tied a bag of supplies to my waist, and donned flippers.

I attached the rope from the first stringer of noodles to my belt and made way into the ice-cold pond. Entering the grotto through the underwater, heart-shaped opening went well. It wasn't until I climbed out of the pond on the inside and began tugging the chain of tubing that the trouble started. The tutti-frutti-colored line of foam had caught on something and wouldn't pull through. I secured the end of the rope around a rock protrusion and dove back in to check things out.

Sure enough, the noodles were hooked on the upper side of the heart. "Ahh! Not now!" In our experimentation, we'd failed to test empty tubes, assuming that snagging would only be an issue with the added weight of the gold. I thanked my lucky stars again for the air tank while I stayed submerged, manually feeding each piece of the colorful snake through to the inside. Once there, I pulled it the rest of the way and up onto the landing near the opening.

I swam back out to the SUV and repeated the process with the other spools until I had four piles of plastic linguini waiting to go inside. I tied the long ends of the four ropes together and pushed them through the hole, leaving the strung noodles in their piles.

Climbing in proved to be more of a challenge than the first time. The saturated wetsuit was slick, and without Gio's hand to grab on the other side, my vertically challenged state became infuriatingly apparent. I used the wobbly, squishy piles to give me a few precarious inches up.

The ropes, though not thick, added bulk. I was afraid Gio would find me stuck like Winnie the Pooh, but frantically kicking my legs gave enough momentum to pry my bum through.

Once there, I hauled the stringers of noodles in one at a time and set the supply bag next to them. From it I produced zip ties and a stainless steel tube with a flared end—a sausage stuffer that had been used in Mangia for generations.

Having learned my lesson about the heavy kegs, I climbed to the top of the stack and pushed two of them off, my feet safely out of the way. By the time Gio joined me, I'd funneled the contents of the four kegs into noodles and cinched the ends closed. I was also shivering so badly I could barely speak.

"*Bella*! You're not using your warmers. Sit down."

I smacked my forehead and replied through chattering teeth, "I was too anxious to get started. I forgot."

"Hypothermia, Kate. What are you thinking? Give me your feet." He rubbed them roughly to get the blood flowing, then took an airtight container from my bag. He put one pair of wool socks on my feet, activated the warming pouches, put them in a second pair of socks, and helped me on with those. He performed a similar act of kindness for my hands with wool gloves.

The efficacy was nearly instantaneous. "Thank your mother again for all of the knitting," I said. "And your dad for thinking of the warmers. I guess being scout master for you and the other Square Pegs taught him a few things."

Thus clumsily clad, but grateful for the heat, my job became holding the rest of tubes as Gio filled and tied them off.

He stopped long enough to kiss me. "Genius." He shook his head and smiled. "Pool noodles! I wouldn't have come up with pool noodles in a million years."

Back in the grotto, I received the now heavy-laden cylinders, as Gio passed them through the hole, and I dumped them into the pond. Thank all that is holy—they floated about three feet under the surface.

His head popped through, following the last noodle. "I'm going to stand right here until you've taken everything out to the other side."

"Why? There's no sense watching me if you can't get through yourself." I strapped my tank back on and left the wool socks on under my flippers.

"I'd knock the wall down to get to you and I'd—"

"Be buried under ten tons of rubble. Then we'd both be

dead!" I took his face in my hands. "Mon amour, Gio, wouldn't it make the most sense to start climbing back up now? Nothing's going to happen, but if it did, you'd be to me sooner."

"I love you, Kathleen Fiona Hannity."

"I love you too, Giovanni Castaldi DiMarco." I climbed back onto the heap of noodles, now much taller and more stable than before, and tenderly kissed the man I loved.

Swimming the coin rolls out of the grotto and tying the long strings at the other side went without a single hitch. When he returned, Gio would use his spool system, along with the winch on his vehicle, to pull the tubes out of the water.

"Ha!" I shouted in triumph. Gio balked whenever I used a kitchen knife as a screwdriver or an egg turner for scraping a wall, but sometimes what was available was way better than having the "right" tool. And what would have been *righter* than neon-bright, spaghetti-shaped pool toys for this job anyway?

I changed out of my wet things in the open air, cold as it was, and into the clothes Gio had sealed in an insulated container with another hot pouch. I climbed into the truck and fired up the engine, waiting for the heater to thaw me out.

I fiddled with the radio until I found the only thing that came in, *Radio Musica*, the Spanish language station. I listened to several salsa numbers, but when the second mariachi song came on, I pressed the off button.

It seemed like I should be seeing him by now. When had I gotten in the truck again? A half hour? Forty-five minutes? I couldn't just sit inside any longer. I killed the engine and hopped out to wait at the bottom of Gio's rope.

And wait.

And wait.

A waving bushy tail in my peripheral vision followed by a litany of excited chirping pulled me out of my fidget. "Mr. Squirrel! How are you today? He is taking a long time, isn't he?"

The squirrel bolted when he heard a wolf whistle and booming voice. "*Santi e angeli*! I've never seen a woman more beautiful in my life, Kate."

"You're beautiful too. You had me worried," I called up.

I thought I was going to pass out watching Gio rappel like an acrobat, pushing off and flying outward in sweeping stages all the way down the mountain.

He removed his harness and helmet and scooped me up in his arms, twirling me around like we were Patrick Swayze and Jennifer Grey. He deposited me gently to the ground, catching my lips with his and holding the kiss all the way down. "We did it! *Finito*!"

"Done! Except for getting it out of the pond, and ten trips back and forth to the cabin." I held him tight.

"No sweat, darlin'. We've got the rest of the day."

38.

Auction House

Gio chartered a plane to Los Angeles. Getting two brief cases full of gold through airport security was unimaginable, and we didn't dare go to an auction house in Colorado. The chances of Gio being recognized were far too high.

After giving the numismatics expert a couple of hours to inspect our sampling of coins, we sat down with him to hear the news."

Mr. Anderson reminded me of Alfred Hitchcock, with his bald head, puffy cheeks, and nasally British accent. "If this is, indeed, a dependable cross-section of the entire collection, then you truly have something quite remarkable."

I squeezed Gio's hand under the table.

The man hummed softly to himself as he looked at a coin under a brightly lit, fixed magnifying glass and set it aside to make notes in his little book. "These are in very good condition, considering their age. Not mint, mind you, but it is very rare to find twenty lire gold coins from the early to mid-eighteen hundreds that look like this."

Gio asked, "So, what do you think?"

Mr. Hitchcock—Anderson—did some figuring on his tablet and frowned in thought.

I said, "I don't like that look. Is something wrong?"

He looked up from his figures. "Hm? Oh, no. I think the value of this collection is quite high. Of course, you could ask much more for it if you had an interesting story to go with it. Where did you say you got them?"

"You wouldn't believe it if I told you," Gio answered. "Let's just say the coins have been in my family for a very long time."

I cleared my throat. "We really don't want to advertise the origin of the collection. We would like to remain anonymous. That's very important."

Mr. Anderson assured us. "Yes. Yes, of course. You might be surprised at the number of our lots that are sold anonymously. We take our clients' privacy very seriously."

After more fiddling with the magnifying glass and his tablet, Mr. Anderson looked up. "If the remainder of the coins are much the same as these, I feel quite confident that we can ask anywhere from four to seven hundred for them."

Gio's face fell in disappointment. "Four to seven hundred thousand? I really thought—I mean from what little I know about it—that this collection of coins was worth several million."

Mr. Anderson stared in incomprehension at Gio for a few seconds before replying, "Oh no, Mr. DiMarco. What I mean to say is that each coin is worth roughly four to seven hundred dollars apiece. These few that I've set aside are worth three times that. If there are many like them, your total would be much higher. You have counted them, is that so?"

Gio said, "Well, we've made a pretty close estimation, based on weight and volume. We figure there are somewhere in the neighborhood of nine hundred fifty thousand individual coins."

A smile slowly oozed onto both of our faces as we did the math. I whispered, "We're talking over half a billion dollars!"

We tried to maintain our dignity and not scream and dance on the table. Gio squeezed my knee.

"Of course," Mr. Anderson clarified, "That's an estimated auction value. If you were to find someone who was an avid collector, I think you could get more for it, especially if you had some sort of provenance to go along with it."

Anonymity be hanged! I was sure that, as far as Aldo was concerned, he'd want the biggest bang for his lire. We could do so much for so many more people. We'd have to deal with the fallout later.

I sang the details like a canary, too excited to hold back. "It originally came from Ruscello, Italy, in Calabria," I spurted out. "Gio's great-great-great-grandfather smuggled it over. He stole his family fortune back from a big mob boss and used it to relocate most of his village to a small town in Colorado. We have his diary . . . "

39.

Tying it Up

I stood in front of the old cheval mirror in Cici's sewing room. Nonna shuffled over, cradling something with her elegantly manicured fingers. "This is something very old. It cannot be your something borrowed, because now it belongs to you."

I took the gold locket Gio and I had found at the twisted tree. "But we gave it to you. These were your grandparents."

"And when I'm gone, there will be a hundred people who will want it, but I think my grandfather and Juliana would want it to go to you. They chose you."

"I don't know about that. I think I must have chosen them when I chose that building." I unclasped the delicate chain and put the locket around my neck.

"Ah, but you were not the first one to live there since Juliana's death. They recognized a special spirit when they saw you." Nonna and I stood next to each other and smiled into our reflections. "Your dress is lovely, my dear. I remember the day Juliana wore it like it was yesterday. Tony and I were cousins, you know."

Lace fashioned a demure Peter Pan collar and covered otherwise bare shoulders, bodice, and long, formfitting sleeves of the dress. The skirt flared from the fitted waist into a bell of satin touching the floor. I wondered how many young brides had worn similar gowns. I was sure I'd seen pictures of Elizabeth Taylor in one just like it. Though probably pure white when Juliana wore it, the now aged ivory tone suited my coloring better. On an online auction, I'd found a tiny vintage veiled hat. The color was perfect, even if the year in which it was made wasn't an exact match for the dress. Off-white gloves with pearl buttons at each wrist finished off the ensemble.

"Yes, I know. Fourth cousins, weren't you? I think Juliana was a little taller than me, but the fit is perfect. I feel honored to wear something Cici has kept so carefully all these years."

On cue, Cici entered the room from behind us, carrying a tray of lemonade. "I'd always hoped one of my daughters could wear my mother's dress, but I didn't inherit her small frame, and I married a big guy. It just wasn't in the cards for the girls. With the way you love old things, and the way it fits you, I know I was saving it for the perfect daughter all along."

Gio and I had been married that morning by Father Michael, with just our parents and Nonna present. We knew Nonna wouldn't be able to think of us as really married without the church ceremony. Now we would be having a bigger wedding out at the ranch for a much larger crowd.

Helicopters buzzed back and forth overhead, the thing we'd hoped to avoid by having the big gathering way out here.

When we'd sold Aldo's cache of coins to a private collector, we were sure that the transaction had gone off without revealing our identities. Sharing Aldo's story—or at least most of it—created a frenzy, and a bidding war ensued. The winning party made a YouTube video about the coin collection that had gone viral. Soon news outlets shared the story about a man in the eighteen-hundreds who once smuggled mob money from Italy and founded a town in Colorado—a town that, to this day, had a population makeup of fourteen percent Italian surnames.

At the height of tourist season, Castle Springs became flooded with the media and curiosity seekers.

Whether or not the new owner was aware of a possible

family connection to the fortune was unclear, but his last name was Santelli.

Before long, there were stories in the tabloids about the Castaldi Foundation, believed to be started by real estate entrepreneur Gio DiMarco. The foundation provided scholarships and funding for small businesses and agricultural endeavors in the Castle Springs area.

The articles cited an increase in funding to the Susan DiMarco Foundation as well, which had recently announced plans to build a new cancer center on the outskirts of town.

When two and two were put together, Gio and I became the target of paparazzi and rabid entertainment news outlets, who were in the area following the jet set at the ski resort.

My mother pinned my little hat down in the back and tucked a stray curl in. "You look beautiful, Katybug." She kissed my cheek and nudged me. "So you and Mr. Yummy had any *alone* time yet today?"

"Mother!"

"I'm just curious. I mean, a lot can happen between town and here, and it's been—what?—two hours?"

I hugged her and laughed. "Don't hold your breath waiting for the details, Mom. Not even the tent of truth could wear me down."

Life-threatening—and life changing—experiences had a way of bringing two people closer together, but when all was said and done, it had been Juliana who convinced me that everything would be all right if I married Gio. The very last night I dreamt of her, we were up in the attic, knitting another project for a child while Tony worked at his desk. She/we got up, stretched, and went to the mirror. She looked deeply into her eyes as she had before, straight into my consciousness. "You want this. You know you do. You will be happy. I promise."

I woke up that morning, realizing it was only two weeks

until the anniversary of taking ownership of my building—or almost taking ownership. On principle, I resisted the thought of getting married just to fulfill some weird rule that Aldo Castaldi set in place, but I kept going back to what Juliana had said. I'd be happy. I'd belong to a family and someday have one of my own. For once in my life, I'd have home and community in a way I'd never dreamed possible. And, though it did turn out to be a moot point, as Sylvia had predicted, my beautiful baby, Mon Petit, would be indisputably mine.

Of course, there was that little other matter, the fact that I was irretrievably, irrevocably, undeniably, madly in love with the deli guy across the street. I fumbled for my phone in the dark that morning and tapped in his number.

"You all right?" He said groggily.

"Yeah."

"Good morning," he growled as he suppressed a yawn, "or it will be soon." His voice had a smile in it, despite the hour.

We listened to each other breathe, as we sometimes did after saying goodbye at night.

Finally I asked, "How would you feel about getting married?"

"Right now? I think I need to shower and shave first, but—"

"How about Saturday after next?"

"I'll be there. I'll be the guy in the tux."

"You own one? Of course you do. I find that very sexy, you know."

"I'll be over in a minute."

I let him in the front door. His hair was sticking straight up, his face dark with stubble, and he was wearing a tee and the brightest plaid flannel pajama bottoms I'd ever seen.

I started to speak and he put his finger to my lips, picked me up and carried me upstairs. He got down on both knees, removed a small box from his pajama pocket and opened it to reveal a beautiful, vintage, three-stone diamond ring.

"Oh, Gio, it's beautiful!"

"My mother gave it to me for you. I had bigger stones put in it—they were tiny, and you deserve better—but the ring was hers. My grandmother, Juliana's. I thought, with everything that's happened, you might—"

I dropped and kneeled with him, face now hot and wet with happy tears. "It's perfect. You know it's perfect."

Gio kissed the tears away, wiping his own with the back of his arm. "Are you going to let me do this thing or what?"

"You're too late," I laughed. 'I already asked and you said yes."

He kissed me. "But I have something all prepared."

"You've told me a hundred times what you wanted—no, what you knew. It's my turn to say it."

I took his rough cheeks in my hands and gazed as deeply into his eyes as he was mine. "Gio Castaldi DiMarco. I never knew until now how it was to love and to be loved so completely, without agenda or reservation. You seem to want me, even with my bag full of crazy." I sniffled loudly. "I was afraid to let you in, and you gave me space but never gave up. I belong here, in this town, in this building, with your family." I smiled. "The live ones and the dead ones. But most of all, I belong with you, right here in your arms and in your life. Will you marry me and make me—and Juliana—so, so happy?"

She hit her mark. The floorboards above us squeaked as though someone were jumping up and down.

And that is how I proposed to Gio DiMarco.

It was standing-room-only downstairs. We got an even bigger event tent for the reception than there'd been for Nonna's party, but for the ceremony itself, Gio wanted me to walk down the grand staircase. This meant packing the family in like sardines, but they didn't seem to mind.

Cici, my mother, and Nonna took the elevator down together. Gina and Giada lined up in their adorable pink dresses. Pink was easy to do, and it made Nonna happy, or so everyone was convinced. Eloise had flown in with her husband and baby Max for the occasion. Her pink maternity dress hugged the new bump of her growing belly. She, Sylvia and Alyssa lined up behind the flower girls, ready for their descent.

Doug, my stepfather, asked, "Are you ready?"

I nodded silently as I took his arm.

Seeing the smiles of those in attendance brought that tight choking feeling to my throat as a fat tear escaped the corner of my eye. My part of the guest list was small. There was my mother and stepfather, Elle, my crew from the shop—but some of those were from the groom's family—and one guest I hadn't anticipated, Chef Henri Leveque.

Henri heard about me on the news and decided to pay me a visit. He wanted to see where I had landed and check out my chocolaterie. He had a show on the cooking channel now and invited me to make a guest appearance. He said that, with the current attention I was receiving, it would boost his ratings and be great promotion for my shop. I was still mulling it over.

Gio was surprised that Henri was not as old and hairy as my caricature implied. Truth be told, I think that made him a little jealous.

Actually, I thought Henri might be smitten with Sylvia. He'd certainly had her show him a lot of ski condos, and I suspected it might take him a very long time to decide on one.

For a fleeting second I thought I caught the smiles of four unexpected guests in the crowd: a woman in a bustled skirt, a man in a bowler hat and striped waistcoat, a beautiful, small woman in an angora sweater and circle skirt, holding the hand of a cool cat with his hair slicked up and back like a young Elvis. But when I returned my gaze, they were gone.

As I made my way down the stairs, trying so hard to do it gracefully, I saw my big strong groom smiling broadly with tears of his own. Oh, how I love a guy who is man enough to cry. Or to be more precise, I loved this one.

There was much dancing to the strangest variety of music ever played at a wedding in the history of all time. Of course, it included swing, boogie-woogie, disco and copious quantities of Barry White.

Every table had centerpieces filled with foil wrapped chocolate coins, embossed on one side with "Mon Petit Chocolaterie" and the other with "G&K forever."

The cake topper was a beautiful white chocolate angel, sculpted by Chef Henri for the occasion. I had to think of it as pure inspiration, because I would never in a million years tell him about the guardian angels who had brought Gio and me together.

During the rounds of toasts, Henri stood to say his piece.

"I have seen Kate blossom since I first met her. She is not the same sad little woman I remember at all. I have to admit, I have always believed in the restorative properties of chocolate."

The crowd chuckled.

"No. No. Really. It was learning to create chocolate that helped to heal Kate from a painful past. It was chocolate that brought her to your beautiful little town, where she met Giovanni—and don't let anyone tell you, ever, that there isn't a little love potion in exquisite, handcrafted chocolate."

Now the gathering burst into laughter.

"As I have always said, 'every day is a good one, as long as there is chocolate,' and I believe it." He looked at me with the smile of a proud father. "I am happy to have helped to create such a fine chocolatier, and I am even happier to have had a tiny, tiny part in helping to create a very fine couple. So much love, you can see it. May they, with or without chocolate, have nothing but good in their lives. And many babies!"

Sylvia's was the last toast of the evening. "Kate, Gio, I knew from the beginning that you were meant for each other."

The crowd emitted a collective "aww . . . "

"I did! You could see the fireworks from a mile away." She hushed the laughter. "I was the cause of some drama in your lives that almost wrecked the magic, and for that, I hope you can forgive me. I've been working hard to make it right, and, Kate, I have something to present to you today."

Marco set a heavy box down on the table in front of me.

"As you know, our family is steeped in tradition. Our ancestor, Aldo Castaldi, began one generations ago. It was his wish that once a piece of property came into the family, it was never to leave. We've honored that wish for almost a hundred-fifty years, and nearly every transfer of property has come with a written stipulation to that effect."

"Yes, I know." I took a sip of water and cleared my throat. "But you added another family tradition to my contract. Now that we're married, it nullifies the perpetuity clause. I'm fully vested in Mon Petit's building."

Sylvia waved my statement away with her hand. "That is absolutely true, but I—we—didn't think that was quite good enough." She opened up the box and held some pages in her hand." This box is filled with legal documents, signed by seven-hundred-sixty-two Castaldi descendants. I've spent the last six months collecting them. The family—those who have remained in the area—the family has decided that all perpetuity agreements pertaining to Castaldi holdings—including yours— are permanently rescinded. You didn't have to marry this moose to take full ownership—but I'm really glad you did."

The raucous cheers of the family—my new family—and the sound of clinking glass, filled the tent.

We decided that when we returned from our honeymoon in Calabria, we'd move out to the ranch to be near Nonna. John and Cici could use a break once in a while, and, honestly, we just wanted to take advantage of every moment we had with her. There was a cozy bedroom in the basement with enough privacy for us, and we planned to fix up the old cabin for regular newlywed getaways.

Nonna dabbed at her eyes as she wished us goodbye. "You have plenty of time to change your mind while you are away in Italy. I would never want you to spend the first days of your life together helping to take care of the needs of an old woman."

Gio bent and kissed her noisily on her wrinkled cheek. "I don't see any old women here. Just a little firecracker in a pink dress."

"Nonna, I barely knew my grandparents. I'm looking forward to you showing me how to beat Gio at pool." I held her hand. "I want to have lots of family stories to tell our children. You've got to help fill in the gaps where Tony left off."

While the party was still going strong, I ran back upstairs to make sure I wasn't leaving anything important behind. As I was searching the sewing room, someone downstairs began playing a soft sonata on the piano at the foot of the stairs. I wondered who played so well. When I got to the landing, the music stopped. There, sitting at the piano bench, were Aldo and Anna Maria Castaldi. Smiling, they looked up and waved before disappearing.

"Everything ready?" Gio waited at the bottom of the staircase.

"Yes," I answered, before getting an idea. "Catch me?"

He grinned like the Cheshire cat. "Always."

I thought of my father and the rope bridge break of my trust. Of Eddie, who had betrayed me in the worst possible way. I knew that Gio was different. That everything that had happened before had led to this moment.

He would always, always be there for me. I could be happily

independent and have happily ever after all at the same time because he was man enough to let me thrive. I threw my leg over the banister and slid down into the arms of my best friend and my one true love.

AUTHOR'S NOTE

Kate and Gio ruled the creation of AS LONG AS THERE IS CHOCOLATE. From the moment my fingers typed "Hey, lady!," I knew Gio was an Italian-American deli owner who admired a chocolatier named Kate, but their surroundings were a bit of a blur at first. One would naturally think of these characters living in New York, New Jersey, or Philly, wouldn't they?

Because I have no personal knowledge of big, northeastern cities—only what I've gathered from movies and TV—I set about finding a place for the story that was more within my scope of experience.

A defining school year of my youth waved its arms wildly to jog my memory.

After spending the first 11 years of my life in the Los Angeles area, I was temporarily transported to an alien, rural Colorado environment to endure seventh grade.

Until then, I'd never seen cattle guards or smiling strangers who waved as you drove by. I'd never seen a middle school with only eighty students or talked on a phone that had a party line. I hadn't yet sat at an old-fashioned soda fountain in a drug store, and I'd never encountered such a high concentration of people with Italian surnames.

I learned that many of the Italian-American families in the area were descendants of homesteaders. (The concept of homesteaders and their descendants was amazing for me at eleven. It was like something straight out of a Laura Ingalls Wilder book!)

When contemplating where to locate ALATIC, I wondered

if Italian homesteaders in Colorado were really a thing, or just something unique to the spot I'd lived in so many years ago.

As it turns out, apparently, they were definitely a thing.

A search led me to a document called "The Salida-Lago Connection: Pioneers from Lago to Salida," which can be found at http://salidaarchive.info. It is a history of a large immigration to Salida, Colorado from one village: Lago, Calabria, Italy.

Today 7.5% of Salida's population are descended from that group of immigrants, in a town with a makeup of 12.5% Italian surnames. The document has photos that show how similar the topography is between the two places. Salida must have felt like coming home to the Calabrians.

Considering these people and their lives brought about the creation of Castle Springs and its backstory.

Castle Springs is purely fictitious. However, there are parts and pieces of other Colorado towns I was compelled to include within. The name is a compilation of Castle Rock, New Castle, and Glenwood Springs.

A few details come from memories captured by me as an eleven-year-old and stored half a lifetime and are, therefore, not to be considered reliable. Other things about Castle Springs can be found in real-life Colorado.

For instance:

- Somewhere between Salida and Aspen is a scenic overlook that has stone "teeth" as described in "The Devil's Maw."
- Since a mine explosion over 120 years ago, an underground fire has been burning beneath New Castle.
- Glenwood Springs has a beautiful, historic, hot springs-fed swimming pool, and caves with stalactites and stalagmites.
- On a farm outside of Silt, Colorado, sits an intriguing stone formation, much like "the fairy ring." I know

about it, because I spent a night there once when I was eleven.

- Castle Rock has, well, a rock, that looks like a castle, if you squint really hard.
- Decades before my years in Colorado, a reported murder/suicide took place in the Victorian farmhouse we saw in the distance from our land. My 11-year-old self knew there must be ghosts living there.

I'm glad the memory of that fateful nine months of my childhood in rural Colorado reared its persistent head. I couldn't think of a happier place in the world for Kate and Gio to meet than Castle Springs.

There are more stories to tell about this little town. Marco & Alyssa, Sylvia & Henri, Nonna & her Giovanni, and others, all have things they still want to say.

And, of course, there are still unanswered questions about Tony and his treasures.

Be sure to look for these and other upcoming stories at:
tanalovett.com
facebook.com/tanalovett

ACKNOWLEDGMENTS

So many thanks to...

Those who read the full manuscript and gave invaluable feedback: Victoria J. Frantz, Kristina Moore, Sara Essary, Julie Keeton Bracker, Tonya Schorzman, Rebecca Zanetti, Carrie Bell, Cindy Talley, AnaMaree Ordway, Sarah Brady, Peggy Strong & Becky Oosting. Your input and encouragement gave this project wings.

The Pens and Needles writers' group on Ravelry.com. You were my group before I got the courage to interact with other writers face-to-face. I wouldn't have gotten this far without you. With special thanks to Julie Keeton Bracker, Larissa Brown, Tien Chiu, and Jennifer Runion.

Coeur d'Alene Chapter of Idaho Writers League, where I learned I could.

Inland Empire Chapter of Romance Writers of America, where I learned by example I could—and how. I'm looking at you, Annette Drake, Arwen Paris, Asa Maria Bradley, Augustina Van Hoven, Cathryn Cade, Danielle Annett, Debra Elise, Griffin Asher, Jennifer Lamont Leo, Jerica MacMillan, Katee Robert, Kathryn Chester, Kathye Thornton, Lisa Berne, Mary J. Williams, Rebecca Zanetti, Robin Connelly, Sarah & Shannen Brady, Shoshanna Gabriel, Tamara Morgan, and Trish McCallan.

Jennifer Leo, for making my first experience with an editor a good one. Thanks for your keen eye and gentle spirit.

Kathy Bland, my friend, writing cohort, and pedicure buddy, who nudges me to write all the words. Your book is next.